LOVE AFTER LOVE

Born in Trinidad, Ingrid Persaud won the Common-wealth Short Story Prize in 2017 and the BBC Short Story Award in 2018. She read law at the LSE and was a legal academic before taking degrees in fine art at Goldsmiths, University of London and Central Saint Martins. Her writing has appeared in *Granta*, *Prospect* and *Pree* magazines. Ingrid lives in London and Barbados.

Ingrid Persaud

LOVE AFTER LOVE

FABER & FABER

First published in 2020
by Faber & Faber Limited
Bloomsbury House
74–77 Great Russell Street
London WC1B 3DA
This export edition first published in 2020

Typeset by Faber & Faber Limited
Printed and bound by CPI Group (UK) Ltd, Croydon, CR0 4YY

Lyrics to 'Old Firestick' reproduced with the
kind permission of Linton Hope

A CIP record for this book
is available from the British Library

ISBN 978-0-571-35620-1

2 4 6 8 10 9 7 5 3

PART ONE

BETTY

Bet-tee! Bet-tee!

He didn't need to shout. I was already behind the car opening the trunk to find the lunch cooler. I took it out carefully along with his newspaper and jacket. Sunil stood waiting as I walked past the driver's door. His swift sharp kick in my shin was half expected.

Slow coach. You can't come when I call you? What, you ugly and you deaf?

Upstairs, I rushed to heat up his food. He was already stinking of rum but the first thing he did was get a fat glass and open a bottle of White Oak. Solo was in front the TV.

Eh, boy. Your father reach home and you can't say good evening?

Hello.

Run and bring my slippers, boy. A man work hard whole week and I come home and have to ask people for my fucking slippers? I have a good mind to beat your ass today.

Before Solo could get up I ran for the slippers.

I ask you for any slippers? Make the boy get up for a change. All he does do is sit down in front the TV.

Solo continued staring at the TV but I knew my baby was frightened.

Solo. What you waiting for? Come here.

Solo walked over slowly and carefully, as if stepping on mossy rocks.

Take off my shoes. And make sure they shine up good and proper before you put them away.

The boy undid the laces, his short, stubby fingers trembling. My baby has only just stopped wearing Pampers. Other children his age can't even do laces yet. But he made a mistake. As he pulled off the socks he couldn't help it. His nose twisted up and the father saw.

You find my foot smelling bad?

Sunil shoved his toes right up in the boy's nostrils, then pulled back but only to gain speed to kick his nose. If you see blood. Solo burst into tears and ran to the bathroom.

Don't cry and run away! Come here!

I froze right there. If he saw my tears that would only make him more crazy.

Solo, bring your ass here. Come. I didn't mean for your nose to bleed. Come boy.

He waited. I was counting the seconds, hoping he would cool off. His voice softened.

Solo. I'm calling you. Come here.

Solo appeared wiping away snot and tears. Toilet paper was pushed up both nostrils.

Sit down. What you learn in school today?

Yes.

I'm right here and I can't hear you. Open your mouth when you're talking. When a person talking soft soft so, I know is something they're hiding.

Yes.

Speak up!

I'm speaking up.

He grabbed Solo's T-shirt and before you could say Jack Robinson the child was on the floor.

Kneel down!

Yes.

Yes, please. What you learn in school today?

I don't know.

You.

The slap hit the top of the child's bent head.

Don't.

His foot rammed into the boy's stomach.

Know?

He grabbed his hair. Solo was screaming. I was screaming.

Leave the child! Sunil! Leave the child alone. He ain't do nothing.

All I want is to find out what he learn in school today. That so unreasonable?

I ran to Solo's bedroom for his backpack, returned breathless and shook it empty on the kitchen counter.

Solo, show Daddy what you do in kindergarten today.

The child was crouched down behind the kitchen counter, crying. I found his letters book and pushed it in front Sunil.

Look how the boy gone and write all his letters so neat neat between the lines. And the teacher told me Solo's best in the class.

Sunil flung the book like a frisbee towards Solo then rocked back and drained his glass. I didn't move a muscle.

Where my food?

In two twos I dished out the stew chicken, vegetable rice and green salad. Sunil used the fork like it was a shovel. When he's like this anything can become an argument and any argument can become a fight.

Like salt cheap?

But I hardly put salt in the food.

He rocked back in his chair. If looks could kill.

You telling me you cook this chicken and didn't put one set of salt in the pot?

Silence.

So, what I tasting? Something must be wrong with my mouth. How I tasting salt so? You know my pressure high and you giving me salt? Like you want to kill me? Eh?

I was careless. I'd left the rolling pin on the drain board. Easy reach of Sunil's chair. That rolling pin might have hit the wall, or the bed, or the chair. But it found me. Doctor said the ulna and the radius snapped in two. My arm was in a cast when we buried Sunil a week later.

At the funeral, I told people it was no big deal. I must stop being so careless with ladders. But I talk half and left half. People used to look at me and Sunil and say, Betty girl, you real lucky. In my head, I wanted to ask if they making joke. Lucky? That man only gave love you could feel. He cuff you down? Honeymoon. He give you a black eye? True love in your tail. He break your hand? A love letter. He put you in hospital for a week? Love will stay the course. He take a knife and stab your leg? Until death do us part.

MR CHETAN

Water lock off since last night. Not a word on the TV or radio about when it's coming back. A lady in the school office was saying how in Gasparillo they haven't had water for a week. What to do? Pay the water truck three hundred dollars to get a full water tank – assuming the water truck even passing your house. I'm not wasting the three buckets I managed to fill up. Half a bucket is all I need to rinse my skin. If you're careful that's more than enough. Trust me. Teeth can brush with a cup of water from the fridge. The toilet is a whole bucket. Nothing you can do about that. Luckily I only wanted to pee. Unless number two is an emergency it will wait until I reach to work.

By the time I came out the road to catch a maxi taxi the Monday morning rush was in full swing. I is a man who hate reaching to work late. Not a single maxi taxi. When one finally pulled up it was a set of shoving and pushing to get on. I was thinking in my mind if to walk up to the junction in case more taxis passing there when I saw Mrs Ramdin's car slowing down.

Come quick, man. I'm holding up traffic.

Nothing's wrong with Mrs Ramdin. She's a little talkative. And you can see the girl she was in her big dark eyes and simple shoulder-length hair. I just prefer not to be too friend friend with people in the main office. Next thing the whole of town all up in your business. I know she so so. Good morning, how you going, but never any big conversation. If I need to book a room for a special class, it goes through her. Things like that. Her husband passed away a good few years now and the whole school got half day off for the funeral. Take the drop? Don't take drop? The driver behind was blowing horn and shouting,

Oh shrimps, woman. Drive if you driving.

What to do? I jumped in the back seat.

Morning, Mrs Ramdin. Thanks for stopping.

Morning. I'm surprised to see you here, Mr Chetan.

She elbowed the boy sitting in front.

Say good morning, Solo. Anybody would think I never teach you manners.

The boy mumbled something. I don't mind. He looked about ten – the age when they start to feel they big.

First time I'm seeing you and I pass here nearly every day, God spare life.

My car's by the mechanic and to tell you the truth this is late for me, Mrs Ramdin. All now so I would be at school already.

Call me Betty.

Yes, Miss Betty. If I'm taking transport I would normally come out a good half hour earlier.

Ain't I just say call me Betty? Miss Betty? Like we don't know one another?

I can't do that. I have too much respect.

Oh gosh. Don't be so.

We edged forward a little then stopped. Trinidad roads aren't made for the amount of cars we have. Move. Stop. Move. Stop. She clearly didn't like silence.

I can't take this traffic every day so.

I nodded although she couldn't see me while driving.

Mr Chetan, sorry, I should have asked how you're feeling. Ain't you took sick leave the other day? You're good now?

Yes, Mrs Ramdin. I mean, Miss Betty. Everything's good, thanks. Wasn't anything serious.

I took out my *Express* and held it high in front my face. If I take a couple days off, why is it anybody's concern? Christ. You can't sneeze without people telling you to take two Panadol.

The new headmaster treating you good?

Now look at my crosses. I don't know this woman enough to speak my mind. Suppose she tells the boss I said so-and-so? Next thing I land up in trouble. I answered from behind the newspaper.

He seems like a decent man. We haven't had too many dealings yet.

Suddenly we picked up a little speed. Whatever was holding up the traffic had cleared away. Miss Betty was concentrating on the road but that didn't stop her from prattling on.

I'm not sure. You notice the label still sew on his jacket sleeve? Oh gosh, man. Pull off the label, nah. Money can't buy breeding. Anyhow, I suppose we should give him a chance. God is love.

I pulled the newspaper so it almost brushed my nose. She took the hint. For the rest of the car ride she and the boy talked until we reached the gates of St Barnabas College.

Mr Chetan, I want to ask you something if you don't mind.

No problem, Mrs Ramdin. Sorry, Miss Betty.

In the fifteen minutes between dropping the boy to his school and reaching ours, Miss Betty chatted nonstop. The husband had died so it was only she and the boy. Well, I knew that already. Things were tight. The house was old but big. She inherited it from her grandmother and it's paid for but she doesn't have much cash. A lodger would be income and company. If I knew anybody suitable I should let her know. A mature, single woman would be ideal. I said I would keep my ears open.

*

On the Wednesday, I found her in the staff room taking a break. Normally I eat lunch at my desk but today I eased up beside her at the long dining table.

Miss Betty.

She looked up from the chow mein noodles she was eating.

Miss Betty, we could talk for a minute? When you're finished your lunch.

She shifted her chair to face me.

You eat already?

I nodded and sat down. Sadly, my story wasn't that unusual in a country clocking forty murders a month. Henry's Pharmacy on Cipero Street is my landlord's business. Bandits came in broad daylight. They knocked him down, buss his head with a gun and tied him up. It was he and his wife there. I never asked but I pray the men them didn't interfere with her. That happened Easter time and made the papers. Not front-page news because nobody died but it was still in the first section. They took it hard and now they're selling up. Everything's going: the pharmacy, the house, two cars, furniture – the whole jahaji bundle. Fort Lauderdale is already home to their grown children and that will be where they settle. I've been renting the little apartment downstairs their house for the last four years. Now I've got to move. Everything I see that I like, I can't afford. What I can afford, I don't like. Maybe Miss Betty's place could be a temporary thing until I find what I want.

I know you prefer a lady and that makes sense. So, if you say no I will understand. But I promise you will hardly know I'm there. You can ask my landlord. All the years I was there we lived easy easy. Not a single quarrel passed between us.

Well, look at that. When I said that word to you the other day I didn't know nothing nothing about you looking for a place. It's true I would prefer a woman but you wouldn't be a bother. Nobody in this office has a bad word to say about you. Not one body. Anyhow, pass later nah and we go talk.

Thanks, Miss Betty. I appreciate that.

Mr Chetan, I know you're teaching math but you don't have to be so serious all the time. You and me are roughly the same age. Neither of us reach forty yet. Calling me Miss Betty makes me sound like an old lady.

I don't mean you're old, Miss Betty. It's a respect thing. Leave me nah.

Well, I only hear people calling you Mr Chetan so I suppose that is what you want me to keep calling you?

I gave her my sweetest smile. In this situation it was best to stay quiet. Let her figure it out.

God is love, yes. I didn't have time to say crick crack, monkey break he back for a piece of pomerac, and boom, the room gone.

Crick crack, look at that. By that evening everything was settled. Moving is next Saturday.

*

Two trips and we moved everything into Miss Betty's house. Her car trunk was chinky for so. One big suitcase and it was nearly full. Lucky thing I wasn't bringing any of the two-three pieces of old furniture I had. Massy had a Rainy Season

Blowout. I said to myself, Chetan, when last you buy something for yourself? I went to town. New bed and an armchair were the main items. Wherever I move to after this I will need my things. While waiting to pay, I saw a cute desk so that passed in the rush too. Normally Massy takes a week to deliver. Don't ask me why but they catch a vaps and dropped off everything the same day. When I told Miss Betty new furniture was coming she wanted to help me choose. No disrespect but when you've lived alone it's hard to take people interfering and this woman looks like she could well interfere. I am going to have to keep my distance or next thing you know she's running my life. If it was woman I wanted, I would've got myself a wife long time. And, of the things I want in life, a wife does not even make the list.

As we turned into the yard with the final carload of my stuff, her son, Solo, was waiting by the black wrought-iron gate. Miss Betty had barely parked when the child was trying to open the trunk.

Mr Chetan. Mr Chetan. I can lift up this suitcase. I can do it.

The suitcase was nearly as big as the child. It probably weighed more.

Leave it, son. Let me do it and you help your mom take things from the back seat.

Miss Betty declared she was leaving the gentlemen to sort out everything and going to take a five minutes. Solo put himself in charge of settling me into the house. I was trying to unpack but the boy kept calling me. Could he show me his room? Two minutes later he wanted to explain how to operate the TV. I had barely packed a drawer when he demanded I inspect the kitchen. What to do? He was only being friendly. Solo showed me everything – down to turning on the water heater if there wasn't enough hot water in the pipe. He was a completely different child from the morning they had stopped to give me a drop. A right little chatterbox.

Mr Chetan, is that the last box you're bringing up?

Yes. You stay. There's nothing else to bring. Ouch. Oh jeez-an-peas, that hurt!

I had stumped my so-and-so toe on the sharp edge of the concrete step. Books tumbled out the box I was carrying. A torch light went clanking down the steps. Solo rushed to help.

You all right, Mr Chetan? You all right?

My toe. Damn. That nail going to turn blue. I hit it and then the torch dropped on top it.

The boy ran after the torch and scooped up the books.

You want ice to put on your toe?

Don't worry. I'll manage.

These steps are very dangerous. My daddy fell down these same steps and died. Right here.

For true? Right here?

I don't remember anything because I was small but I know he fell down.

I'm sorry.

Sometimes he used to drink, get drunk and fall down.

You mustn't say that about your father.

But Mammy told me that happened.

I hoped Miss Betty wasn't listening. Her window was open so unless she was sleeping hard she must have heard. Children these days.

I'm sure your father was a good man.

Just please be very, very, very, very careful on the steps. Okay? Especially if you come home drunk.

You're not going to see me drunk. I take my Carib or a Stag now and then but I'm not a drinker. And Solo, you must be careful on the step too. If I knew about your daddy's accident I wouldn't have let you run up and down with boxes.

I'm accustomed to the steps. Nothing will happen to me.

He bent down and picked up a large plastic bag.

A boy in my class said he does thief Carib beer from the fridge and drink it in the back yard.

I hope you never do that.

Mammy said that is the one thing she will give me licks for. I can do anything but that.

It took the both of us till evening to put everything in place. Of course I could have done it all much faster but Solo refused to leave my side. I didn't mind and, although this boy's blabbing nonstop, half the time he's muttering to himself. At dinner Miss Betty acted like she hadn't heard what Solo said about his father. Still, it bothered me. People like to run their mouth – especially when it's nothing to do with them. No, I wouldn't want that for these two. About half past eight I asked Solo, please, let's knock off for the day. What wasn't put away could wait.

Solo, you can help me again but not too early. It's Sunday tomorrow.

Okay. I won't come in your room and wake you up then.

Before you go, come let me whisper something in your ears.

He smiled and came close.

You mustn't go around telling people that your father used to drink. It doesn't sound nice, especially since he's passed. And it will make your mom cry.

He leaned into my ear and whispered back,

My mammy won't cry for that.

BETTY

Friday night is pizza and TV. You should see Mr Chetan and Solo – happy as pappy and I'm like a Wednesday in the middle. They don't care that a film's boring for me. If I don't want to see the car chases and the shooting I best go in my bedroom. Funny how Mr Chetan made it clear he was only staying here for a few months. After a year I noticed he stopped that talk. I'm glad. He's a help, plus he's security. People know a man living about here. I wish I could say a good-looking thing like him by we because of my charm but hands down it's because of Solo. Them two real tight. He's not a father but he's a natural at fathering.

With Sunil dead and gone long time, my riding partners through thick and thin, Deedee and Gloria, are forever behind me to get out and meet people. They find I'm too young to stay home. Their thing is gambling. Two of them don't let a weekend pass without showing their face in the casino. Well, I surprised myself and had a good lime. We stuck with the slot machines them. My rule was to stop when I reached my limit. If you see games. Cash Hunter. Slot Father. Dog Ca$her. Moola Rouge. When we were fed up playing we sit down, eat we belly full and relax we-self. Tonight we're not going far. South City mall has a brand-new casino. But them girls' foot hot for so. We've hit casinos all about. Grand Bazaar. Couva. Penal. One time we reach quite Woodbrook. And is only Chinee people

18

running them. How Chinee people reach from so far to open all these casinos in little Trinidad I don't know. It must have a story behind that.

In the casino my arm started paining me bad. Gloria noticed me rubbing it.

What happen, girl? Your arm like it giving you trouble.

You have anything I could use?

I have a cream. A muscle relaxer. Problem is if you put it on here, people on the other side of the casino will smell it too.

Don't worry then. You see from the elbow to the hand? Remember I break them two bones years ago. Every now and then it will pain me. And if rain fall? Worse yet.

I saw Deedee walking between the machines towards us. She'd been watching live roulette.

A white fella just take them for a whole ten thousand dollars. Ten thousand. We better go make friends.

I had to laugh. Not one of us have a man and we are unlikely to find one here. The pickings these days real slim.

You win anything, Gloria?

Girl, tonight's not my night. I played Wish Upon A Jackpot and I tried my luck with Gold Raider but nothing doing. Must be the full moon. All you might think I'm making joke but I've never won a red cent when the moon full.

I reminded them it was past seven. The dining room was now open.

Betty, tell me something good.

I gave one long steupse – sucking air and spit through my front teeth to make a hissing noise because is vex I vex.

Paco and the Popping Peppers and King Cashalot gone with the few dollars I had in my purse. Anyhow, God is love.

Over dinner I was rubbing my arm again. Gloria pulled out the smelly cream and a pack of Advil. I shook my head.

Leave it. And the doctor them can't do a blasted thing. They say that is how it is. At least it doesn't pain me steady.

Deedee put down her fork.

How I never thought of this before? Betty, you need a good jharay by somebody who know what they doing. I feel the hand hurting because somebody put maljo on your head.

Hush your mouth. Who would want to put bad eye on me? Sunil's family? Half of them in New York anyway. You can't put maljo from so far.

That is the thing, Betty. You wouldn't even know they do it.

Deedee and Gloria too sweet but I'm keeping quiet. One pain and they're ready to get me jharay. Thing is, worse than the pain in my arm is Sunil's spirit in the house. The man in the walls, on the stairs, in the rooms. Before he passed he must have put he bad eye on me for truth. Years ago I went by Reverend Lutchman and asked him to say prayers for the spirit to cross over for all eternity. I don't know if it's because he was just ordained, or the fact that he's Guyanese, but his prayers didn't do a blessed thing.

We left the talk there but it had me thinking. Not counting our son, this pain in my arm is the only lasting thing Sunil left me. When he was alive I was too shame to say anything, and, once he passed, I was even more shame. What kind of woman does bad talk she dead husband? And Sunil was good-looking. You have to give him that. A fair-skin Indian with thick, black hair was a big catch. No one said it but I knew. Why would a hot man like that settle for a mook like me?

*

Saturday afternoon I finished cleaning the house, washed clothes and cooked. Sweet breeze was blowing so I sat down on the front porch. I wasn't there a good ten minutes when Deedee's car pulled up outside. She was busy waving from the front seat. Gloria came out and stood by the gate.

Me and Deedee had a panchayat and when we done the talking we decided you need a full jharay. Not just for your arm. Everything from your head come down. Let we go by a pundit in Williamsville. Deedee swears he's the bomb.

Hush your mouth and come upstairs. If you're lucky I will give you some of my chicken pelau that just come off the stove. It make with pigeon peas I pick this morning.

We'll take the pelau to go. Change your clothes and come. We're waiting.

What about Solo?

Sister, please. Solo tall like you. He could look after himself. It's not like you're leaving the island.

They carried me far up in the country where the trees and grass were a deeper green than in San Fernando. We drove past giant, whistling bamboo groves and tall, laden breadfruit trees. By the time we reached Williamsville the place was making dark. Deedee said relax because jharay can only happen after six o'clock anyhow. Either then or before six in the morning. Pundit was living in an upstairs wooden house. The place was small but neat with vegetables planted up on one side of the yard. A line of washing, all whites, was hanging under the house and parked next to it was a beat-up yellow Corolla. Somebody was home for sure.

Deedee went in front. Set next to the gate was a bundle of bamboo poles with solid coloured, triangular flags attached. I may have lost most of my Indian culture but I knew these were jhandis. The flags were yellow with one-one in between in other colours – red, black, blue and white. Some were faded and torn from months, possibly years, of blowing in the rain and hot sun. A few looked new. My ma would have known the god worshipped by each colour. I read in the Sunday papers that this flag business is now only a Trini-Guyanese thing. People like my great-great-grandmother brought it from India but modern Indians stopped doing this long time.

Pundit! Pundit!

A round, sleepy face peeped out a window.

Pundit, like you're resting? Is Deedee. How you going?

The man welcomed us in and Deedee explained my pain. Pundit agreed it was the correct thing coming to him. One glance at me and he said I carried a bad aura. Well, thanks for that, pundit. I mentally prepared for a long, confusing set of prayers on my head but it wasn't too bad. Pundit made a little parcel out of a piece of white cloth and inside he put five garlic cloves, five bird peppers and a shake of salt and pepper. He tied that and passed it over me, front and back and then around my head. Five times he did that while chanting prayers in Hindi. He could've been chanting the alphabet for all the Hindi I knew.

Next he got a cocoyea broom. Cocoyea broom is easy to make. Strip some coconut palms of the leaf them. Take a good set of the hard centre strips, tie up one end to make a handle and sweep with the next end. Best yard broom ever. Pundit took five pieces of cocoyea broom and passed that over me the same way. Five times again. More chanting. The only difference was that he blew on the cocoyea after each rounds. When that was done, he put the cloth bundle and the cocoyea stick on the ground, took a box of matches from his pants pocket and looked me in my eye direct.

Daughter, you know your Bible?

I was a little surprised because this ain't no Christian thing and he better not blaspheme here today. I nodded.

Yes, pundit.

You remember what scripture say did befall Lot's wife?

I nodded again but he started off anyway.

> The woman turned into a pillar of salt. The Lord tell them
> straight. Do not look back at Sodom. But she disobeyed
> and the Lord punished her. Well, today you come like Lot's
> wife. I'm going to burn everything I used. All the evil that's
> on you will burn away too. But you mustn't look at the
> fire. You hear me? One look and the evil will come back
> more strong. If that happen even I go can't help you. You
> understand?

On the drive back home it was pitch black. Clearly no government minister have house and land out here or they would've
made sure to put in street lights and have the bulbs them
working. Whole road Gloria and Deedee prattled nonstop
while the radio belted out soca hits. I felt exhausted. But God
is love. They dropped me home and drove off happy happy. I
don't know why but as I started walking up the back steps I
got into one set of crying. Instead of coming from my eyes the
tears like they were shooting up from inside my heart. I sat
down right on the cold concrete steps and covered my mouth.
Solo mustn't hear. Or Mr Chetan. Truth is I believe Sunil's
spirit, his nasty bad eye, ain't ever leaving me no matter how
much jharay I get.

MR CHETAN

I understand a kitchen. I'm not saying Miss Betty can't cook. But give Jim his gym-boots. She hand nowhere near sweet like mine. Two of us coming home from work, same tired, so I took over the cooking three times for the week. As it's Sunday I decided to do my nice steamed kingfish, callaloo with salt meat, rice and, just for Solo, a macaroni pie.

While the pie was in the oven I went on the porch. Solo was there swinging in the hammock, head in the iPad as usual.

Why's lunch not ready?

Excuse me?

It's past twelve o'clock.

I am not your slave, young man.

Well, if you're cooking you should try and finish on time.

I told myself, Chetan, breathe. Teenagers.

Solo, don't speak to me like that. Don't speak to anybody like that.

The boy jumped out of the hammock and stood too close. Our eyes were nearly level.

You can't tell me what to do. You're not my father.

I bit my lip and turned away. But he wasn't finished.

> What kind of man is always in the kitchen cooking or
> sitting around reading? What happen? You're a buller man?

That was a body blow. I retreated to the kitchen. His footsteps
drummed hard on the wooden floor and a door banged.

I left the food in covered serving bowls, told Miss Betty I
had a headache and went in my room. Half of me wanted to
punch the little shit. How the fuck he dare treat me like that?
And what he know about buller man? But anger was only part
of the pain. And Solo might be catching up to my height but
he's still a child. I took up the book I was half way through and
settled in for the afternoon. If I couldn't lose away with a good
book I think I would go loco.

I dozed off, only waking because someone had noisily
opened my door. It wasn't quite dusk but the dim of the room
suggested the sun would soon be leaving the sky. Solo crept in,
carefully balancing a mug of tea. He rested it on the bedside
table and stood there, wordless, staring at the floor. I took a
sip. It was perfect.

> What's happening with you, Solo?

He didn't look up.

> I might not be your daddy but I do care about you. You
> know that.

Solo dug his hands into his pockets.

> This rude behaviour is not you. Not my Solo. And your
> mammy told me the school called her in because you keep

getting in fights. Something happened? You know whatever talk go on between us will stay right here.

He nodded, hesitated, then turned and left quietly. What worries me is that he is basically a sweet child. I've never seen him knocking about with the boys who smoking weed and drinking. If anything, he's too much of a loner. I finished my tea and strolled onto the porch. Solo was alone in the hammock.

Where's your mammy?

She went out. Not sure where.

I sat on a stool close enough to rock the hammock.

I ever told you about how I was a postman in London?

Solo's eyes opened wide wide.

No.

Yes, man. I was a postman. And before that I was a cab driver.

Solo's entire face smiled.

A black taxi?

Yup.

Wow.

The stories I could tell you about people who sat in my cab. Ha. You think is two crazy people I bounced up? When I first went to London things were hard. Jobs you wouldn't take back home you were glad for over there.

Please don't give me one of them look-how-hard-we-had-
it-and-how-easy-life-is-for-young-people-today stories. I
get enough of that from Mammy.

I laughed.

I had a friend. I'll never forget his name. Rupert Maclean.
White people wouldn't usually take the time to say good
morning to a little coolie boy like me. But Rupert would
always come to the door and have a little chat.

I gave the hammock a push. Every time it swung back I gently
sent it off again. Never mind this rudeness. If I was the kind of
man to have children I would want one like this boy.

To be honest I didn't have a big set of friends. Brixton
and Shepherd's Bush were full of West Indians but I was
always a man to stay by myself. But you see Rupert? He
encouraged me. Showed me how things worked. If it
wasn't for him I might still be a postman fighting up in
the cold.

So how exactly did Rupert help you? He gave you money?

Nah, nothing so. Every day I'm delivering the mail and over
time we got to talking and he asked where I was from and
how I reached there. He showed an interest then.

Solo sat up in the hammock.

He had a good heart. I told him how I stopped school
at sixteen and he asked me why I didn't try now. Well,
who would pay my rent? But he kept behind me. Do the
studying part time. He got leaflets for me. Always saying

how he could tell from talking to me that I could better myself.

Remembering Rupert made me a little sad.

So, what did you do?

It took some long years but I did evening courses and eventually I got my degree. Since I was small I was good at maths so I did that. Thanks to him, when I came back I could get a job teaching. Rupert Maclean. Fate put him in front me.

Solo let his head fall back into the hammock.

Why you didn't stay in England? If it was me I would've stayed. Anything to get away from here. Trinidad's so boring.

I stopped pushing the hammock and got up. I wanted to say something but the words were hiding.

Mr Chetan, if you leave your mouth open so, you'll catch a fly.

I closed my mouth and bit my bottom lip. It came out as a whisper.

Home, boy. That's important.

What did you say?

Home. Home is where your navel string's buried.

BETTY

I only fell asleep minutes past one. Still, my eyes opened wide wide at five on the dot. That internal alarm never fails. As soon as the clock strikes five a recording goes off in my head: Betty, when you're dead you can sleep all you want. While the good Lord give you breath, get your backside out the bed. Start the day.

That it was Saturday didn't change a damn thing. I could have done with a little half hour extra. Under the blanket was well cosy and nice. But hear what. Enough rules gone through in the past twenty-four hours. What is one more? I'm staying horizontal. Well, I'll get up to wee wee, open the window for the breeze and then it's straight back under the blanket. Since last night I'm all over the place. A married man. Me. I go from nothing to this level of sin. One minute I feel guilty and the next I'm high – the kind I imagine comes from smoking weed. Not that I ever went near that. Last night. Have mercy. Now that was a first for me.

How to explain? Maybe I can plead temporary insanity. It wasn't drink. Two sips of red wine is hardly drinking. Something misfired in my head and messed me up real good. Jesus, I hope nobody saw us. He wouldn't tell anybody. Or maybe he will because men like to boast to one another. That is a sure way for things to come out. I could text later. Or call. What if the wife answers his phone? Best to wait till Monday. Maybe he'll ring later. If he gets a chance. He didn't say he would. I'm assuming any decent man would ring or text to make sure everything's cool. Imagine if he rang and Solo picked up my phone? The child would get suspicious one time. And what if Mr Chetan finds out? I would feel so shame. Oh shit.

My bedroom door creaked open a little, then a little more. Solo's head poked through. When he saw me awake his face lit up and he dived into the bed.

You don't find you getting too big for this?

Nope.

I squeezed him tight. His long body was warm. I planted a noisy kiss on the top of his head. Only when he's half sleepy I can steal away a few kisses. Otherwise Mister Man feels he's too big for love up. The days of getting a goodbye kiss by the school gate gone long time.

I remember one time we took you by a friend and they asked you how old you were and you said, four and three quarter. And the person said, well, that means you're still four and you said, no. Four and three quarter. You had everybody laughing.

And what else?

I remember that your favourite toy was a mop. Always mopping. You even had your own small mop because you wanted one like mine. People used to say I was using you as child labour.

I squeezed my baby and kissed his forehead.

Go back to sleep. It's not even six o'clock yet.

I prefer your bed.

Sleep here then.

He pulled one of the two pillows my head was resting on.

You didn't come home till late late.

My stomach did a backflip.

I told you I was going out with church people.

Technically that was in the vicinity of truth. Technically. I was trying to breathe normally, buying time to see where this talk was going. God is love. Solo snuggled down and fell back asleep. No more questions – at least not now. But what doesn't come out in the wash will come out in the rinse. Hopefully this washing and rinsing won't happen until we get we story straight. When will I see him again? How will I see him? He can't come here. Obviously, his house is out of the question. I'm not sleeping in another woman's bed. And I'm not holing up in no car again. We were an easy target. All it would have taken was one worthless bandit on the block. How exactly would I explain that? Worse yet, suppose one or both of us took a bullet and ended up dead. These days they don't just rob you. No. After they take your money, and whatever jewellery they want, is a bullet in your brain.

And my son? Mr Chetan would want Solo. I know that. Since he's not blood I can't ask him to stand in for me. My parents would take him in but I don't trust them to bring up my boy properly. I know for a fact Sunil's family don't care.

None of them does take up the phone and check to see if we're alive or dead. His brother, Hari, was the only one who was halfway decent but he wouldn't take Solo under his hand. When me and Sunil first started to talk and thing Hari was already married. But having a ring on his left hand didn't stop him knocking about with all kind of other woman. To besides, he gone New York and forget us. I don't mind for me but Solo is his nephew. It would kill him to buy a birthday card or a Christmas card and put a stamp? Anyhow, nothing bad happened last night, for which I must give thanks, yes. Today could have been the start of a completely different story.

I eased out the bed quiet quiet even though I knew Solo was asleep. If I stayed he would pick up my anxious vibes. Once coffee begins trickling through my veins I'll be fine. The neighbour opposite is an early riser too and we exchanged good mornings across the fence. She's an artist plus she brings out a small carnival band every year. Old-fashioned mas with proper costumes. As an extra bonus, she's also mad no ass. I like her. Sheets of plyboard were all over her driveway. I leaned over the porch bannister and asked what she was making. The woman watch me with a straight face and said she was making her coffin because normal coffins are too boring. Her final resting place will be decorated with flowers, vines and trees she plans to paint. I didn't know what to say. She can't be fifty yet and she don't look sick. Maybe she was giving me a six for a nine but with her it could well be the truth. Madness. Making your own coffin? That's a new one on me.

Kiskadee song is the main noise in this early morning half-light. Perhaps because they are here every morning I'd stopped hearing them. Today I heard them clearly. My whole world

seems brighter, lighter, but this can't happen again. I should be
on my knees begging forgiveness. He is a next woman's man.
Mind you, he said they don't have relations. Not like that. People living in one house but passing each other like two jumbie.
She should know better. A nice, fit man like that. Well, if she
won't look after her husband then she should expect somebody else will do the looking after for she. It was me this time.
Next time it could be someone who takes him for good. And
it's not like I'm some young girl scoping for a sugar daddy.
True, he paid for the Chinese food. But. But. But. Betty Ramdin, every thought has a 'but' in it. Watch how your life will
turn inside out, upside down, if the man's wife finds out. What
if she reached by the school and started to make noise? Or she
came by the house? Imagine the shame. Nah. That won't happen. How she go know? Like I said, by rights if she didn't want
the man to stray, she should have taken care of business. It's
not like I'm whoring down the place. As God is my witness,
this is the first time I've been with a man since my husband
and he passed long time.

Footsteps from inside told me Mr Chetan was up. A few
minutes later he drifted onto the porch.

Morning. Coffee? I'm making.

Thanks.

He returned with my coffee. I could bet house and land that
it's exactly the way I like it – strong, a tups of milk and a few
grains of sugar, hardly worth putting in but it makes all the
difference to me. We sat in silence. It was killing me to say
something; to make an excuse about last night. Of course, I

don't need to explain myself to a soul. I'm a hard back, forty-year-old woman not a teenager who broke her curfew. It's my business what I do.

Last night Solo was trying his best to stay up for you. I told him to leave you in peace. I said it's once in a blue moon she takes time for herself. Did he message you?

If? I put the phone on silent because he was texting every five minutes. Checking up on me. My father and my husband both done dead, God rest their souls. I'm not letting no man rule me.

Mr Chetan sat there sipping coffee and skinning his teeth at me.

Miss Betty, relaxing is not a crime. Live a little. Best to do things while you still have your own teeth in your mouth.

I nearly sprayed the coffee I was drinking all over myself.

Don't make me laugh. I'm a long way from false teeth. And you're a fine one to talk. When last you went out? Once you have a book or TV you don't go nowhere. The only time you move is if Solo begs you to go football. I lie?

I need a second coffee.

While he was in the kitchen my mind travelled back to last night. Behind my eyes it was all there. Sunil would never in a million years do the things that man did. Have mercy. I swear he mistook me for a ripe Julie mango. Jesus, Mary and Joseph. That was something else. My whole body was on fire. A voice put that memory on pause.

We out of sugar?

No. Try the cupboard next to the fridge.

One more time. I want that feeling one more time and then I'll let go. He wanted to know what I liked. I never even knew I was missing this until now. Sunil was the same two positions in the same order. Once he was done that was that. And he never, ever did it sober. Always had to have drink inside him. Last night, well, that was a whole next universe. From looking at the man you would never know. People might say he's average. Not so. The man's smoking hot. Lethal. For months now he would pass and touch my arm or my back and his hand would linger a tups longer than was strictly necessary for a Bible group friend. I didn't want to admit it but even the lightest touch would zing through my spine. Now that I've had a taste I just want one more. Sin is sin. I know that. Just one more time and I could finish with that. Lord, why you show me this only to torment my soul?

MR CHETAN

I didn't say a word to a soul. I got up easy easy, put water and a couple beers in the cooler and slipped away before the rest of the house was awake. In traffic the drive can be all kind of two and a half hours. But on a Sunday before six o'clock? Man, I was dipping my toes in Maracas Bay in under two hours. Whenever I can spare the time that is my spot. Half the pull is the beach and half is the spectacular drive to reach there. If your heart's weak, or you're timid, leave the driving to others. The roads are narrow and winding as they hug the sides of the Northern Range. Lose the fear of being pushed off the precipice by some crazy-ass driver and enjoy as each hairpin twist unveils another breathtaking view of lush green mountains rising from the turquoise sea.

For once I would have preferred an even longer drive to clear my head. Only a handful of people were on the beach. Come this afternoon it will be a different story. A clump of coconut trees to the left had my name on it and I settled down with my cooler and beach chair. Two minutes of my feet wiggling around in the sand and any fretting or worries vanish one time. Add to that the roaring sea and I chill right down. I pulled in a lungful of the salty air. People busy swallowing one set of drugs to cope with life when what they need is a regular dose of the sea.

As the tide was going out the beach was wider than usual and perfect for a stroll. Maybe it was the vastness of the sand, or the postcard-perfect bay of sea and sky blues – whatever it was, it made me still inside. With that peace filling my lungs I set off to cover the length of the bay. The few people strolling gave each other plenty space with the unspoken understanding that if you're walking this long beach alone, at this hour, you're not looking to make friends.

Different days see me here for different things. Sometimes it's to recharge. Mostly I come to forget. Today I have a purpose. It's time to make up my mind once and for all. It's not the first or even the tenth occasion I've pounded this sand threatening not to leave until I've decided one way or another. Normally I don't have a religious bone in my body but if the big man up there is listening, please, send me a sign, any sign. These 3 a.m. awakenings, staring at the ceiling, can't keep happening. It's barely eight o'clock yet and my mind is exhausted.

The sun was beginning to hint at the sting it would inflict by midday. I planned to finish my walk then jump in the sea to cool off. From my starting point in the middle of the bay I headed left to one end where a small river emptied into the sea. Within minutes I was lost hearing only the pounding rhythm of the breaking waves. Footprints of a man walking ahead of me, a little larger than mine, formed a trail and I began stepping into them, my imprint mixing with his. It was a childish game. I soon noticed the owner of the footprints – the colour of wholewheat toast and sporting an unruly afro. Surely he must know that those tiny pum-pum shorts are plain distraction for man and woman alike. I couldn't tell his age. He ain't young but he was in decent shape. Snatches of his profile when he glanced around or looked out to sea showed sideburns and a sculptured beard. Early forties maybe? Sweat glistened off his chiselled cheekbones and collarbones. A thick moustache partly covered his cherry thick lips and once again I was butting up against that eternal dilemma. This is what makes my knees weak and my heart race. Why can't I want something else? Why can't I lust after what I have at home instead?

My whole life has been a lie. What do I get staying as I am? Nothing. Alone forever. Imagine a man my age without a full adult relationship under his belt. And if you ask me, that boat's probably sailed. Maybe in my head I did once, sort of, have a thing going but nothing was ever said. Occasionally, I chance a club in Port of Spain. Even though it's far from San Fernando you never know who you might bounce up. Feeling alive, no, feeling anything at all, is mainly a few intense, crazy minutes in a restroom in the grocery or the mall. When I think of it like that it doesn't seem worth it. Yet it's those few moments when I'm complete – the whole me. But with Miss Betty, with her I could have something else, something precious.

Pum-pum shorts stopped at his pitch in the sand. With a towel he slowly wiped the glistening sweat from his face and hairy chest, then spread the towel on the sand. My chair was further on. This man might be what I want but he is not what I need. Not today. Want and need were jamming. I commanded myself to keep walking. Just keep walking. In the middle of this battle he turned. We connected. He turned away then looked back at me a second time. I gave him the look, the one that lingers a couple seconds too long, the one that says, I am horny as fuck for you. Even something so subtle out in the open is risky. Imagine my shock when this hot thing, sweet as demerara sugar, returned the look. I stopped, pretending to take in the sea view. Inside I was grinning from my mouth to my groin. Out of the corner of my eye I knew he too was snatching a glance at me. Me. I walked over and sat near enough to talk but not so close that I was in the man's space. Neither of us said a word. The tension was building up. Was he feeling the vibes? Had I got it wrong? I needed a word or a movement, something to justify me staying here. I found myself announcing to the wind,

The sea looking real good this morning.

He nodded, smiled, but didn't speak. Damn. One more minute listening to the pounding roar of waves crashing and I gone. Maybe because I was good with walking away, the panic eased. With each awkward, passing moment I was sure this heavenly doux-doux darling would leave. No worries. I came to the beach for peace. The sensible thing would be to make tracks. But my cock and my head had different opinions. When I should have been moving on I began shifting ever so slightly closer. Still nothing. Well, I tried. Head, heart, cock – all of we accepted this brown sugar god wasn't happening. I was about to go my way when he announced to the wind and the sea,

Time to test out the water, yes.

With that he stood up. I threw off my T-shirt and together we walked into the water. He was a stronger swimmer and soon far beyond the breakers. I treaded in the cool water and watched him go. It's right here he was coming back. The closest person to us was a distant blob. Pum-pum shorts swam towards me. I smiled and swam away. He ducked under the water then popped up right behind me like a big fish. His hands went searching. It was worth the wide grin he flashed that my swim trunks had vanished. Neither of us talked while we played, always vigilant because even the Caribbean Sea can't cover our crime. Tension was rising inside me until his finger in my ass reached that spot, that fucking amazing spot. He flicked his head towards the shore. You should see how fast I was out the water.

Fear, anticipation and horniness were surging through my veins. I had to smile to myself. The number of times I'd come to Maracas hoping for a little piece and never a damn thing. But this morning, when I came for peace, this honey trickled down my skin. Now see me hustling on the sand behind a strange man I cannot resist.

In the public changing facility was a long, wide bench down the middle. Lining both walls were cubicles with swing doors that didn't lock. Apart from a mash-up pair of rubber slippers forgotten under the bench there was no sign that anyone had been in here today. Giddy with nervous excitement, I whispered that anyone could barge in and catch us.

Relax. Nobody coming here this hour.

You sure? What if somebody came in?

We good. The beach wasn't busy.

His soft voice contrasted with the strong push of his fingers from the top of my spine to my butt. The surge of electricity it brought was all the courage I needed to follow him into the end cubicle. He began kissing me all over then sucking me. Oh fuck, he was good. But if someone walked in and found us we would get beat up today for sure for sure. We should stop. But I couldn't. Oh Lord, my body was trembling with pleasure. I kept being on the verge of coming and then a creak or a thud would stop me. I wasn't ready to take a knifing up. Over and over I almost came then pulled back. The tension got too much and I finally let rip. Every cell in my body was grateful to this brown sugar god. No time to bask in the feeling. I did a quick survey and listened for a moment. Coast clear. I returned the favour while he stroked my head and neck and in no time his body buckled and braced against the side of the cubicle. If things were different, I would have thanked him for making me feel unbroken, unmarked. Not here and not to a strange man you fucked in a public facility. Instead we showered quickly. Pum-pum shorts left ahead of me. As he did so a man burst in. That was close. As I rushed past, our eyes met – mine petrified and guilty, his nasty and questioning. Talk about perfect timing and a whole heap of luck.

I hurried back to the shade where I had plonked my chair. The smell of fish frying at Richard's Shark and Bake filled my nostrils. I must have that with a little chadon beni seasoning, garlic sauce and slight pepper. Life was stirring on the beach. A young family arrived and set out their chairs and picnic within my canopy of coconut trees. Their little one ran to the water's edge, dipped her toes and ran back screaming that the sea was cold like ice water. My body spent, and my mind empty, I sat down and drifted in and out of daydreams. A group of pretty pretty, half-naked girls walked past. How different, how strange, would it be fucking a woman? And to be clear, it wasn't women in general. It was one particular woman and my closest friend. I love her as much as I can love anybody. In time the rest will surely fall in place. We'll be a family. A real family. That will make up for everything.

BETTY

The England football team are in Trinidad for a friendly. I hope they understand there's nothing friendly about them coming here. I don't follow football and even I know we ain't making joke. Put aside all what happened long time when we were a colony. The thing that nobody in this country can forgive is how England throw us out the World Cup in Germany. But we're waiting for them. Mr Chetan's taken Solo. The two of them were excited like Christmas reached early. When he was buying tickets, he asked if I wanted to go too. Me in Hasely Crawford Stadium with twenty-five thousand people? Thanks but no thanks. Besides, I was looking forward to being home alone. That was before I checked the date. Tuesday is 2 November. Today is Sunday and I haven't gone anywhere near Paradise Cemetery. I messaged Deedee. All I did was mention All Souls' Day coming and she piped up,

When we going to clean Sunil's grave?

Deedee, you is a godsend, yes. I could manage by myself but I won't say no to a little company.

Pass for me. We only cleaning the grave today, right?

Yeah. Tuesday evening I will go back with flowers and candles. If we put out things from now it bound to get thief.

43

By the time we got to Paradise Cemetery the place was buzz-
ing. If the dead think it busy now wait until All Souls'. Like all
who weren't taking in the football were weeding graves, lime
washing tombstones and generally making the plots them
look nice. It's a respect thing. In church this morning Reverend said that it's only in Trinidad that All Souls' Day is a thing
for everybody. Christian, Muslim, even Hindu – all of we does
be busy cleaning grave and lighting candle.

Betty, I'm tackling from the middle go up and you clean
from the middle go down.

Madame Deedee, I know you since high school so don't
treat me like a stupid bobolee. You gone and choose the
end with less weeding. Scoundrel.

Hush and put your hand to work.

Rainy season was heavy this year and the grave's well over-
grown. Most weeds I could pull out with my hand but one
patch like a tree had taken root. Probably seeds from one of
the many samaan trees in this cemetery.

Nobody ain't bury in this plot next to Sunil. I wonder who
own it.

Me.

What? You buy that?

Sunil bought it long time. One for him and one for me.
When my time come is right here I resting.

No way. Sell it. Swap it. Give it away.

It's no big deal.

I turned and pushed my small garden fork into the stubborn roots of a weed. Deedee was quiet but I could feel a heaviness between us. We worked away for a few minutes. I said to the ground,

He didn't start off bad, you know.

Deedee kept pulling up anything that had roots in the plot. I know she heard me.

When I first met him every week he would show up looking proud of himself and hand me one or two fresh roses. At our wedding I met his neighbour and she told me all them roses came from her garden. No matter how much times she told Sunil no more roses he would keep coming back boldface boldface. And neighbour claimed she was the first to know when he was going to propose. That Saturday, instead of one rose, he asked her for all the roses she could spare.

Deedee stood up and stretched her back. I looked at her face.

You don't believe me?

It's not that I don't believe you.

She sighed.

How he went from Rose Man to what I remember? It wasn't two times I went hospital to find you mash-up mash-up. It not good to bad talk the dead but more than once I wanted to kill him myself.

It was the rum. When he wasn't drinking he could be sweet sweet.

Yes, but what about the time he knife you in your leg? Why you didn't call police for him I will never understand.

Deedee, we're by the man resting place. Leave it alone. Where I was going to go? Who else would want me and my small child? My own mother said licks showed Sunil loved me. To besides, you can't play sailor mas and 'fraid powder.

She didn't say a word but moved around to tackle a next set of bush. Most of the weeds had been cleared and already the whole plot was looking respectable. Come Tuesday night Solo and I will light candles. My red ginger lilies are big enough for me to cut a few for decoration. And I mustn't forget to bring two pack of candles, a box of matches, and a container for the flowers. Deedee's voice interrupted the list I was busy making in my head.

I only have one more question and then I will stop asking.

I buss a smile and shook my head.

You never have only one more question. But it's all right. You is like my sister. Ask what you want.

Why you always putting yourself down?

I stopped and folded my arms.

I have more than one mirror in the house.

Well, you should look properly. And stop wearing all them

tents. I would kill for your figure even though you make baby. What is my excuse for this roll of fat?

I took a deep breath.

Sunil had a way he used to watch me cut eye and say the two of we were like Beauty and the Beast, only he was the beauty and I was the beast.

He never dared côme with that talk in front of me because he knew I would've put him in his place.

She shook her head.

Ah Lord. Beauty and the Beast? That making me so vex I don't want to clean his plot at all at all.

You're not doing it for him. You doing it so nobody can point their finger and say all kind of thing about me.

Let we hurry up and done. After all this hard labour, I deserve a lie down in your hammock.

SOLO

I don't know what the plan is because this Dev that Mammy's taken up with is a married man. The absolute worst part is that his two sons go to my school. At least we're not in the same class. The older one has the most massive round head you will ever see in your entire life. I mean, it's like he dropped down from Mars. They does call him Brains because that big head he have real empty. And his boys know about me too. They made sure I found out Dev took them to Disney at Christmas and that they're going to Toronto for all of July with their mom. I know the gang that they lime with are always laughing at me. One time Brains pointed me out to a woman. From the way she looked at me that had to be his mother. Face twist up like she stepped in dog shit. I wanted to ask the bitch if I do she something. It's not me she husband busy checking.

Today was the last day of term. At the exact moment me and Mammy were driving out the school gates, guess who was coming through? Yup. His wife. With the traffic preventing us from bolting I was sure war would break out. Would she cuss Mammy? Would Mammy cuss back? Anything was possible. Since Dev came on the scene Mammy's changed up. Six months ago I wouldn't have imagined that my sweet mammy was capable of cussing in public. Now I'm worried she will be the one to start the cussing. My hands were gripping the edges of the car seat tight tight and my chest hurt. If these two started carrying on I will transfer to another school. Simple as that. But all those Sundays in church paid off. The Lord took pity and the woman didn't clock us until we had almost gone past each other. Now that was luck. In Mammy's words, God is love. As my breathing returned to normal Mammy decided to rev it up. She poked my leg.

You realise that was Dev's family we just passed?

Yeah.

That woman ever tell you anything?

No.

She children does bother you?

No.

I don't know what she's vexed for. Driving a brand-new car. I have the same old car for donkey years now. You hear me complaining? I never asked anybody for anything.

I looked out the window. This was nothing to do with me. So the man bought his wife a new BMW 3 Series, in metallic silver, with the upgraded rims. Sweet. Mammy nudged me.

Solo, you know she living in one big house in Bel Air with swimming pool and jacuzzi. What more she want?

I don't know why but I found myself yelling at her. I wanted her to please, please, please, shut the fuck up. Please.

He's not your blasted husband!

What you just said? Eh? And shouting at me? Don't say

blasted. Have some respect. Since when you feel you could talk to me like that? You're still a child, Solo, and I am still your mother.

Dev's so dotish. Dumb and dotish.

You're not too big for me to wash out your mouth with blue soap. He's very nice to us.

Nice to you.

What you mean by that exactly? Look, child, this rudeness better stop now for now.

I don't know what to think. Most of the time I don't mind him. Monday evening we played football together in the back yard. June public holiday he took us to Blanchisseuse Beach. Yeah, Dev can be fun. I don't mean to be nasty about him. It comes out of nowhere and I can't control it. Take last week. He and I went to collect pizza because both Mammy and Mr Chetan were too tired to cook. I felt totally angry with him even though he was doing something nice. He can't keep coming by us and then leaving for his real home late in the night. Either stay or go back home and remain in your own house. Stop hanging around and being nice. I don't want to have fun with him if it's not for keeps. Maybe Mammy was reading my thoughts.

It's time Dev made a decision. If he doesn't love the woman then he should leave. For everybody's sake.

Stop talking to me about him.

I have thought about what it would be like for us all to be a family – Brains and his brother included. Could we live happy together in the house with the swimming pool and jacuzzi? I can't see it working. I hate them and they hate me right back. They think I'm a nobody and I think they're losers. But what if Dev and Mammy got married? We wouldn't have a choice. Of course Mr Chetan will move with us. I would tell them point blank. I'm not going anywhere without Mr Chetan. What would happen to Dev's wife? Maybe he would build another house for her or maybe he would leave her there and build a bigger house for us.

Solo? You even listening?

What?

I'm pulling into Jazz's Bakery. Get two sliced loaves. If you want a currants roll or piece of pone, buy for yourself. I don't want and Mr Chetan shouldn't be eating all that sugar.

Inside Jazz's the place was packed like free bread was sharing. Pushing. Shoving. All this to get cake and bread for the weekend. Height was an advantage. I could see the woman serving near me. Cuteness for days. From the tight, low-cut jersey she had on she knows she's hot. I stretched my hand clear above the head of the lady in front and touched her shoulder. If you see the sweet eye I get.

As I got close to the car Mammy leaned out the window.

They had the bread?

Yup.

I slammed the car door.

While you were in there I was thinking. Maybe she

wouldn't mind if Dev left. After all the hullabaloo the main
thing is she's not happy and he's not happy. They would
both be better off in the long run.

Have mercy. Mammy was still on this. I twisted my body so I
was staring out of the window with my back turned as much
as the seat belt allowed. Take the hint nah. Stop this foolishness and stop including me in it. I wanted my normal, steady
mammy instead of this crazy bitch she's become. Mammy
and I used to do everything together. We went to the grocery
together. We went to the movies together. It was us two and
sometimes Mr Chetan. Now she and Dev go for drives alone
and they don't ask me if I want to come too. When they're
liming on the porch together they don't say I can't rock in the
hammock but I get the vibes. Three's a crowd. And I hate to see
them holding hands and Mammy laughing at every dumb-ass
thing he says. They even went Tobago for a long weekend. Mr
Chetan and I had a good time at home but imagine leaving me
to go away with him? If a year ago someone said this would
happen I would've laughed in their face. But now?

I'm telling you. If that woman have something to say, she
better have the guts to say it to my face. All she good for is
to talk behind people back. But she don't frighten me. She
thinks I don't know anything. Well, I know a few things.
Matthew, chapter seven, verse three. Before looking at the
mote in thy brother's eye, think about the beam in thine
own. God is love.

As we turned into our street I saw Dev was waiting. No hiding that bright red truck parked up in front our house. I don't

want to see him. Mammy's gone from angry to skinning her teeth from one ear to the next.

Why is he here again? Like he forgot where he living? If nobody's home, he should go.

Shut up, Solo.

So boldface. And he's not even waiting in the truck. Why he feel he can open the gate and park his ugly backside on our porch?

I said shut up. Shut up, you stupid child.

Well, that got me vex. She yelling at me over he?

I'm fed up of him. His wife's not missing him?

Stop talking like that.

No. Why should I stop?

Why are you being so rude? I can't have a friend pass by me without you carrying on?

Dev opened the gates so Mammy could pull into the parking space under the house. Opening our gate like he's living here. This is my house. He should fuck off. We were hardly out the car and Mammy was apologising in a stupid voice that we weren't home earlier because we went for bread. He feel because he have money he could come here whenever he catch a vaps?

Solo, say good afternoon to Uncle Dev.

Yo, Dev.

Is Uncle Dev to you.

He took the bags of bread from Mammy and the two of them kissed on the mouth right there as if I'm invisible. I heard Mammy telling him she loved the tight jersey he had on as it showed off his six-pack. Is true the man buff but why they have to carry on so for? Suddenly, like Mammy remembered I was there too.

Solo, you didn't say good afternoon properly to Uncle Dev.

He's not my fucking uncle.

Screw them. I grabbed my backpack and lunch box, ran straight past them and up the stairs. They can wait till thy kingdom come. Uncle, my ass. Mammy's apologising. They must be upstairs in the living room. I heard her saying, oh, she can't understand what happened to me recently. Seems I used to be a good child and now I am a bad-tempered teenager. Yeah, right. If you ask me she's the one who has turned into a wormy, rotten guava.

I slammed my bedroom door hard enough for them to know that I'd heard everything. Enough bull. Not now. Not ever. But he's probably eating with us and then staying for dessert in the bedroom. Disgusting. From now on while he's here I'm not coming out my room. If Mammy thinks I'm sitting at the same table with that asshole she had better think again. Her choice. If she makes a scene I will make a scene right back. I. Don't. Care. If he doesn't like it he can jump in his stupid truck and go home. Nothing's stopping him.

One loud knock and my door opened. I should have locked the effing thing. Dev walked in boldface boldface with a big plastic bag from Sports World.

I bought something for you.

I couldn't look at him.

The man in Sports World said all the young fellas wearing these sneakers. It should fit. Your mammy texted me your size. I kept the bill in case it's too small for your foot.

Without raising my head I could see his jeans and the bag. He stood there like he was waiting for me to say thanks. I didn't say boo.

Okay, I'm leaving it right here. Try it on and let me know if the size good. Like I said, I have the bill so we could always carry it back and get a next size.

He left, closing the door soft soft, and I could hear them outside. Mammy was saying thanks for the sneakers.

You're spoiling Solo.

That is a small thing.

What he say?

Nothing.

He didn't say thanks?

Leave him alone. Boys that age can act funny.

I didn't know exactly what was happening but I heard whispering and then Mammy laughing loud loud.

Dev, stop that. The neighbours can see you.

The two of them are just nasty. Imagine in front of me and Mr Chetan her hand does be on his leg right near his pants crotch. And he's not backward. I've seen him putting his hand all up inside her top. Yuk. Carrying on like that. Disgusting.

I opened the Sports World bag to find a shoe box. Size 8. White Nike sneakers. Real expensive, only they are never going on my foot. Full stop. I wanted to fling them straight at his blasted head. You know what Dev gone and done? He gave me the exact same sneakers he'd bought for Brains and Brains's little brother. I don't want to look anything like them. When fellas at school see the three of us in the identical shoes they going to laugh their belly full. Trust me.

Dinner time came and Mammy called for me. Ignoring her was easy. The more frantic she got, the happier I felt.

Solo! Now! How many times I must call you? Come to the table.

From behind my locked bedroom door I yelled back.

I'm not hungry!

That was a lie. I was starving. So what? I'll go in the pot later when everybody's sleeping.

What you mean you're not hungry? Boy, come to the table.

I'm not coming. You can't even cook. Mr Chetan cooks better than you.

Stop being so rude and come to the table now.

No! And stop calling me!

I heard Mr Chetan telling her to leave me alone and enjoy her food while it hot. Sure. Go ahead and forget about me. I don't need any of you. My headphones can block out this house and everyone in it. It certainly blocked the noise of Mr Chetan calling for me. It was only when he was banging hard hard on my bedroom door that I finally heard and unlocked it. I don't mind talking to him – but only him.

What?

He came in and gently lifted the headphones off my ears.

You want to eat now?

Not hungry.

You expect me to believe that? You is a man who don't mess with his food.

I'm not eating while that man is in the house.

Fine. Come play a game of chess with me instead.

No.

Dominoes, then.

No.

What about checkers? You beat me last time.

No.

You want to watch TV in my room?

No.

He sat on the edge of the bed.

Dev's gone.

That's early for him.

He and your mammy had a quarrel.

I picked up my iPad.

He said he won't come here if you don't like him.

You believe that? He was probably looking for an excuse because he had to go home early.

Why you showing the man bad face? I only see him being nice to you.

I didn't do anything to him.

You're sure? I'm asking because your mammy's crying and I don't like to see that.

She's crying because the man gone home to his wife.

That's not fair. What's bothering you?

Nothing.

Then for your mammy's sake try to be pleasant and polite. Please. For me. Do it for me.

I rubbed my temples to stop the headache that was developing.

What's the point? He's not going to be here forever.

You don't know that. I don't know that. And I bet you five dollars even they don't know. Big people business complicated.

What, you think it's right that Mammy's hooked up with him?

When you get older you'll realise that life's not so black and white.

So, it's all right?

Solo, it's not as simple as wrong or right.

Well, what you feel going to happen? Don't think I haven't heard all the bull he does be saying about leaving the wife. His wife's driving a brand-new BMW. They went Florida for holidays. That is his family. We are not his family. If Mammy believes his bullshit, then more fool she.

Mr Chetan ruffled my hair and stood up.

You're a funny boy. One minute you're a baby and next minute you're playing big. Come out of the room for a quick game of checkers with me and then go get a plate of food.

I said no but I was smiling.

If I had to get a new father it should be you. But you and Mammy don't seem the slightest bit interested in one another.

Mr Chetan let out one laugh and pulled me close.

Can you take out some food for me? Please.

Okay, lazy bones. Make me fetch and carry for the little Maharaja of Simonette Street.

MR CHETAN

As I drank my second coffee I wondered if today we might talk. It's been on my mind to say something to Miss Betty when the time's right. Solo's going on a school trip. Without him around she might open up a little. The break-up with Dev was a good few months now and it's still bothering her. For all the big talk Miss Betty never had the gumption to take a stand and make Dev choose. Being his long-term deputy wasn't her style either although I personally think that set-up has its merits. He didn't choose and she couldn't settle. Part of me wishes they had had a big bust-up where everybody cussed and carried on. At least then the relationship is dead. End of story. Take your pain in one hit. You recover faster than if the relationship drags on for ages. And those two dragged that carcass from one hurricane season to the next. Drip by drip he stopped coming over. She doesn't mention it but her eyes don't lie. Miss Betty's still hurting.

And Solo is a next one. Getting him out of this house is hard work. It might be easier to hook him up to a crane. Happiness for him would be staying in his bedroom forever with headphones and iPad. It's Saturday but it's a school thing and he better go if he knows what's good for him. He'll get in trouble if he breaks biche and misses this outing. Poor fella. He's finding it hard to fit in and he's forever angry. When I went to wake him up he started sniffling, pretending he's stuffed up.

I'm feeling real dread. No way I can go out today.

I felt his forehead.

Solo, you're not sick. Get your little tail out of the bed.

Honest. I'm not making joke. I'm getting a cold.

Two Panadol and jump in the shower. You're not going to cut cane. You'll have fun. See the Pitch Lake. Buss a lime on the beach. It will do you good.

For a teenager to be by himself all the time is unhealthy. Apart from not wanting to go on the excursion, the bus was leaving from the school yard at 8 a.m. Solo's not a morning person. He whinged. He whined. He carried on like a cry cry baby. I assume this is a phase. What I don't want is for it to become a habit. He mustn't go through life being 'fraidy 'fraidy. Trust me. I know it's no life. Besides, I was up early o'clock to make the little wretch saheenas and aloo pies for his trip.

Once Solo was gone Miss Betty mapped out the day. I was given my orders – weeding the beds and planting out the tomatoes we've been growing from seed. We have a little vegetable garden at the back of the house. Let me rephrase that. Miss Betty started a vegetable garden and I got roped in as the hard labour. Skinny me as the muscle. I don't want to put goat mouth on it but days like this are as good as having my own family.

I pulled on my rubber boots and went out back. Miss Betty was already on her knees weeding the okro. That was the first thing we planted because in two twos they're longer than your hand. I fingered the row of plants, checking the leaves for white blight spots or holes where insects have nibbled. By next month-end we should be feasting on our own fried okro with hot sada roti or using it to make callaloo soup. The pigeon peas, pimento and sweet peppers are already bearing. Two steel drums, cut in half horizontally and laid end to end, have every seasoning you could want. I'm talking thyme, Spanish thyme, rosemary, chive, sweet basil, marjoram, coriander, flat leaf parsley, curly leaf parsley. The chadon beni need a haircut before it takes over. But not everything we've put in the ground has been a success.

Something is eating the pumpkin vine, Miss B.

I saw that. It could be the birds.

Whatever was attacking the pumpkin should move over to the spinach instead. When I was little the neighbour used to grow endless spinach, only they called it by the Indian name, chorai bhagi. Strange the things you remember. We have enough spinach to sell in the market. Everyone on our street got a share. People at work got plenty. Open the fridge right now and it's overflowing with the damn thing. To hear Miss Betty you would think spinach was heaven's chosen plant. She tells anybody who asks, and a few who don't, that since she started having spinach daily her skin's clearer, she has more energy and she's regular as clockwork. Not me.

Mr Chetan, you plan to keep walking around like an inspector or you're going to put a hand?

Your problem is you're too anxious. Relax. I will finish this in two twos.

She rolled her eyes at me but I caught the little smile that came after. I like when she pretends she's vexed with me. Best I start weeding before she gets mad for real.

Agriculturists may not agree but in my experience weeds are always the fastest-growing plant whatever the conditions.

An hour of kneeling down, crouching over these rows and rows of plants, and I was desperate for a beastly cold Carib.

A Carib for you, Miss B?

So early? Only a glass of cold water, please.

When I came back with the drinks Miss Betty was poking two small bags of sargassum fertiliser. Me? Only thing I wanted to examine was a second Carib, while rocking in the hammock.

Miss Betty, the fertiliser is enough?

It will stretch. No way I'm getting up from here to go in traffic for more.

I could always go.

You ain't going nowhere. Pulling a fast one. I look like I born yesterday? You leave to buy fertiliser and next thing I'll get a call saying, oh, you took two wrong turns and don't know how but you land up in Maracas Bay.

She wagged a pointy finger in my face.

I'm watching you good.

All right, all right. Cool yourself. I was only making joke.

You going to weed that bed of spinach?

I'm leaving that for last. Damn spinach will shoot up even if the weeds choking them. But check out this pretty little pepper tree. The thing ain't reach a good three foot yet and it's laden with Congo pepper. Just now we'll be making pepper sauce.

By eleven o'clock the sun was stinging the back of my neck and my middle-aged bones were telling me they had been punished enough.

Hear nah. How about we call it a day? Tomorrow morning bright and early, when it's not making so hot, you go find me right here.

No way. Once you leave, this garden ain't seeing your face again for the weekend.

Have a heart, woman. While you're in church, I will finish up. Promise. Cross my heart and hope to die.

Go along, go along. You don't have an ounce of stamina. Them years in London made you 'fraid a little hot sun. Leave. I'm good.

You sure?

Go bathe your skin in some cold water before you get sun stroke.

In my room, I cooled off under the high-speed fan. Not being able to deal with the heat is something I can't admit as a born and bred Trini. Give me the cold over this hot sun any day. Miss Betty's still going strong outside. Me? I'm dead out. My back done tell me I've put in a full day's labour. My watch however claims it's barely 11.30 a.m.

*

I shifted to the patio to take the breeze. A good hour passed before she collapsed in the hammock next to mine, a nasty-looking green smoothie in her hand.

Hitting the spinach hard, I see. Mind you don't turn green like Kermit the Frog.

This is a healthy blend of spinach, banana and apple juice. If you know what's good for you, you would put down the Carib and drink a glass too. We might all be getting older but I'm not going down without a fight.

She sipped her drink and I scanned the newspaper.

You want to go to Movietown, Mr Chetan?

Not really. If it's company you want I'll go. What do you want to see?

I haven't even checked what's showing.

She took another gulp of the green liquid and waved for me to hand over the papers.

And pass your glasses one time.

I took off my glasses and pretended to hand them over. Just before she touched them I yanked them away. She sighed and put her hand out, palm up. I slowly reached out but she was fast and snatched the glasses. With victory in her smile she put them on even though they swallowed her narrow face.

Miss B, you don't think you should get your eyes tested soon? Like next week.

Nothing is wrong with my eyes. And I'm not wearing glasses. Full stop. Make me look more ugly. Now and then when I can't see something I can borrow yours.

I wouldn't say Miss Betty's pretty. After seeing her daily, and looking all how, my mind's changed. She's handsome. Even this minute, with her wet hair pulled in a bun and wearing my oversized glasses, she is attractive in a weird way.

So, what are you dragging me to see then?

Give me a fat chance. I'm still looking.

But Miss B, I was enjoying my papers. There's a good article on the Venezuelans coming here for work.

Hush. Keep quiet for five minutes. And don't start me on the way we treating Venezuelans. They vex because the Venezuelans showing them up and working hard.

Sighing, she looked up.

It's only one set of stupidness showing. It wasn't so much the cinema. I wanted to go out the house little bit. You don't sometimes wish you had a person to lime with?

So, what happen? I'm not people?

You know what I mean. Somebody who is into you.

Dev's on your mind?

No answer. Another swig of the green slime. How she could stomach that I will never know.

Girl, stop worrying your head. Every bread have its cheese.

So, what you saying? Sunil was my cheese?

Not that mouldy cheddar. Sorry, I shouldn't say that.

She shook her head.

It's just the two of us. Say what you want.

Well, you don't have to eat mouldy cheese. Fresh cheddar in Massy supermarket every week. You only have to get out there and look.

At least she smiled while she drained her glass.

You see me? I'm done. From now on is bread and water for me.

You mustn't say that.

She gently rested the empty glass on the floor.

You know what? I honestly think Sunil is my cross to bear until I'm six feet under. Like I can't shake him off.

From what you've told me that man should have been locked up. Nobody should feel they can treat another human being like that. Not your wife. Not your son. Especially not your wife or your son.

Miss Betty was next to me but her eyes were far away.

The Dev thing didn't work out but you know something? After you met him I find you're walking taller, with your back straight. And you're taking a little better care of yourself. I like your hair the way you have it now.

Yeah, right.

I'm not lying. You're looking good. For your age.

She whacked me with the newspaper.

Watch your mouth. To me everybody that comes in your life there to teach you. Dev was the Lord's way of reminding me that things in that department shut down for good. My life is me and Solo. Period.

What if Dev pulled up here right now and said that he's left the witch he married and is you he wants to make a life with?

Nothing doing.

You're sure about that?

Even if that witch flew away on a broomstick and took she two big-head children with she.

We both well laughed hard. But soon Miss Betty looked sad again and sighed.

Sunil's always in the background. That man's spirit was bad. No. Like I said, I'm done with all this love business.

I sat up in the hammock.

Watch me. I have a theory. You have some people who know when they see a good cheese. They don't wait. They bite it straight away. Right. Then there are other people who think the cheese is so-so. It's not tasting quite right but it's not too bad either. So they say, what the hell, and eat it. But then you have the third group who never went near the cheese. Them so? When they hit a certain age they does start bawling down the place. Where my cheese? Who take all the cheese? I ain't even get a little piece of cheese.

Miss Betty rocked back laughing.

Half the time you're quiet as a mouse but when you're ready you well know how to talk foolishness.

All I'm saying is don't end up asking where the cheese gone when you never went looking in the first place.

You're full of big talk today. You even remember what cheese tastes like? I've never once seen you with a girlfriend.

I eased myself up out of the hammock and stretched out my hand for her empty glass.

You want anything else?

I'm good.

I'm going to take a five in my bed. If you're feeling for Movietown tonight I'm cool with that.

Girlfriend? Hopefully that talk won't come up again. Or maybe the answer is simply: Miss Betty. I keep going over this. It's funny but in all the years I've been living here not a single harsh word has passed between us. I had my doubts but we clicked so easily. Almost convinces me to try. In fairness, she's not put out vibes that she liked me that way. Maybe she's waiting for me to make the first move. Why is it always the man who must make the first move? She's not backward. If she wanted me she's had plenty chances. Every day. But when she asked me about a girlfriend, why didn't I say something? It would have been so easy. But no, Chetan. You had to run and hide, leaving the woman high and dry.

I slumped into my chair and picked up the book I was reading. If I sat quietly and read this moment would pass. Hopefully she's already forgotten she even asked me that question. My mind kept drifting and I reread the same two paragraphs at least three times. I had to settle my spinning head. A happy, comfortable life was feet away. This isn't a huge sacrifice. Look at all I could have. A ready-made family. Solo as my son. My son. Our DNA may be different and yes he can be stubborn and moody but he's my boy. He's growing up and the mother needs to cut those apron strings. When my time's up, whatever little I have is his.

I don't know what to do. I just don't. I've had this argument with myself so many times and it never gets any easier or clearer. There's no peace. It's like travelling in a maxi taxi on the wrong side of the Solomon Hochoy Highway. Swerving, screeching, overtaking on the inside, never slowing down, driving on the hard shoulder. I need an ease-up.

A tap, tap, tap on the door snatched me from this half dream.

What about a sandwich? And a brownie? Solo didn't take all.

In no time she was back with a tray. Four neat triangles of tuna sandwich, salad and fresh lime juice to wash it down.

You did that for spite.

What?

You know I hate salad.

Stop acting like a two-year-old and eat the thing.

She had used one of her special bone china plates – the ones that live in the tall glass cabinet. I didn't know if I should say something or pretend not to notice. She remained standing, half in, half out the room.

Thanks for all this.

Okay. Let me leave you to your beauty rest.

That's the thing about this sweet woman. I didn't know I wanted a tuna sandwich. She knew what I wanted before I did.

I can't say how long I sat staring at that wall, thinking about the little cracks on the right-hand side that need filling and repainting. Without moving I filled and painted the cracks over and over. I began to have flashbacks to pum-pum shorts man from Maracas Beach. I tried to push him away and think of Miss Betty. When I couldn't I shifted to the patterns made by the hairline cracks. I thought of squeezing the tube of ready-mix filler, putting a tiny bit on an old knife and forcing it into the open gaps. Before the filler was dry the image living in my head, his profile, his smell – they filled my insides. Again I pushed him aside, imagining opening the tube of filler, putting some on the old knife, dragging the knife along the crack lines. Each time he returned. His hard chest, his strong legs, they stopped me from getting further to the part where the filler has dried and I can sand it down twice – rough followed by smooth sandpaper. Forget repainting. Replaying the rough, muscular way he handled me made concentration impossible. When I think of Miss B it's not the same. She's someone I want to protect, look after, not throw around the bedroom.

BETTY

I was walking back to the car toting a full basket of vegetables from the outdoor market when I remembered Red Man. Last week he promised. You never know. Today self I might get a shock.

I say like you're not doing market today.

Red Man, look how I nearly gone home without seeing you. But my mind tell me I was forgetting something. You have any?

Mistress, I had it out right here and the amount of people who wanted to grab it from me. I had to hide it up or you wasn't getting nothing.

From a cooler by his feet he took out a thick parcel of newspaper. Inside were twelve of the ugliest fish God put in the sea. Each no bigger than my hand, the cascadoux looked like something that should have gone out with the dinosaur. For a start cascadoux doesn't have scales. They are armour-plated. I'm not joking. Two rows of dark grey armour like the fish ready for a sword fight. And each side of its ugly mouth there are these long spikes. Ugh.

I cleaned out the guts, Mistress, but I left the head them. Some say that is where all the flavour does be. Other people does be frighten. Whatever you want. I could cut them off easy easy.

Leave them. I could always chop them off if I change my mind.

A man passing behind me stopped.

But Red Man, how you could treat me so? I buy from you must be half hour ago and you never said you have cascadoux.

Oh gosh, don't take worries. This was a special order. You know how long this lady been begging me to bring cascadoux for she? And these days it does be real scarce.

The stranger turned to me.

Family, you're taking all this sweet cascadoux. So what I go eat?

Sorry. Today is curry cascadoux in my house.

Hear what. I find you look like a nice, reasonable woman. Let me do you a favour.

He tapped his chest.

I will pay for all the fish. All. But then I go take half home and you go take half. Free. Just so. You can't get better than that. Free fish and everybody happy. What you say?

I had to smile.

But you real boldface. Buy my fish from under my nose? You're mad or what?

Cool yourself, family. You don't have to get on so. I try a thing. And you're sure sure you can't share that cascadoux?

My cascadoux and God face is two things you ain't ever seeing.

It's been donkey years since I tasted cascadoux. Must be since early marriage. If Sunil saw lines of these mud-covered fish selling by the roadside near Caroni he would buy and bring home. Of course then I had to clean everything myself but as it was so fresh it would eat nice nice. I done know Solo will turn up his nose. Have mercy, this fish seriously ugly for days. If I didn't know how sweet it does taste I wouldn't want to eat it either. Only thing is you can't cook cascadoux now for now. It requires preparation.

*

Solo! Come, please. I need help, son. Solo!

He needs his hearing checked. Mind you, if I was calling him for KFC you would see speed.

What?

What? It's what, Mammy. And stop with that grumpy voice.

What you want? I'm doing homework.

Go in the garden and cut some seasoning, please.

Why you can't get it?

I'm not asking you again. I want a dozen chadon beni leaves and two-three pimento peppers.

He rolled his eyes and turned to go. When did the devil switch my darling doux-doux for this rude man-child?

And bring a bunch of chive too, please. Oh, and some thyme. A good handful of thyme.

It's a lucky thing I wasn't in a hurry because Solo like he was waiting for the herbs them to grow.

Here.

He dumped a sweet-smelling bag on the counter. All from my garden. I love that.

Why you don't look to see how I'm cooking cascadoux? You never know. One day you might want to make it yourself.

No. I was doing my homework and you interrupted me. When is dinner?

It's not even close to dinner time.

Well, I want food now.

You can't go five minutes without eating. Take an orange and cool yourself. And you better be studying in there and not playing on no computer. Exams are just now.

Yes. Yes.

If you don't do well in the exams you ain't getting into no college. Without proper qualifications you will face plenty catch-ass.

He peeled the orange over the sink.

Uncle Hari doesn't have any big qualifications and he's living good in New York.

Yes, your father brother set himself up in America but you have no idea what kind of hard work he had to put in to make ends meet. It's not like he went there and land a big job just so just so.

Solo took his orange and left. I heard the click of the key turning in the lock. Mister Hard Ears feel he big and know everything. Don't mind me. I'm only the mother. Children always think their parents are dumb dumbs.

The muddy water smell of the fish only disappeared after a good wash with two limes. Into the blender I threw the chadon beni, chives, thyme, an onion cut up and two cloves of garlic. That mix perfumed the whole kitchen. Two chopped-up tomatoes went in the mix. These tomatoes are down to Mr Chetan. He didn't take to gardening at first. But he planted them out, checked on them every evening after work, and now we're eating the sweetest tomatoes grown from seed. I'm not boasting but fact is fact. Tomatoes in the market can't touch these for flavour. Inside each fish I stuffed the green seasoning and tomato mixture. That will sit in the fridge until it's time to curry them down in the pot.

When cascadoux's starring nothing must upstage it. Boiled rice to soak up the curry, a little fried plantain on the side and we good to go. Mr Chetan will never say no to a piece of fried plantain. I peeled two, cut them in half and sliced them. Not too thick and not too thin. It must fry without burning. I hope Mr Chetan gets home soon. He's so sweet. Whatever else he does on a Saturday he makes it his business to go to the grocery for things like washing powder, foil, napkins and soap. For me that is a real ease up. Once market is done I can relax myself. I lucked out on that one. Now, if only I could get lucky in other ways, life would be perfect. Whatever, he's not interested in me like that.

I took out the big fry pan and put it on the stove. We've switched to olive oil for most of the cooking but certain things demand ordinary corn oil. It took three batches to fry out the plantain. I could have squished in more slices and finished in half the time but what would be the point of that? Monday to Friday everybody hustling. Today I'm taking my sweet time and cooking something different for a change.

Truth is the plantain's only frying for one person. It's hard to tell when it happened but over the last few years, piece by piece, I think I catch feelings for Mr Chetan. He's gentle. In a country with so much crime and selfishness he's soft. And he loves my son. It's the little kindnesses he adds to my life – like making me a smoothie or helping in the house when I'm tired. The idiot is still calling me Miss Betty. Occasionally it's shortened to Miss B when he's being playful. Anyhow, horse dead and cow fat and still nothing has ever passed between us. After so long I guess that plane has taken off.

The warm plantain will stay covered with a little foil until we're ready to eat. Shame we never got together. We make sense. Oops. The rice. I almost forgot that. Just in time I turned off the heat and covered the pot. Mr Chetan's already living with me so no surprises there. We've seen each other in the morning pre-brushed teeth and pre-shower. And I still like his gentle smile and the way he looks at me directly in the eye when he's talking. Love? I thought I loved my husband

and look how that turned out. Did I love Dev? The thought of him still makes my stomach flip. And I ain't going to lie. We fit together in the bedroom like he was made for me. Lust or love? Best to leave love out of the talk.

Cascadoux must be eaten as soon as it comes off the fire. I yelled to Solo that dinner wouldn't be long. Time for my skin to catch a little water and wash away the day. Back in the kitchen I found Mr Chetan snooping around, lifting covers.

Hands off the plantain.

Two tiny pieces were falling off the plate. All I did was rescue them.

Behave yourself. Now shoo from here.

In my favourite iron pot, I fried a chopped onion, two-three cloves of minced garlic, and two tablespoons each of curry powder, turmeric, geera and garam masala. I also threw in a handful of curry leaves, a nice hot pepper and two pimento peppers sliced up thin thin. Once that began sticking I poured enough water to mix everything. I love that moment when the water hits the pot. It does be like a curry bomb exploding. I wouldn't be surprised if the neighbour's house is smelling of curry too.

Now for the cascadoux. My ma called this chunkaying the fish – mixing so it's covered with the curry. I must teach Solo that word or my generation will be the last to know. Fish is a thing that does cook now for now so I watched the pot carefully. Eight minutes later I poured a can of coconut milk and threw in some fresh, boiled pigeon peas. The spicy aroma must have been why Mr Chetan reached back in my way.

I tired tell you to stay out the kitchen when I'm doing my thing.

Lord, woman. You're making a man hungry.

He lifted the lid slightly and inhaled.

Where'd you find cascadoux?

I have my ways. You like it?

I'm embarrassed to admit this. I've never had cascadoux.

No way. Well, today self we're fixing that.

He dipped a teaspoon into the sauce. From the smack of his lips I knew it real lash.

We sat down to eat, the three of us, and as I thought, Solo took one look at the fish and said he wasn't touching it. Could he get a ham and cheese sandwich? I showed him how, starting from the head, you slide your fork under the scales and they peel off easy easy. Underneath is bare sweet flesh. My child said the fish head was frightening to look at. Mr Chetan promptly broke them off and put them on his plate.

Mammy, this is real hard labour for a little flesh.

Yes, but that little piece of fish sweeter than all the rest of fish put together. Carite, kingfish, red snapper, barracuda. Not one of them can touch cascadoux for taste. And Solo, this is a special fish. They say if you eat it you will never leave Trinidad. Even if you leave you will always return to die.

Whatever. Give me a good stew chicken over this ugly thing any day. Cook chicken tomorrow nah.

You're trying my patience. Eat what I put in front you and
stop asking about what cooking tomorrow. You see me?
Come tomorrow I mightn't even feel like lighting the stove.

Mr Chetan leaned across to Solo.

Don't worry, boy. I will cook chicken for you. But try with
the cascadoux. Your mammy went to a lot of trouble to get
the fish and cook it for us.

I gave Mr Chetan a cut eye.

Go on. Spoil the child. Monkey know which tree to climb.

Solo continued to pick pick at the fish but honestly I wasn't
paying him much mind. Food like this had to eat without
obstructions like knife and fork. Once I cleared the flesh I
went down on the fish bones and well sucked them dry. And
the fish head? Sucked that too.

Mammy, you could leave a little. If we had a dog the poor
thing would starve.

We don't have a dog and you're not getting one because is
me will end up minding it.

Solo nudged Mr Chetan.

You're not worried a fish bone will stick in your throat?

He grinned but couldn't reply because he was busy with a fish
head. From his grin you could see this fish was boss. Curry
was trickling down his forearm. It's only after I had wiped the
drips with my own fingers and sucked them did I realise what
I had done. I swear it was the sight of all that yummy sauce. I

wasn't thinking. God is love, yes, because Mr Chetan ignored me and kept eating. Solo didn't seem to notice. We continued but I had tasted something even sweeter than the curry and, boops, bam, without a word, everything shifted. I didn't think anything had changed for him but it had. When he next looked at me his brown eyes were softer.

We finished dinner, both of us focusing on Solo. House rules are clear. The cook doesn't wash wares. While Mr Chetan and Solo cleared the dishes, washed and packed away, I lazed on the porch, taking the night breeze. Tasting his skin probably meant more to me than to him. The softness in his eyes I may have imagined. It wouldn't be the first time I took a six for a nine. Oh Jesus, the salty taste of his skin. That was real.

Inside my belly a heat was rising and it wasn't from the curry. I stretched out on the recliner, my whole body slowly catching fire. From the kitchen I could hear raucous laughing and dishes clanking. They had better not break any of my good plates. And hurry up. I was a hot mess. Inside this one body a hot craving and a deep dread were throwing blows at one other. I didn't know what to do. That's when he appeared with two small glasses and a fancy bottle.

You refused to try my Chai Rum before.

It's no secret I'm not a drinker and here he was offering me rum neat. Maybe because I needed to calm myself, I took the glass and sipped like a pro. But wait. This rum tasted real different for truth. Man, I could get used to this.

Where you get this Chai Rum from? I've never tasted anything so. When they say a drink's smooth this must be what they mean.

See, I knew you would like it. They're making it right here in Trinidad. Now, before the next sip, I want you to do something. Your hands clean?

Yes.

All right. Throw a drop of Chai Rum on the palm of one hand and rub your hands together.

I did what the man told me.

Sniff your hand. Check out the aroma.

I pulled the fumes deep into my nostrils. Definitely a rum, only it didn't burn my nose like the nastiness Sunil used to guzzle. Mr Chetan took my hand up to his face and inhaled.

Now you can take a sip.

Mellow, slight sweetness, it slipped down my throat like honey. Once inside it lit my chest, my belly and down below. I raised my empty glass.

I probably shouldn't but as we're home. It's not like I'm driving anywhere.

His hand was heavy when pouring. I wasn't going to object because right now I needed a little something. Mr Chetan rocked back in his hammock.

Come by me.

I got up and dragged my chair next to the hammock so I was beside him.

Where's Solo?

In his room watching a movie. He said he's finished his homework.

I never know what's going on behind that bedroom door.

You really want to know what a teenaged boy is doing when the door's locked?

We laughed.

And watch out. Just now it's girlfriends on the scene.

Fingers reached out and coiled strands of my hair. As I sipped my drink, I calculated how much I should move my arm, my head, my lips. A single unnecessary movement might stop the flow of those fingers massaging my scalp. And as they moved from my scalp to my neck we talked for what seemed like hours. Exactly what was said I couldn't repeat. All I remember were his fingers stroking my hair, my neck, sliding over my breasts. The world was vibrating. Maybe I had two or three more refills. He dipped his index finger in the glass and with the wet tip traced my lips. It was too much. I looked him in the eye.

Move over.

He pushed himself up and opened his legs. The only place I wanted to be was wrapped in that space. I snuggled into his warm body. If he had put two fingers inside me I would have come straight away. Sweeter, hotter than anything, was the feel of his body closing around mine. Between the drink and the lust I was light-headed. We felt like familiar lovers. He leaned in and we had the longest, deepest kiss. His tongue might have been inside my mouth but it tingled every piece of my flesh.

Even my toes quivered.

I staggered to standing. It wasn't the booze. This might be what they mean by swooning and I was glad for the moonless sky. He should fuck me right now, right here. Grabbing his hand, I pushed him against the balustrade.

You want something, Miss B?

What you think?

I guided his fingers.

You're soaking wet.

Holding hands and tiptoeing, he led me to his bed. As we passed Solo's room he put a finger to his lips. How was I supposed to be quiet when he was making funny faces? He had barely locked the door behind us when we both started throwing off our clothes and rolling around on the bed together. I know size doesn't matter but I had to check out the package. Not bad. Not bad at all.

Who would have known his kisses would be like melted chocolate? Sly devil. Keeping that silky tongue to himself. I wanted to eat the man raw. And forget about how the rum smell. Sniffing his skin was getting me high. I wanted him inside me now now. My hands reached down expecting him to be rock hard but he wasn't. The drink was playing with him. And some men take longer. Besides, we're not as young as we used to be.

I pushed him onto his back and climbed on top. I had this. Chetan had the most beautiful smile as he lay there, eyes closed. I slide down and I sucked on him more than I had the cascadoux. His moans, I loved the sound of his moans. Even when he was hard I didn't stop. I wanted that music in my ears. He pulled me up, licking and biting me all over. I took his cock and stroked my pussy. We were nearly there, nearly there, then braps. My boy went limp.

I drank too much.

Chill. We're not in a hurry.

Lie. I wanted this all like yesterday. With a huge sigh he rolled off me.

Let's take a break.

No, sugar. We're not taking a break. We're going for gold.

Call it what you want – Dandool, the Gorgon, Jeremiah, the Sledge, the Punisher, Big Ben, Hot Beef Injection, the Slayer. I didn't care. It just had to get up. Tactics were required. My brain rifled through each tip and trick I had learnt with Sunil, Dev and every porn movie I'd enjoyed. I went down on him with a strategy. Before long the sweet music of his soft moans filled my ears. My thighs were slippery with wetness. Oh Jesus, I wanted this man inside me now now. He moved on top and tried to enter me. But one thrust later his hardness had weakened. I could sense he was panicking. It was probably over. Peas-an-rice, what did a girl have to do to get a fuck around here?

I tried rubbing my pussy on him, kissing him, biting him. Nothing. Using his hands, he tried to wake the sleeping soldier. Nothing.

You know how long it's been since I get a little something?
Eh? I find the Lord could've shown some mercy.

We looked at one other and burst out laughing. If only he
would go down on me. I was so close to exploding.

Lick me.

I've had too much to drink. Come for a love up.

Wait – it was fine for me to suck him like it was going out of
style but he couldn't go down on me for a two minutes? Selfish
bastard. I didn't have him down as a taker. Suddenly I clicked.
My boy needed a pill.

You does take anything to, you know, help?

I don't need Viagra.

I pulled the sheet up by my neck. Whatever Chai Rum was
still in my blood evaporated instantly.

Really? So it's just me you can't fuck? Fine. But you should
have worked that out earlier.

No. No. That's not it at all. I care about you. It's me. I'm
drunk. It's me.

Don't give me that. You changed your mind half way and
have me here like a fool.

He sat up.

I have something to tell you, Miss B.

Really? What? You have a woman hide up somewhere that
you forgot to tell me about?

He burst out laughing. That got me more vexed.

Go ahead. Laugh till your belly bust.

I turned away and immediately he scooped his body around mine. Even though I was mad no ass I took the cuddle. My heart softened. I moved to see his face – odd, sad even – and tried to gently kiss him but he shook his head.

I want to tell you something.

I sat up and brushed his cheek with the back of my hand.

You know the saying all food good to eat but all talk ain't good to talk? If you have something you want to keep private that's fine. I have things I keep to myself too. Big things.

This you need to know. I'm gay.

I felt like I was free-falling through the air.

I'm gay. I've always been gay. I tried having a girlfriend once but it didn't work. I can't help it. This is who I am. Seems that even being with you can't change that.

He put his head in his hands.

I'm really sorry. I wanted this to work. You and me. Nothing would have made me happier. We're so close as it is.

I would have given anything to be fully dressed. He didn't look gay. He didn't act gay. Mr Chetan, a buller man?

You talking foolishness. You're not gay. We had a little challenge tonight. Could happen to anybody. That doesn't make you gay.

I'm telling you the truth.

What's going on? You're in this bed with me right now, right here, and you know you're gay? This is some kinda blasted game to you?

On my list of regrets this one's going straight to number one. I felt I might burst into tears or punch his fucking face. It could go either way.

Miss B, you know I care for you, right? I care for you more than I care for anybody else. I promise you that.

Tears started flowing and they wouldn't stop. Soft kisses on my forehead only made me feel more wretched. Anger dissolved into snot and tears.

Were you fantasising about a man while we were doing things? Next thing you'll be eyeing up Solo.

He looked at me with shock and pain in his eyes. I stared right back. I wanted to rip out his heart and push it through a shredder.

I love him like my own son.

I bit my lip and whispered,

I didn't mean it.

He pulled me in close. Big, ugly tears spilled down my face and neck. He cared but he didn't want me. My body wasn't enough. It's never been good enough. I blurted out,

You sure sure you're gay?

He flipped me around, looked down at his limpness then back up at me.

What you think?

We both burst out laughing. I tried drying my face with the sheet.

This ain't easy, you hear. Look at me. I'm naked, drunk and, heaven help me, I just tried to fuck a gay man.

He squeezed me tight. This night had no back door.

MR CHETAN

We were in one of hell's inner circles. Even if she didn't want coffee I needed it injected directly into my veins. It took a whole heap of coaxing and cooing to get Miss Betty tucked up under a blanket before I could throw on some clothes and tiptoe to the kitchen. She needed to sober up and get in her own bed to sleep this off. The rest we'll figure out.

Until tonight I'd lied to myself that I wasn't a hundred per cent gay. Maybe I was eighty or even ninety per cent. Now that longed-for space to have a family had vaporised. If I ever need a witness to swear that I am a queer, a whole queer, and nothing but a queer, it's Miss Betty I'm calling. Poor woman has had chapter and verse.

Why you didn't say something before?

Her voice made me jump, spilling hot coffee on the counter. She was standing behind me in her peach nightie.

Why? I never told anyone. I thought it would go away if, you know, we had something going.

She sat down across from me, reached over and gripped both my hands in hers.

It's my fault too. I didn't stop to ask myself why you've never had a woman.

Miss Betty took my hands to her lips and kissed them with a new sweetness I'd not felt before.

When was the last time you were in love, Mr Chetan?

I'm in love with you.

Yes, well, thanks for that but it ain't going to work. You know what I'm talking about.

I sighed, opened my mouth, then shut it with another sigh. Why dream of the past? When you've dug a pit in your heart and buried your feelings, sharing memories isn't easy. Where to start? Miss Betty would be well within her rights to wash her hands clean having discovered the real me. Too much for one blasted night. While these thoughts were whirling around, giving me an instant headache, she got up, climbed into the chair beside me and wrapped me tight tight in her arms.

Look, we tried. And for the record I put in some serious effort tonight.

I grinned. She wasn't lying.

But God is love. You and me will keep living like family, unless of course you find some hunk and leave.

That's not going to happen.

Who knows? You're still hot. I say so.

I squeezed her. My honey. Best to keep it simple. People have all kind of families. Maybe we could do this even if the bedroom's absent from the equation.

Ever so slowly her compassion coaxed snippets and stories. When did I first know I was gay? In primary school. While the boys were sweet on Jenny with hair in two long plaits, I only had eyes for shy Tony. Even at six years old I knew that wasn't the way for others. I sipped the strong coffee. Simply admitting Tony, speaking the words out loud, was a huge release. No one knew. It surprised me I could even remember that far back.

Can I tell you something weird?

You don't find you tell me enough weird things for one night?

We laughed again. I told her about my father's friend hugging me. I must have been about ten. His cologne was a deep, musky, masculine scent. In a split second I knew this was the smell I wanted. Isn't that odd? None of the perfumes my mother or my aunties wore ever affected me that way. All these years later if I sniff anything similar it's an immediate turn-on.

When I asked you about being in love you didn't answer me.

Love's not easy, is it? And a closet queer? Worse yet.

Don't give me that. You know you're hot. How much hearts you break?

Me? Break hearts? More like get mine mashed up good and proper.

She harassed my soul until I told her about Mani. We met in secondary school. I was a shy, awkward boy. He was the opposite. For whatever reason he took me under his wing and that was that. Bullies had to go through him to get to me. From day one I was in love. Of course, I never let on.

Mani was your first love?

I told her about the time when we were fifteen and I slept over at Mani's house. We were play-wrestling and it became more. Much more. We did things to each other, things that felt real good.

He didn't have skills like you but you know what I mean.

Miss Betty blushed.

That he wanted me was one of the happiest moments of my life. Now when I think of him it's only with shame.

But why?

It's painful.

Miss Betty took our empty mugs and began washing up. I found a clean dishcloth to dry.

Miss B, you ever did something that left you feeling utterly ashamed?

You don't own shame.

I put away the mugs and turned to catch her looking at me with such tenderness that my eyes started to water. I blurted out,

My mother found out about Mani.

I put my head on that kitchen table and sobbed like a baby. It was much worse than Miss Betty's rum-fuelled crying earlier. She stayed by me, strong and silent. Between sobs I explained how my mother told my father and as punishment they sent me to live by distant relatives on the other side of the island. The only thing my mother ever said about it was, 'I know what you are.' And that was that. My family stopped being my family. Miss Betty kissed my wet cheek.

Maybe you should look up Mani.

He's probably married with a string band of children.

Or he might be single and ready to mingle.

I got up, washed my face at the kitchen sink and dried it with a paper towel.

Now you know why I don't visit family. I don't have any. Is shame they shame to know me.

Let them go. From where I'm standing your guts hard like a calabash. Look at all what you've gone through and you still ended up a decent man.

She looked down at her feet.

You have nothing to be ashamed of. The only one in this room that should be full of shame is me. Not you.

What you talking about, Miss B? You're too sweet for that.

That's not true.

She paused and stared at the wall. Her whole body seemed to shrink and double over. The drink was still in her system.

I should be sitting down in jail.

Stop exaggerating. It's not like you killed anybody.

She unfolded and we locked eyes. I could see her swallowing hard.

What if I had?

I brushed the stray hairs off her forehead. Her face had turned grey.

Sunil died right here. In this house. But he didn't fall just so.

I'm sorry but the man was a drunk. You can't save someone when they love rum more than anything else.

You can't know what it was like to live with him. I never knew if I was going to rub up with the nice Sunil or the nasty Sunil. And once he was drinking he could flip from one to the next like a light switch. I was scared all the time. Sunil broke my arm. He cuffed me in my face so many times. One time he burnt my hand on the stove. I had plenty horrors with that man. When he was fed up beating me he would turn on Solo. And Solo was only a baby. That is where I draw the line. Do what you want to me. I is a big woman. But don't touch my child.

I held her hand while she spoke to the floor.

It was Solo's fifth birthday. I made a nice cake. We sang happy birthday. Only the three of us. Even then Solo knew that his father could change in a second so he never wanted any little friends to come over. I tried to get Sunil not to drink but he said it's his son's birthday and nobody was going to stop him celebrating. Then he got nasty. I put Solo in his room. I was so vexed. It was the boy's special day. For once in his life he couldn't put his son first? I saw him leaning up on the post at the top of the back stairs, cigarette in one hand, rum in the other. Happy as pappy. Not a care in the world. I don't know what came over me but I pushed him. By the time he landed at the bottom of the stairs he was dead.

I was stunned. It was then we heard a sob, turned around and there was Solo. How long he'd been standing there I couldn't say. From the look in his eyes it was clear he had heard every word.

PART TWO

SOLO

As the plane hit the runway I buss a smile for the first time since leaving Piarco Airport. Man, is gone I gone. I didn't just wake up one morning, catch a vaps and leave. Let me make it clear. It's not like I had a choice in the matter. I wanted to dust it out that effing house the same night I found out. But where I could ups and go as a schoolboy without a red cent to my name? High school done now and I put what I made working part time and Mammy put the rest. She didn't suspect a thing. All these years she had me like a stupid kunumunu. If I didn't hear she and Mr Chetan all now so I still wouldn't know the blasted truth. Making the world think my father caused his own death. Well, partner, me and she done. From now on she is my mother in name only and I don't want to see she face as long as I live. I don't want to see she, hear she, nothing, nothing, nothing. This ain't no joke. She could suck salt. If I never saw Trinidad again it wouldn't trouble me. It's not big enough for all two of we. Let she stay there and rot.

Whole flight I was checking out a family in front. You should hear them loud loud complaining that American Airlines giving people the same chicken and pasta meal since before their children were born. I tell myself them is the right people to stick to. At least if I got lost it would be with people who know the runnings of the place. My chest felt tight. From now on is me looking after me. I balled up my fists and curled in my toes to keep it together.

And it was a good thing I kept up with them, yes, because man this JFK ain't play it big. From the plane to immigration was a good ten minutes fast walking. I couldn't believe we were still inside one airport. If I walked this long in Piarco Airport I would have reached the carpark by now. As soon as we glimpsed the immigration hall they had guards directing traffic. American citizens and green card holders one way with no queue. Others get to use a machine but we so had to jam up in a line that twisted out into the hallway. The backpack was cutting into my shoulders. I wanted to fling it off and kick it along on the ground in front me. It's not like we're rushing going anywhere. But when I looked around most people were holding on to their bags. The last thing I wanted was for the guard to look at me or my bag. Next thing you know police with gun are all up in my face and I get deported before I even see Times Square.

Must be nearly an hour we waited, inching up one way, back down, then up again and back down. And check this out – not a man cut in. No cussing. Nobody was resting on the ground. The security wasn't harassed to see if they could ease up this one or put that one in front. If this was Trinidad all now so fight would have broken out with shoving and pushing boldface boldface. The one little piece of excitement was when an officer opened the barrier and sent people to the empty side for citizens only. People snatched up bag, child, old grandmother and ran. In the rush a woman mashed the corn on my little toe and a next one whacked me with a PriceSmart shopping bag. All the rushing and pushing got the officer vex and she started shouting in English and Spanish. I made out a few words: 'por favor', 'ahora', 'seguridad'. And she sounded just like Señora Jane from school. I could picture her saying that after all the Spanish she taught me, day in, day out, I should be able to understand what the woman was saying. My view was I took the B in Spanish and ran before they changed their minds. Besides, this security guard was only talking fast fast.

In the rush I gone and lost the family I was trailing. They got through to the other side and were skinning up their teeth happy happy. The time it took me to move three-four yards they'd done gone. Strange, I felt they had abandoned me. It's so weird being alone. Not a soul knew me from Adam. When Mammy tried to kiss me one last time I said, no, don't embarrass me. I can't un-know what she did and I cannot, will not, forgive, ever and ever, amen. But when Mr Chetan came and hugged me up tight, I ain't go lie – that was dread. I didn't dare look at him because I knew I would freak out and maybe he'd guess what was really going on. He's a man who knows things.

I reached the top of the line and the officer sent me to join a next small line of people in front a booth. Why every officer must have a gun? I was nervous enough without adding guns to the mix. Of course I got the slowest line. People waiting for the booth next to me were zipping through fast fast. Click, bam, click, bam. Passport stamped and they gone their way. Not the pig I was easing up towards. That fat face was red red like he was overheating. He ain't business that we've been standing up now for over an hour. It could take whole day for all he cared. He was taking his cool time checking every single stamp, on every single page, of every single passport. Where you were from didn't matter. It had people from all about waiting to get through: Mexico, Haiti, Jamaica. I even saw a passport from little Dominica pass in the rush. You know how scarce that must be?

I was standing up good good when my left leg began shaking a little. I didn't trust this guy. But it might look bad to shift over to the faster line. I dug my fingernails hard into my palm until it hurt. That little pain in my hand was enough to stop the shaking. Only two away from the slow-coach immigration officer but that was like being behind four people in any other line. I swallowed hard and realised my throat was dry too. I mustn't look worried. They'll think I'm hiding something and I had nothing to hide. My Trini passport was exactly the same as every other, plus that visitor's visa is the damn thing self. Don't mind it took a whole two days lining up in the hot sun. It's valid for ten years with multiple entry.

When it was my turn all I had to do was give him the same story I gave Mammy. Uncle Hari, my father's brother, had invited me for holidays. I'm planning to lime with my cousins who I last saw when all of we were little. We'll check out the sights, including a ferry ride to the Statue of Liberty. When the holidays are done I'm dusting it back to Trinidad. Mammy was fooled. And Mr Chetan. I'm not proud of that. I was sweating. The officer shouted next and I crossed the red line.

Good afternoon.

He didn't look up or reply good afternoon dog, or good afternoon cat, to me. Nothing. I handed him my brand-new blue passport. He opened it up to the picture page, shoved it down on a scanner and stared at his computer screen. He still hadn't said boo yet. When he opened his mouth I jumped.

What is the purpose of your visit to New York?

Now his beady eyes locked on to me like he was Superman's brother and had X-ray vision. But I kept my cool. Uncle Hari said always be polite and respectful. Remember you're coming in the people country and they don't have to let you in if they don't like how your face fixed – visa or no visa.

I'm spending a month. I've come for holidays by my uncle.

What's your uncle's name?

Hari Ramdin. I have a letter from him. You want to see it?

No.

He went through every page of my passport even though it was clean as a whistle, and while he was doing that he let go a set of questions in my tail. Who living at this Queens address? What does your uncle do for a living? How long are you stay-ing in the United States? Do you have a return ticket? Are you aware that you are not allowed by law to work or study while in the United States? Have you ever been to Canada? Have you worked on a farm recently?

How much money have you brought with you?

You mean cash?

Yes. Cash.

Five hundred dollars.

I reached into my jeans pocket, sure he wanted the proof.

I don't need to see your wallet.

Instead he skin up the passport like it was a picture flip book before picking a page right in the middle. Then clink, bam. Now that was bad mind. Why he didn't pick a page in the front and start from there?

Welcome to the United States. Have a nice day.

It wasn't until later I dared peep at the stamp. I got a clean six months. The stamp took up an entire page. Wow. I told myself, yes, man. Solo, boy, you're going places.

I was so relieved when he handed back my passport that I walked off in the wrong direction. You think they're not checking your every move? Within seconds an officer was shouting at me, pointing to the signs for baggage claim. I could see where they were pointing but I was scared. One more wrong turn and who knows where I could land up. Mr Chetan had warned me that when they see a brown-skin young fella travelling alone, they're automatically thinking terrorist. Them think all brown and black people make one way – thief, murderer, rapist or terrorist. And over here police real like to shoot first and ask questions later.

The escalator to baggage claim took me down into a next set of confusion. At first I panicked because there weren't that many bags going around the belt. But then I saw people digging around in a stack of suitcases at the side. I spotted my bag one time. Mammy had tied a bright gold ribbon in a bow on the handle. Earlier that had got me vex. Treating me like some country bookie who wouldn't recognise his own black bag. She don't have to know but that damn gold bow really came in handy, yes. But it didn't have to be big and gold for everybody to know we is Indian. I yanked it off and threw it in the trash. Embarrassing. Well, that was the last embarrassing thing she will ever do me because me and Madame Betty Ramdin overs. We done, done, done. Imagine all these years what people must have said behind we back. Calling my daddy a drunk whose own foolishness got him killed when all along it was that bitch. Well, Betty, if you spit in the sky it must fall back in your eye.

Searching for the exit I bounced up yet another long line. Fucking hell. This one was a free-for-all. People were driving their luggage carts like they were motor cars. Twice somebody's cart hit my ankles but I didn't say nothing. Right by the exit a stout lady officer took my passport. She watched me cut eye while asking if I had any foodstuffs or plants. I played innocent and shook my head. No. But that was not true. Anybody leaving Trinidad for America must carry up food. Mammy had sent Uncle Hari dhalpourri roti, curry mango, curry goat, curry duck and a dozen Ali's doubles. Left up to me I wasn't taking she food but Uncle Hari wanted it. Miss Officer like she was itching to search my bag but the line behind me was pure madness. Probably more to save she-self the hassle I got through. I don't think I breathed steady until I was outside. But I made it outside.

Uncle Hari wasn't there. In between the Yankee talk I heard plenty West Indian accents but not my father's brother. Maybe I took so long to come out he got fed up and left or I wasn't looking properly. I checked one side. I went the next side. Above all I tried not to look lost in case thief targeted me. Bad things always happening regular in America. And New York? Worse yet. Man, people say this place so big and busy you could get rob, stab and nobody would business.

Uncle Hari's cell number and address were in my phone, plus, as back-up, I'd written it on a tiny piece of paper. It's real easy to thief a man phone although this one didn't have a signal. Looks like my Digicel plan doesn't work up here. I'm giving Uncle Hari half hour and then I could always take taxi. How much for a ride and where the hell I was supposed to find one? He's coming. He wouldn't forget Sunil's only child in the airport. I found a bench in the waiting area and angled myself to scope out the place. The backpack I locked between my legs and one hand gripped the suitcase handle otherwise next thing my bag will get snatched. I missed Mr Chetan. He is a man always on time. If he said he was picking you up at four he was there all quarter to.

Ten minutes scanning the waiting area rolled into twenty minutes. Half hour came and went. Uncle Hari like he well forgot me. Forty minutes. Forty-five. Fifty minutes. I could feel my left leg getting jittery again. I started thinking that Uncle Hari changed his mind. Taking me in was too much and he didn't have the heart to tell me. By now I had landed in America a good two and a half hours. Maybe he wasn't serious. All them months I was texting. He was texting. Talking on the phone outside in case Mammy heard anything. Uncle Hari promised so where the ass was he? I felt my head paining me. Fuck Uncle Hari. Fuck Uncle Hari.

Someone tapped my shoulder and I nearly had a heart attack. A fella who could pass for Trini asked if I was Hari's nephew.

Your uncle waiting outside. He can't park so he said to tell you to come. You can't miss him. He's driving a green car with a black top.

I said thanks and rushed to the nearest exit. Outside was a traffic jam of yellow taxi cabs blowing horn and everybody was trying to find a place to stop. In the far lane I saw Uncle Hari waving from a green Honda. He looked just like his pictures.

Boy, I watched you crossing the road and it was like seeing a young Sunil. You're the print of your father.

He shoved the suitcase and backpack in the trunk and we took off at one speed into a four-lane expressway. I ain't go lie, for a split second I thought we would crash into the oncoming traffic. I don't care what people say, Americans drive on the wrong side of the road.

You thought I forget you?

I knew you would come. I was cooling myself until you reach.

Boy, I was hustling to finish some things before I picked you up. Plus, we're putting in the cabling for a big office building and the job's already two weeks behind. Anyhow, don't study me. How was the flight? How's Betty?

She's good. Half my suitcase is food for you.

Any curry duck?

That was the first thing that got packed.

And customs didn't try to take it away?

They didn't search me.

You're real lucky.

He looked over and slapped my leg.

If you know how happy I am to see you. Sunil's young man reach New York.

I didn't know what to say. Nobody had ever talked to me like that. I smiled.

You know, one time I was coming through JFK and they buss open my bag and want to tell me I can't bring in my food. I say nah. All you not getting my good curry duck that I buy from Mona's in Marabella. Ask the children if I lie. I sat down right there in the airport and lick down the food. I know them officers. The scamps them does want the thing to keep. Well, this Indian wasn't giving them nothing.

We zoomed past plenty identical, red-brown, high-rise apartment blocks. Huge billboards showed off the latest car models. Some cars I had never even heard of. Lincoln Navigator. Chevrolet Volt. And everything looked to be the wrong size. I felt I had shrunk like Super Mario after losing his mushroom. One more hit and game over. Ordinary cars seemed stretched and the SUVs looked like they'd been lifting weights to beef up.

I think I mentioned already how me and your aunty not together. My friend Sherry living home by me now. And you won't make out your cousins. Is years all you ain't seen one another. Katherine should be home by now. She works in a pet store. Anything to do with animals and she's happy. Ian is our nerd who knows all it have to know about fixing computers. Sometimes he will be with a company if they have a lot of work but mostly he finds his own jobs.

So, where's Aunty living?

She moved far. New Jersey near her sister. I will ask the children to carry you one day to see she.

By now we had left the expressway. Cars were still oversized but the buildings were more normal, like two storeys high. The shiny skyscrapers I'd glimpsed in the distance were another side of New York. Here nothing was shiny at all. The shop fronts looked dirty and many were boarded up. And was only black people walking about or driving cars. Uncle Hari turned off the air con and lowered the windows. A rotting garbage smell catch me straight away. He didn't seem to notice. As casually as I could I buried my nose in my T-shirt. Suddenly his cell phone buzzed loud loud. Uncle Hari let out one long sigh.

A man can't get five minutes' peace.

He pressed the speaker button.

Sherry, what happen? I'm on Foch Boulevard.

A woman with a perfect Trini accent didn't sound too impressed.

So long you leave to go airport and is only now you coming back? Where you went? The flight delayed?

You-self know how busy JFK does be. Anyhow, I have Solo here and we heading home now. Ten minutes.

He clicked the off button and nudged me with his elbow.

Don't say nothing about waiting in the airport.

Me?

He winked.

We Ramdin men must stick up for one another.

I liked how that sounded. The Ramdin men. That was new.

From the main road we turned off into a residential street. Things didn't look too hot. The houses were crooked and mash-up. Plenty fences had good rust on them. And people living here like they don't have lawnmowers. If you see how high the grass was. We parked outside a light brown house with an unpainted wooden front door and no front yard. A window on the second floor was boarded over. Compared to this my Trini house was a mansion.

From the voice on the phone I had expected Sherry to look, well, older. Not so. She was prettier and younger than I thought and hugged me like I was a long-lost nephew. My cousins, Katherine and Ian, said hello quick quick and vanished back to their rooms. I felt more shy than usual. Either they're not business with me or they don't want me here. Sherry pointed to my room at the top of some steep, narrow stairs and said to be careful. If I had a few beers inside me I might trip over my own feet. My stomach twitched and a disgusting, bitter taste hit the back of my throat. Wasn't her fault. She wouldn't know what had happened to Daddy. But all I could see were the back stairs in Trinidad. Daddy standing there with no clue this was going to be his last moment on earth. What I didn't know then was that every single flecking time I used those stairs that same thought would fly through my mind.

The boarded-up window in my new bedroom made the day instantly night. Sherry felt for the light switch. One naked bulb lit up the place. Must be a fifteen-watt because it was real dull. They had made a bedroom at one end of a long, low room. The other end was piled up with all kind of old box, a Christmas tree, a chainsaw. It even had a broken baby's pram. Why they had that heaven alone knows. My bed was a narrow folding cot next to an empty bookshelf.

Make yourself comfortable. We'll fix the window but your uncle was busy this week. You remember I showed you the bathroom when you came in?

I nodded.

Take your time. When you ready come down.

Uncle Hari's head poked out from the top of the stairs.

Your suitcase.

I rushed to take it from him.

We ain't have big house like all you in Trinidad but it's home. Up here is yours. Nobody will come and bother you.

I tried not to let it show but home I had a queen-sized bed, a desk and massive cupboards. Even our storage room by the garage was better than this. I opened the suitcase and handed them Mammy's food parcels. Uncle Hari's eyes opened big big.

Way, boy, this is Fourth of July, Thanksgiving and Christmas all one time. Sherry, heat up some of this for me, please.

I hadn't wanted to bring Mammy's food but I was glad now. Who knew a little Trini home curry would make Uncle Hari so happy?

When they were gone I sat on the bed not knowing what to feel. In my head New York was the Big Apple, shiny skyscrapers and bright neon lights. I know Uncle Hari had said things were tough here but I didn't know it was this bad. But he also said that with hard work you could make a new life. Well, I'm here. First thing Monday we'll see about a small job someplace where they don't ask too many questions, like if you have a Social Security number. New York, I reach.

BETTY

On the drive home from Piarco Airport, I don't think either me or Mr Chetan talk two words good. My mind was all over the place. Long time, and I'm talking about when I was small small, going away, even to Tobago, was a big deal. Whenever someone was travelling we would line up in the airport's waving gallery to see them off. A few times my father took all three of us – me and my two brothers – for a drive to the airport just for so. We would sit down in the waving gallery, enjoy the breeze and watch the planes take off and land. Big quarrel would break out over where to go if by some miracle we were leaving on an airplane. I was always heading to England. We have family living there in a place called Kent. One brother wanted to go Canada. Guess where he's living now? Edmonton. Left and never came back. I'm not sure my little brother ever put his big toe outside Trinidad. Weed smoked out his brain.

The waving gallery went when they built the new airport. Today we said goodbye inside the terminal. I whispered two prayers that my son finds the correct gate and doesn't end up on a flight to Timbuktu. He's a bright young man and I'm sure he didn't catch no trouble. I mean, if he got confused and missed the flight ain't he would've called? My mind won't rest until I hear Hari have him.

Solo's usually right where I can see him. Well, he's getting big. I better get used to the house being over-quiet. Half the time his head was two inches from the iPad but at least he was here. I don't know what to do with myself.

Statue of Liberty, Empire State Building, Central Park – my baby going to see all them things. He couldn't stop talking about meeting his uncle and cousins. I hope they treat him good and send him back to me in one piece. America's full of Bad John who could do all kind of thing to my child. But God is love and as back-up my prayer group put Solo on their list. The other day I was passing the Catholic church on the Promenade and I ducked in quick quick to light a candle. When it comes to divine intervention I like everybody's god. A blessing from the Virgin Mary can't hurt. And trust me, if I hear anybody having puja I'll be front and centre asking Brahma, Krishna and Vishnu to keep an eye on my boy. I want him back safe and, please, without a Yankee accent.

Of course, he'll be home before I've turned around twice, but, like I can't focus. He gave Mr Chetan a long tight hug and a big kiss goodbye. I moved in to kiss him after. You know the boy pushed me away? Oh, I'm embarrassing him. It's partly his age but only partly. I ain't go lie – his behaviour didn't surprise me. In the year or so since he found out what happened with his father, I don't think he's given me so much as a cuddle that I didn't thief. If my boy child still keeping any love for me he hiding it deep deep. Seeing more of the world will help him understand life better. And who knows? Time apart might heal things between us. We could really do with some healing.

In under an hour we reached back San Fernando to a house bellowing silence. Mr Chetan drank a glass of water and shut his door. I went to inspect the garden. A few months back I planted a bed of ixora at the side of the garage where it will get hot sun. Most people have the red ixora. That doesn't do it for me. Mine have bright bright orange flowers and when I tell you it pretty for days. But as I looked I realised one or two leaves had yellow spots. Nothing a dose of fertiliser can't cure. I was picking off the bad leaves when I heard a baby laughing. Next door must have visitors. I couldn't quite make out what was going on but it had the baby bussing out laughing every few seconds. Talk about sweetness. If I had to choose the best sound in the whole world, hands down it would be a baby laughing.

Maybe because my baby is now a young man and he doesn't laugh hard so, maybe because Solo often looks at me with pure hate, maybe because he's now gone, but suddenly I couldn't see too good. Water was springing from my eyes, wetting my cheeks. The day we brought Solo home is clear clear like yesterday. Six pounds, one ounce. We didn't know how to look after this piti popo. That first week Sunil was frightened to even close his eyes in case Solo stopped breathing. We have a picture taken right in the back here – Solo less than a month old and perfect. His tiny vest and socks were like dolly clothes. In the picture Sunil is holding the baby, pride plastered across his face. Every day he would rush home after work, change clothes and take Solo for a walk. Nothing he liked better than showing off his baby son to the neighbours and pointing out the child is the print of him. Have mercy, I couldn't imagine then what life would throw my way. Tears started up again. I dragged an old plastic chair under the chenette tree and stayed there until it was making dark. Don't ask me why but I started singing to myself, quiet quiet so nobody would hear and think I'd gone mad.

Dodo piti popo
Mammy gone to town
To buy a little sugar plum
And give baby some.

Look at me. Husband dead. Child out in the world by himself. Betty, is what you going to do with yourself now, girl?

SOLO

I heard them stomping around, getting ready for work. Ian and Katherine were quarrelling over who takes longer in the bathroom. Sherry was hustling to leave for her nanny gig with a doctor's family in Manhattan. She gave Uncle Hari one good buff about coming home late every night. If he so much as sneeze by a next woman and she finds out, she's leaving his ass high and dry. Uncle Hari wasn't taking her on. He had his own complaining that only yesterday self he bought a big thing of orange juice and now when he want a glass it don't have a drop in the fridge. Around eight I heard a knock and Uncle Hari opened my door.

Hey, boy, you sleep good?

Yes, thanks, Uncle.

All of we leaving for work but stay home and rest yourself.

I want to start looking for work.

Relax. Let me make some calls and we go fix up. Don't worry yourself.

He took a step closer and looked around.

You have everything?

Yeah, man. I'm cool.

Take a walk later. Go and see where everything is. Stop & Shop, MTA, post office. Nothing far.

So, when I go out the house, turn left or right?

Either way and then if you go a little bit you will meet up the main road.

Okay.

And I already tell you. Make yourself at home. It have food in the fridge. It have TV. Take a few days and settle yourself good.

Four times that front door banged shut. My body relaxed. I was surprised because I didn't even know I was feeling tension. They were gone for the day but I couldn't help walking quiet quiet while I checked out the place. Not that I was hungry but I opened the fridge. Uncle Hari was right about no orange juice. But far down in the back it had cranberry light. Cheese was a strange orange and already sliced up. Home our cheese is a yellow block marked New Zealand Cheddar. And these people could well drink milk. Soy, two per cent, strawberry flavoured. We fridge only had UHT milk. I took a little sip of the pink strawberry milk. Oh, God, oh. That tasted bad. I rinsed out my mouth twice.

In the choke-up living room I sat down on the couch. Last night we had crowded up in here, watched *Law & Order* and ate Mammy's food, or rather they ate the food. I wasn't touching anything she made. Something jooked my leg. A spring was sticking through the cloth. That could well cut bad. And the place real dusty. They have too much things everywhere.

I flicked through must be close to a hundred channels. Every noise frightened me. I don't know why but I was tired enough to sleep for a week. Just when people were heading to work I was crawling back to my cot.

*

You telling me whole day you spend inside? You never even open the door and see nothing? What happen? Like you frighten somebody go do you something?

I stayed quiet. Sherry opened the fridge and started pulling out vegetables.

You called your mother? I heard Hari reminding you.

No. Mr Chetan called and we talked but I didn't speak to Mammy. I'll try tomorrow. She won't be home now.

How you mean she not home eight o'clock on a Monday night? Like she foot hot?

Mondays is church group and she don't miss that. Reverend said she running the church more than he.

And this Mr Chetan. Hari tell me he renting from all you?

He's like family.

He and your mother together?

No.

You sure?

Yeah.

You like him?

Yeah.

I think you're holding back and that is Betty's man.

It's not like that at all at all.

If you say so.

*

Uncle Hari's face was vex. Today I had said for sure for sure I will check out the neighbourhood but honestly I didn't like how outside looked. I forced myself to bathe, put on sneakers. When I peeped out the window it had police parked up opposite waiting for what I don't know. Another police car cruised by. I told myself the best thing for me was to keep my little tail quiet inside. Uncle Hari twist up his mouth.

You're acting like you never saw a police car before. Around here police does be patrolling up and down. What, you think they go hold you just so?

I wanted to say that in my street police does only reach if something real bad happen – like the time they rob the big orange house on the corner.

I here twenty years and I promise you this place safer than Trinidad. True, now not like long time. I remember running to the Stop & Shop and not bothering to lock up.

I wouldn't do that today but it still safe around here. To besides, we glad when police make a pass and check that no crook them causing mischief.

Sherry looked up from her phone.

Hari, carry the boy for a walk and show him where to find the Stop & Shop. At least make sure he know that.

We ain't reached the end of the road good and I had stumped my big toe twice on the broken pavement. And what surprised me was how more than half the street lights them weren't working. I thought in a rich place like America as soon as a bulb blow the government would fix it.

On the main road blue buses were pelting up and down. Uncle Hari told me to look good because is bus I'll be taking to move around – especially the Q8 and the Q24 – as they stopped right near our street. In Trinidad, I never, ever took bus. Never. None of my friends did. Bus was for people who didn't have a car – not even a reconditioned Japanese car that selling cheap cheap. But if that is what people does do here then fine. From now on I'll take the bus.

We strolled around with Uncle Hari showing me this, that and the other. As we passed a cafe with bright bright lights he pulled my hand.

You ever had a sticky cinnamon bun?

I shook my head.

You can't let the family know I carried you here. With the diabetes I shouldn't eat sweet things.

Me?

With my hand I zipped my mouth shut.

> If Sherry had she way, the red meat would go. The liquor
> would go. The bread, the orange juice – everything. The
> way I see it, God put me on this earth to talk and laugh and
> live happy. I prefer a few years less than to live to a hundred
> and be miserable.

When I saw how big the cinnamon buns were I thought we
must be sharing one. No star. Uncle Hari said he can share
anything but he food is he food. If I wanted to see him vex vex
just push my hand in his plate.

> This tastes like the iced buns we used to get from a bakery
> in Mayaro. You know about the time your father and I
> camped down there?

I shook my head.

> I don't know too much about Daddy.

> I was about fourteen so he had to be near seventeen. I don't
> know how we got our parents to agree but they let us go
> camping. Just the two of us. I still remember that as one
> of the best weeks in my life. We pitched tent on the beach
> and in no time we bounced up with some young American
> girls staying in a house nearby. Two sisters. Whole week we
> limed with them. They even invited us home for dinner.
> That was the first time I ever kissed a girl with tongues and
> thing. I left there feeling like I was a big man.

It was so weird talking about my daddy. I had a million questions but I didn't know where to start.

I know Sunil and he girl spent a good bit of time alone in the tent but no matter how I begged he never told me if they had sex.

Uncle Hari took a bite of the cinnamon bun.

You know what I think, Solo? I think he didn't tell me because it was his first time. Looking back, that girl knew what was what. Not Sunil. And you know he was always real good-looking. He looked like one of them Indian star boy.

I tried to nail down Daddy's face in my mind. What passed through my mind was me, Mammy and Daddy walking up a hill. Maybe San Fernando Hill. Breeze was blowing sweet. I can see the green green grass. At the top Mammy wanted to take a picture. Daddy hugged me up tight tight. My head reached by the top of his leg and I held on by his knee. We were happy. Definitely happy.

We both concentrated on the cinnamon buns. I licked the melted icing from my fingers.

You like it? I told you it was real nice.

I didn't ask but just so Uncle Hari began telling me about when he landed in New York. Long time, you could get papers now for now. His St Vincent partner was busy checking a girl working in Social Security. Now, with computers and all them things, it couldn't happen so again. Then it cost him a good $500, which is like $5,000 these days, but that was the best investment he ever made. Up to today it's that same Social

Security number he's using. Nothing's wrong with it. Katherine and Ian were both born Yankee so they never see trouble.

When I came up here it's not like anybody helped me. In fairness I never tell them in Trinidad but I real catch my ass. You think is two toilet I clean? I did janitor work, kitchen work, cut grass, all kind of thing before I got settled.

Uncle Hari, I'm not afraid to take whatever work it have.

We go see about that. Up to now you've had it softee softee. You don't even realise how easy you've had it. I told you once and I'm telling you again. You're here without papers. Don't think you getting a job jumping up in people office wearing suit and tie.

I know.

And I don't know what gone on with you and your mother. Take your time. See if you like New York.

I've made up my mind to stay.

You're saying that now. Wait until a cold breeze bite your tail.

Uncle Hari went down on the cinnamon bun like he hadn't seen food for days.

I don't want you to get vex with me and I'm not your father. But if Sunil was alive I think he would want you to finish your education. I wasn't bright like him so I had to find my way. The best thing is to spend a little six months, save up your money then go home and get a qualification.

It's easy for him to talk. I looked out the window at the people walking by. Everybody had purpose. They knew where they were going. Apart from Uncle Hari nobody was expecting me anywhere.

I can't live in Trinidad. Not now.

Uncle Hari licked his lips.

America's no bed of roses. Things expensive.

My stomach dropped.

The second I start working I'll pay rent.

He smiled and I saw a piece of bun stuck between his teeth.

Watch me. I don't want nothing from you. You are my nephew and you come like my next son. While you're under my roof you're not paying a red cent. And who don't like it too bad for them.

He licked his fingers then grinned at me.

Every time I look at you I seeing piece of Sunil. No lie. Especially in the eyes. It's frightening how much all you look alike.

You have any pictures of him when he was growing up?

It have an album somewhere, yes, but it's to put my hand on it. Long long time I ain't look through it.

Now that is something I will hold him to.

Anyhow, I talked to my partner, Dennis. I say, boy, my

nephew reach. He's not accustomed to doing labour work but he have to start somewhere. Dennis said no problem. They're finishing off a building and he need a hand painting. You're good with that?

Painting? Who you think painted our house last Christmas?

He raised an eyebrow.

For true?

I nodded.

You're not easy. I glad to hear you does help with the house.

He will want a Social Security number?

Nah, nah, nah. He don't worry with that. Seventy dollars a day. Cash.

He wagged his finger at me.

And don't make no trouble. Do whatever the people ask you to do.

I'm ready to start in the morning.

I like your style. By the way, tell me about this Mr Chetan. He and Betty in thing?

*

Friday I got paid. Four days' work and I had 280 US dollars. Cash. This was real bread. I sent Mr Chetan a text. He was surprised I was working. I said it was only a holiday job and left it at that. Okay, my shoulders them stiff stiff but so worth it. And in a strange way I liked it so. When my wrists paining and my shoulders them hard like rock I don't think of a single thing. Trinidad, Mammy, even Mr Chetan doesn't cross my thoughts. My mind does be blank. Dennis have me working with a Grenadian. Lucky for me he's not a talker either. On a morning he puts on the radio and he cool jamming eighties tunes whole day. Thank the Lord I didn't get put with the men on the floor above. They always cussing loud loud. Every man Jack is West Indian. Come to think of it, I ain't meet a single white person since I came up here. And round by where we living? Worse yet. Is mainly Trini and Jamaican and I've even heard a few Bajan accents.

Solo, how much Dennis pay you?

Before I could answer, Uncle Hari raise his hand.

Sherry, I find you well fast with yourself. How much the boy make is he personal business.

So, what happen? He's not putting a hand for groceries or something for rent?

Last time I check is my name on the lease.

Well, I'm not working to mind a big man like he.

Not now, Sherry.

Not now, Sherry? Why not now? First, you say the boy was coming for a little holiday, then soon as he land your tune changed. If he's staying a whole six months he should damn well pay rent and food. You hear me?

Yes, Aunty Sherry.

Stay out of this, Solo.

Look, the boy and all saying he don't mind contributing a little something. He knows nothing free up here.

Uncle Hari's face was set up like rain about to fall. He got up.

Sherry, come in the bedroom.

I'm watching my show.

I said come in the bedroom.

What you carrying on so big and bad for?

She rolled her eyes.

All right, all right. Hold your horses. I'm coming.

I tiptoed to my room. As I went past their door I tried to make out what they were saying but I couldn't. Although it was only 9 p.m. I went in my bed. The tiredness of the week was hitting me hard.

The next morning when I came downstairs Katherine was cooking scrambled eggs and looking upset. Even first thing in the morning, with her long hair scrunched up in a ponytail, she was still cute with them two dimples. And that girl's addicted to her Zumba. Ian and Uncle Hari were waiting for food.

Morning.

Morning, Solo. Sit down. You reach in time.

Ian watched me cut eye. If he was living in Trinidad people would never call him Ian. When they saw him coming it would be Slims or Slim Man. He could lick back real big food but the man fine fine. Touch him hard and he look like he go break in half. People say the same thing about me. I guess it run in the blood.

You need help, Katherine?

Get some cutlery. Like you smelt the food?

I smiled.

Where's Aunty Sherry? Take out cutlery for her?

Katherine shared up the eggs on four plates. No one said boo.

She's sleeping?

Uncle Hari sighed.

Sherry's not here, boy. I don't know where she's gone.

BETTY

I woke up early. My head pounding me and my nose dripping like a standpipe. All about my body was feeling mash-up mash-up as if a bus ran me over. Worse yet, I had had a horrible dream about Solo as a baby. He was bawling nonstop and nothing I did helped. A woman was trying to take the baby away, saying I wasn't a good mother. I patted the bedside table looking for my phone. No phone. Every bone in my body hurt when I got up. How the phone ended up in that little crack between the bed and bedside table I don't know. I had to bend down on all fours to find the damn thing.

Three messages and none were from Mister Solo. What was going on in his mind only the good Lord was privy to. I blew my nose hard and mercifully my left ear popped open. Up to last night I asked Mr Chetan if Solo messaged him. He said no. Solo thinks he can live just so in the people country? I have a good mind to go New York and bring his backside home but Mr Chetan said that will only make things worse. He's probably right. Solo have age now. I can't force him to do nothing.

Jeez-an-ages, me head hurting me. Taking the few steps to the bathroom I thought I might faint. The one box of cold and flu tablets I found was nearly empty. Usually I leave a glass by the sink but it wasn't there. I must have taken it to the kitchen. No way I had the strength to walk further than my bed. I washed down the tablets with water straight from the tap. Where the hand towel gone? You see me? I'm not able today. The end of my nightie doubled as a towel to dry my mouth and hands. God is love, yes. I made it back in the bed without collapsing.

What got on my nerves was that I didn't have energy to do nothing but it wasn't like I could sleep sound either. I tossed, I turned, I dragged the blanket over me until it was tangled up good and proper. The place was making real cold. It was only then I noticed the window open. Whole night it was open. Even with the wrought-iron burglar proofing that was a dangerous thing. These days bandit does walk with cutting tools or push a gun through the barrier and force you to open for them. I wanted to get up and close the window but didn't have strength. I stared at the window, hoping some obeah would make it close itself.

I must have dropped back asleep because voices woke me up. Mr Chetan was talking to a man soft soft. I heard footsteps and giggling like two schoolchildren. Keys jingled and the security gate by the front door squeaked open. I couldn't make out what they were saying. He must think my ears deaf that I don't know when he have a man in the house. I was wondering if I knew this person when Mr Chetan knocked and pushed open the door.

I woke you up?

No. Come.

He bounced in happy happy but as soon as he looked at me his face changed.

You're still sick?

Boy, I'm fed up. It's two days now this fever coming and going. And my head's hurting. My nose running.

You took Panadol?

Who were you talking to just now?

You take anything? Just a friend.

I drank the last two Panadol must be an hour ago. I didn't hear anybody come in.

Don't worry yourself. I'll make you some fresh ginger tea with honey and lemon. We have that nice honey from Mount Saint Benedict.

He sat down on the edge of the bed and felt my forehead, then my cheeks and the sides of my neck.

You're roasting hot.

I'm freezing.

Nah. We're getting rid of this fever once and for all. If it was only one day I would say leave it but this going on a little too long for my liking.

He stood up.

Time to rinse yourself in cold water and after that I'll go to the pharmacy and see what else they have that you can take.

You mad or what? If you think I'm getting out of my bed to go in a cold shower you better think again.

You need to deal with this fever. Come, babes.

I sighed and took his hand. In the bathroom he turned on the shower, tested the water then looked at me. I tried a last beg.

Oh gosh. Let me shower later, nah. This fever go pass by itself now for now.

Without asking he gently lifted the nightie over my head. I couldn't remember when last I shaved under my arms and even with my blocked-up nose I smelt sweat mixed with Vicks VapoRub. Too weak to care or resist, I took off my panty. I didn't want him doing that. What surprised me was, even with my sick self, I felt a twinge in my chest. Imagine he could see me buck naked and he's cool for days. No awkwardness or a tups of regret. I closed my eyes and ducked under the shower.

Oh Lord! Like you want to kill me? This is ice water!

Cold water will help bring down the fever.

Easy for you to say.

He hovered around while I soaped myself. As soon as I locked off the shower he rushed to hold up a fluffy, clean towel for me.

I'm not dead yet. I can dry myself.

He wiped my back gentle gentle.

Let me go make up the bed before you get back in. It looks like you had a wrestling match in there.

At least my aching, shivering body wasn't smelly any more. I got a new nightie and eased back into the bed. Ginger tea reached and he left for the pharmacy. I kept studying who might be the friend I'd heard earlier. Sleep drifted over me. What felt like only minutes later, Mr Chetan was asking me to sit up and wash down two yellow-and-red capsules with cold tea. I didn't check the name of the medicine. I took them, sank under the blanket and was out for the count. I don't even think a 'thank you' came out my mouth.

Whole day I drifted in and out of sleep. By late afternoon I finally opened my eyes properly. Sitting in my old Morris chair next to the lamp, his foot on the bed, was Mr Chetan, reading the *Sunday Newsday*. Everything felt damp – the sheets, the pillow case. My nightie was wet like rain fall hard on me. I still felt weak but it wasn't the same earlier sickliness.

How you feeling, babes? You conked out hard.

I was snoring?

Snoring? The noise you make could wake the dead.

Boy, what kind tablet you gave me? That thing knocked me for six. What's the time? I slept whole day?

It's minutes to four. I've never seen you take to your bed like this.

I pushed off the blanket to get out of bed.

Don't try to get up. You're hungry?

You could warm up the corn soup? I'm getting up. You don't see how my clothes wet? And the sheet them wet too.

Everything's damp.

You sweated the fever from your body.

He left and I towelled myself dry and put on an old house dress. Slowly, I pulled off the sheets and threw them in the laundry basket. My stomach was rumbling loud loud.

In the kitchen the two of us sat down to eat. Sometimes I still catch myself eyeing him up, checking to see if I'd missed an obvious clue about his sexuality. Should I have known from the fact that he's a boss cook? No, the cooking wasn't the give-away. It was the limp cock.

Eat up, Miss B. I don't want you fainting on me. San Fernando General is no place to lime on a Sunday evening.

I don't know how I will manage if you get somebody and leave me.

Why do you think that?

I just feel kind of left out these days. You seem to have man in and out.

He blushed and looked away.

Nobody will come between us.

I tried to smile. There was a time I believed that completely. Now? I wouldn't put my head on a block for that. He's been coming in all hours of the night from I don't know where.

All right, I'm heading back to my bed.

Mr Chetan reached for my empty bowl.

Take two more cold tablets. You want anything else? More ginger tea?

No. No. I'm good, thanks.

I was planning to go out tonight but I don't have to.

Some handsome man?

Wait nah. You're jealous?

A little. Sometimes.

He buss a kiss on my greasy forehead.

You will always be number one. You hear that?

Fine. Now go enjoy yourself. If it's anything I will call you.

Promise?

Promise.

MR CHETAN

Rain came down hard for the second day in a row and I was bored cooped up in the apartment. It was the right thing to move out but the timing wasn't great. I'm not sure the timing would ever have been good. Miss B and I needed to be free to meet other people otherwise it was like we were in a sexless marriage. We both need to breathe. It would ease things if we knew what Solo was planning to do. He should have come back months ago. Fingers crossed we'll see him soon. His mother's pining away for him bad. I miss him too but at least he's talking to me.

As usual I landed up crawling around the internet. Well, I got a little shock when I saw the face. Older, but that was the man self. I could see the sweet cleft right in the middle of his chin. It must be him. Don't tell me Facebook have more than one Mani Boodoosingh with a sexy chin like that, hailing from Point Fortin and went Ishmael High School. I had a good maco. Studied at University of the West Indies, St Augustine. Yup. Works at Carib Brewery. Possible. Relationship status – nothing. Check my boy. He was hot from long time. But now? Wow. And look at the cute moustache and the little designer beard. I could've kissed the screen. We might be the same age but he could pass for somebody much younger. Easy. And the man's fit. Looked like he is friends with the gym. I'd better start lifting myself. One other thing was obvious. He real liked his job. Nearly every picture he posted was something to do with Carib beer. Drinking a Carib. Wearing a Carib T-shirt. In a carnival fete wining down the place, Machel Montano on stage. And what you think he was waving in the air? A Carib rag. This man happy too bad, yes.

I know I shouldn't trouble trouble but jeez-an-ages, this wasn't any old fella from Point Fortin. This was Mani, my Mani. When I tell you I was in love – sick with tabanca for him. We had both just started high school, feeling big, and they took us on an outing to the Wildfowl Trust in Pointe a Pierre. I can still remember us close close together whole day. Any little touch from him would set off an explosion inside me. Mani was my riding partner right through school.

The real intel I was digging for he wasn't giving away free on social media. I checked his timeline up, down, sideways. No woman or child was big and up front. At least that is something. A woman with short short hair, squeezed inside clothes a size too small, popped up a lot. Tagged as Hazel. That must be his sister Hazel who I remember as an annoying little girl. Always nagging to play with us no matter what we were doing. But the thing that had my head confused was a tall black fella who was also starring in plenty pictures. Tagged Patrick Murphy. Sometimes it was him and Hazel but enough were him and Mani alone. Hazel's boyfriend? Nah. Maybe it was Mani's blasted boyfriend. I checked every post, picture and like to figure out how this Patrick person fitted into Mani's life. I can't have my fantasies crushed before I even had a chance to meet the man. If that is his boyfriend I wonder if he knows about Mani's first time? I could always fill him in since I was there. Fifteen, horny and clumsy. He kissed me first.

I'm not going to risk friending Mani only for him to turn around and blank me. Who is you? Worse yet, he remembers me and could not care less. Since finding him I've lost count of the number of times we've talked, laughed, kissed, fucked – all in my daydreams, of course. A man's allowed to escape. The scenario I liked to play over and over is us bouncing up. He would watch me. I would watch him. Then he would ask me if I am so-and-so and be overjoyed to see me after all these years. We would talk for hours. It would be the most natural thing to end up fucking. It's foolish. It's schoolboyish. But say what. My fantasies aren't bothering a soul.

I mentioned finding him to Miss Betty when she came to visit. She went on Facebook one time. I waited for her reaction but she was holding back.

Well? What you thinking?

He's all right.

Just all right?

Not bad-looking if you like them gym bunny types.

Not bad-looking? Miss B, this man hotter than your pepper sauce.

She didn't look too happy about that.

But you don't find he's nice?

Look, this is Facebook. Everybody know fisherman don't say he fish rotten.

I sighed. As usual she had hit bullseye.

True. I give you that.

Wait until you meet in real life. Otherwise how you will
know what kind a man you're dealing with? Posting all
these pretty pretty selfies. That's a pappy show. People don't
live so. You here bazodee over a man you ain't seen since he
was in short pants.

I shut the laptop. We settled back with fresh passion fruit
juice she'd brought and I changed the subject. What happened
between us is in the past but she probably doesn't want to
hear me carrying on about a man who is clearly the hottest
employee at Carib offices on Eastern Main Road. Things would
have been much simpler with her. What to do? That's life.

The other night Miss B called me all half past ten in the night,
screaming down the phone. I thought something had happened to Solo. Turned out there was a scorpion in the kitchen
and she was petrified. This woman has gone through so much
horrors and survived but one little scorpion and she bawling. I
jumped in my car and whole road I was cussing, imagining the
stupid little scorpion. Well, partner, if you see this thing – one
ugly, massive creature. I caught it and she shouted at me to kill
it dead and pelt it outside. Now, it was nasty but I don't see why
people have to kill what not killing them. The scorpion didn't
sting anybody. Being big and ugly is not a sufficient reason for
the animal to dead or else half the population would lose their
lives. For the sake of peace, I made it look like I was going to
kill it outside. When she thought it was dead, I had let it go far
away in the bush. If that scorpion had sense it would be north
of the Caroni River by now.

So, Mr Chetan, what you do to the place since I was last here?

The bedroom. I painted the walls and fixed it up little bit. My landlord loves me. All he has to do is pay for the paint. By the time I'm done this place will look real nice. I don't mind as long as he doesn't turn around and try to raise the rent.

I showed off my walls covered in 'Quiet Cove' – a calming pale blue. I've put up new curtains and bought a lovely bedspread from Grand Bazaar with a paisley pattern that picks up the exact blue as 'Quiet Cove'. Miss Betty's face was twisted up all how.

Tell me something. Why you never fixed up by me like this?

I looked away. For all our closeness, that was her house I'd been living in. I couldn't tell the lady how to decorate she own place.

Watch me, I'm giving you notice today. When I'm ready to fix up my living room you're coming to help me choose colours and thing.

As she walked over to the window I saw her eyeing up my bedside table. Apart from my lamp and the book I was reading, the only other thing was a framed photo. It had lived on her bookshelf. Me, Miss Betty and Solo in front the Christmas tree. Time flies, yes.

Good to know this is where my picture ended up.

Hands off. It's my picture now. I like having you and Solo close.

She picked up the frame and stared at our younger selves.

I fed up call, text. Nothing doing. You know if he does even
look at my messages?

I shook my head. No point pretending. Solo's not taking her
on at all. But he's young and acting stubborn. I can't believe he
will cut off his poor mother forever. The anger will work its
way out his system. Miss Betty looked like she was ready to
cry. I leaned in and hugged her tight.

Don't get yourself upset. Time longer than twine. Come see
how I've changed the kitchen. I need more shelves but since
I finished the bedroom I've been kind of lazy.

We ate, we talked and when it was near six she said she better
make tracks before it started making dark.

The way things going it's not safe to be on the road late.
You saw on the news what happened in Lange Park? As the
man turned into his own driveway the bandits them were
waiting. And like everybody carrying gun these days.

That was the one where they shot the couple?

Yup. They robbed the people and shot them right in their
house. Town say it was an inside job and they had to kill
them otherwise they would've been able to identify them to
the police.

We walked out together. By the gate she squeezed my arm.

Call Carib and ask to speak to this Mani who you so love
up on.

I wasn't expecting that.

I can't. He won't remember me. We're talking nearly twenty-five years ago.

Write a letter then. Whatever. Stop stalking the man.

You see me stalking anybody?

She laughed and rubbed my arm.

You know you want to see the man. Do it while your teeth in your mouth and not in a glass by the sink.

SOLO

During the week it's one long hustle – work, home, eat, sleep, repeat. I don't have the energy to think. Come Sunday things slow right down and I don't always know what to do with myself. By lunchtime Uncle Hari's usually home for us to eat together. Ian fixed a spaghetti Bolognese today. Once I drowned mine in parmesan cheese it wasn't too bad. Up here they real love their pasta. Three-four times a week I will eat something like lasagna, ravioli or spaghetti. I texted Mr Chetan pictures of all the pasta I have been eating and he said at this rate I will turn Italian soon.

I can't help thinking of Sundays at home. You getting baked chicken, stew red beans, vegetable rice, fried plantain, macaroni pie and green salad. And Mr Chetan was always making pone or sweet bread or fudge. Aunty Gloria or Aunty Deedee might reach lunchtime and all five, six, they're still on the porch. Even with my door closed I would hear them laughing and kicksing around with Mammy. I rubbed my temples. I want some kind of magic that will wipe all of this from my freaking mind. This is now home. I want to be here.

As soon as we were done eating, Ian looked at Katherine.

Sis, I cooked. You know the deal.

I pushed back my chair and reached for the dirty cutlery and empty plates.

Katherine, I'll do it.

We'll do it together. Have you seen the kitchen? It's like super messy.

While she packed away the leftovers I filled the dishwasher. That still left a good few things to hand-wash. I tackled the scrubbing and Katherine did the drying. Without thinking I asked Katherine to turn on the radio. Back home I wash, Mammy wipes, and the radio plays Heartbeat 103.5 FM.

What station?

Forget the radio.

I'll put on my playlist.

Her music is better than Ian's pop. Underground indie rock bands. Sick.

A bunch of us are going to play crazy golf tonight. Want to come? It'll be fun and you'll meet my friends.

I don't know how to play.

It's not like Tiger Woods golf. You're hitting the ball in these weird holes. And they have DJs. Come. It'll be great.

Nah, I'm good.

You always say that.

She took the colander I just washed and began drying it.

What did you do for fun in Trinidad?

Nothing.

What? You must do something.

I didn't know what to say. I loved hanging out at home until that night when every fucking thing changed.

She put the colander in the cupboard and reached for the wet plastic bowl.

Come with me. Just once. If you don't like it you don't have to come again.

Next weekend.

I don't believe you.

I made the sign of the cross.

Cross my heart and hope to die, stick a needle in my eye.

She laughed at me.

I still don't believe you. Since you came you've been hiding in the attic.

We could lime next weekend. For truth for truth.

Katherine leaned over and pinched my cheek like I was a baby.

Aww, you're, like, so super shy. And FYI, my friends don't bite.

My face turned instantly hot. I kept my head down and tossed clean pot spoons on the drain board. Out of the corner of my eye I saw Katherine taking she time drying each one slow slow. I was studying what excuse to give next time she asks me to go out when Uncle Hari bounced in.

I'm heading out to buy my lottery ticket. Mega Millions ain't had a winner for a while and the jackpot is now over a billion. A billion. My partner just called. He say the lines them long long so I'd better move fast.

Dad, you can play online.

Nah, nah, nah. I want a proper ticket in my hand. And watch me, I'm going to win. I have a system. I'm playing everybody birthday plus Sherry's birthday and the Mega Ball is the month I born. So that giving me . . .

He took a piece of paper from his wallet.

The Hari Ramdin lucky numbers are 6, 22, 19, 10, 30 and 7. All you want any tickets?

No thanks, Dad. I'm good.

I shook my head.

All right, the last train leaving for Mega Millions. I gone.

I heard him shuffling around and then the bang of the front door.

Okay, Solo, you go first. If you won the lottery what would be, like, your luxury thing?

Nothing.

Come on.

This girl was confusing my brain.

Okay, I'll go first. I would go to Bloomingdale's and have a total makeover. Everything from makeup to shoes.

I bit my lip.

You must want something.

I don't know. Maybe a little apartment.

It has to be a really big apartment because you're winning millions.

Okay, big with a room for chilling out and listening to music and another room with a massive TV.

Oh yeah, I want a home cinema too.

And I want a waterbed. This friend of mine, his parents had one. It was so cool.

Katherine buss out laughing.

A waterbed? Seriously? I don't think they even make those any more.

Well, you asked me and I'm getting a king-size waterbed.

You're too funny.

She left the kitchen and came back with a few dirty bowls and mugs.

Somebody left these in the living room right where they were watching TV.

Don't look at me. That was Ian and Uncle Hari last night.

I started washing the mugs.

So, let's say you got your apartment and your waterbed.

And my home cinema and the massive stereo system.

Okay, you got all of that. You wouldn't remain in construction?

Nah. No way.

Well, what would you do, Mr Mega Millions?

Don't know.

I would quit my job and open, like, a super high-end dog hotel and spa.

What madness is that?

Oh, you would be surprised. Trust me. The people who come into the pet store spend loads of money on their fur babies. It's a thing.

I guess I could open a restaurant where you get the tastiest Trini food in the whole of New York. And Mr Chetan would come and run it because he's a seriously good cook.

Speaking of Trinidad, do you remember us visiting?

No. Sorry. I was small small.

If I was six, then you were maybe three or four? We visited your house and Ian and I played on a swing for hours and hours.

We still have that swing in the back.

Aunty Betty made me take turns with Ian. And she had to hold you the whole time. You wouldn't let her put you down.

How you could remember that if you were six?

She shrugged.

That swing and you clinging to your mom stayed with me.

I didn't cling to Mammy.

You did. You were, like, totally a mama's boy.

I scrubbed the frying pan extra hard. I could well imagine gripping Mammy's leg and she picking me up. A wave of pain hit my chest and I swallowed. I had to remind myself that I don't miss her.

How is Aunty Betty these days? Have you spoken lately?

Hear what, Katherine – I don't know and I don't want to know. I'm in America, she's in Trinidad and we're keeping it just so. I managed to whisper,

She's good, I suppose.

Is she still worried about you being attacked in the Big Apple? Dad said she's freaked out that you'll get mugged or something.

I shook my head. Mammy will have to work out how to stop worrying by she-self. And she must stop with the interfering. I straightened my back.

She's carrying on like I can't take care of myself. Here is probably safer than parts of Trinidad.

She's only being a mom.

Yeah, well, I overs that.

Thank God the sink was empty. I looked up.

We're done.

She was smiling at me sweet sweet. I didn't expect that.

Come for a hug.

She squeezed me tight and I realised it had been a long time since I'd got a hug up. From my toes to my head felt warm, safe and for a few seconds my whole body let go. But I caught myself. To make it in New York I can't be no softee softee man. The second she let go I bolted to my bedroom and locked the door. Monday coming now for now.

BETTY

I must be call Solo a hundred times but he not answering. I don't know if to stop calling or what to do. He have age so he could do what he want. I must accept that. You make your children, look after them and hope for the best. But oh gosh, man. Any fool knows that reaching adult age is not the same as having the sense and experience. And if anybody needs some good sense knocked into them it's that boy and his hard head. Who going to help him up there? Hari?

I sat down the other day. The house is always quiet quiet. I know writing letters is old-fashioned. People hardly even send Christmas and birthday cards. I should probably be tweeting or Snapchatting but the thing with a letter is that you can't ignore it. No simple delete button. If the postman drop a letter you must want to know what it says. I'm banking on that. I started putting down a few words. I wrote one line then I scratched it out. I wrote a next one but it sounded stupid. It wasn't easy but I kept trying.

I hope you have a job where people are treating you good and you are not overworked. You were always shy in public and I worry that people will take advantage of you. Not everybody who smiles at you is your friend. Remember that. I wish you wouldn't cut me out of your life like this. I miss you so much. Every time I think about you I start crying.

Solo never gave me a chance. He didn't believe my side of the story. Better watch what I write. For him life is black and white. It must look like I literally got away with murder. As if I sat down, took my time and studied how to kill the man. Took out a hit on Sunil. Bought rat poison and put it in his food. Poured Gramoxone down the man's throat. It happened in a flash and our Heavenly Father knows I carry this guilt in my heart and on my back forevermore. Get away? I didn't get away. I went from one kind of hell to a next.

And Solo was too small to remember how I protected him from the licks and the cussing. He was a baby. He can't know how his father would lock us in a room whole day because he didn't like the dress I was wearing or he thought I gave him a cut eye. Whatever happened to me I always protected Solo. That must count. And what about his education? Without a qualification in his hand Solo ain't going nowhere fast.

Son, you've made your point. Time to end this stupidness. Come back now and apply to UWI or UTT and get a degree in something. You are breaking the law. You want them to deport you like a common criminal and bring shame on us? What will people say? You ever thought about what this doing to me?

The only person he was thinking about was himself. He would have preferred to grow up with that drunk bully of a father? If Sunil was alive by the time Solo reached his teens he would've been getting blows regular regular. I was the only one who put him first. He didn't grow up with a set of man moving in and out this house telling him to call them Daddy.

I got up to make coffee and as I passed Solo's bedroom I couldn't help myself. The room still has his feel. He doesn't know how I fixed it away nice for whenever he comes back. I hope he comes back soon. I must tell him everything's waiting for him – new curtains and a fresh coat of paint in a nice shade of cream.

Maybe as an only child he got spoilt up a tincy wincy more than was good. But the teen years? Jeez-an-ages, he should have had a brother or a sister. I wanted more. I tried all kind of thing. I even went vegan for six months because Deedee's sister swore that is what helped her get pregnant. Nothing doing. Doctor said she couldn't find anything wrong. No way I was going to tell her the amount of wickedness Sunil had done to me. The shame would have been like getting the punches and kicks all over again.

Of course big man Sunil refused to go to a doctor. Nothing was ever his fault. All that drink he poured down his gullet, I wouldn't be surprised if even his sperm them were punch drunk. Instead of swimming they were probably passed out. No sense in complaining now. The Lord gave me one and I'm grateful. It isn't Christian to question His plan but I find if He was going to take away my one child from me He could've given me a next one who would stay home.

Half the time when I think of Solo I want to bawl down the place and the other half I want to wring his neck. From the time he left this house he knew what he was doing. Going New York for holidays my foot. And dotish me thinking that was what he deserved after exams. I never went New York. But I bought him a ticket. He study that? Smiling up to my face when he was scheming with Hari behind my back. But if

I write that he will get more vex. Time to cover your mouth, Betty.

I wonder if Solo would change his mind if Mr Chetan was the one to put pressure on him? I'll mention how much Mr Chetan misses him. It's the truth.

I am worried about you, Solo. I am missing you and Mr Chetan is missing you. I told him to pray that you will come home soon and he said he prays for your safe return every night. Not a day goes by when we don't ask God to guide and protect you.

Whatever stupidness I wrote it, done full up three pages. In the letter I was patient and reasonable to keep Mister Solo happy.

I read my letter over and I was vexed with myself. Tiptoeing around Solo. Man, to hell with that. He should know the truth that with Sunil I was never sure when he would explode. One minute we might be sitting down talking good good and next minute he would be bellowing in my face calling me a cunt and accusing me of going with man I barely knew. Sometimes I got away from a beating by grabbing Solo and the two of us would jump in the car, hoping Sunil would be asleep by the time we came back. He didn't want a wife. He wanted a punching bag.

Once I married and left my mother's house you think I could run back with story about Sunil? I told my mother he beat me and you know what she said? You're playing big woman and have husband? Well, take what the husband giving. I don't know why she was so mean because she had a good home life. True, my father had he little outside woman, yes, but he didn't throw it in she face and he never raised his hand.

Deedee and Gloria weren't close to me the way we're tight now and yet they were the only ones who encouraged me to take my child and leave. I didn't want to leave. I wanted Sunil to change. What I thought I needed was a big person to talk to Sunil. Imagine my shock when the church elders didn't believe me. Sunil Ramdin does beat he wife? Nah, man. No way. That had to be people bad talking a decent, upright man. And the Indian people would whisper that it was black people who had started that talk. They would rather fight about coolie and nigger than stop a man putting licks on a woman. I will never forget how one time a woman in the church had the nerve to look me straight in my eye and tell me that if your husband doesn't put two good lash on you every now and then, how you will know he loves you? And what about that quack doctor Sunil used to carry me by whenever I needed a patch-up? Is only money he liked? Not once did he ever so much as ask, Mrs Ramdin, how you always falling down so? This is the third time in a month your husband say you slipped on the wet tiles. Whatever Sunil said happened was what he marked down on the file. People like he were born missing a conscience.

Before Solo cuts me off forever he should know these things. I've tried saying them before and it didn't seem to sink in so I'm putting it in black and white. I wrote down everything. Later I read it over and thought, nah. It's the boy's father. He doesn't need chapter and verse. All he must realise is that I didn't murder the man in cold blood. The rest? I will bide my time.

Nobody lifted a finger to help us. They never asked why I was always falling and bruising myself or breaking bones. When push came to shove, they preferred to mind they own business and let me take my licks. I used to think that one day when Sunil drank too much rum he would end up killing the both of us. You were a baby so you don't remember how bad things were. I know what I did was the biggest sin and I live with that weight on me every day but losing you, my angel, is worse than any pain. It's only you I have in this world. Please, son, find it in your heart to forgive me. Come back home. I love you.

Mammy

MR CHETAN

I watched Mani on social media for months and it should have stayed right there. Seeing him has brought back all the sweetness of that boy. We had nine whole months together before it ended. Ma saw us kissing. I was terrified but she didn't say a word to me. Weeks, months, went by and nothing. But the woman was biding she time. Once I finished my exams in the June she told my father. He came home early one day. I was in the back yard. All he did was call me but from his voice I knew straight away. I remember thinking I should run. But run where? As he got closer he rolled up his sleeves. Right in the yard, with the neighbours looking, he knocked me down on the ground and pinned me in the dirt with his big boots. Loud loud he was shouting,

> No son of mine is a buller. You hear me? I raise you to be
> a buller man? Eh? Answer me. I raise you to want totee up
> your bottom? Man, I go beat the fucking shit out of you
> today self. You nasty pervert. You kiss-me-ass mother cunt.
> I going to beat you so bad you go beg me to kill you.

I was screaming for help. He held me down and my mother gave him rope. They ripped off my pants and the two of them together hog-tied me right there. I saw the cutlass coming down on me and I thought I was going to die. He spared my life but until you get planasse with the side of a cutlass you don't know real licks. When they threw me out to live by relatives I hardly knew, part of me was relieved. True talk – to this day I tote around that pain and humiliation.

Seeing Mani has made me realise how much that is still strangling me, making me 'fraidy 'fraidy. Always worried people will talk. They're probably talking anyway because by now I should be married with house, child and dog rather than living alone without even a pet goldfish. Mani and me is pure fantasy. Never happening. I told myself – settle for what the internet's offering. My favourite site had a biblical name. Adam wasn't business with Eve. Adam was looking for a next Adam hiding in the Garden of Eden. Well, papayo, adamlookingforadam.com have plenty man busy winking and messaging. I didn't put up a profile picture but not everyone was bashful so. The best was a parent at the school. Up to last week I saw him looking like Daddy dearest with wifey and three children. But his picture up on the site boldface boldface.

And talking of school – Saturday is the blasted staff Christmas party. At least they holding it at that sweet little hotel in St Joseph Village. I like their cooking but does that make up for them half-drunk men? Whole week I've been taxing my brain for a good excuse to miss the damn thing. And the worst part is the pressure to bring somebody. Anybody. Even Miss Betty has a date. I shouldn't say it like that because she's lovely. Gloria's fixed her up with some bachelor cousin visiting from England, looking to retire here. I hope Miss Betty knows that he so really looking for a nurse with benefits for when the time come and he can't wipe his own bamsee.

And I'm not calling names but a certain female teacher has been bringing a man to all school functions and that man is not the one she walked down the aisle with. Years now she's been doing this. Always some excuse why she husband stayed home and this kind gentleman, out of the goodness of his heart, brought her. Who she feel she fooling? Everybody knows she's stepping out with a deputy. Even the husband must know by now. But let me reach with a decent man like Mani and watch how trouble go start. They might have Gay Pride March and all them kind of thing in Port of Spain. I glad for them. But try that south of the Caroni River and see if you don't get pelt with bottle.

*

The Christmas party was exactly as expected. I hated seeing Miss Betty laughing with that dotish, wrinkly buffoon. She could do better than that. A lot better. Once I had licked down a pastelle and tasted the black cake (it needed plenty more rum), I slipped out what I thought was an exit and ended up lost in the people hotel. A security guard showed me how to get back to the main entrance.

Let me walk you out.

Thanks.

You have far to go?

Nah, man. I'm right in Duncan Village.

For true? I live close to Duncan Village.

He gave me a long hard stare that melted into a sweet eye and the cutest little smile ever. I looked around. It was busy and somebody from my school posse could pass by any minute. But there was no doubt in my mind. He had given me the look.

This is my car.

We locked eyes again.

I know you from somewhere?

He shook his head and brushed my arm even though there was plenty room as he turned to head back to the hotel.

I would have remembered you. Anyhow, you know where to find me. I do security work weekends when they have functions.

I raced home and went straight on the computer. Yes. I knew I had seen him before. I knew it. Look, my boy right there: jackhammer77. I sent him my picture. Up to him now. I'm willing and waiting.

SOLO

Habib? Habib Khan?

She was about to call out a third time when I got up. It's me the woman's calling.

Here.

Hi, how are you? You want to put two drops in the left eye, three times a day, and keep doing it for five days even if you think the eye is better.

I hate putting thing in my eye.

I could show you how to do it but you're better off checking YouTube. Loads of videos there on the best technique for getting the drops in. You'll be fine.

I took the small bag and handed her a twenty-dollar bill.

That's twelve dollars straight and eight dollars is your change. Have a nice day.

This better work, yes. Blink and it's like something's scraping my eyeball. Four months of dust from that building site. I shouldn't be surprised the eye red and paining me. Dennis, Uncle Hari's contractor friend, said he's done for at least a month. Once work starts back up he will check me. I'm praying it's soon. Meantime your boy holding down a small work at Blue Parrot in King's Mall. General kitchen helper, $5 an hour, but hey, as Uncle Hari said, it's an honest dollar. I texted Mr Chetan and told him. He had a good laugh because at home he would buff me for leaving my dirty wares in the sink. He can't believe I have a job washing dishes from 5 p.m. to midnight, six days a week. It's good he knows I'm not afraid of hard work. He's stopped asking me why I'm working. I think he understands and he doesn't hassle me about it, so we're good. He did drop that Mammy was wondering when she will hear from me. I'm not messaging her. She could stay right there and wonder.

It was Ian who got me the fake ID I used for this job. He's cool once you get to know him. Plus, he knows his shit when it comes to anything online. He hooked me up on this website where the fakes are so good they offer a thirty-day money back guarantee. Trouble is you can only pay in Bitcoin. Ian got a friend of his to sort me out for an extra five bucks. Two days later, boom. ID card dropped in the letter box.

I look like a Habib Khan to you?

Ian leaned over for a fist bump.

Hey, man, this is dope. They probably took that Social Security off some dead guy. Seriously dope.

Blue Parrot people only know me as Habib Khan but I kept forgetting that was me. Sometimes it took three-four times before I realised, but wait nah, is me they're calling. I bet the manager thought I was playing hard ears. That would explain why he was always digging me about how long I took to wash wares. He has this rule that you can't take toilet breaks. A

Jamaican fella who up here long time said that was illegal. He
could talk. Me? I will wait till my ten-minute break unless it's
a shit-yourself-now-for-now situation. If I could quit this very
minute, I would. But it's not like I have another job waiting. A
dollar is a dollar.

*

Uncle Hari, you hear anything from your friend Dennis?
He have any construction jobs going?

Boy, Dennis said things real quiet.

Me and this Blue Parrot work can't hold out much longer.

What you go do? That's life.

I can't stand the place. They're full of attitude.

Hold some strain. I have a next friend with a hand in
construction. Let me ask a question.

Thanks, Uncle Hari.

And while we talking, let me ask you something. You call
your mother?

I texted.

He wagged his finger in my lying face.

Because you're not keeping in touch is me taking the
blows. I had to put she in she place the other day. You
won't believe this. Betty turn around and say she going to
call police and report me for kidnapping. I said, kidnap?

How I could kidnap a big man? Solo is nineteen. He reach here of his own free will and is you self who help him buy the ticket. This ain't no little child we talking about. If he wanted to go back Trinidad tomorrow I self would drive him to the airport.

I didn't know if to laugh or cry. That was Mammy all over. I could see her shelling pigeon peas and telling Mr Chetan she's going to call that Hari and give him a piece of her mind for snatching away her one child. And Mr Chetan would be talking her down, saying, don't upset yourself. Well, Mr C, she did it anyway.

Mammy won't call police. She won't go that far. But if she ever gives you that kidnap talk again ask her what was the real reason I left. See what she says then.

And what was the real reason, Solo?

For a nanosecond I wanted to tell him. Imagine the commess if he found out. His big brother? Now you talking police. Fact is I hate her bad and if I never saw her again that would be fine by me. Putting her in jail? Tempting. But I can't do that.

I just want to live my own life without her stifling me.

*

When I checked the time it was minutes to eight. On a Sunday morning. But somebody was banging loud loud on our front door. It sounded like Sherry shouting for Uncle Hari. Well, partner, since me living here was what caused the bacchanal, and their relationship capsizing, I stayed quiet in my room. That didn't mean I wasn't interested. I eased my bedroom door open to hear better.

Hari, open the blasted door. Open up. You know I left my key.

Uncle Hari was home. Katherine was home. Ian was home. Yet nobody was answering the door.

Hari, I said open the blasted door.

I could hear her rattling the door handle.

Open the door. Your car here so I know you inside. I want my black shoes. I forgot them in the wardrobe. Hari, open the door.

The entire street could hear her.

Hari, I know you're inside. Open the damn door. Open up. I don't care if you have your whore in there. I want my shoes now. I have a funeral to go to and I need my black shoes.

Uncle Hari's bedroom door creaked open. I could hear movement. Suddenly Uncle Hari was coming up my steps.

Solo? You waking?

Yeah, yeah. I'm up. What's happening?

Put on some clothes, quick. I'm sending Mala up by you. Let me deal with this madwoman outside. Like she's not leaving without them shoes.

Who the hell was Mala? I pulled on jeans and a T-shirt just in time. A sleepy woman, must be only a few years older than Katherine, tiptoed in. Her blouse was crumpled and she had on a tight denim skirt that wasn't zipped up all the way. How the ass Uncle Hari pull a hot thing so?

Sorry about this.

No problem.

Hari didn't say nothing about a wife.

I wanted to say that she was way too hot to be with a man old like her father. Instead, I whispered that the woman carrying on outside wasn't his wife. Uncle Hari was downstairs opening drawers and cupboards. I heard him asking Katherine if she knew about any black shoes Sherry had left. Mala came and sat on the bed. Her bare legs touched mine and I swear I got a little electric shock.

She won't come up here?

Nah. You're cool.

The girl slipped her arm in mine. I froze. She was warm and smelt so fucking good. Downstairs Uncle Hari opened the front door and Sherry stormed inside shouting. Mala gripped my arm tight. My stomach flipped.

Why you didn't answer me? Eh? Is woman you have in here? You think I give a shit if you fucking some whore? Where she hiding? Eh? Where she? She in the bedroom?

Like you gone mad? You see anybody here? And carrying on like this on a Sunday morning. Look, I don't know what

blasted old shoes you making all this ruction for but take
them and go. Just go. You're making a scene for nothing.

One set of stomping around and doors banging.

I tell you to take your shoes them and leave my house.
Please. Please. You're embarrassing yourself. The whole
neighbourhood hearing you carrying on like a wajang.

You have somebody here. I could feel it. Where you hiding
the sketel? Eh? Hello? Hello? Don't frighten. I ain't come
here to beat up nobody.

Stop this stupidness. Oh gosh, man. I'm talking to you easy
easy. Leave my house. You're causing a ruction.

Hello? Hello? Where you hiding? Let me tell you now, I
used to live here so I know every nook and cranny. I go find
you. Blasted jamette.

The big coat cupboard door slammed so hard I thought Sherry
had gone and broken the hinge.

Stop embarrassing yourself.

Don't touch me.

Oh gosh, man. I barely touch your back.

If you so much as lay a finger on me, Hari Ramdin, I swear
to God I'm bringing police for you.

You want to call police? Eh? Here. Take my phone. Go
on, use it. When they reach is you they go be locking up.
Disturbing the peace. Trespassing.

Shuffling, walking and then crying. Loud ugly crying. I glanced at Mala. She put her hand over her mouth and shook her head. I nodded to show I understood. Poor girl never meant to cause the raw pain in Sherry's bawling.

You feel you could treat me like dirt. I go do for you, Hari Ramdin. Wait and see. This ain't done.

The front door slammed. Bradam. I felt the whole house shake. A car door banged. An engine started. Wow. Uncle Hari catch a good break there. Cat don't have as many lives as this sweet man.

*

Seventeen days left on my six-month immigration stamp. And it's falling on Thanksgiving Day itself. This is it. If I stay in Uncle Sam's country a day longer I become one of those illegal immigrants Fox News so worried about. They think we're terrorists living off Social Security rather than working we ass off. And I am staying. Once I turn illegal, if I step out the country, that is it. No way I'd get back in. Simple as that.

Uncle Hari said to think it over. Think what over? Still, this was a serious move so I texted Mr Chetan. He said the same thing. But then again he wants me back home. I told him if I miss anybody from Trinidad it's him. I don't have a choice. And because I'm not texting, Mammy's been writing. The letters make me so angry it's like the anger is right up under my skin. I can't keep it down. One night I clenched my fist so tight it bled.

The back steps. Lying all those years and every day she's

up and down them same steps. I dream those fucking steps all the time. And on my birthday. Maybe it would never have happened if it wasn't my birthday. Why that day? And how did it happen? Were they quarrelling? Who hit who first? It could have been an accident but I don't think so. I feel she knew exactly what she was doing. Imagine she's smiling up in church when all the time she's broken the highest commandment. I'm staying. If that means being illegal I'll work out something. Plenty people get through. Plenty. A Guyanese man that Uncle Hari knows bought a genuine birth certificate. Cost him $3,500. One of Katherine's friends married a gay fella to get papers. Money passed although I don't know how much. That route is marriage for at least three years. Or five. Whatever. I haven't dated, much more find a girl to marry.

Dennis is still quiet. Uncle Hari said he heard Dennis gone Grenada because he's building a house there and he might not come back till quite April. I am proud that I lasted six fucking long weeks at Blue Parrot. That is one place not seeing me again in a hurry. Don't think is only me. Same day I quit two others left. One of them told the Puerto Rican manager how he should stop acting like he's white because real white people does shit on him the same as us. That was a new one for me. So, America have white people and people who look white but not white enough? This place crazy for truth. That leaves me taking the Q10 bus, then the F, to join the Bay Center janitorial team. They make it sound like it's a big deal: the janitorial team. All it means is I have a cleaning cart with two different types of mop to go around the mall cleaning up soda, vomit, chewing gum. Blasted chewing gum everywhere. I used to chew gum but this job's put me off for life. Toilet rota every three hours. Rich, respectable-looking people walking about the mall but put them in the toilet and they become disgusting creatures. I wonder if their bathroom home does be the same way. Throwing the nasty toilet paper on the ground? Peeing on the seat? Somebody has to clean it and that somebody is me.

One thing that's better here than at Blue Parrot is that the supervisor real like me bad. My first day she walked by and said, hi, how are you. I don't remember what I said. Some foolishness. Whatever. Trouble started one time. She went on and on about how much she loves my accent. The Trini accent is so gorgeous. It's not 'broken' like the Jamaican one. She joked in my ear that she doesn't understand half of what the Jamaicans say. But my accent? Cute. Super cute. Take that in your pipe and smoke it.

Today she gave me a little wink and whispered that my accent is not the only cute thing about me. I swear I'm telling the truth. Gross. The woman isn't exactly Mammy's age but with all them crisscross line on she face she can't be too far behind. Connie O'Reilly. I asked Uncle Hari what to do if she puts more moves on me. All he could do was laugh his belly full.

Solo, like an American passport go drop in your lap, boy.

That was not funny.

As soon as Ian reached home he was up in my room digging me for information.

I can't believe you're dating some older woman? How come you told Dad and not me? I'm your older, wiser cousin. Let me give you some tips on dealing with the ladies.

I never said anything about dating.

I thought it wasn't true. In that case you want to go on a double date with me? Two Guyanese sisters. Long hair. Very pretty.

Nah. I'm good.

Until you meet these girls you're not good.

Ian, I have to get up early.

I'll text them that you're on.

No. Don't do that.

Okay, but you're missing out. Later, cuz.

I pulled the blanket right over my head and curled up tight. I just wanted to fall asleep.

BETTY

I stood in his bare room. Every last stitch of Mr Chetan has been gone for some time. It's like he hadn't lived in this house all those years. Not a cologne, a piece of clothes, an old book. When I say nothing, I mean nothing, nothing, nothing. Even his sweet smell had vanished. I can't get accustomed to this loneliness. I walked around and the place felt lifeless with just me. It's so quiet that the quiet is loud with the kind of sounds you don't hear when people are in and out. First Solo and soon after Mr Chetan. Everybody's gone and left me. This weekend I took to my bed and cried for two days straight. After Solo had ups and gone New York I didn't know I had this much heart left to mash up. Of course, it was the right thing for Mr Chetan and for me too. I understood that. No way we could keep living under one roof while he's busy checking this man and that man. Time he had his privacy. That's my brain talking. My heart? Maybe I don't like seeing him with other men but I still want him here. Forget the romantic aspect. I done know that's never happening. I want my companion back right here, right now.

Once he left I stopped cooking. I don't want to cook for me alone. Mr Chetan was the real cook. He liked doing that to relax. If I stew chicken then whole week I'm eating it until I feel like I'll turn into a hen. Deedee especially is always passing on top tips like cook and freeze portions then rotate what you take out from the deep freeze. That good for she. If they ever stopped selling sliced bread and New Zealand Cheddar, I will starve. That would be one way to permanently lose the ten pounds I put on and take off, year in, year out.

These days all I seem to do is work, home and sleep. I never used to be a woman to stay in my bed long. Now? I could win Olympic gold for sleeping. Both Deedee and Gloria have been encouraging me to do something with myself but is what. The church already gets enough of my time. Other people should be putting a hand to help. I have my plants and my vegetable garden. Just the other day the neighbour was saying I should specialise in growing seasoning to supply restaurants. Growing the herbs is fine. I could do that with my eyes closed. But the hustling to get people to buy? I'm not in that. And none of these things will make the house feel less empty.

The ladies forced me to go on their Friday night casino lime. Mark my words. On the day of reckoning they will find that Deedee and Gloria skipped church on a Sunday more times than they skipped casino on a Friday. I don't want to lime. All the laughing and talking doesn't feel like it has anything to do with me. So I don't have to answer too much questions, I simply stick on my Betty Happy Face. Lovely, reliable Betty. People don't want to hear how isolated it does feel sometimes. And I can't go around saying I'm lonely. That would be another set of shame to add to being a widow with a son who gone he way. So Betty Happy Face going through hard no matter how miserable I feel.

Unfortunately, my Betty Happy Face slipped while me and Gloria were in the ladies' room at the casino.

Betty, what happen? I find you're not looking yourself. You're missing the buller man?

Don't make me regret telling you he's gay.

I'm only making joke. That's staying between you, me and Deedee.

Then please stop with the buller man talk. He has a name. Use his name.

My voice cracked and two rivers started flooding my face. I mopped my wet cheeks and swiped off half the makeup it had taken me ages to put on.

I'm sorry. I didn't mean nothing bad. You know Mr Chetan is my boy.

He's a kind, decent man and all you could do is call him names like he's from the gutter.

Sorry, Betty. You know is only joke I was joking.

The tears would not stop.

Oh, Betty, please don't cry.

Why do people always say don't cry when you're crying? I want to cry. Crying is all I want to do.

Betty girl, never mind. Ain't he does come visit? And he's not far. It's not like he left the country.

The house gets so quiet.

Listen to me. You managed by yourself before and you will manage again.

But I had Solo then. Now is me and me alone.

She wouldn't believe me, and I would never admit it, but when Mr Chetan left it was the first time I had ever slept in a house by myself. Ever. Like in my whole life ever. Before I got married I was never alone in the night and after it was the same.

Stay and fix your face. You can't be playing the people them slot machine and looking like Dracula's wife.

Thanks for that.

I got some wipes, cleaned up and began reapplying a touch of foundation.

Gloria, you know what really hit me hard?

What?

My whole life I looked after everybody. I looked after Sunil. I looked after Solo. I even looked after Mr Chetan little bit. And now? Look at me, in my forties, and I don't have a damn thing to show for myself. It's like I had my uses and now I'm nothing to nobody.

That's not true.

Really? Who I have? My son doesn't bother with me. Mr Chetan's moving on with his life. He's happy. But me? I alone must face everything.

Look, you don't need anyone. And stop talking like you're over the hill. Give yourself a chance.

I slapped on a little powder and passed the lipstick on my mouth.

Let me stop moaning, yes. Plenty people have it a hundred times worse and they don't complain.

Don't worry, girl. Stick with me. Tuesdays after work we're going to the dutty wine exercise class. Throw some waist to the beat and you'll forget everything and everybody.

I looked away and rolled my eyes. She's trying to help. When Tuesday reach, I will remind her that me and dutty wining have never been friends and we not starting now.

MR CHETAN

I follow Mani every few days when I flick through my Twitter, Insta and Facebook. He's recently posted from Miami – in a bar, Carib in hand, with a caption: look what I found. Up to last week I was wishing it's me he would find. But that was before Jackson. As soon as he picked up my message online we hit it off. Every night for the past week we have been talking and texting. His voice alone has me weak. I said if he wasn't police he could do phone sex easy easy. My boy asked if he could practise on me first. Saturday morning, exactly one week after we met, I was shaved, smelling sweet and looking sharp in a white linen shirt and my good jeans, ready for Mr Sexy.

Although he was keen to meet it took a little negotiation to decide exactly where. He didn't want to meet in south. Being gay and in the police was extra pressure. It's so bad they don't even acknowledge gay people exist in the force. I understand where he's coming from because I live with the same anxieties twenty-four seven. All it would take is one stray look or touch and people would run their mouth. It's exhausting. We needed a public place that was private enough to talk without feeling people were minding your business. After endless tre-le-le and tra-la-la we agreed on a cute coffee shop on the Gulf View Link Road.

From the second I saw him my head went bazodee. My memory didn't do the man justice. A little taller than me so probably six foot. Fit with skin smooth and dark like eggplant. This block of black marble was way out of my league. And yet we didn't have a single awkward moment. I couldn't get over it was me, stupid little me, on a date with this hotness. In my prayers I had asked the universe to take away this loneliness hoping for Mani. This was some second option. My first real date and I didn't want it to end. What would happen next? I might never see him again. He seemed to like me but I didn't know the rules. Was I supposed to ask him back to my place? This wasn't no ordinary hook-up. Don't get me wrong. I wanted to fuck him bad bad. I just didn't know if I was supposed to wait or if it was expected. Three and a half hours later we finally left the coffee shop, laughing and joking like we've been tight buddies from ever since. Neither of us said anything about meeting again. We shook hands, quick hug and that was that.

Instead of driving off I sat in my car replaying parts of our conversation and trying to memorise the way he laughed with his eyes. My phone rang. Jackson:

Chetan, it was real cool meeting you.

Yeah. You too.

We should link up.

For sure, man.

Silence. I could hardly breathe. I wanted to ask. He beat me to it.

You want to see where I'm living? It's nothing posh. I'm just a poor man.

Where are you now?

You saw where I park? I'm still there. Follow me.

*

I followed him then, and the next day, and the day after, and the day after that. We were inseparable like bamsee and bench. All we did was work and fuck, fuck and work. One lunchtime we even managed to run away by me for a quickie. Another time I tried to sneak a little suck and he stopped me.

Don't do that nah, man. We're in the car.

Nobody can see us.

That's not the point. Nobody ever tell you that you mustn't have sex in a car or else the car will develop problems? And look nah, I just spent a thousand dollars to get this engine fixed.

I buss out laughing only to realise that the man was dead serious. He's too cute.

Miss Betty noticed I was looking tired and thought I must be coming down with whatever virus was going around. She wanted to bring food and stay to look after me. I had to make up all kind of excuse to keep she far from my place. Hands down I was having the best time of my life.

BETTY

Hari, don't lie. I know you is the one keeping Solo from talking to me.

No, no, no. You got that wrong. I is the one always saying, call your mother, call your mother.

You rush him to New York and expect me to believe that?

I'm tired telling you Solo is his own man.

Don't get me vex today. Solo's behaviour is because you backing him.

Betty, my nephew asked if he could come and stay by me. I said yes. End of story. You and Solo better sort out your business. I have nothing to do with that.

From long time you didn't like me. You took Solo for spite.

You know what you are? You are a controlling bitch. Now stop fucking bothering me.

Click. The man end the call. He ain't change one bit. And he better not be encouraging Solo to drink. It was drinking with Hari that turned Sunil. When the two of them went liming I wouldn't see Sunil before all three, four in the morning. Marriage and a new baby made no difference. Hari still expected Sunil to lime like a bachie.

At eighteen months Solo still wouldn't sleep unless Mammy was in the bed too. Sunil pulled an all-nighter drinking. Instead of going to sleep he started to keep one set of noise. Oh, I was always putting the child before him. We're not even sleeping in the same bed. All I was thinking is if this child woke up now, that was the end of sleep for the night.

Come nah, babes. Rub my back for me, nah.

To stop him disturbing the baby I let him lead me to our room. Next thing Sunil's straddling me, trying a thing.

Behave. You're stinking of rum.

Take some of this.

Go to sleep.

I ain't sleepy. Come nah, man.

No. I'm not doing it with a drunk.

Wataps. My cheek stung from where he'd hit me.

What you just call me?

Shock had locked my jaws together. I couldn't say anything. But this time I saw his hand coming and braced myself.
Wataps.

Say it again.

My jaw was still locked tight.
Wataps.

If you don't talk I go slap you again.

Wataps.

You asked for that.

He rolled off me, grabbed a pillow to himself and was snoring like a truck in less than a minute. When he surfaced later that day he said it wasn't him. It was the rum. From that minute he was done with the drinking.

You're my tamarind ball. You know that. You know I love you.

Hari wasn't giving up his drinking partner without a fight – especially now the partner's excuse was helping me with the child. War started up. My weapon was a baby turning into a little chatterbox who thought his daddy was the best daddy in the whole world. For a few months me and the chatterbox won every Friday night battle. Christmas reach and Hari threw a pastelle and rum punch lime for the family. Everything was going good good until Hari noticed the punch Sunil drinking was virgin.

Sunil, you can't come by my house and drink juice. What kind a thing is that?

Sunil looked at me.

Don't dig no horrors. I'm cool with this.

Nah, man. People does be begging for a taste of my rum punch.

I know that, boss. I've had it before.

I could see the way Sunil was eyeing the glass in Hari's hand. He was serving the rum punch in some tall glasses with nutmeg sprinkle on top and the Angostura bitters slowly mixing with the festive punch. I knew he wasn't going to be able to hold out so I spoke up.

Hari, boy, I think we heading out, yes. Tomorrow is work.

Hari ignored me.

Sunil, take a glass and come sit down.

Well, now I was vex.

Hari, ain't I just said we going? This child have to bathe.

Hari still wasn't taking me on. I picked up my handbag.

Sunil, you have the car keys? Goodnight, everybody.

All three of we went home. But Lord, that was not the end. Hardly the start. New year, new campaign. Trinidad doesn't miss a beat between Christmas and Carnival. It's one fete after another. Hari hounded Sunil to go liming. Hounded. Eventually he gave in to his brother.

What you want me to do, Betty? He's family. I go have to see him some time.

By Ash Wednesday the routine was set with drinking from Thursday through Sunday. It broke my heart. I asked Sunil to give up for Lent. He said nah. Jesus would want him to take a drink. Ain't was he-self that turned water into wine? First Friday of Lent, in front Hari, I threw my arms around Sunil's waist.

Babes, what about your tamarind ball. Ain't you love tamarind ball?

He looked me in my eye.

I don't even like tamarind ball.

That night he came in drunk, picked a fight and gave me one hard cuff that split my lip. From then the licks never stopped. Hari had won the war.

SOLO

What happen? You're not coming home, baby?

No.

Why you doing this?

Doing what?

Oh gosh, boy. Your six months coming up in a couple days.
It's time to done whatever this is and come home.

No.

Why, Solo?

You know exactly why.

Silence, except she was breathing hard. I wanted to end the call.

Come back nah. Come back and go university next year.
You have the grades. Get a degree in something. After that
you could go America, Canada, all about. But you need an
education.

Me and school overs.

So what? You're going to spend the rest of your life washing
wares? Painting house? Anybody from your school doing
that now? Eh? Everybody trying to better themselves and
you're there throwing away your life.

I could hear her crying softly.

Son, you're vex with me. I get it.

Now her voice was trembling.

That is one thing. But that is not a reason to wreck your whole future.

I'm making good money.

What kind of money you're making? You could pay rent? Bills? Put food on the table? If Hari kicks you out, how you go find your way up there all alone? And you're not legal. Answer me that.

I don't need nobody. And besides, Uncle Hari's not going to kick me out.

You have that in writing?

We is blood. And he ain't a liar.

Well, if I was you I would feed him with a long spoon. All these years Hari didn't have time to post a birthday card or send something come Christmas. Now you like a son? You know your mind but I would take him with two big pinch of salt.

Well, she's leaving out half the story. I think she never wanted me to have anything to do with Daddy's family. He has family living right in Trinidad. Why we never visited them? For all I know I've passed them straight on the road and didn't know we were related. But if I let go my mouth I might say things I regret. She could go rot.

Solo, all these years I've been holding back from talking to you because you were little. But now you have age is time we talk straight. Since that night when you heard what I said to Mr Chetan.

My heart started racing.

I've been trying to explain again and again that what you heard is not the whole truth but you don't want to listen. You know me. I'm not a violent person. I don't go around making trouble for anybody. When you were little life wasn't easy. You won't remember what it was like with your father but small as you were you were afraid of him too. I'm not saying he was always so. It was the drinking. Once he had rum inside him he used to go crazy.

Stop right there. Uncle Hari's told me so much about Daddy that I never knew. He used to take me everywhere with him when I was small. Every football game. Every cricket match. People used to say they never saw a father have his child with him no matter where he was liming.

I'm not saying he wasn't ever a good father. And he loved you, baby. Solo, these things are not black and white.

She let out a big big sigh like the world weighing her down.

Look, believe what you want. Wasn't only me who get licks. And that is where I drew a line. I see all kind of trouble but I always protected you. I was protecting you that night of your birthday.

Nah.

I jabbed the off button on the screen and don't ask me why but I punched myself. Hard. Right hook landed on my jaw. I punched again. This time I knocked my ear real hard. It was stinging. I aimed a blow right at the pain.

Harder.

Again.

Harder.

Again.

How hard can I hit myself?

Again.

Do it again.

Again.

When my hand was paining me too much, I kept up the blows by slamming the side of my head on the wall. Bang. Bang. Bang. Every blow was pain but then, and this is the weirdest thing: I liked the pain. I wanted the pain. I wanted to see how much I could take before I had to stop. Nothing else mattered. Everything I was feeling before, everything Mammy said, it all vanished. I concentrated on the blows. What she said didn't sting so much. I crawled my way up the blasted steps to my room. But you know what? My head might be spinning with pain. My ears might be stinging. My hand might be burning. But my mind was clear. I buss one hard sleep. Monday could've fallen on Sunday and I would've been none the wiser.

It was dark when I went in the bed and only slightly lighter when I got up the next morning. My shift started seven o'clock. As I turned to check my phone one hot jabbing pain passed through my jaw and neck, down by my shoulder and up the side of my head. With the camera on selfie mode I had a look.

Ouch. Not cute. It wasn't so much the swelling as the rainbow
of colours on my cheek, starting with blueish purple under
my right eye and crimson by my ear. I just touched it and it
hurt for so. Last night I don't remember it hurting this much.
If anybody saw me now they would think I lost a fight with
some Queens Bad John. How the ass I was supposed to leave
the house without people seeing me?

Lucky thing I managed to digs out before the rest of them
woke up properly. But the luck ended when Connie O'Reilly
spotted me coming in. The million-dollar question was whether
my super cute Trini accent would save my ass. I would even
have flashed her a sweet eye if my eye wasn't swollen.

Did you get mugged?

Nothing so, Miss O'Reilly. The front door swung open and
stupid me was behind. I got one hard lash.

She sighed.

Customers in the mall can't see you like this. I'm sorry but
I'm going to have to ask you to leave. You can't work like
this.

You're firing me, Miss O'Reilly?

I'm not but you can't come back until that bruise has gone
down and you're looking normal.

Please. I'll keep my head down. No one will notice. If I
wrap up in my scarf no one will see the bruise them.

Habib, you have no idea how much trouble I would get into
with my boss. I could be fired if I let you out into the mall.

I felt real dotish. What would Uncle Hari say? The man might make me pack my bags and leave one time. He's done everything for me and this is how I end up. Jackass Mammy's blasted fault. I wouldn't be here doing low-down work in the first place if she didn't do what she did.

Wait a sec, Habib, I've thought of something.

I held my breath.

I might be able to put you with the cleaning crew on the fifth floor. Those offices are empty on a Sunday. And if you don't mind night work you could move from the day team to the night shift. Clock in at ten at night and clock off at five in the morning. What do you think?

Right that minute I could have kissed her. And you won't believe what jumped straight out my mouth.

God is love. Thank you so much.

Same as if Mammy was saying it. I blinked her away.

Thank you. You don't know how much I appreciate this. I will work whatever time. And it won't happen again. I don't get in fights, Miss O'Reilly.

She winked.

You've got a girlfriend, Habib?

No.

Sister?

No.

Well, here's my top tip. Go to Walmart. In the cosmetics aisle you'll find foundation. Comes in all different shades. You want to get something near your skin tone. Put a little on the bruise and you won't see it. Works a dream.

You would think I learnt my lesson good and proper. I mean, beating myself up is real dumb if it costs me a good work. But the beating did other things for me – things that I wanted bad. I did it a next time. And again. Only difference was I quickly learnt to hide the marks. I wish I could explain how it made life easier. Licks shouldn't make you feel peaceful inside but, for me, that's how it was.

*

I called Mr Chetan. We talked long. His old car finally conked out for good and he's thinking of buying a Honda somebody at school is selling. I wanted to tell him about the beating. And I've started cutting too. But where to start with something so? He might get vexed. He asked if Mammy has told me more about my daddy. I shut that down one time. Like I don't know he and Mammy will talk? You see me? Right now I can't take on this bullshit.

The day before Thanksgiving, Mammy must have called about ten times. I clean forgot to block her. When she wasn't getting through with the ringing she moved to texting. That blasted woman like she's stuck on repeat. Begging. Don't overstay. Come back Trinidad. Home waiting for you. I'm the only thing she has in the world. Whole day I ignored the craziness. Everything was going good good until I was walking from the bus stop to home. Just so I suddenly catch a vaps and called. I didn't even bother with hello.

I want to ask you something. If I didn't overhear, you ever planned to tell me the truth?

I could hear her hard breathing.

I was going to tell you. But I had to wait for you to be the right age to understand.

What age would that be exactly?

Please, son. Look at it from my side.

You're not getting out of it so. I'm asking you. What age did you think I would understand what you did to my daddy? Twenty? Thirty? Forty?

Two of we were quiet, wanting to know where this would land. While we waited on each other I slipped my hand under my clothes. Sweater, shirt, vest, I kept pulling until I felt warm flesh. I pinched hard. All I could hear was her breathing. Harder. I scraped and scraped one spot until my nails cut into the flesh. When I pulled out my hand it had blood. Mammy was crying and saying she sorry over and over. I didn't answer back. The sting of the scrapes drowned her voice. Besides, I was now outside the house. I clicked off and went inside.

That night was hard. I wasn't booked to go back to Trinidad. Every few hours I woke and checked the time. Part of me wished I could go back home. Not by Mammy. If I lived with Mr Chetan that could work. Just dreams though. I'm in New York. Sounds real dope. But check this room. And how am I ever going to find a good job? How many years before I find a way to get legal? I scraped the scabs forming on my stomach. I scraped and scraped and scraped myself to sleep.

It became my thing. Now I don't even try to sleep without a good half hour to cut my arm or land a few punches to my leg. It clears my head. But I'm careful. The story nearly jump out when Ian and I were clearing rubbish from the yard. I accidentally pulled up my sweatshirt. He saw and asked how I got the cuts on my belly. I said they were nothing and he left me alone. Madame Katherine, on the other hand, is not one to hold back. I forgot to put a plaster on a cut and blood seeped through.

Solo-Rolo, you know you have blood on the front of your T-shirt?

I panicked as she tried to lift the edge of my T-shirt, and managed to yank it down fast fast.

Girl, move nah.

You have a bad cut. Tell your girlfriend not to rough you up so much next time.

Uncle Hari's ears pricked up one time.

Solo, is girlfriend you get and you ain't tell me nothing?

Katherine's playing fast. There's no girlfriend.

Dad, don't believe him. That mark only got there one way. Let me have a look, lover boy.

She was only playing but I pulled away.

Come on. Let's see what she's done to you in the heat of passion. Bet she's a screamer too.

Katherine, you're embarrassing the boy. He's now learning to handle these American women them.

They were wetting themselves laughing as I escaped upstairs and locked my door. Me? Have a girlfriend? Nice that they think so but they're sweetening their tea with salt. How exactly would I find a girl? Katherine knows it's none of the friends she's always pushing on me. Plus, a man working nights and sleeping in the day. When exactly I'm supposed to have time to check woman? All it have for me is to reach home when people getting up, settle down with a razor blade and cut under my foot or my stomach or my arm, whatever, until I get an ease up. People don't know my shame. You're not supposed to slice your flesh. To add to the shame, sometimes the cutting makes Little Solo wake and I do that too. Why does cutting relax me and even make me horny? I must be a special kind of freak.

Katherine and Uncle Hari were still downstairs laughing and making fun of me. I heard them. One day they'll figure out the truth and then nobody will be laughing. I can't face anybody finding out. Even with my fingers deep inside my ears I couldn't drown out their voices. I ducked as I walked past the little mirror hanging on my wall. Ever since I started this cutting I avoid mirrors. I don't want to see Solo Ramdin, aka Habib Khan. I hate him.

BETTY

As we turned in by Deedee's sister's street I could feel the excitement on my skin. Cars lined both sides of the road, making it hard for traffic to pass. Before we even reached the house we could make out one set of tassa drumming along with the high-pitched jhal and little cymbals, keeping time.

They've gone to town on this Hindu wedding. Like they found their roots.

Nah. You don't see what's going on here? Is show off they showing off.

Deedee's nephew was marrying a girl with funny-looking teeth. Like the teeth them too long for the mouth. And you see the two in front? They had white streaks that made the rest of the teeth look yellow yellow. I don't know why she family didn't go dentist and get the teeth whitened or see if they could paint all one colour and done the thing. When you're in love, different coloured teeth don't matter. You might even find it's cute. But wait seven, eight years and it will be a different story. Gloria said not to mind the teeth. At least the boy won't get horn.

Worse than the girl's teeth was her religion. Deedee's people are Presbyterian and not normal Presbyterians. Her grandparents helped set up the local Presbyterian church. Her nephew looked up and down the whole of Trinidad and Tobago. Instead of taking a nice Presbyterian girl down the aisle he had to fall for a funny-teeth Hindu dulahin demanding a proper three-day Hindu wedding. Deedee's side are not having their son marrying in dhoti and turban. He had to be in a three-piece suit, the girl in a white dress, and pictures taken in front a three-tier cake from Camille's. Anything less and the Erin Village Presbyterian Church's congregation will be bad talking them behind their back from now till thy kingdom come.

Tonight was the Matikor where we ladies put down some wutless dancing, talk foolishness and eat we belly full. Sunday is the full temple wedding starting early. Once that's done everybody will head to a hotel in Claxton Bay. From there Deedee's family will run the show. Reverend Mahabir will bless the couple. By then the boy will have changed into a suit and the girl will be floating around in a white wedding dress. As we dance the last dance everybody's mother and father will have got almost all they wanted. If it was my son I would tell him and the girl to go in the registry, sign what you have to sign and we'd throw a small lime at home. All this three-day wedding when the young people could well put that money to buy house and land. If it was my son. Then again, it doesn't look like me and Solo will ever argue about marrying in a church, temple or mosque. For all I know he might done be married and I wouldn't know nothing.

Once Deedee's side accepted that the Hindu wedding was happening they turned more Hindu than the in-laws. They were up and down Chaguanas buying sari, kurta pyjama suit and salwar kameez. And Trini people like to dress up. The same outfit not wearing twice. In the rush, I even picked up a lovely purple sari with a silver paisley pattern. That's for the main wedding day. Deedee bought a heavy green silk sari with gold embroidery. It looked like it came direct from Bollywood. For some reason, by the time she reached home and looked at it twice, she mind changed. Oh, the colour made her look like she was swimming in callaloo soup and just so I get it. I won't say boo but you see the replacement yellow sari she bought? Now she's drowning in dhal.

We had to push past one set of people to get inside the front yard for the Matikor. If you see people. And man, the tassa drummers were going hard. Over to the side of the house I spied a tent where people were getting into some serious eating with their hands. Nothing sweeter than Indian wedding food. I'm talking curry channa and aloo, pumpkin, bodi, chataigne if it in season, curry mango, dhal, rice and dhalpourri roti. Gloria caught me eyeing up the people food and tugged my elbow.

Manners. We can't tackle the roti before we say hello to the family.

The invitation was for 5 p.m. Luckily they meant 5 p.m. Trini time so six o'clock things were now starting. Behind the tassa drummers a procession headed out into the road. At the front was a little girl balancing a big tray on her head. Five women surrounded her – Deedee's sister, her mom, an aunty, a cousin Aisha and another woman I didn't know who was the ringleader. The rest of us fell in behind. I waved to Deedee in the crowd and she shouted back.

I say all you wasn't coming. The Hardi now starting.

We stepped in with a grinning Deedee and headed up the street. Nobody would know this is the same highfalutin Presbyterian.

How all you know what to do for the ceremony tonight?

Girl, my sister hired a tyrant.

She pointed to an older woman, orhni covering her head and tucked into her dress band.

That is Miss Harridyal directing proceedings. Whatever she tell me to do, I doing.

Vibrations from the tassa drums were making my flesh shake. It was like a hammer breaking up all the loneliness I was carrying. Stepping to the rhythm, our group kept walking up the road. A car slowed down and followed alongside while dropping a Drupatee tune on us about rolling up the tassa.

The drummers stopped in front a purple house. Jhandis planted by their gate meant we had reached by proper Hindu people house and not our pretend bunch of Christianised Indians. A middle-aged woman was waiting and greeted us with clapping and some wining to the tassa beat. She led the way to a little pipe she had in the front yard – the kind of low pipe you would attach a hose when watering the palm trees out front. It was on full blast.

Way! Look how they're wasting water. Somebody tell the lady to lock off the pipe.

Deedee rolled her eyes.

You really don't know nothing? According to how Sita and Rama got married you're supposed to collect flowing water from five rivers to wash down the groom. Miss Harridyal said as we don't have no five rivers the next best thing is to go by this Hindu neighbour and catch running water from their pipe.

And what if you didn't have a Hindu neighbour?

She rolled her eyes again.

Where in Trinidad you wouldn't have a single Hindu neighbour?

Point taken.

Miss Harridyal began chanting Sanskrit prayers and doing things I couldn't quite see. I know she lit a diya and she put red sindur on the married women's foreheads. The lady of the house handed Deedee's sister a hoe and she dug up some dirt which Miss Harridyal wrapped in a leaf and that too went on the tray. She never stopped chanting her prayers. Deedee's sister also collected some of the running water in a small brass cup.

Suddenly the tassa paused and when they started back, man, they ripped into the rhythms. That was the signal for the old ladies let go some rude jamming. I was shocked. Waist was shaking. Dress got hitched up. I never thought these respectable-looking women could get on bad so.

Check that old lady. She wine till she nearly had sex with that other old lady.

Wait till she get two drink in she head later. Is then you go see action.

Gloria nudged me.

Let we buss a little wine, nah.

I'm not dancing in the people yard.

Gloria was doing a thing with she hips.

Betty, this is a durga puja. You're supposed to get on bad.

I looked at her blank. Nobody ever told me about this.

We're dancing to make sure the bride and groom get down
to the business and make grandchildren. It's part of the
puja.

Gloria put her hand around my waist and knocked my hips.

Girl, come on. For the young people.

Them old girls doing enough wining for everybody.

I was saying one thing and feeling another. The drumbeat was
vibrating in my chest and getting under my skin. I swayed but
I kept it in. Next thing Deedee reached over and put her arms
around the two of we and buss a wine. My girls weren't holding back. They threw some waist like in the Indian movies we
have on TV every Sunday morning. I joined in. For the young
people. I danced for the young people's happiness.

MR CHETAN

I slipped out the bed easy easy to let Jackson sleep. Whole week he was up and down to Port of Spain for a training course. Starting in San Fernando, to reach Port of Spain for eight you can't be behind the wheel later than five or else is pressure in your tail. Traffic for so. Much better to take the water taxi and in fifty minutes you'll get dropped in the heart of town. My poor doux-doux darling still had to wake up so early to catch the 6.30 a.m. water taxi. I told him to stay the nights by me and I will do the dropping and the picking up from the terminal. We managed it that Jackson's car wasn't parked outside my apartment from evening to morning. The street's quiet. People notice things. And the old lady living two houses down from me? She is Queen Macociousness. My landlord warned me that she's such a good maco she will know your business even before it happened. Well, forewarned is forearmed. Me and Jackson don't even walk out the apartment together. I read in the papers that two men were beaten up when the neighbours realised they were a gay couple.

I love having him here and not only for the sex although it guaranteed he was putting down a work on me every evening. And when he wakes up in the morning? Same thing. But it's more than that. In the bathroom his toothbrush is next to mine. Little things like that make the place feel complete. I straightened his deodorant, cologne and comb on the shelf then turned on the shower for the hot water to soak my skin. Lavender-scented shower gel is my favourite. I always buy it. Now if I could bottle Jackson's smell hands down I would bathe in that.

Back in the bedroom he was awake.

Why you went in the bathroom so early? It's Saturday. You left me alone.

I wanted to do market early to leave the day clear.

You're bound to go?

Yeah. It's half the price of the grocery and things does be fresh fresh.

Like you don't remember what today is?

You think it's only you remember? Of course I know today is three months since we met.

His eyes flashed a smile.

Come back in the bed, let me give you a very happy anniversary. Come, choonkalunks.

Man, that towel get dropped so fast. Market will have to wait. Jackson decided we should have our anniversary picnic on San Fernando Hill. I wanted us to celebrate at the Temple in the Sea. But he'd made up his mind. If it's one thing I've discovered it's that the man is stubborn. Once he's fixed on something you can't get him to budge. He could see I was disappointed and promised we'd go to the Temple in the Sea for the four-month anniversary. It's okay. Whatever my boyfriend wants I want too.

On the way to San Fernando Hill we stopped by Charlie's. Not many things can beat a hot hops bread and black pudding from that shop. That, plus a few cold Stag, and we headed up San Fernando Hill. I had forgotten how tranquil it is up there and how far you can see from the top. The whole city and way beyond were sprawled out at our feet. Unfortunately, we weren't the only people who thought it was the perfect afternoon for a picnic. It took a while to find a vacant bench offering privacy and still look out past Pointe a Pierre to the Gulf of Paria and, as it was a clear day, Venezuela.

Privacy meant we could talk without people macoing. It didn't mean we could sit close to one another. I put the cool bag of beers between us. Trouble might come anyway but at least we're minimising the risk. These days every Tom, Dick and Harry carrying gun and they ready to use it if you so much as look at them the wrong way. And Jackson being in the police is an extra consideration. A buller man in the force? You mad or what? On my three-month anniversary, instead of holding my beautiful lover's hand or kissing his neck as we watched the orange sun set over the Gulf of Paria, he was at one end of the bench, I was down the other end, and there wasn't a damn thing we could do about it.

Sunset turned the sky orange, red, pink and yellow. I told Jackson it was gorgeous because of us. Even the sky was celebrating our love.

Hey, Jackson, you ever see the green flash right before the sun dips below the horizon?

I've never even heard about that.

Watch. Keep watching as the sun goes down. Keep watching and you might get lucky and see it.

As the yellows and pinks deepened to purple and blue we concentrated on the line where the sky touched the sea. I'm not sure if it was the two Stag in my head but sitting there with Jackson felt perfect.

Chetan?

He was whispering. I whispered back.

Yes, honey?

I love you.

I love you more.

I turned away from the horizon to look at him, really look. Was he for real or was this god mamaguying me?

I want us to be together all the time.

Me too.

We should look for a place together.

And how we getting away with that?

Don't dig no horrors. If we take a two-bedroom it will look like two bachelors renting together.

Every morning waking up together.

Let we go, Chetan. I feel to do something very rude to you.

Officer, can you rough me up, please?

He winked at me.

Actually, let's wait. I want to see this green flash you were talking about.

Man, don't bother with that. And you don't always see it. Come hurry up before I sexually assault you right here.

All right. Cool yourself. We're reaching home just now.

From that night Jackson and I began planning our life together. Seriously planning. I'm talking details. He would look for a transfer to either Arima or D'Abadie – anywhere in the east. Out of the nineteen primary schools covering that part of the country I was bound to find a job. We took drives scoping out where would be good to live. I called a few agents and we should be able to afford to rent a nice small house. Nobody knew us around there. We would be starting fresh.

If Jackson wasn't spending the night by me I went by him. That didn't happen often. I get the vibe that he doesn't too care for people in his space. When he's by me I make him coffee. I'll check his uniform's ironed properly and the shoes shining till you can see your face. All he has to do is eat, bathe, dress and go to work. He doesn't have to make the bed or wash a cup. Nothing. However, and I'm not complaining about my choonkalunks, when I go by him none of that happens. He lives like a teenager. Most of the time he doesn't even remember to buy bread. In the morning we're hunting around to find something to eat. And I'm never alone in his apartment. When he's ready to go to work I must leave too. What does he think I'll do in there? Anyhow, I mustn't complain. Maybe I'm a little over-sensitive because he's my first proper relationship. My bad.

The other night I was on Facebook. I hardly check it these days and Jackson doesn't do any social media.

So, who you checking on Facebook?

Nobody. I like a few posts and that's it. I don't actually post anything myself.

He leaned over to look at the screen.

Who is this Steve posing in front Soong's?

That's the PE teacher.

Hmm.

What you going 'hmm' for?

Nothing.

I don't have anything to hide. You could look. I want to watch TV anyway.

He took the laptop and I turned on Netflix. I figured he would take a quick look, realise there was no reason to be jealous and hand back my laptop. Not so. When I couldn't take it no more I asked him what was so fascinating about my Facebook.

Who is Mani Boodoosingh?

Sorry?

Your search history only has one name. Mani Boodoosingh. Who he?

That's somebody I grew up with in Point Fortin but I don't think he'll remember me.

You and he was in thing?

I looked away.

Of course not. I was a boy then. What you take me for?

Well, you should add him as a friend.

I don't think so.

Yes. Add him.

No. I don't want to.

Look, I'm going to add him for you.

I couldn't believe it. He sent Mani a friend request from me. My mouth was open like I was ready to catch flies.

What happen, Chetan? Why you're looking at me so?

I was blue vex to the point where I couldn't speak.

Cool yourself.

I was searching my head to know what to say to this man. I still couldn't talk.

If you didn't have anything going with the man, then what's the big deal? You yourself said he probably won't remember you, in which case he will delete the request.

I was having to consciously keep my breath steady. Best thing I could do was to concentrate on the TV and ignore him. He still had my laptop. I wanted to snatch it back. At the same time I didn't want it to look like I was having a tantrum. Minutes passed and he still hadn't handed back my laptop.

Please close my laptop.

Why, choonkalunks?

Just close it.

You vex? Eh, choonkalunks? You don't want me to see what you have on your computer?

I lost it.

Hand over my fucking laptop. Now.

But eh, eh. What you getting on so for? Here. Take your blasted computer.

I grabbed it and put it on the coffee table. Jackson steupsed, got up and went to the door where he had left his sneakers. He tied his laces, opened the door, and left. No goodbye dog, goodbye cat. Nothing. For the next two whole weeks I didn't hear a peep from him. Just like that we went from being together every spare minute to being ghosted. That was rough. I felt he had ripped my heart out of my chest then taken a knife and chopped it up fine fine like he was chopping parsley. I am learning the hard way that come see me, and come live with me, are completely different things.

SOLO

As I got off the subway at Columbus Circle the sun went straight in my eyes. If you see how peaceful and nice the place was looking. Central Park was dazzling white, covered in snow; the sky clear blue. Everything was pretty pretty to make up for the place being damn cold. This is not my first winter and I know that a beautiful clear sky meant no cloud cover to keep the city warm. Give it another hour and here will be completely different. Traffic will build up and the cab drivers will start honking horn. All that snow on the ground will turn brown from people hustling to reach to work on time.

Mr Chetan said he couldn't handle winters. I took a selfie and wrote: 'freezing my ass off'. Whenever I send him a message my mind automatically jumps to Mammy. Only for a couple seconds. She's never seen snow. Maybe by now she has. Who knows. We don't talk. Letters come now and then. No point in writing back. She made her bed, I made mine and now it's too weird to even begin to talk.

I didn't come Midtown to lime. Work is on a construction project quite down by Wall Street. Honestly, if I reach 34th Street I reach far and by the time work's done I'm escaping before the mad rush. But Chips asked for a breakfast meeting at a diner – corner of Ninth Avenue and 50th Street. If it wasn't for this new fella on the site, Trevor, I wouldn't even know Chips was born.

Trevor joined the crew on the Wall Street site when Dennis took on extras to finish the job. He's a good bit older. Late forties maybe? We're painting this massive reception area but Trevor's easy to spot. His bald head's always plastered down with a mash-up, faded red cap with 'Mount Gay Rum' on it. We were joking and I told him to get a new cap before this one falls apart completely.

Yo, Trini. Watch your mouth. It don't have a shop in the world selling this cap. Not even them big, expensive stores on Fifth Avenue have this. The onliest way to get one is if you sail in a race Mount Gay's sponsoring.

You could sail?

If I could sail? Man, in Dominica I had my own boat, *Sayamanda*. You ever went sailing?

No.

Come Dominica and I go show you. My boat could catch some good speed. Check it out.

He took out his iPhone. Even through the cracked screen Trevor's photos posing with his fancy boat were sick. I can't even guess how much a boat like that costs.

So Trevor, what you doing fighting up here?

Hurricane Maria. Flattened Dominica. Better to wait it out over here than to catch ass back home. Things rough for the small businessman like me.

I was in New York when that hurricane passed and Uncle Hari was involved in some fundraising. Trevor said people lost everything. But he's always laughing and smiling with everybody. Nice man. If he goes to the bodega for a soda one coming for me too. And he is forever asking me to come by them for Sunday lunch so I finally went. Of course he had to be living in Brooklyn. Where else? Trini Indians happy to stay in Queens. Around by Trevor is more Jamaican, Bajan and a few small islanders. Don't quote me but I think Trevor's wife is a Bajan. I didn't meet her. Extra shift at the hospital. You know how it is. And the children had gone to a birthday party, which left only his parents in the apartment.

The whole time I was there they sprawled out in front the TV. Now and then Trevor would look over at me.

Trini, make yourself comfortable. What about a next beer? Take some more food. You want watermelon?

Granny made a chicken pelau. I'm sorry. Back home what she made wouldn't qualify as pelau. Where's the seasoning? I learnt from watching Mr Chetan. And Mammy. Our pelau would be bubbling up with chadon beni, pimentos, chive, thyme, flat leaf parsley and topped with a fat Congo pepper to flavour the pot. Whenever I catch a vaps and cook a pelau you can bet whichever woman Uncle Hari checking he will drop she one time and digs home. And like chicken scarce in Brooklyn. I had to hunt for two little piece. Yes, I'm bad talking the people, but hear what. They served the food on paper plates. Granny must have seen my face because she said something about paper plates saving on the washing-up. Well, each to his own. If somebody pass by us in Queens we would never, ever give them Sunday lunch on a paper plate. We poor but that doesn't stop us from doing things properly.

Lord, I'm starting to sound like Mammy.

And act like her. She kept the house neat and put away and was always complaining that I was untidy. Katherine and Ian are like how I was then and I am now like Mammy. Except I don't quarrel with my cousins the way she used to bawl at me. But shit, man, how hard is it to put a plate and a glass in the dishwasher? And if I didn't give the living room a vacuum now and then I swear we would choke on the dust. Oh, and a next thing. Seasonings and herbs are expensive up here. Every time I pay for things like chives I remember how I used to go in the back yard and cut whatever we needed. It's not the same but I've lined the windowsill in the kitchen with pots of herbs. So far I've managed not to kill rosemary, basil, mint and parsley. As Mr Chetan's in his own place I don't hear about our garden and I don't ask. Funny, I thought it might get easier being away all these years. That's a joke. In some ways it still hurts as much as it did that night in the kitchen. I've come to accept pain as a second skin covering my whole body.

As soon as I walked in the diner Chips clocked me. Because I know he's a big-up I was expecting the suit and tie but don't ask me why I also imagined he would be built like a basketball player. Chips couldn't be more different. He was a neat, small black fella with a trendy moustache and beard circling his mouth. He called out to me,

Trini! I know you people a mile off.

Chips?

The one and only. Let me buy you a cup of coffee.

The server poured me a cup. Chips asked for orange juice.

I can't explain it exactly but I like Trinidadians. It's cause you all blend in more than, like, the Guyanese people. Know what I'm saying?

How you mean?

See the Guyanese? They might look okay but once they start talking with that bad accent they got, you know they're not going to fit in. And the people from, like, India and Pakistan? Man, they're the worst. They don't even try. I'm black so you know I'm no racist but, man, you can't go around New York not speaking English and shit like that.

I gulped some coffee before it got cold.

But hey, man, you guys come here and you blend in. Know what I'm saying?

I forced a smile. Soon we were down to brass tacks.

It's going to cost five thousand dollars. Cash. It's expensive. But it's worth it.

All one time?

Yup. Up front, my man.

But my cousin's friend got hers for half that. Let me see. It was three years ago. Yes. About three years ago because I had just come up. She only paid, like, I want to say, two thousand five hundred.

Well, Trini, this is the United States of America. You're free to do business with anybody you like. Only thing is I can't help you for no two thousand five hundred. That won't work.

See, even three years ago I would say things were different. Easier. Now we've got ICE and shit like that going down I've got to use more resources to get you what you're asking for. People have got to get around some super tight computer security to produce this documentation. You need the right connections. And I've got the inside. Know what I'm saying?

He straightened his jacket.

I'm a businessman. I'm not one of those guys hanging on the block. One minute they're there and next minute you can't find them. Here today, gone tomorrow. You call me in three months, six months, and you say, Chips, I can't get a Social Security cause this birth certificate is messed up. You know what I'd do?

He took a loud slurp of orange juice. Mammy would say he needed to learn table manners.

I'd fix the problem. Or. Or, I'd give you a refund. No questions asked. That is how sure I am. And once I get you in the system, you're in the system for life. Know what I'm saying?

In Trinidad people say that good things not cheap and cheap things not good.

Exactly. You got it. Nobody will be able to tell the difference between your birth certificate and mine. Your record's going to be in the computer as if it's been there from the day you were born. Me, I'm Brooklyn born and raised but nobody's going to know the difference between your birth certificate and mine. I guarantee. Know what I'm saying?

His phone rang and he switched it off. Seconds later it rang again. He got up and patted himself down. Turns out his second phone was ringing.

Hey, sorry about that. Like I was saying, it's up to you, bro. You gotta know how you want to spend them hard-earned dollars of yours. If you know somewhere cheaper that's your call, man. But what are you gonna do when you find out that the birth certificate you paid two thousand five hundred for is a fake? That is two thousand five hundred straight down the toilet. Plus. Plus, ICE is going to hear about you and they're going to put your ass on the next plane out of JFK.

I drained my coffee. It's not like I had a ton of options. Once I have a birth certificate I can apply for a proper Social Security, in my own name, like a normal person. Hey, I could even get an American passport.

Let me think about it.

That's cool. You think about it. All I'm gonna say is that it might seem a lot now but it's an investment in your future, bro. An investment like buying stocks and bonds. Help get your foot on the ladder. Know what I'm saying?

I understand but let me think it through. We go link up.

You do that, bro. I can fix you up quick if you start the process this week while I've got space in my diary. Later down the road I can't make no promises.

At work Trevor was waiting for me. I asked him if he was sure, sure, sure Chips was the real deal. Five thousand would wipe me out clean as a whistle.

It's he who fixed me up. All legit. Chips is the man.

I need to check this out with my uncle first.

Why?

He's more like a father than an uncle. Look, I'm not a duncey head but this is a big thing for me.

Chips won't be too happy about you telling any and every body about his services. You understand where I'm coming from? You is a big man. You don't need permission.

I don't need permission but I thought of calling Mr Chetan. Problem is if he knows I'm trying to make this permanent he might tell Mammy. Not that it should come as a shock. He said he never tells her what we talk about, but then again I'm not there to know if that is true. And you know what? She did what she did and I need to do what I need to do. Time for me to concentrate on myself and my Ramdin family. Full stop.

*

Whole week I could hardly sleep. The only time I got a little ease up was when I cut myself. Yes, yes, cutting is bad and you're not supposed to do it and call your mental health provider blah blah blah. I wouldn't cut if I knew what else to do. How do I get a little release from everything? And I'm not advertising. You'll never catch me in anything except long sleeves and long pants. One time I made the mistake to hook up with one of Katherine's friends. I was nervous. But she? Wow. She knew what she wanted. Everything was cool until

I pulled off my T-shirt. It was like flicking a switch. She took one look at my arms, said something about not being able to deal with that and shut it down straight away. I won't be trying that again any time this century.

Maybe the cutting will get less eventually. For now, it could be the hottest day in the middle of August, I'm wearing long sleeves. I cut yesterday and those weren't too bad. All my gear is stashed away in a little wash bag – Band-Aids, bandages, Polysporin and razor blades. The bag lives between my boxers so nobody will find that. Last night I only needed a quick spray of Polysporin and two Band-Aids. Tonight, Band-Aids weren't enough so I put on a bandage. Home accustomed to me saying I hurt my hand at work and work accustomed to me telling them I hurt my hand at home. Story done.

On top of all this Chips commess another thing dropped in my lap. Uncle Hari went to see his ex-wife and I don't know who say what but the man land up in the kitchen hugging a whiskey bottle. Katherine was at the gym doing some charity Zumba marathon that I had to give her $10 for and Ian was out. My bro have it bad for a Colombian señorita. She's cute with enough front and back. And she's super friendly. Lucky dog. A computer nerd and he managed that. How? The brother left the house looking real sharp and drowning in so much aftershave the girl will smell him a mile off.

You want a coffee, Uncle Hari?

Nah. I'm sticking with the twins, Johnnie and Walker.

Them ain't no friend to have.

I'm not like your father. I can hold my drink.

My stomach flipped. The coffee machine seemed extra loud.

> Sorry. You know what I mean. I does drink but I know
> when to stop. He used to drink to blank out. Poor fella.
> We family were good at pretending nothing bad ever
> happened. Nobody had the courage to talk to Sunil about
> his drinking. And I'm including myself in that category. I
> never said a word.

I think I nodded. I know I didn't speak because my voice was
locked down inside my throat. I wanted to grab my coffee and
run.

> But aside from that, your father was a good man. A good
> man to you and your mother. And a loving brother. Bright
> for so. He didn't leave brains for me. Every prize-giving
> Sunil used to lick up everything.

I took a sip of my coffee. Questions, I had a million questions,
yet my jaw was locked and my chest was pounding.

> Sometimes I wonder if I could've helped Sunil. After I left
> he fell out with all our sisters, over what, I don't know.

Uncle Hari poured himself a half inch of whiskey, sniffed it
then took a good swig.

> I don't know why I'm telling you all this foolishness for.
> Your father wasn't an easy man. But when it come to me it
> was a different story. When I reach in secondary school he
> was already in form three. Everybody knew not to trouble
> me. If they so much as touch me by accident Sunil would
> beat their tail. And some big brothers wouldn't want to

hang with you but not him. He carried me everywhere and did everything for me.

Uncle Hari looked up from talking to the whiskey glass.

We have ice? Put two block of ice in my glass, please.

I got up, found a small bowl and filled it with ice from the freezer. I was about to find a spoon when he held my arm.

Sit down. Sit down. I go use my hand.

Through my T-shirt he was squeezing exactly where I had cut. Fuck.

You know that your father lived by our grandparents? He didn't live with us.

Why?

My three sisters were already born when my grandmother took in sick. She was sick for a good few months and my grandfather needed help. But my father said our house was too small to bring she by us. So, the story is that Ma took she three little girl children and went to live by she parents during the week and weekends she would come home. All right. Let me wet my tongue.

He took a gulp.

Well, thing and thing happen and next thing Ma had Sunil. Only trouble was Sunil didn't look nothing like we. We father was dark. Ma was dark. So how come this child come out fair fair? You see how you fair and I dark? Well, you get that colour from your father.

So, all you don't have the same father?

Nobody ever said that but from a baby Sunil lived by
my grandparents. You put two and two together. Sunil
heard talk that it was a man from the same village as our
grandparents. Some old boyfriend Ma must be had as a
young girl. But the saddest part of the story is.

He stopped to knock back the last drops of whiskey and suck
on an ice cube.

The sad part is we will never know the truth because the man
died in an accident when Sunil was only a few months old.

And your ma never said anything?

You mad or what? Which woman's going to confess she make
she husband wear a jacket? No way. And besides, whatever
happened they made back up because I came along.

All I could think was poor Daddy and how I would feel in his
shoes. He had plenty to deal with. It's no wonder he drank.
Uncle Hari got up and gave me a bear hug.

Watch me. Everybody family have their own problems.
Don't mind what they look like from outside. Inside, all of
we going through the same shit. Now let your uncle go and
take a sleep.

The plan had been to ask Uncle Hari what he thought of the
Chips business. Not any more. I know half was the whiskey
talking but I'm glad things came out. Same way my daddy
coped by himself, I can deal with this alone. I've learnt my
lesson. No matter what I'll always be alone.

BETTY

Gloria's cousin from England has been visiting Trinidad on and off for years and I never took him seriously. He's a good ten years older than me. I wouldn't call him ugly and he's not stupid. Very polite – opening car door and things like that. But oh gosh, the man dull like a washing machine manual. Then the last few times he was home he's called saying Gloria suggested I might be able to help him as he wants to retire here. I couldn't see what help I was supposed to provide but for Gloria's sake I went with him to look at some land. Wherever we went I gave him my two cents about the area. He liked Tortuga. I agreed that would be a good place to settle down. It's high in the Central Range and my uncle Lesley who lives up there swears that the views and the breeze beat back the whole country.

This Good Friday gone the man passed by me looking sharp in a nice linen shirt and smelling like a perfume store. He wanted company to check out another piece of land, this time in Manzanilla. I'm not sure why I went. As it was a public holiday things by me were quiet and the drive to Manzanilla is always relaxing. So I jumped in the car. If I'm not careful I will end up with this Mr England (Mr Chetan's name for him) by accident.

We followed the coast road, taking in the beauty of mile after mile of beach lined with coconut trees. If this country didn't have five hundred plus murders last year alone we would be in paradise.

We're coming up to the police station, Betty. Can you look out for a sign, please? 'Land for Sale' or something like that.

Turn right. You see it?

The property was in a great location – five minutes' drive to the beach and near the police station so hopefully bandits will think twice before breaking in. I knew all about here like the back of my hand.

I have family from around here.

Really?

I remember coming this side for holidays and running through people cocoa estates and coconut estates.

I bet you were pretty from then.

My great-uncle used to tell us stories about the American soldiers living down here. Right here in the bush they used to train in jungle warfare.

I never knew that.

Mr England suggested we stop for a picnic and take a sea bath. With curry chicken roti from Patraj in one hand and a sweet drink in the other, we settled down under a coconut tree. For me this salty sea breeze was my childhood. I took a picture of the beach.

Who are you sending the picture to?

Mr Chetan. And he will forward it to my son in New York.

Why you don't send it straight?

I looked at the blue sea. New York was far far away.

It's a long story but we're not talking.

I don't know how anybody could not talk to you.

As soon as he finished eating, Mister Man took off his shirt and wanted me to follow him in the sea. I put him straight. This bath suit was only for show because we were on a beach. No way I was going in the water. The sea was making rough and the currents here are dangerous for so. And this man has clearly been living away too long because he forgot what day it was.

You don't know you're not supposed to bathe in the sea on Good Friday? Especially before six o'clock in the evening.

You believe that nonsense about turning into a fish if you go in the water?

I know that is dotishness but every year people drown on Good Friday.

Well, I love the sea and I'm going in. Come with me.

No way. Besides, the sea don't have a back door.

Come in. I'll look after you.

Nah. I'm good right here. I will watch you.

We reached this far and you're not going in the water? That's not making sense.

But I'm happy sitting on the sand. Honest. You go if you want.

Mr England kept harassing me. It seemed easier to put my toe in the water than to keep arguing with him. As we walked into the sea he tried to hold my hand. I hugged myself and stepped out of his reach. The man swam away. I stayed in water up to my knee and watched as the idiot got knocked over by wave after wave. He did look like he was having a good time and he didn't drown, thank God. But we didn't escape the Good Friday curse completely. On our way home he bounced the car fender.

You know I only scraped the car because I took my eyes off the road to look at you.

Stop talking foolishness. It's punishment for going in the sea.

Problem is I liked the foolishness. It's been so long since I've had time alone with someone, anyone, who had an interest in me. And nothing's wrong with him as such. After he dropped me home he sent one long text saying how much he enjoyed spending the day together and how we must do it again. I wrote back saying thanks and that I had a good time too. Well, he took that as the lights changing from red straight to green. No exaggeration, I am getting at least three texts a day. One in the morning to say hello and asking what I have going on. Lunchtime he will text asking what I'm eating for lunch and who I'm talking to. In the evening it's another long text. Did I watch TV? Am I going to sleep early? When can he pass by to see me? He even sent Gloria to make his case. I told her to let him know I wasn't looking for a man.

Oh gosh, Betty, what wrong with you? The man in love.

He's okay but I'm not feeling the vibe.

You could learn to feel the vibe. Unless you're holding out on my family because you already have a man we ain't know about.

Really, Gloria? And why you jooking me so about him? I said I'm happy by myself.

But you're not happy.

Okay. A little lonely. That's all.

Your problem is you have too much false pride. A man throwing himself at you and you busy bussing style.

Maybe Gloria's right. Too much pride. What exactly was I waiting for?

MR CHETAN

I ain't able. Jackson walked out on me cool as Gokool on a Thursday night. For the next two weeks? Silence. Not a peep. This Tuesday gone I was packing up to leave work when he messaged that he was coming over. Dry so he breezed back in with fresh coconut water but not a word of apology. This was after I had taken to my bed, feeling like shit, for more nights than I will admit. I was sure we were through. Now Jackson's twinkling up them eyes at me, acting like nothing ever happened. So when I was crying my heart out, I was doing that for no good reason? Before I could say my piece, he pushed me back on the couch, unzipped my jeans and sucked the pain away.

This stress is a new thing for me. I never knew people could blow hot and cold so without reason. And don't think he will talk about it. He moved on long time. The only way he knows how to say sorry is to do things. He asked me to come stay by him and in the morning coffee reached me in the bed. And he had bread in the apartment. Now when we're watching TV my foot's getting massaged. My neck's getting plenty kisses. When we're apart my boy is busy texting steady – mainly what he wants to do to me. I love it.

We're back talking about living together. Jackson has put out feelers for a transfer. His job is the harder one to move. Once he's fixed I will go by the Ministry of Education to check out what going on. And we might not know which house we're moving to but we're sure it will be in one of three streets. Under all the talk, I never thought I would be planning my future with a man. It feels natural, like we were meant for one another, and all this before we've had our four-month anniversary.

This time we're taking in the Temple in the Sea that was postponed from last month. I've been before but somehow Jackson's never reached there yet. I can't wait to show him the gigantic Hanuman statue. Once we check it out, and the temple on land, I want us to sit down in that peace and watch the sun set. If nobody is around I will whisper in his ears the story about the man who built the original little temple out at sea, all by himself, brick by brick. This time we won't take our eyes off the horizon and we'll catch that green flash.

The anniversary reached and things started off good good with some heavy working up in the bed. When I turned around to ask what time we should head up to the Temple in the Sea, he looked at me like I was dotish. Oh, he didn't know that plan was set in concrete. He wanted to carry me by his grandparents. Obviously, he can't tell them who I am but I'd be the first man he was taking to meet his family. When he put it like that I couldn't get on bad. This relationship business ain't play it hard but I'm learning. My face probably showed I was a little vex because Jackson gave me a hug up and promised that for sure for sure, next month's anniversary we were going to the Temple in the Sea. But today we're heading south to Fifth Company Village.

Is shame I shame but I had to run and find out which part of Trinidad we were going. Fifth Company Village was a tiny dot. Blink and you miss it. At least now I know it's near Moruga, which still claims fame as the place where Columbus first landed. Never mind we now know the man didn't even put his big toe on our soil. As he was passing on his way to South America, gold in his eyes, he looked out, dropped the name La Isla de Trinidad on us and kept sailing. I asked Jackson if he knew how Moruga people felt having had one story for centuries and then finding out it was fake news. He laughed.

Keep that talk to yourself. My grandparents wouldn't like you bad talking Columbus.

I smiled. Of course I wasn't going to bother the old people – especially the first time I'm meeting them.

All right, Jackson, but listen, we can't go with we two hands swinging.

We'll pick up something on the way.

No, man. I'm meeting the in-laws.

Honey, do what you want. I'm going to wash the car.

While he was outside with bucket and soap I made three killer coconut sweet breads – one to take, one for home and one for Miss Betty. She says my sweet bread is the bomb. The secret is balancing the candied fruit and the raisins with the coconut. Get that wrong and it's either too sweet, not sweet enough or people asking if coconut scarce. Thinking about her hurt my conscience. You know how long I ain't pass to check how she's doing? Months. Jackson has me giddy. Tomorrow this sweet bread getting dropped. Poor Solo has also taken a back seat since I've found love. It's about two weeks, going on three, that

I ain't even send the boy a one-line text. What to say about my boy? Gone quite New York to work construction. And it's not like he doesn't have brains. Sense alone should tell him to get a degree. That is what does happen when you let anger eat out your insides. Poor thing. Life ain't easy. I must call this week.

I had a neat shave, creamed up my face and was a little heavy with the cologne. I don't care. Better that than to go by the people house smelling founkie. I put on a red jersey and my good jeans and walked outside. Jackson's face swell up. He didn't like the red.

Well, come and pick out what it is you want me to wear.

Fine.

He chose a light blue polo shirt. The last time somebody chose my clothes for me I was in diapers. I ain't sure he'll get to do this again.

Warm sweet bread wrapped in a tea towel, a bottle of rum for his grandfather, and we hit the road. I know they're clueless about us but we know and this is a day we'll talk about when we're old. Whole road Jackson talked a set of rubbish. He's sure a new fella at work is gay. Thing is the fella doesn't have time for Jackson at all at all. I said the man must think Jackson making a play and he ain't touching that. Another policeman? No sir. But my doux-doux darling's accustomed to giving sweet eye and having men drop to their knees – me included. The amount of lovers he's had makes me feel like a saint.

I'm waiting for him to ask about Facebook and Mani. Nothing so far. At some point I will tell him that Mani accepted his/ my friend request. His temper's too unpredictable for me to tell him I got a message as well. Talk about bad timing. Mani remembered me and asked to fix up a lime. One minute my love life's in drought and next tropical downpours are on the horizon. I'd like to see Mani only because I've thought about him so often in the past. Is that stoking fire? Mister Jackson will not be pleased and this time if he storms out he mightn't come back.

As we hit the Moruga road we dropped down in a pothole nearly the width of the car. Jackson got vex one time.

> You know how long this mother-ass government say they going to fix the road? This is what poor people does have to put up with. You think it have road like this anywhere else in the country?

> Cool yourself. It must get better.

He watched me cut eye.

> Wait and see. This ain't nothing. You don't remember how the people blocked the road to protest the state it was in? It made papers. And on top of that it had a landslide that mashed up a house and licked way the road.

We bumped and rattled along for another few miles with Jackson cussing away that he had a mind to send the blasted government a bill for the damage this drive was doing to his suspension. He had a point. By the time we turned off the Moruga road and up a small hill I was feeling queasy. Jackson rubbed my leg.

> Sorry, choonkalunks. Now you see why I don't come down here regular.

He beeped his horn and we got out in front an old-time wooden house, propped up on stilts that looked like they were ready to walk the house down the hill. Five concrete steps tacked onto the front porch were the only solid thing anchoring it to the land. My heart went soft soft. I knew this kind of home with its crooked floorboards and chipped lattice roof trim that a man in the village would have hand-carved so long ago. He would also have carved the spike at the front and back of the roof too in case the devil thinks he's a smart man and tries to come through the roof. Those spikes are there to split his ass in two.

An old lady in a rocking chair on the porch slowly got up.

Jackson? Is you there?

She might be missing half she teeth and wearing Coke-bottle glasses but I thought I could still see piece of Jackson in her. Something in the shape of the face and the nose.

God bless the little bit of eyesight I still got. Jackson, boy, so long you ain't come and see your old grandmother. I should chalk your foot.

She hugged him up tight, eyes full of water. Only then she eyed me.

You bring a friend?

Mama, this is Chetan.

She looked at me, then at Jackson, and asked him if I was a police too.

No, Mama. He's a maths teacher.

I leaned in and gave her a hug.

Nice to meet you, Mama. I baked a sweet bread for you.

She turned to Jackson.

He talking truth? He could bake?

I handed her the loaf.

It make this morning. Just for you, Mama.

We pulled up two white plastic chairs that were stacked in the corner.

Your grandfather gone walking in the garden. This year he will make eighty-five years and I still can't get him to stay quiet. Just now he go come back.

She looked at me.

You know how much years I have? Guess.

I don't know. You're looking so young.

Don't try to sweet talk an old lady. Last year I make eighty-three years so this November go make it eighty-four, God willing.

So, Mama, you're keeping well? What've you been doing with yourself?

Boy, you know I can't move around like I uses to. I does still try to go in the garden to see what going on.

I saw my chance.

I used to live in a house with a good-sized garden. We had okro, spinach, peas.

She cut me off.

We does plant everything here. All what you call out and more. Everything. Sweet potato, yam, dasheen, cassava, fig. Help me out, Jackson. What else we have in the back?

Hmmm, well, you have passion fruit. You have limes. Pawpaw. I know you always grow seasoning. And you used to have chickens. You still have any?

Nah, man. Long time now I stop minding fowl. Too much trouble. Mongoose thiefing the egg and all kind of thing. Take something to drink, nah. You must be thirsty after that long drive.

I relaxed in the tiny porch, feeling the breeze on my face and recovering from the bumpy drive. It was heaven listening as Jackson and Mama caught up on who now born, who passed, who making baby, who take in sick, who make a jail, who left the village, who have horner man and get cutlass in their tail, who lose their work, who still here fighting up, who never changed.

Just then a tall old fella came around the side of the house, a ripe breadfruit in his hand. I could see where Jackson gets his beautiful, shiny, eggplant-dark skin.

You won't believe this but I was in the land good good and my mind tell me somebody reach by the house. And look at that. You reach.

Papa, long time I ain't see you.

Jackson? Boy, you're looking sharp. Like police work treating you good.

Papa leapt up the front steps like a man twenty years younger.

I brought a friend with me. Chetan, this is my grandfather. Everybody around here know him as Papa Elliot.

We shook hands and I handed over the bottle of rum.

Jackson, I like this friend already.

Once the drink was flowing Papa Elliot and Mama started jamming poor Jackson. Oh, when was Jackson going to find a woman and give them a few great-grand? And why I ain't married either? Mama knew a lady in Princes Town with a set of daughters needing to marry. Before we headed home she was going to find the telephone number and Jackson must go see if he liked any of the girls. Papa Elliot had a better idea.

Jackson, if you have problems getting married you know your papa here for you. I'm retired but people does still come by me to give them one of my remedies. Just this morning I made up a Shining Bush tea for Miss Maynard. She have the cold real bad and the antibiotics the doctor give she ain't helping at all at all.

I was there skinning up my teeth when I wanted to scream: he's already married. This is my man. Mine. Mine. Mine.

All you can't stay bachelors much longer or else no woman go want you. I will make an oil to help all you get wife.

Mama got up.

I'm going to put on the light inside.

Papa rocked back and looked at me.

> Chetan, it wasn't yesterday I learn how to heal, you know.
> Ask Jackson. When he was a boy I was busy. People would
> come with their worries and wanting an oil fix up or for me
> to do prayers for them. My father showed me, and he father
> showed him, and he father before that showed him. So it
> come down as a family thing. But these days people not so
> interested. None of my children learn what to do. When I
> dead and gone none of them will carry on with the healing.

I looked over at Jackson, grateful he had brought me here. I
wanted to be part of this family who Papa Elliot could trace
back to America and who had lived in this same village since
1816. Imagine knowing your family from so far back. And
when it's my turn, what can I, a coolie buller man, offer Jackson? I can't take Jackson to meet Ajee and Aja for them to tell
him how five generations ago we came from India on the
Fath Al Razak and how my great-great-grandmother worked
on a coconut estate only ten miles from here. To them I dead
long time.

SOLO

I can't believe Daddy and I have had the same kind of separation from family thing. That's so weird. Lucky thing I have my little piece of Ramdin family, yes. Thing is, I'm going with Chips kind of behind Uncle Hari's back. If it backfires I couldn't face him. Not after all he's done for me. But using this set of fake papers and fake IDs was costing me. Every time I need a new one is all kind of $200 and $300 plus the worry that ICE might buss a raid. Katherine said it takes time to get regular. Three years is nothing. Five, six years is more like the average. The average. She knew people who took, like, ten years and change to get their papers fixed. Even then it still cost serious money.

At least I can talk to Trevor. He's a big man and he's gone through this shit already. I can't have better to advise me. Funny thing but back home I would never have met people from all these other islands. Up here it doesn't matter if you're Grenadian, Bajan, Trini or a Vinci. All of we is one. And Trevor knows the pressure of up here compared to back home. Chips better not be fucking with me. This money is three years' hard work, saving every red cent I could. Go in my room now and check what I have. Three pairs of shoes. The winter coat I'm wearing is the same one Ian gave me when I first came up here.

I turned it all around, inside out, upside down and a week later I called Chips. The cash had to be delivered to an address in Brooklyn which Trevor said was right by where he's living. Bus and subway with that kind of money? You might as well be wearing a sign marked 'Rob Me'. Best he carried me to the bank and after he would drop off the cash to Chips directly.

I brought a brown padded envelope for the money. Even so, the envelope was bulging. I'd never seen that much cash in my whole life. Just to be extra safe the envelope went inside an old grocery bag. If you saw me walking out a bank wearing old clothes and carrying a Stop & Shop bag you would never think I had this kind of money on me.

Trevor, make sure you put it in his hand. Don't leave it with anyone to give him.

I gave Trevor the bag.

Five thousand in there.

He nodded.

Don't dig no horrors. I won't give the money to a soul other than Chips himself. I'm driving straight there now.

As he drove off I caught a look in his eye. You know what? The man looked like he'd won the lottery. Totally happy. I stood on the sidewalk and couldn't move. I had such a bad feeling about this yet my feet were like two lead pipes. I felt like vomiting. No. He wouldn't take my money. He wouldn't. My hands were shaking as I got out my cell phone and dialled. Come back. I'll take the money to Chips myself. The call went to voicemail. For the next ten-fifteen minutes I stood in the parking lot outside the bank and tried Trevor's number constantly. Nothing. Phone like it was switched off. I jumped on the subway and headed to his apartment. Granny peeped through the door with the chain on.

Trevor? Trevor not here. He must be home.

He doesn't live here?

No. He in his own place. I don't have room to mind all of them.

What's his address?

She sighed.

I wish I could tell you but I don't know it.

You don't know it? Nah. Granny, don't give me that. Please. It's important. He has my money.

She made what looked like the sign of the cross.

I don't know where he living. They does move around so much.

You have a cell number for him?

Damn. It was the same number I had already. Did she have a next one? Of course not. I asked if she would call from her phone but she didn't have any credit. What about her husband? Yes, he might. Only trouble is he gone out to play dominoes. Sorry she couldn't help. The door slammed and the double locks clicked.

Inside my body began to heat up until my skin was on fire. If I could slit open the flesh the heat would escape. Fingernails weren't enough. Razor blade. I needed a razor blade. On a rush-hour subway ride home there wasn't much I could do. I started with my little finger and chewed through the short nail to the flesh underneath. I almost missed my stop and had to skid through the doors before they banged shut.

Outside the train station I checked my phone for a signal. One missed call. It was Trevor.

MR CHETAN

Solo sent me a selfie and, no lie, I got the shock of my life. The boy looked maga maga like he's not eating. He said the weight dropped off just so. How you would lose all that weight if you're not starving yourself? And he had no colour in his skin to the point where he could pass for white. I don't know if it's winter have him so. But you know what upset me the most? His eyes. The pupils were dark dark and they had a crazy look in them. The first thing that passed through my mind was the boy taking drugs. I called him and we had a long talk. As we were saying goodbye I asked him straight: Solo, you on drugs? He claimed he's not in that. He had tried a little weed and it didn't do a blasted thing for him. We had a good laugh. He told me after a few puffs, he sat there waiting to experience a higher connection. Instead he felt real hungry and licked up a large Domino's by himself.

But under all the jokes and ol' talk I could tell he was lonely down to his bones. I wanted to catch a plane there and then, pick him up and bring him home with me. I told him, like I have many, many times, he always has a place by me. His answer never changes. Not even his pinky toe touching Trinidad while his mother's alive. Solo's not easy, you hear. Stubborn for so. And I know he won't get out and meet people. New York is a big place. Imagine how many people lined up on Tinder, waiting. If he doesn't want that he could find a chess club, play football – anything to have a little fun. Not Solo. He's too 'fraidy 'fraidy. I know exactly how he feels and that is why I want better for him. If his cousins didn't take him liming now and then I think he would stay in his room every weekend.

At least he's texting more often. It makes my heart glad that we still talk and he hasn't chopped me out his life like he has Miss Betty. Whenever I don't hear from him for a while that is my first thought – he's done with me too. I don't need reminding he's not my son but I want to be as much of a father as I can. Anyway, his mood seems more upbeat. This morning he dropped a text on me early o'clock that has totally confoffled my brain:

how old wer u wen u had yor 1st girlfriend?

I looked at the text. I read it. I read it again. And again. I turned off the phone. I switched it back on. The text ain't moving. He thought he was asking a simple question. Solo, boy, this is not easy. I could make up a girl and feed him some bullshit story and done with that. Or, and I can't believe I'm even thinking this, I could tell him the truth. Solo's not a child. He's been living away, fending for himself. He knows things. Maybe it's time to done with the secrets. I want to tell him about Jackson. Imagine we've been together nearly a year and I've never told Solo how I'm so bazodee over a certain policeman I could eat the man raw. He might find it's no big deal. His generation's not dotish and backward like mine.

Or, it could be our last conversation and he cuts me off too.

If he could wash his hands clean of his own mother, then who is me? Of course she shouldn't have done what she did.

But now he has some age and he still can't put himself in her position. The number of times she ended up by the doctor or in hospital because that drunkard beat the shit out of her should be enough for Solo to have a heart and forgive. He hasn't. At least not yet.

I've never heard him insult gay people, yet you can't discount all the years growing up in Trinidad. He could have had his head filled with all kind of prejudice. With my own two ears I've heard intelligent people, people with big job and PhD, saying things like, be careful with your little children around gay men. And that is the least of it. Next thing you know my boy looks back at our time together and thinks that I wanted a piece. All his memories of me would suddenly seem disgusting. Even from the pulpit I've heard how gay people are filthy, spreading disease, into bestiality, not right in the head. What else? Evil. Gays are pure evil and an abomination in the eyes of the Lord. The other day a teacher right here in my school said give her a gun and she will deal with the gays. You heard me? A gun. She so should get locked up but you think anybody even bothered to report her to the ministry? I wonder what she would do if she found out about me. Would she shoot me dead?

All these things were running through my mind and yet I couldn't shut down the idea of telling him the truth. Whole day my head was spinning like a clothes dryer. He might be okay or he might not. Even if Solo wasn't cool in the beginning he could come around. I went one way and then the next. Yes, I will tell him. No, I'm keeping my big trap shut. Evening reached and I still hadn't replied. Miss Betty crossed my mind and I thought of asking her what she thought. The thing is, she likes to know Solo's in touch with me but it also makes the woman jealous. Nah. Bringing her in this talk would add more commess and confusion.

After two days I decided to tell him. But how to say it?

I am gay.
I have always been gay.

I deleted that. Start again.

I am gay.
I can't help being who I am.

Too apologetic.

I've never had a girlfriend.
I might be gay.

After hours – and I mean hours – my final, final draft was this:

I am gay. But I am the same
person you always knew.
Nothing has changed.
Please don't tell anybody.
You know what T&T is like.

I could almost taste the relief of telling Solo – like licking down a tall glass of ice water after a day in the hot sun. That feeling as the water wets your throat and spreads throughout your body, cooling your arms, chest, stomach, legs, patching the body back together after the sun had done its best to burn you alive.

Just then Jackson came in. I told him what I was doing. Father, was then the bacchanal started.

What trouble is this. Chetan, you gone mad? You have any blasted idea what will happen if them men in the station find out I'm gay? You think they go give me a little talk and leave it so? Eh? Tell me. What you think they will do to me when they find out a buller man in the force?

He went on and on. If I told Solo, how I know he wouldn't tell somebody else? All he had to do was tell one person who then mentions it to another person. We people love to maco. In no time that talk would reach Trinidad. People will be shoo-shoo-ing under their breath: Chetan is a buller man. And guess how long it will take before they put two and two together? Next thing town say, you know Jackson in the police? He's a buller man. Yes, it's true. Well, if it ain't true then why he always liming with that Indian buller man?

Solo's a quiet fella. He doesn't have any set of friend to spread we business.

I never see more. Like you get extra dotish overnight? How the mother-ass you know that for sure?

He was all up in my face.

If you don't care what happens to me then think about your-self. In which fucking universe the Presbyterian Board or the Catholic or the Baptist them go be happy to have a gay man teaching little children? Answer me that. They go kick your ass out of there so fast you wouldn't know what hit you.

Jackson, please sit down. Your stomping up and down giving me a headache. And stop jabbing your finger in my face, please.

He stepped back, arms folded, watching me hard.

Oh, sorry. I'm giving you a headache. Poor doux-doux darling. You want me to get two Panadol for you?

He stormed off to the bathroom and I pulled out my phone, erased the earlier text and sent this:

> I started late.
> Don't use me as your example.
> You will find someone soon.
> Any woman would be lucky
> to have you. Nite son.

From the bathroom I could hear Jackson still quarrelling.

> Never mind I will get beat up or raped. Never mind I will lose my work. What about my family? Eh? You want my family to disown me? My grandparents had life hard and you want them to have to deal with this before they dead? Just because your family don't want you doesn't mean I have to lose mine.

Jackson said a lot more things, but I stopped taking it in properly. Something about how Solo is not my son and he didn't understand why I was so attached to the boy. If that is what I want, I could count him out. I think he asked me if it's not hard enough being gay and what did I hope to achieve by coming out. He didn't get why people like me were always running from jumbie only to butt up with coffin. As he was shouting and cussing I suddenly felt exhausted like I had done ten laps of the Savannah. Jackson kept yelling and stomping around the room barking at me. I felt myself becoming smaller and smaller until I was a tight ball.

SOLO

Chips have
$$ will contact
in 7 days. Wife
mother dead.
Heart attack.
Gone Florida for
funeral. Trevor

Trevor's blasted text only made me feel worse. Mother-in-law dead my left foot. I look like I was born yesterday? You're texting a man whose grandmother died twice. Once she died so me and Ian could buss a lime by his friends in DC. Poor old lady had to die a second time because some asshole was bullying me to work Labor Day weekend. Sorry, death in the family.

Trevor's phone was permanently busy and although my texts were delivered he hadn't read a single word. I tried staying awake that night. Just in case. I wouldn't want to miss a message or a call. Around about quarter past three in the morning I heard the ping of a text arriving. I woke up one time. The phone had fallen on my chest. No Trevor. But Chips had replied.

Trini – $1K on
account. Get

rest to me
asap. Chip$.

What the fuck? Only a grand? What happen to the next four
thousand? That is all my savings. I messaged back. Chips
checked again and confirmed: a thousand straight. In a brown
envelope sealed? Yup. We had to do face to face. Two that
afternoon in the diner was the earliest he could offer. Usually
I am careful not to make noise. Not now. I banged my head
on the wooden bedside table over and over and over until
I was exhausted. It should split open. Let my head split in
two. Stupid. Worthless. Dumb fuck. I deserved the throbbing
pain as if someone was sawing into my skull. My eyes couldn't
focus. This is what you get for being a dotish, duncey, freaking,
asshole, Solo. Who will save you now?

*

If you asked me how I reached the diner on Ninth Avenue and
50th Street the next day I couldn't say. By hook and crook,
I got there, a massive headache still paining me. I ordered
coffee only to forget to drink the thing before it was cold as
dog nose. Well, this is it. No money, no girlfriend, not a damn
thing to say I is man.

Trini! What's up, man? You're dreaming? I was waving and
you didn't see me.

Really?

I saw you from across the street and I waved and you
looked right through me.

I can't see you from so far.

Chips ordered orange juice. I asked for a glass of tap water.

So, I got your money. I don't know what you're so worried about. I don't usually take instalments but I can deal. We're cool. But you can't get nothing until I've been paid in full. Know what I'm saying?

That is the thing. Chips, man, I gave Trevor the whole five thousand to give you.

Five grand? No, bro. See, I sent you that text cause I didn't get no five thousand dollars. Like I told you, Trevor put one thousand down and said you'll be sending the rest soon.

That's a blasted lie.

You calling me a liar?

No. No. Not you. Trevor.

See, I'm a businessman. I've got a reputation. I ain't got no reason to cheat you. If I'd taken your money why would I meet you, bro? Why would I even be here?

I told him how it went down – blow by blow. While I talked he watched me dead in the eye. Even while he was drinking juice he never stopped looking at me. I stared right back. He didn't say a word but while I was talking he did this weird shit bending each finger, one by one, back and forth, back and forth, until each one made a popping noise.

Chips, you hearing me? Tell me something nah.

He sighed.

Bro, this is heavy, man. I got to make some calls.

But you believe me?

I'm not saying I believe you and I'm not saying I don't.
We'll talk.

When? When we go talk? This is all my money. All. I told
you. I'm wiped out.

Trini, we'll talk. Might not be today but tomorrow. Or the
day after. Definitely by the day after.

As much as I begged, Chips refused to say more. I had no
choice but to wait. On the way home I stopped at CVS for
Tylenol and a box of plasters – the extra-large ones with med-
ication that promotes healing in seven days and were at least
twice as effective as the next leading brand. My handiwork
needed attention. When the cuts get pus it's not too right-
eous and Jesus above knows I can't afford to go doctor for
antibiotics.

If I hadn't been fleeced and fucked over by that cunt Trevor,
or Trevor and Chips scheming together, or Chips working a
one-man scam, if things were different, I would have stayed in
my bed the rest of the week. But joke is joke. This was no time
to get Dennis vex. Next thing I gone and lose my work. Nearly
three years I've been regular crew with steady work. Boss man
doesn't deserve to be jerked around.

Of course Trevor didn't reach to work. By lunchtime I casually asked if anyone had heard from him. Dennis overheard
and let out a long steupse.

Look, in fifty-six years my instincts have never been wrong. But I so wanted to get this job done quick that I told myself to take a chance. And look at what happen. In the middle of work the man ups and gone quite Philly. Some cock-and-bull story about he mother take in and they put she in hospital. I bet nothing wrong with he mother.

I wanted to vomit. Mother in hospital my foot. And Philly? Since when Brooklyn is in Philly? Well, I could state as a fact, before a court of law, that two days ago I saw Granny, talked to Granny, and everything about the woman I could make out said she was healthy as an ox. Crook. Motherfucking scoundrel. What kind of man will see another man struggling and rob him blind? I can't understand this thing.

Chips was quiet for a good few days – not even a text. In the pit of my stomach I knew it was hopeless. Apparently Chips doesn't do refunds but the deposit remains good – years, if that is how things go down. This is a business. Know what I'm saying? Yeah, well, I'm seeing how business is done in America and it's killing me, man. It's killing me.

BETTY

She is Deedee's niece by marriage because she married Deedee's nephew. For too long me and Gloria have been calling
her 'the funny teeth girl'. It's reached the point where neither of
us remember her actual name. I feel it's a flower. Rose? Maybe
Jasmine? Gloria thinks Rose sounds familiar. Anyhow, we're
both feeling shame because the girl had three free tickets to
the Caroni Bird Sanctuary which she gave to Deedee with spe-
cific instructions to take her friends, Aunty Betty and Aunty
Gloria. That was kind of Rose/Jasmine/Funny Teeth but I said
no thanks. Deedee wasn't taking that.

Betty, give me one good reason why you don't want to go
and I won't force you.

Easy. I'm happy right here in my house. I will cock up my
foot and watch Netflix. Water my plants. Shell some pigeon
peas. Trust me, I'm good.

Don't make me call the Lord's name on the Sabbath.
That is precisely why you're coming out. Liming with we
should not be in the same category as staying home in
front the TV.

Well, I 'fraid snake, and Caroni must be full of snake.

We're going to the bird sanctuary, not the snake sanctuary.

And we'll be on a boat with a guide and other people. You'll be safe. I promise.

I didn't want to talk truth. It's a hard place for me to visit. But when Deedee and Gloria gang up on me so it's easier to pack my mosquito spray and jump in the car with them. They don't need to know all my business.

If Madame Deedee knew who we would bounce up when getting on the boat she would have stayed with me and watched two movie. In front of us was none other than her old boyfriend, John. And not just any old boyfriend. This one cancelled a big wedding with her. Now look at the man – happy happy with his little family. Deedee's still by she-self and because of that blasted man she's allergic to commitment. We said awkward hellos and settled down for the tour. I whispered in Deedee's ear,

Relax. Look at the ugly girl he ended up with. You ten times prettier.

She nodded slightly, like she was in a straitjacket and couldn't move. Poor thing. For the next two, two and a half hours, she was trapped. Gloria leaned in.

I've been before and the tour don't last long.

Deedee rolled her eyes and put a finger to her lips.

Shhhhh. The guide said to be quiet.

Slowly we motored up a canal with tall, dark mangrove growing out of each bank, sometimes touching overhead to form an arch. Along the way the guide pointed out this bird or that animal hiding in the tangle of roots and branches. Only thing

I saw good was an anteater that looked like a tiny teddy bear wrapped around a branch. Deedee was ignoring the wildlife and staring at the ex's back as he pointed out things to his young daughter and his wife. I felt for my girl, yes. She won't be coming back here in a hurry.

It ain't easy for me either. Last time I was here Sunil brought me. That was well over twenty years ago. Our first real big date. Remembering the good times like this gets to me. He picked me up in his father's car and paid for everything. I felt like a big woman even though I was barely nineteen. Whole boat ride he hugged me up tight. In public. We were instantly a couple. Talk about romantic. I know Deedee and Gloria right here but loneliness punched me in the stomach. Suddenly the guide boomed.

Look up. All you see the boa constrictor? Wrapped around that branch. It's sleeping. All you seeing it?

Well, now Deedee had to rescue me because I was ready to jump in the water and take my chances with the caiman them. She let me hide my face in her shoulder until it was clear the nasty snake couldn't fall and land in the boat. Gloria joined the cuddle.

Ladies, we ain't even reach half way and we done see two different kind of snake. One in the boat and one in a tree.

At least that made Deedee smile. She seemed to breathe again. The guide cut the engine and tied up the boat in the middle of a huge open swamp. For the next half hour all fifteen people on the boat sat in silence and watched the sky as wave after wave of bright orangey-red scarlet ibis flew past us to roost together in the nearby trees.

The boat I took with Sunil must have stopped around here too, although I remember the trees being taller. While everybody was concentrating on the birds them, Sunil was concentrating on me. He managed to sneak one hand under my top and for the whole time the boat was parked he was feeling me up. I was wet down there and ready for more action. Another first for me.

I looked over at Deedee. She was holding it together, but I could see that the silence and fading light, the water and the romance of those magnificent red birds swooping over us was a lot to handle. If you had to bounce up your ex after all this time I find God should arrange it to be in a crowded supermarket on a Saturday morning. He and the wife should be vex with one another and the child throwing a tantrum on the floor.

With dusk coming fast hundreds of scarlet ibis flew to us and settled on the trees like red Christmas decorations. I was back with Sunil, thinking of the way we'd hardly talked when we'd watched this, and how when we were heading back in almost complete darkness he'd leaned over and whispered in my ear how much he liked me. And then he asked if I like tamarind balls.

Yes, I like tamarind balls. Why?

You are my tamarind ball. You're sweet, you're soft and you're spicy all one time.

Later in the car the kissing got hot. He asked if I was a virgin. Of course I was. Then he asked if I wanted my first time to be with him. Well, he didn't have to ask twice.

We married a year later. I was twenty – younger than Solo
is today. What the hell did I know about life? I didn't want to
wait. We were hot and sweaty for one another. I was sure sure
this was love. Now I can see what I wanted was my independ-
ence, and marriage was an escape from my parents. Marrying
Sunil wasn't just Sunil. It was keys to my own house, a family,
a new life.

I'm glad Solo hasn't repeated that mistake and settled down
too young. He sure wanted to get away from home though,
but he's managed it another way. Still, it's not what I wanted
for him at all at all. Now I'm worried for him again. As soon as
these ladies drop me home I'll call Mr Chetan. He may have
some news from my child. Solo might be a big man, off fending for himself, but he's still my baby.

MR CHETAN

Tell me something, in the whole of San Fernando it only have about fifty-five, fifty-six thousand people – plenty less than a place like Chaguanas. So how come you could break up with a man and not bounce him up again? I mean never – not even pass him on the road when you're driving or see him in the mall? And the mall was a place Jackson used to go regular. Trinidad's too small to hide for long. The other day I went to the beach – just me, my book and two-three beers. As I was pulling into Maracas Bay carpark my mind told me to stop by Richard's for a shark and bake. As I opened the car door I saw a couple who live two houses down from Miss Betty. You can't even buy a fish sandwich on the other side of the island without seeing a string band of people you know. Everyone except Jackson.

Don't laugh. I feel it's obeah keeping me from seeing him. Most people go by the obeah man when they getting horn and want their lover back. Maybe Jackson took out a reverse spell: please make sure that stupidee Chetan stay out of my life. In fact, make it so I don't ever bounce him up again. You see that Papa Elliot? True, he is into the herbal medicine. But Jackson explained that wasn't all he did. Back in the day people used to come from all over Trinidad to see Papa Elliot and they weren't doing that because their foot was paining them or a rash wouldn't clear up. He was respected. Some were even frightened of him.

Part of his healing was calling on the spirits and the ancestors for help. Depending on your problem, he would send you home with ingredients for a spiritual bath, or a bush bath as they call it. Most popular were the Money Drawing, John the Conqueror and the Uncrossing or the Reversible baths. As for his oils, Jackson remembered Papa Elliot couldn't make them fast enough. When I tell you we laughed at the names of them oils: Man Trap, Bossfix, Influence Over Evil, Jezebel and the one I liked best, Bewitching. I'm certainly not bewitching anybody these days.

Yesterday I went by myself to the Wildfowl Trust in Pointe a Pierre. As I was walking around thinking of Jackson, I remembered him telling me Papa Elliot's remedy when bad luck was sticking to you. As I seem to be the kind of unlucky that could cut his hand on wet paper I thought maybe it was time for the extra help. For the thing to work I had to collect seven branches from seven different trees. Among the ducks and the peacocks strutting their stuff I got a piece of bamboo and broke a piece off a poui tree. Five more were needed. I heard the great kiskadees before I saw their beautiful yellow feathers in between a mahogany tree. Further, near the pond, was a cashew tree where a blue-grey tanager was nesting. Real pretty. Four down and three more trees to go. I found a cherry tree but the cherries were too green to eat. Collecting seven branches wasn't as easy as I thought and they were closing soon. Two more and I could do my own good luck spell. It was right in front me and I wasn't seeing but I hadn't taken a branch from any of the palm trees. Six down. As I walked towards the exit – boom – a tropical kingbird showed me a guava tree and my lucky seventh branch.

All seven pieces had to be burnt. Outside my back door is a little two-by-four space you can't really call a garden. I stacked my wood, said the Lord's Prayer, and set the bundle on fire. Thankfully the neighbours weren't looking out. I still whispered. Just in case. This is Trinidad and someone is always macoing. Over the fire I quietly chanted,

> *bad luck be broken as these words are spoken*
> *bad luck be broken as these words are spoken*
> *bad luck be broken as these words are spoken*

I thought about why I hadn't fought to keep Jackson. I didn't apologise. I never asked his forgiveness. That night I think we both heard the final whistle blow. It couldn't last. I understand that now. Doesn't make it hurt any less. Everything happened so fast and back to front. 'I love you' came before we got to know each other instead of after. And he liked to get his own way too damn much.

To finish the spell, ashes from these burnt branches had to be thrown in a river or nearby moving water. After that my luck should make a U-turn. Fingers crossed. By now it was night but I didn't care. I jumped in my car and drove to the creek where they do the open cremations.

We were together for over a year and it had taken me nearly the same amount of time to stop driving past Jackson's block of flats. I've never seen him or his car and his place has always been in complete darkness. Thank God. Imagine the shame if he saw me. I have no reason to be all down in the back by where he's living unless is maco I'm macoing. I wonder if he moved to Arima like we'd talked about? Maybe he met someone else and went off with them. Who knows? The one place he is still alive is Grindr. Would it hurt to swipe right? I haven't. But I ain't go lie. Some nights I've been tempted.

Part of the fault was mine for sure. I should have stood up for myself. Honestly, half the time I didn't know how to act or what to say. He was so confident compared to me. I find this hard to admit but it was like that even with the sex. I can't explain it. No question I always found the man was very doable. From the start he knew what he wanted and how he wanted it. I went along like a puppy grateful for any love up. He was a top so I became a bottom. I had a lot of fun but I don't know if it was truly me. I took what was given and didn't ask for anything more or different. And I always felt less than Jackson. He was buff while I've always been maga maga like I don't eat. If you saw me you wouldn't think I was gay. I'm not hot. I don't dress flashy. Grateful. That was the problem. I was always grateful that he wanted me but I never knew why exactly.

I parked and walked from the creek to the bridge. In the moonless night I couldn't see where the ashes landed. The currents would take them out of the creek and into the sea. Was this love? I don't know. It real hurt for sure. Maybe love wasn't for men like me.

MR CHETAN

Sadness does reach in a racing car but when it's time to leave it walks slow slow. Miss Betty knew I was down because she harassed me until I said, yes, all right, I will go liming. She had tickets to the Oval for a one-day match. I like my little cricket and I have nothing against going with her but she already had a posse. From the time I pulled up in front her house things started going wrong. A strange car was parked up under the house. In my spot. Freaking Mr England. He looked a little too comfortable for my liking, getting everybody drinks and acting large and in charge. You can preach Peter, you can preach Paul, I'm not changing my mind about him. He's a worthless scamp. Miss Betty's a big woman. If she doesn't mind nursing that dog in ten, maybe fifteen years tops, then who am I to stand in the way of true love?

But Miss B will always be my person so I brought her a mango cheesecake. Mr England watched me cut eye.

You made that?

Before I could open my mouth, Deedee pushed in.

You don't know Chetan does bake like a boss? Forget all them posh bakeries.

She kissed my cheek and I felt my face get hot. I get embarrassed when people try to big me up so.

I'm not lying. This man hand sweet too bad. Long time we used to get plenty sweet bread, cake, pone, brownies, all kind of thing, especially if Solo asked. We used to beg Solo to say he wanted so-and-so when the child didn't want nothing. Is we who wanted it.

Mr England twisted up his nose.

Baking cake? You wouldn't catch me dead doing that.

My body went cold. Part of me wanted to pelt the cheesecake in his face and the other part wanted to drive straight back home. What exactly was his point? Baking made me less man than he? Miss Betty grabbed the cheesecake from my hands.

Let me put it in the fridge. Very professional-looking. Thanks, doux-doux.

She turned and wagged her finger.

And I'm warning all you. Don't ask me for a piece because I'm not sharing. This make for me and me alone.

Mr England snuggled up behind Miss Betty, holding her waist like a love-sick dog.

But you won't mind feeding me a piece?

Instead of slapping the dotish, crinkle-face toad she buss one lovey-dovey smile. Have mercy. We ain't left San Fernando yet and I'm fed up with all of them.

*

Even with my bad mood I had to admit that from the Scotia-bank Stand we had a fantastic view of the action just square of the wicket. Windies were playing India and all twenty thousand seats had people in them. I can't talk about places like Lord's or Edgbaston cricket ground but I don't think they have good bacchanal like we do beyond the boundary. They probably have afternoon tea specials. We had the Trini Posse Stand's soca blasting and a set of woman wining down the place. Our stand wasn't backward neither. Plenty Trini flags were waving in the air. Mankind blowing whistle and horn. If a fella hit a four, or better yet a six, the noise hit the roof. And who didn't bring any noise maker were busy shouting about who can't catch, who sleeping at the crease and where they find that dotish captain. He can't see he should put another man in the slips? I sat with Miss Betty on my left and thank God on my right was one of the few quiet men in the whole stand. He'd stuck in earphones and was taking in the radio commentary.

I took a picture of the grounds and shared it with Solo. He prefers football but I reminded him of the time the two of us came here for a Twenty20 game. And I told him it looked like the nuts man, Jumbo, had retired so no chance of the freshest pack of salt nuts in the whole of Trinidad. And I missed Jumbo performing in the stadium. That man could pelt straight. He'd aim at a customer and you could bet the bag of nuts was landing exactly where he intended. People say Jumbo was the best bowler the Windies side never had.

For once we weren't playing too badly. Bravo, a flashy, left-handed batsman, was in with the equally flamboyant and very hot Denesh Ramdin. That is man. They started to put pressure on the Indian pace bowler, Ishant Sharma. But my boy Bravo like he tell himself is me and them today. He saw a fast ball coming, flicked his wrist and sent the ball past the third man, who tripped trying to catch it. Four runs. Nice. Next ball he angled his bat again. This time the ball went through the fielder's legs. A next four. And the partnership kept going with Denesh opening his shoulders to swing some huge sixes. One of them even landed on the roof of our stand. Man, the crowd went wild – the whole crowd, that is, except for Mr England. I leaned over.

What happen to you?

I'm supporting India.

But wait nah, ain't you born here?

Yes, but we can trace our ancestors right back to the exact place in Bihar they came from.

I let go one steupse.

Oh, you mean you know which part your dirt-poor relatives catch the boat to haul ass half way around the world for the opportunity to cut cane in this hot sun.

I had more to say about how he was always talking up England and look how his *Windrush* ass reached back right here. Miss Betty stepped in. The three ladies wanted a next Stag. I took my time, walked around, then headed for the bar. Coming towards me was a face I knew. My heart stopped. I was afraid to even breathe. It was him. Mani. I'd seen his Facebook pictures so many times that I was a hundred per cent sure it was him. He saw me, a second of hesitation and then he smiled. I knew he couldn't place my face.

Mani? You remember me? Chetan.

Wait nah, man? Chetan? Ah, how you going? I can't even say when last I saw you. It's been a lifetime.

You're good? I think we became Facebook friends a couple years ago.

Oh yes, yes. I remember now.

I could hardly breathe. If I didn't act now I might never see him again.

You have time for a beer?

Only if it's a Carib.

He pointed to the logo on his T-shirt and smiled.

I can't right now. I'm working. We have some VIPs that I'm taking care of.

What do you do?

Public relations. Professional schmoozer. And you?

I felt my heart racing.

Teaching. Right in San Fernando.

I exhaled.

You're looking well, Chetan.

You're the good-looking one.

I said that? Shite. My mind was jumbled. I didn't want him to go but I didn't know what to say. I blurted out,

Your face ain't change.

We both laughed.

Look, I have to go back to work. Take my number, nah?

I could barely keep my hands steady to type the digits into my phone. When he asked for my number I drew a complete blank. I could not remember my own phone number. It came back, but for a moment I probably could not have told him my name.

When I got back to my seat Miss Betty looked at me funny.

Why your two hand swinging? I thought you went to get some Stag?

Oh shoots. I bounced up a partner. We were talking and I clean forgot I was getting drinks. Two minutes. I'm coming back.

She was about to say something when my phone pinged twice. A text from Mani. I started chewing my bottom lip. The corporate box had space and if I wanted to come sit by him for the rest of the match he would meet me downstairs. I told Miss Betty I was heading home. She didn't buy that.

You lie. Someone just messaged you.

I looked down.

Tell me I lie.

My face was still burning when she held it in her hands.

Gone. Behave yourself.

*

After the match we propped up a bar on Tragarete Road, not far from Queen's Park Oval, talking and laughing nonstop. Just when I was sinking into this comfortable, cosy feeling with him, Mani dropped a bomb. He has a husband. He didn't say friend, boyfriend, partner. I laughed. Like he forgot where he was living? This ain't Europe or America. One day they might scrap the buggery laws. One day. But gay marriage? Nah. That was a whole other story. Well, my boy explained that yes, he is legally married. Happened in New York, where Patrick is from. Out came the phone with the wedding pictures. Talk about sweetening my tea with salt. I had to hear about the virtues of darling Patrick, who is some bigshot.

But I find Patrick look like he could pass for a Trini.

Parents are Grenadian but he was born and brought up in the States.

I hoped my face wasn't giving away my heart. The little fantasy of me and Mani will now come true just as soon as chicken get teeth. But married? Why he had to go and settle down? I would've thought he had plenty people lining up to take a bite of that sweet spot in his chin. I done see the amount of men and women checking him while we've been sitting here and he's lapping up the attention. But Patrick or no Patrick, right now he was with me and we had years to catch up on.

I asked if people know he's married to a man. He said at work it was never discussed but he didn't hide Patrick either. What had my head spinning was his family. All of them apparently love this Patrick fella. Mother, father, sister, brother – even the grandmother. The grandfather was not easy but he's dead so we don't have to count him.

So wait, nah. Let me get this straight. Your family don't have a problem with you and Patrick? They know?

Yes and no.

How you mean?

We don't talk about sex. I will never have one of those conversations with my parents. But Patrick comes to every-thing. Christmas. Easter. Diwali. He's automatically included.

So, take your brother. If he had to introduce Patrick, what he does say?

I think he would say, this is Mani's friend, and done with that.

I rocked back in my chair.

I can't believe you're so lucky. And what about his parents?

Okay, well, Patrick's family are crazy. Just how we don't talk about anything, they like to talk about every single thing. I've been there when his sister is having her periods and the whole household will have an opinion on what she should take for cramps. I don't think I have ever heard the word period in our house. My sister used to hide her tampons in a black plastic bag.

I rolled my eyes.

So Mani, why you think it went one way for you and a next way for me? Eh? That make sense?

He looked embarrassed.

> I mean to say, your family and my family are the same country Indian people. The same. We come from the same place. Same everything. So how come your family take things so cool?

He looked at his glass.

> Bro, I can't answer that. With some people that's how they stop. No rhyme, no reason.

Well, I wasn't buying that. We both knew the reason. It boiled down to love. His family loved him no matter what. He was their son. Full stop. Mine? Man, one look at me and all they saw was a big mother-ass tumour they had to cut out now for now.

I could see Mani was shifting in his chair and looking around the room like he wanted an escape route. He drained his glass.

> Tell me about you.

I gave him my story. He stayed quiet for a good long while. When I finished I said:

> You asked.

He sighed.

> Yeah, but I never realised all this went on. I'm so sorry. I never knew. And to think it was partly my fault.

> Nah, man.

I knocked his arm.

I used to like you real bad.

I can't tell you how sorry I feel. That was real horrors. I always wondered why you ups and left just so and didn't bother to get in touch.

He shook his head.

Chetan, I don't know about you but a beer can't deal with this news. What you drinking?

We moved on to Johnnie Walker Black. He wanted to know everything.

At least tell me you're happy now.

I'm taking things easy. It's a little lonely sometimes but that's life.

Well. that set him off. He had a million suggestions of websites and bars for a hook-up. I told him I was tired of that.

You don't find you just want to have a person you could talk to? But you know that already, Mister Married Man.

I don't know if it was the Scotch but suddenly I felt angry with Mani. What did he care? He had someone waiting home. He could fuck off back to Patrick. I said goodnight.

The drive home was one continuous traffic jam and I cussed every fucking driver from Port of Spain to Chaguanas. I was tired so I listened to some shit on the radio. By the time I reached home my head was hurting me bad. I took two Panadol, washed them down with a neat Scotch and lay down on top the bedspread. You see me? I'm done with today.

BETTY

What happen? Like you stop answering your phone?

I barged in, scanned the living room and studied him. Both he and the place were a mess.

I would hug you up but it look like you forgot where the shower is. And shave nah, man. I tired telling you that hair on your face don't take you.

He stared at me and I could tell he wasn't overjoyed. Politeness stopped him from saying it out loud but I knew he was probably asking himself – what the ass this woman think she doing coming to my flat and bossing me around? When he didn't move, I squeezed his arm.

Go nah. While you're surprising your skin with water, I'll put out lunch.

Supposing I'm happy like this? I don't have chick nor child and it's Carnival long weekend.

Please tell me you're not serious.

Anybody ever tell you you're damn interfering?

Only you. Now go and wash off that bad energy.

Grown men can sometimes be such children. If you see how he sulked off to bathe. Worse than a teenager. Mind my own business? He is my business. I heard him from the bathroom complaining.

The hot water not working.

Good. A blast of cold water is the right thing to shock your tail out of this mood.

Whatever was going on with him I ain't leaving until I get the low-down.

He took his cool time getting ready. Just as well because I started from one side of the apartment. I stripped the bed and put on clean sheets. Books went back on the shelf and I put the cushions on the couch the way they were normally fixed nice nice. The kitchen's a disgrace. That is how I knew he was truly in the dumps. If it's one thing he cannot abide it's a nasty kitchen and this one had dirty dishes piled high and smelling up the place. By the time I was done putting away and wiping down, the place was still not up to normal standards. At least it looked like you could live here without catching something.

I heard him lock off the water long time so he must be done in there. Now he's hiding in the bedroom. Even if he's not hungry, I am. In the cupboard I found a pretty checked table cloth – perfect for the dining table. I brought a pot of Oil Down I made that morning plus I had leftover mango talkari which he loves. Whatever you're eating, if it's served like it matters, people enjoy the food more. I'm saying this from experience. If I had this Oil Down in front the TV it would taste completely different. This is too good not to serve right.

Cinderella finally emerged, sweet-smelling, shaved and in a clean shorts and T-shirt. Without a word he kissed the middle parting in my hair.

When did you start going grey?

I find you well fast with yourself.

He buss a next kiss on my head.

Nothing wrong with going grey. Of course, I'm still a young boy because I don't have a single grey.

Sit down and leave my head alone. I bought the box of dye but I haven't bothered to use it yet.

Leaving your hair grey is a fashion these days. You might be one of those women who looks distinguished with grey hair.

Or I might look like an old witch. I'm not taking chances.

He looked around the apartment.

Why you gone and do all this cleaning? I would've done it.

I gave him a cut eye.

Eventually. I would have done it eventually.

He sat down and for the first time when he looked at me he was the Mr Chetan I know.

What did I do to deserve you?

I lifted the lids.

I made Oil Down Trini-style. Not the Grenadian way. I could only manage a one-pot dish today.

Smells delicious.

Eat nah, man, and done with all the long talk.

I do a decent Oil Down, if I may say so myself.

Okay this Oil Down has a slightly different colour from mine and it has a richer taste. How you do that?

If I tell you my secret I go have to kill you dead.

He smiled. That was more like my darling doux-doux Mr Chetan.

I cook the breadfruit with the dasheen and plenty pigtail but I put in two things you mightn't use. When I'm throwing in the seasonings and the coconut milk, I add a Maggi cube. Yes, a simple little Maggi cube. Then, five minutes before it's ready, I stir in a tablespoon of Golden Ray margarine for colour and flavour.

Well, it's eating nice.

I left the curry mango for last. It can only be eaten with your hand. We have knife-and-fork Indians who don't use their hand but them ain't my friend. I chewed and sucked the sweet, spicy flesh until it was dry.

Wow. You made this mango talkari?

Of course. Who else?

I thought maybe Mr England.

He can't cook.

But he's satisfactory otherwise?

I ain't make up my mind good yet.

In no time he had licked back a plate of food and was digging in the pot for seconds. I smiled. It's nice to cook and eat with somebody for once.

What you smiling for?

Just you.

I'm obeying Chetan's First Law.

Which is?

He rubbed his flat belly.

Better belly buss than good food waste.

I shook my head and smiled. One Oil Down and my friend was back in the groove. I'd been feeling a little lonely myself. Carnival Monday and the whole place seemed to be either playing mas or gone Tobago to get away from mas. I was in between and nowhere. Maybe next year I'll join the girls. All now so Deedee and Gloria were probably a little tipsy while jumping up with their band, Lost Tribe.

While we ate I tried, casually as I could, to bring up Solo. I've been trying to put the past in the past and speak to Hari without getting vexed. I know he's good to Solo. The other day when I called he made a joke about Solo not having any friends. Under the joking I felt from the way he said it he wasn't joking at all. The man cares. It was something in his voice, like he think things aren't right with the boy.

Take more mango talkari, nah? You hear anything from Solo?

Up to last week me and he talked. He sounded fine. You know he likes to keep by himself. I don't think I'm much help.

He changed the subject.

So what's the latest on Mr England? He asked you to marry him yet?

Hush your mouth. And I don't want to talk about that fool.

I looked him in the eye.

While I'm here, text Solo for me, please. Find out how he's going.

He washed his hands and sent the text.

It's the middle of a weekday. He probably won't text back till later.

Not much I could do but wait. Time to focus on what was going on with the man right in front of me.

Anyhow, I came today because you, mister, have me a little worried. What really going on?

Nothing.

I let out a long sigh.

Don't try that. It's been a good few weeks, no, months, you've not looked yourself. I'm glad to see you eating today but you've lost weight. Your face hollow hollow. And you're more of a hermit than usual. I told Deedee the other day that the last time you looked half way happy was at the Oval. You met your friend, the Carib man. What's his name again?

Mani.

So, what happen with you and Mani?

Nothing.

Oh Lord, put a hand. Is me, Chetan.

While we tidied away the dishes he explained how seeing Mani had flooded his head with long time memories. Some days he didn't want to get out of bed at all. I listened without saying boo.

You must be thinking, first he doesn't want to talk and now it's like he's eaten parrot bottom.

No. Keep talking. Not every day you can carry your own bag of cocoa. That's why we have friends.

And you have Mr England now.

I opened my eyes big big and shook my head.

Nope. I like my own space. My days for all that done.

A phone pinged. It must be Solo. Chetan held the screen at an angle and I couldn't do a thing.

Solo says he's fed up with the cold. Hopefully winter will done soon. On his way home. Later.

That's all?

He put the phone in his pocket.

You ever know him to talk plenty? I'll let you know if I get a next message.

I'm so grateful you and Solo still close. Sometimes that is the only comfort I have.

MR CHETAN

We talked and talked until the place started to make dark. Miss Betty left me with the remaining Oil Down and a tight cuddle. While she was here I did feel lighter, brighter, and watching her drive off only made the loneliness come back ten times worse. But I put that aside because something going on with Solo and we needed to talk. His message was weird. I read it again slowly to see if I'd missed something:

> I fed up with the cold.
> Hopefully winter will
> done soon. Man from
> work stole all $$$
> and trying 2 get it back.

What the ass was happening? How could someone thief my boy's money? And he works so hard.

Solo wasn't picking up my messages. I surfed the web with one eye and looked for a reply with the other. To torture myself I opened Facebook and Twitter. Yup. Mani had posted earlier in the day. He and the wonderful husband, Patrick, were playing mas dressed in nothing more than leopard-print, pum-pum shorts and a small belt with a piece of fur hanging down in the front. Like that was hiding anything. Mani had gone all out and was showing off his six-pack with leopard spots painted on his chest and stomach. I wish I didn't find him so damn hot. Whatever. He has his life and I must stop resenting the man for being happy. And as Miss B said, I've been down long enough. Time to gather up Mani and everything to do with him, with my family, the whole jahaji bundle. I wish I could burn everything and throw away the ashes like I had those seven branches. For my sanity I had to move on or I could end up in St Ann's Psychiatric Hospital, aka, the madhouse.

But how do I move on? What will help me? I slumped on the couch as wave after wave of loneliness numbed my insides. Lord, I was real desperate for a man, any man, to press his hard body against mine even if it was only for a little ten-fifteen minutes. I've made do with strangers before and it'll have to be enough again. Tonight I needed someone. Being Carnival Monday, I had to be careful as there was more chance of bouncing up a drunk bigot who wants to fuck you up – pelt bottle behind you or beat you. I never do anybody a thing but simply being me is illegal, immoral and perverted. If anything happened to me town will say, the queer deserved it. What he was doing in the back down there in the first place? People won't stop to think we're only in the dark hiding because we aren't allowed in the light.

I'm careful. The popular websites are safe – as secure as a hook-up like this can be. My choice is either to be alone or check out that man winking at me online. I don't feel any attraction to him but beggars can't be choosers. Who knows? I try to convince myself it might be fun. In two twos business was fixed. Whole drive to the location I tried to feel excited. It was not working. I dug deep, imagining the release a good hard fuck would bring. How will I ever scrub Jackson and Mani's faces from my mind?

A little after midnight I pulled up outside a dingy-looking rum shop somewhere in the back of Princes Town. A man waved and walked towards my car. He was shorter than I expected and wearing an ugly flesh-coloured T-shirt that didn't suit him at all at all. As soon as he opened the car door the fumes of whiskey and sweat hit me. But even drunk he was surprisingly polite, which was strange and made me try to see beyond his bloodshot eyes. Big mistake and still I couldn't turn him down directly.

Hey man, you looking like you've been liming whole day. You must be tired. I'm cool to leave this for another time.

Relax.

Hear what, I think I've changed my mind.

Oh gosh, don't say that, nah.

His hand moved down my chest.

Relax. I go take care of you. You don't have to do nothing. Promise.

I exhaled, pushed the car seat back and unzipped my jeans. He did what he said he would. The release and tiny connection with another human was as lovely as a cool dip in the sea on a blistering hot day.

That night I slept solidly for the first time in weeks. In the morning I checked my phone. Solo had still not replied.

SOLO

Twice I went by Trevor's parents and twice Granny alone was there and refused to open the door. That didn't stop me. I said what I had to say to the apartment door. She and the door refused to budge. Okay, if that is how she stop. It's not my neighbours who hearing all this bacchanal.

Haul your ass nah, boy. And stop coming here. My Trevor ain't take your money.

Then how come he's hiding?

Trevor would never take so much as a toothpick that didn't belong to he.

Well, he thief a mother-ass more than a toothpick.

I knew it was useless but I didn't know what else to do or where else to go. She ain't helping me if I was the last man alive. Even as I was thinking that I laughed to myself. No way Mammy would protect me like this if I had robbed somebody. God would stop her.

Granny was either peeping out or she knew my knock because the next time I rocked up, before I could say boo, she was ready for me. From now on she's done listening to my falsehoods about Trevor. I don't know what I'm talking about and if I didn't move my stinking coolie backside before she count to ten, she was calling the cops. Bothering a respectable

281

pensioner who never do nobody nothing. Cunt. I gave the door two hard kick before leaving. And what's this coolie business? Bringing that racist shit with them quite to America. What happen to all of we is one family?

As I walked to the train station it was making so cold my brain was paining me. I thought, for kicks, let me text Chips. And then I told myself, send Trevor one and all. I stopped right there on the sidewalk, in the freezing, windy cold, and sent them one long string of joined-up cussing. Chips read it. I could see that. No reply. Fuck you too, bro.

If I lived here for the rest of my life I don't think I will ever get accustomed to this damn freezing weather. The wind had to be coming from the Arctic direct. I might as well not be wearing a jacket because my bones them were freezing. All inside my sneakers icy icy. Old timers have a saying that you don't appreciate what you have until it's gone. I get what they meant. I said bye-bye to sunshine, my nice house, an easy life. Correction: I had to say goodbye.

Up ahead I saw the subway entrance. Something inside me knew tonight was different. I wasn't getting on the train. I couldn't. The closer I got to the station the louder a voice inside was telling me to keep walking.

But I'm freezing.

Keep walking. What exactly you're going back to Ozone Park for? That is your home?

It's home now. After all this time and the bad blood with Mammy, I can't leave.

Keep walking.

I walked and I walked in that fucking bitter cold while this merciless voice cussed me whole road.

You feel you is man? I don't know anybody more dotish than you.

Part of me wanted this to end now for now and part of me knew I didn't have the courage. If I had had that kind of strength I would have done it long time.

Facts is facts. You're a burden to everybody. Fucking useless. What will Mr Chetan say when he hears you lost all your money just so? And look how you gone and proved Mammy right. She always said you wouldn't make it up here.

I didn't have a plan. From the main street I turned off and walked through an underpass and into a park with empty swings. I headed towards a huge tree and, even though the cold was biting me, I sat down right there. The bark wet my pants. Not that I cared any more. I just wanted this nightmare to end. I didn't need a voice telling me what a dumb fuck I was. I knew that already.

I was out of razors and I needed more. Now. Right now. I got up and headed back to the main street. CVS, Walmart – anything so would do. I know the cashier doesn't give a rat's ass but I still threw a pack of spearmint gum on the counter. Wasting money because she would have cashed the razor blades on their own without looking up. No one gives a shit about anybody. I read the other day how a man in Manhattan killed himself with poison. He sat in his car rotting for nearly a week before anybody realised something was wrong. That is the country I'm living in.

I don't remember reaching home. The one thought I had was that this was it. I had given it my best and my best wasn't enough. Normally I cut longways down my arm. Every cutter knows it's safer that way. Well, I'm done worrying about that.

My breathing slowed. With the first cut across I instantly felt an ease up. Only with this could I relax myself. I moved down my arm towards my wrist, forming a pretty pattern of short, parallel lines of blood. If you've never cut you won't understand the pure relief that flowed with the blood. A lot of blood. I lay back on the bed and the tears wouldn't stop. Faces swam before my eyes – Mammy, Daddy, Mr Chetan, Uncle Hari. I'm so sorry but I've had enough licks. I'm done. I can't take no more pressure.

Uncle Hari interrupted. He panicked. I heard a lot of shouting. I think Ian drove. Uncle Hari kept asking me what I'd gone and done. I didn't have the strength to explain and he wouldn't understand. Even if I wanted to speak, my throat and chest had grabbed hold of my words. As we walked through the main hospital doors into Emergency, Uncle Hari held me tight.

Listen good. When we go inside I'm handing them Ian's ID card. You hear me? If they put your card in the system and anything suspicious come up, police will reach one time. You understand me? Tell me you understand.

I didn't respond.

Ian, give him your wallet. Don't look at me so. Just do it. Quick.

The whole wallet?

Hurry up, man. I have to do all the thinking in this family?

The Haitian nurse looking after me said I only just missed an artery. I missed. I fucking missed. Six hours, six stitches on the biggest cut, four on another and a pile of leaflets later, Katherine was unlocking the door for us. She gave me a hug. I didn't hug back. I still hadn't spoken to either Uncle Hari or Ian – not even to say thanks. Especially not to say thanks. How was I supposed to face them? I was so shame. They knew everything, had seen everything. And to put them through Emergency. I never wanted that. Never. My mess took up the whole night and in a couple hours they had to go to work. All because of me.

I wanted to go to work too so I wouldn't have to think, but even the weather was vexed with me because a snowstorm hit the city and the whole of New York shut down. I was waiting for Uncle Hari to say he can't have me in the house again after what I did.

Instead he parked himself in a chair and said he was there in case I needed anything. I said I was fine but he didn't budge.

*

In the afternoon Uncle Hari came in holding out his cell phone to me.

Somebody want to talk to you.

I took the phone because, well, what choice did I have? Can't even kill myself properly.

Solo? Baby? Solo?

Hi.

Is Mammy, darling.

I hadn't heard her voice in years. It sounded older and sad. My stomach dropped.

How you keeping? Your uncle called me. He said you not feeling yourself. Solo?

He shouldn't have bothered you.

He called because even if you're not talking to me I am still your mother and I love you, darling. I know you can't forgive me because of your father. I understand. But let me help you.

She started crying.

As long as I am alive I am your mother. You hear me? I love you. You want me to come up? I could get a flight tomorrow. Let me come and look after you.

No.

For a second I felt sorry for her.

I'm okay.

I could hear the tears in her voice. I bit down on my lip.

Solo, Uncle Hari said it might be good for you to have a little company. I could bring up some nice food for you. You used to like my food.

I shook my head and rubbed away the water filling my eyes.

Solo. Is only you and me. Please. You know how hard it is for me knowing my one child's suffering and I'm not there to help?

Hard for her. Well, it's hard for me too, Mammy. I took a deep breath. This was too much.

Please don't come. I can't see you. And if you come I promise, on my father's grave, I will leave and nobody will hear from me again.

I passed the phone back to Uncle Hari. Why the hell he did that? I don't want her seeing me like this. Who else knows I'm a complete failure?

The snowstorm eased off and Katherine went out. I prayed they would all go out. Instead Ian replaced Uncle Hari and sat in my room on his laptop. Uncle Hari paced the house, up and down, like a jumbie was haunting him. Sweet Katherine came back with a big box of Krispy Kreme doughnuts for me. With my sweet tooth I would normally polish off that whole box by myself. Not now. I'm not eating a single one. I don't deserve treats. Besides, my appetite's gone. Ian left and I had a few precious minutes alone before Uncle Hari came back in my room.

I could put on the light?

He flicked the switch before I could answer.

What happen? I heard a noise. That wasn't your head banging, was it?

His voice is naturally jokey. Not now. I pulled up the blanket. Uncle Hari was staring at me with this weird expression. Sympathy? Pity?

I wasn't doing anything.

Is me you talking to, boy.

I looked at my bandaged hands.

Solo, I know you is a big man but that don't mean you can't tell me if something's wrong. We is family. Ian bigger than you and he does come and tell me all his business. What happen? It's woman troubles? You know when it come to that I is the king. It ain't have nothing I ain't pass through yet. Give horn. Get horn. Woman get she-self pregnant. You might think I does only be the one to leave but I've had my share of tabanca.

He tugged my foot through the blanket.

So, what happen with you? Tell your old uncle.

I couldn't speak. Simply opening my mouth would mean crumbling like a biscuit. My head hurt so much. I chewed my lips.

Solo. I can't replace my brother. But with him gone you come like my son. It don't have nothing you can't tell me. I wasn't there when you were little.

He broke off and eased himself onto the edge of the bed.

When you wanted to leave your mother's house ain't I said come by me? I never asked you why. I never questioned you. And to tell you the truth I would have preferred to see you stay with Betty and go to college. Don't get me wrong. She is not my favourite person. Once Sunil married she like he gave up on the rest of the family. I don't know why I telling you that now. You see how my mind does go all about the place? Your uncle getting old.

He was rubbing my foot through the blanket.

Truth is I wanted you in America by me. I don't have much but you know I would give you the same as Katherine and Ian. I don't play favourites.

We sat quiet quiet as I swallowed and bit down on my teeth as hard as I could. Not since those first early days in New York had I felt this fucking miserable. And was me, myself and I to blame. Uncle Hari sighed and got up.

All right, get some rest. You want anything?

I shook my head. Only the dumbest, most dotish moron would be in my position. Maybe Chips got it wrong. Maybe if I closed my eyes tight tight this nightmare would end. I'd wake up never having met Trevor or Chips and certainly not cleaned out my bank account.

In the dark again I curled up and let myself remember my bedroom in Trinidad and the two hammocks on the front porch and playing chess with Mr Chetan. He would be fast asleep now. I shouldn't but I called. The worst part was I woke him up and then I couldn't speak. All I did was cry, and cry, and cry. His soft voice offered me a ticket home or he could come to me. Mainly he just said, it's okay. When the crying eased up I managed to say bye. He said, I love you, Solo. And he said how I could come and live by him if I wanted. I'm a big man now. I didn't have to live by Mammy. I clicked off and cried so hard I thought I would never stop. I can't keep living like this.

MR CHETAN

On a normal day I can reach by Miss Betty in about fifteen minutes, twelve if the road's clear. I made it in nine. Hazard lights on and I drove like a madman. She was bawling like ten Tarzan and I couldn't understand what she was saying. All I heard was Solo and suicide. The relief I felt when I knew he was alive and safe couldn't make up for those minutes when I thought he was dead. Years shaved off my life. The neighbour on one side heard Miss Betty and ran over. I got there just in time to stop the lady from calling an ambulance because she was frightened Miss Betty was having a nervous breakdown.

Calming her down wasn't easy. Over and over I had to remind her the boy ain't dead. He was safe. He was being looked after. I spoke to Hari because I couldn't get any sense out of Miss Betty but he and all wasn't clear about what happened before he carried Solo to Emergency. He was damn clueless about why Solo would want to kill himself. No one could get anything out of the boy yet. He must be feeling so weak. And in between this I had to keep Miss B from charging off to the airport for the next flight to New York. She was getting on so bad I took her car keys. If she went behind a wheel in this state, the only way she was coming back home was in a coffin.

Hari heard all this commess going on with the car key and he thought that was the perfect moment to take a turn in my tail and start one big set of quarrelling. Seems when he first

290

called to tell Miss B she let go one set of bad words behind him that this was his fault and if he hadn't taken her son from her this would never have happened. Instead of understanding it was the shock talking he apparently said she was the world's worst parent. Why else would Solo run from Trinidad in the first place?

Hari, all of we need to cool down.

Cool down? Cool down? Don't tell me about cooling down when that blasted soucouyant, Betty, done suck the life out of Solo.

But how you could blame her? What she do? Eh?

Monkey don't see he own tail. She bring up the boy so. Have him stick up by she alone when he had all of we.

Now is not the time for that kind of talk.

I should have told my late brother, God rest his soul, she was trouble. You know the kind of family she come from? Corbeau can't eat sponge cake.

Hari, done that now. You're insulting the woman for no reason.

While he was talking this nonsense in my ear, Miss Betty was busy screaming at me to tell him all kind of nastiness and I was in middle trying to make peace. I asked Hari if the two of them could please take a five minutes to catch themselves and calm down. I promised to call back. I had to go see about Miss Betty.

I want my son. You don't understand how I'm feeling. You can't. I need to go to my son.

She started wailing again.

It's my fault. This is punishment for Sunil. I know it is.

I held her tight tight.

I want to talk to Hari. Call Hari again.

I don't think you and he can talk now.

I ain't asking you. I'm telling you. Call Hari now.

When I passed her over to Hari, I thought she would talk quiet and get him to put Solo on the phone. No such luck. Within seconds the two of them started back with the blaming. I got her to use the speakerphone so I could try to part the fight. She turned on me and I started to get abuse coming and going. Oh, how I could take Hari's side? His family knew Sunil used to beat her bad and they never tried to talk to him or stop him drinking. Everything she did was for Solo to have a good life.

Hari wasn't taking that. He let her know that from the time Sunil married her he changed. He stopped seeing his family. She was the one who made him drink. She kept Solo far from anybody named Ramdin even though that was the child's name too.

Between the two of them they jook one another until all the decades of bad blood bubbled out that cell phone speaker.

When Miss Betty finally spoke to her son I rubbed her back and forced myself to smile. It broke my heart. Solo real harden. He didn't give an inch and cut the talk down quick. The poor woman broke down. I wanted to cry too. Is true that child will eat mother but mother don't eat child.

The only person who hadn't spoken to Solo was me. Hari wasn't in favour and, as much as I was vex with the man, he made a good point. Solo needed time. Miss Betty stood up to go in her bed and she nearly collapsed. I had to hold her to walk to the bedroom. After I settled her I was going to make some chamomile tea but I realised that can't work. I gave her a shot of whiskey. No way I was leaving her alone so I went to my old room with its new bed, new bedside table and chair. Strange how there was nothing of me in this room that had been my little nest.

I dozed off, woke on the first ring and jumped up when I saw Solo's number flash across the screen. No words. He just bawled his heart out on the phone. I begged him to come back. He could live by me easy easy. No reply. After a while I realised all he wanted was someone to hear his pain. I listened and hoped he couldn't hear I was quietly crying too. After, I sent him a text:

Solo – remember that
laugh and cry does
live in the same place.
I love you. Chetan

BETTY

I don't care what people say, sometimes you get a sign. In Trinidad we don't get hit by earthquake so. I was walking from the car to the hairdresser when the whole place started to shake. Cars were bouncing up and down. One huge concrete building was swaying back and forth like a dolly house. I looked around me and the faces I saw were looking as scared and shocked as I felt. I heard glass smashing but not a single scream. All my energy was on keeping my footing steady while Mother Earth did she best to shake me off. What had me most frightened was how long it lasted. Later the news said it measured a massive 7.3 and went on for a whole two minutes. Well, I can believe the 7.3 part. Only two minutes? Nah. They had to be using a different kind of clock. No one died, and it didn't cause any big set of damage. Imagine if I was inside getting my hair cut and the building collapsed and killed me dead dead? I would have gone to my grave without ever seeing Solo again. God is love.

I should have known that a bigger shake-up was coming. Solo cut his wrists. It was an attempted suicide for sure. I'm still in shock. He won't talk to me and there's not a damn thing I can do. My son was in so much pain he thought it was better to take his own life and I can't help him. At least he has Hari and Mr Chetan and I know they will do their best. What is the point of being a mother if you can't protect your one piece of child? I don't know what to do with myself. Mr Chetan stayed over a few nights but he has his own life.

Mr England found out about Solo from Gloria, I guess. I didn't bother to ask him how he knew. He parked himself in my living room.

Betty, come sit by me and stop saying I should go. Come, honey.

I sighed.

Please, I have a lot on my mind.

He moved from the couch and perched himself on the arm of my chair. Next thing he was hugging me up tight.

That is why I'm staying right here. You need someone to look after you. Give you a little tender loving.

I'm fine.

No, you're not fine and you need me. You need me to stay here with you and protect you.

He began massaging my shoulders, then his hands were inside my T-shirt and on my breasts. Suddenly I wanted him to stay. It's been so long since anyone was sweet on me. His tongue slid inside my ear.

Stay if you want.

I already told you I want. I'm not letting you out of my sight.

SOLO

Dennis came a few days later to see me. Uncle Hari made me sit with them in the living room. I pushed myself into an end of the couch while they worked out who playing who this cricket season and which side going to get their ass cut. The new bottle of Johnnie Walker Black Dennis brought soon had a proper dent. I stayed as long as I could bear it and then begged for an excuse. One good thing in these last few days is that once my head hit the pillow, I drop asleep before the sheep have time to line up for counting, much more jump over the fence. Dennis told me to take a whole two weeks home to rest myself and he slipped me an envelope with full pay. He didn't have to do that. I nearly cried.

Night and day somebody was always home with me. It looked like Ian got the work as chief babysitter. He had to pick up a client's computer from New Canaan, quite the hell in Connecticut, and he begged me to come for the drive. If I didn't go he would have to wait until Katherine came home from work and then the traffic would be shit. I told him not to get on like an ass. I was fine by myself. Apparently not. Uncle Hari had him under heavy manners. I couldn't stop the man doing his job properly on top of everything else. At least he will put on music in the car and we don't have to talk. Sometimes I tell myself, look at Ian. He's quietly doing his computer thing. I mean, the man is a nerd but that doesn't stop him stepping out with the ladies. Every few months is a new woman and every time he says, this is the one – until he meets the next one. He's no gym bunny. Average-looking. But he's happy in his skin. Now, why I can't be like that?

Before lunch we hit the Hutchinson River Parkway with Moodymann vibing. An hour in, right after we zoomed past Port Chester, he turned down the music.

Solo, you need to help me out.

Yeah what?

Dad said I can't come back home until I get you to tell me what really going on. What's upsetting you?

I looked out the window.

Let me see. His exact instructions were to drive to Boston if that is what it took. Just don't come back home until you know what's eating up your cousin. So, I'm asking. What's happening, cuz?

My heart began racing.

You're going to help me out? New Canaan is maybe another half hour. Once I pick up the stuff can we turn around and head home? Or do we keep going north? Up to you.

I turned and glanced at him as he concentrated on the road ahead. An eighteen-wheeler overtook us, spraying brown slush all over the car. Suddenly I felt bone tired. If there was a bed I would fall asleep this minute. No such luck. I was trapped in his blue Prius. What to do? He got the whole damn story about Chips and Trevor. Give him his due – Ian listened and never called me stupid or dumb. We picked up McDonald's from a drive-through and ate in the car right outside the house.

Now listen, when we go inside I'm telling Dad. Don't worry. He'll help.

You think he'll throw me out?

He looked at me and I could see a grin even though the Quarter Pounder with Cheese was covering half his face. I waited while he chomped away, ketchup spilling out the sides of his mouth.

Where do you get these crazy ideas from? You think he would do that to Sunil's only child? Please. Sometimes I think he loves you more than me and Katherine. No. You're stuck with us, cuz. I was more thinking about what's going to happen to Chips and Trevor if Dad finds them.

Ian and Uncle Hari talked for a good fifteen-twenty minutes behind a locked bedroom door. Uncle Hari found me sitting at the kitchen table. If he was vexed, he hid it good.

You and me need to have a serious talk.

I braced myself for whatever was coming.

Boy, I eh go lie. If I catch either of them smart men I don't know what I go do to them. I so vex. They have no conscience. No decency. To rob a man blind so.

I put my head down and concentrated on the diamond-patterned linoleum.

But let me ask you a question.

I half looked up.

You let them get to you so bad that you try to kill yourself?
They're worth your life, Solo? A young man like you?

My stomach flipped. Well, everything's out now.

Boy, everybody does make mistakes. But you have to learn
not to take it out on yourself.

He sighed.

Anyhow, I have a friend. He is the rightest person to handle
this. It's a little while we ain't talk but that don't matter.
Leave it with me.

He was on the phone for a good time.

You ever hear about the Flatland gangs?

I shrugged.

I see fellas liming in the projects.

My friend Pluto started off hustling a little weed. Well now
I hear is more than weed he's pushing. I don't like to go cap
in hand to nobody but this is not something I can handle
by myself. Who Pluto don't know, not worth knowing. As
soon as I mentioned Chips right away he knew the creature
I was talking about.

I'm sorry you had to ask for help because of me.

Nah. Don't hurt your head. Help for you is help for me.
But you must promise me.

His voice cracked and he wiped his eyes.

Promise me you won't try nothing like that again. I felt like
you cut my heart when you did that. If something's wrong
come and see me. I'm not a monster.

I didn't want to be more of a burden than I am already.
And I felt stupid. Nobody else would've lost their money
like this.

That is what you think. One day we'll sit down and I will
give you some stories. You think is two catch-ass I pass
through?

Pluto took over and we left him to do his thing. What kind
of name is Pluto anyway? He might find Trevor and I hope to
high heaven he doesn't beat up the old parents to get to him.
And supposing he does get back my money. Does that mean
I'm now in debt to this big-time drug dealer? I was scared to
ask Uncle Hari anything. Pluto was a last resort. And he did it
for me. For me.

MR CHETAN

I went with my fast self and messaged Mani happy birthday. Facebook's fault again. Otherwise, why the hell would I get in touch with him? Whenever I remembered that evening in the pub I cringed. He must think I'm a self-pitying piece of shit. Imagine my shock when he sent a text. Party's happening by him and I must come. He was being kind, I thought, but then my boy followed up with another message giving directions and saying sorry he hadn't been in touch and please come for the lime. Even if he'd forgotten, I'm a firm believer that cockroach don't have no business in fowl party. He has his fancy husband and their friends would be all kind of highfalutin people. Not where I belong. And what about his family? Seeing me would be like seeing a jumbie and I'd have to dodge a million questions.

At the best of times I'm no fete man. I live quiet – work, home, read a book, watch a little TV, eat, sleep. Now and then I might check out the scene online although I'm getting tired of that. Miss Betty I see all the time. Weekends I must have my sea bath at Maracas or, if the water's too rough, I head further east to Blanchisseuse Beach. And that's me done. Too simple for Mani and them.

I couldn't make up my mind. Seeing Mani alone would be cool but that wasn't on offer. A little house fete could be okay. And check me, in my forties and I'm now going to a gay people party. Just the idea was messing with my brains. Even if all I did was show my face for an hour and dust it back down the road, that was something I should do.

If I was going to do this I wanted to do it properly. A man can't look all how. As the Gulf City Mall stores opened on Saturday morning your boy was there. Don't think it's only women seeing pressure to look good and have nice thing. A fete full of buff men in tight tight clothes, showing off what five days a week in the gym could do to a body, ain't easy. The amount of time I spent looking for a shirt, anybody would think I was buying a wedding suit. I was coming down the escalator when I spotted it in the window of this choke-up little shop. White linen with a Nehru collar made it regal but rolling back the sleeves showed off the surprise – a sweet blue-and-white print on the inside of the cuff. That had my name.

For a big man I was anxious and restless like a teenager. The invitation was any time from six in the evening. To me that meant don't reach by people house before 7 p.m. I rocked up all 7.30 p.m. and people were still showing up around midnight.

Mani was a sweetie. Patrick shook my hand and I took an instant dislike to the man. His hand was clammy. That was a turn-off.

Patrick, I told you about bouncing up Chetan at cricket after all these years.

Mani was watching me straight in my eye.

Chetan, you know you're the oldest friend I have.

Who you calling old? We're the same age.

You know what I mean. We go way back. Not many people can remember what I was like aged eleven.

I didn't have to see Patrick's face to know he didn't like his husband saying that to some strange coolie boy from down south. The man gave off a coldness like he knew things about me. Instead of getting stressed out I surprised myself and relaxed. Mani introduced me to everybody and an older man even flirted with me. Even more amazing was that not a soul batted an eyelid. Part of me was thinking I might at last have found my posse. Or not. The only other time I might meet nice people like this would be someplace like a gay bar in Woodbrook. Problem with that is any and every body will know about you one time. Just going there makes you a target.

I loved Mani's home. Whoever did the decorating had great taste. The furniture was simple, quality mahogany like you used to find long time. Mani must have inherited these because you can't buy beautiful morris chairs now. But the money clearly went on art. Every wall had something interesting. One I could have looked at whole evening was an amazing photo of men playing Blue Devil carnival mas. Mani saw me looking at his picture.

You like this one?

If it missing, know is me who thief it.

His shoulder was touching mine. I didn't want him to move.

Maria Nunes is the photographer. She has a whole series of the Blue Devils from Paramin Village. Look her up.

I was trying to act cool and sip my beer when someone came up to him, whispered in his ear and Mani stormed off.

I don't know what went down but about ten minutes later Patrick and Mani came out together. Mani looked blue vex. The husband was cold like a freezer. I think if you stuck him with a pin you wouldn't get blood. I didn't like him before and now I hated the man. The fella next to me was the one who had spoken to Mani.

Boy, I feeling bad, yes, because is me who buss the mark. But I find that real dread. Is the man party. All their friends here.

What happen?

I thought I was opening the bathroom door and I opened the spare bedroom door by mistake. Patrick was with a man. No lie. I saw it with my own two eyes. Hush. Mani's coming.

He had on a forced smile.

Everybody good for drinks? Chetan, what are you drinking?

I'm good. Remember I living far.

Mani went into overdrive getting drinks and passing around snacks. I felt for him. The fella next to me started back up.

Everybody knows Patrick is not the most loyal man on the planet. Everybody except Mani. This is not the first time. Anyhow, that is their business. You can't know what does go on in private.

Suddenly the night was over for me. I didn't want all this drama. I tried to slip out without saying goodbye but Mani spotted me and walked me out.

Let me be your bodyguard. I don't want anything happening to you. I think I've caused you enough problems in life.

That's not true.

We reached my car without saying much more.

Thanks for inviting me. You have a nice place and great friends.

Yeah. We must link up soon, okay?

Yeah, man.

I got behind the wheel, put my hand out the window to give him a fist bump. Instead he gripped my arm and came in for a raw, passionate kiss. I was too shocked to kiss back properly. He smiled.

I'll call you.

BETTY

Mr Chetan forwarded pictures Solo had sent him a few weeks after recovery. If you see how the boy looking like a man. The baby face gone. And I hate to admit it but he was the print of his father at that age. Handsome for days. It was a little shocking seeing him in a big winter jacket in the snow when I'm accustomed to him living in short pants and T-shirts. I spent a long time looking at the pictures of the teenager who had turned into a man clean out of my sight. I showed Mr England.

Look at my big son.

He needs to put on weight or the next hard breeze will blow him away.

Yeah. He was always on the maga side. If I so much as smell cake I put on five pounds but he could eat big food and never get fat.

I scrolled through the photos.

I love, love, love this close-up of his face. I'm making it my screen saver.

Oh, so you'll make his picture your screen saver but not mine?

He's my son.

And I'm your boyfriend.

You don't find you too old to be bothering if I have your picture as my screen saver?

For the whole morning Mr England's face was swell up big big. Lunchtime I had cooked nice food and he hardly said two words to me. I don't have space in my head to take on this man and he foolishness, yes. After lunch he sat down in front the TV and he still wasn't talking to me. I snuggled up next to him.

Honey, why you quiet so?

You know why.

You can't still be vex about my screen saver? It's a picture of my son.

So? I'm not important too?

I took a deep breath.

I'm very tired and you're not enjoying liming. Why we don't talk tomorrow? We could go for a drive somewhere in the afternoon.

You're putting me out?

No. But you don't want to be with me so best you go home.

I'm not going anywhere.

Something inside my stomach turned. I didn't have the strength for an argument. All I wanted was my bed. If he was staying that was fine.

I dozed off, only to be woken by his hardness pushing against my bottom and his fingers between my legs.

Oh gosh, you can't see I'm sleeping?

Darling, sugar. I have something for you.

Later nah. Let me take a five.

I didn't mean to upset you. You know it's only because I love you more than anybody else could ever love you. I can't help myself.

He rolled on top of me. I was vex and tired. Today he ain't getting nothing. You know what the man did? He straddled me and started singing about how much he loved me – all a little off-key but my boy went through hard. What to say? He get a piece. A good piece.

*

I switched from the Thursday to the Tuesday prayer group. Sometimes it's good to shake things up. One of the regulars – everybody calls her Tanty – had stopped coming to Sunday morning church. When I tackled her she said she had switched to the six o'clock Sunday evening service. No offence but that evening service wasn't even a quarter as good as the one morning time. Their organist and the singing don't ever be together on the same beat. Reverend Luke usually leaves the evening service for an elder so you know the sermon is pure hit and miss. I pushed a little and she let go but not before I swore on my son's head to keep my mouth shut. Tanty's son is an addict and the boy's always in and out of jail. Last time he came out he was living by she. Her eyes were full of water when she told me how the boy thief she sou-sou hand. Every last cent that she was saving to fix up her house went up his nose.

She was punishing bad until she found help. I wasn't to tell anybody. Well, she was right to be hush hush. Even I who don't know about Hindu people thing recognised that as devil worship with all kind of evil like blood sacrifice. How Tanty could call she-self a Christian and be doing this? Next thing she was inviting me for the following Sunday to a temple in Tunapuna.

Me? You mad or what? Tanty, I'm not in that.

Kali worship is not what you think. Blood sacrifice and thing is ol' talk.

I twisted up my mouth. I'm so bad lucky already I can't go bringing obeah on my head as well.

Maybe because she confided in me, Tanty wouldn't leave me alone. I asked how she could be in our church and same time worshipping a bloodthirsty goddess.

Betty, you never hear about getting a second opinion?

How you mean?

When you ask God for something and like he deaf, you don't ever wish you had somebody else to turn to in your time of need?

I gave her my Betty Happy Face. I pretended too well because she carried on talking. I tried to change the topic.

Tanty, tell me something. You lose weight?

Fifteen pounds. Another five to go and I good.

And I find your skin and all looking nice.

Hush your mouth. Mamaguying an old woman like me.

She bent over and whispered,

> I ain't take nothing. All I do is keep up my devotions to
> Mudder Kali. Three days before you go temple you can't eat
> meat, drink alcohol or have sex.

Most importantly her son had gone back to rehab. She used
to come to prayer group meeting looking sickly and dowdy.
That overs. So long as that craziness stayed outside we church
I was glad for she.

I thought I was in the clear but every blasted week after
prayer group she would hold me down for a talk. Tanty said
she wasn't the only non-Hindu to go to Kali puja. She had met
Catholics, Anglicans, Baptists and even Muslims. Everybody
had their faith but they came to Mudder Kali for that little
extra help. Black, Indian, red skin and dougla mixed when
it came time to worship Mudder. One time Tanty even saw a
white boy in the temple but he was only doing research.

If I had to ask Kali for help I might see if she can't get rid of
Mr England for me, please. No question he loves me. No question. If anything he loves me a little too much and I'm not sure
I can give what he wants. Always by me. Always texting. I can't
get five minutes to myself before he's wondering where I am
and if I'm leaving him. But all joke aside, the one thing I would
want from Kali is for my son to come back home to me. If she
could do that then I would be worshipping night and day.

SOLO

Loyalty's a knock-out punch. Pluto threw a few punches and bradaps – Hari's nephew got fixed up. If it wasn't for Pluto all now so I would still be scratching around without a hope of getting back my money. And when I say punch I mean that literally. Pluto didn't beat up Trevor himself. Nah. Pushing fifties, bald like a baby and keeping a little belly – he was no match for a hard-back strong man like Mister Trevor. Not that he wouldn't try. If any of the massive gold rings he's always sporting – three on the left hand, four on the right – connected with your head, you would black out one time. The real reason he didn't break Trevor's jaw himself was because my boy loss away in Florida by a baby mother. I mean to say, who wouldn't prefer the Sunshine State when New York's in a polar vortex? Better yet, this little vacation ain't coming out of his pocket. By the time Pluto's associate in Boca Raton had landed Trevor in Emergency the man had already breezed through half my money.

Chips was more reasonable. The two grand Pluto got back, plus the one grand Chips already had, was enough to get my birth certificate. A one-time special. But I wanted to make sure that didn't mean the birth certificate was only going to be three fifths as good. We met at our regular diner, me with a coffee and he with his orange juice.

It's gonna be the real deal. But Trini, you never said you

were with Pluto's crew. I would've given you a discount up front, bro. Made me look bad in front the man. Know what I'm saying? You've gotta tell him I didn't know who you were.

Don't take no horrors. Pluto's cool.

You make sure the brother's cool cause I don't want no trouble. I'm just a simple businessman trying to earn a dollar.

I didn't put you in the bamboo. All I want is a birth certificate. That's all.

Your product's on fast track. So, you put a word in for me with Pluto. I don't have no beef with nobody. Know what I'm saying?

I should have been reassured. I should have been able to wait it out because Uncle Hari had Pluto behind the job. Only cutting helped. I couldn't give it up. It's how I manage. The shame and guilt didn't ease when I took out a razor blade, but I don't have anything else. Whiskey made me sick. A couple times me and Ian shared a joint. That didn't do one fart for me except make me eat like a pig. And recently I've worked out how to hide the cutting. My scalp. Only trouble with that is you have to leave your hair greasy. One time I forgot and shampoo went inside the cuts. Oh jeez-an-ages. That sting bad.

Ever since the Emergency night Uncle Hari's been checking my room. He thinks I don't know but little things catch him. Sometimes a book that was on the floor magically goes back on the shelf, or my jeans that were thrown away on a chair ended up neat neat on a hanger. A man don't have any flecking privacy. But I look for that. No stray blades in my room any more. For him to find what he's looking for he'd have to go all up inside my wallet and that wallet living in my back pocket. Bloody tissues I flush down the toilet or I throw them in the outside bin. Once or twice there was blood on the pillow case. That is what the Chinese laundromat there for.

Chips came through with the birth certificate and, as Mammy would say, God is love. It was the authentic, real thing self. I got through with the Social Security office and I could breathe. But don't think I wanted to cut myself less once I was legal. Maybe that's just how I'm made. I texted Mr Chetan to tell him the news. He said if I was happy then he was good, only he missed me. Like Uncle Hari he didn't seem to trust that I was doing all right. And then Uncle Hari asked me straight if I had stopped with the cutting. I left that right there. No way I wanted to lie to him. I can't stop. Or is it that I won't stop? I don't know. I'm tired.

Uncle Hari was so relieved you would think it was his papers that came through.

I always say dog don't make cat.

How you mean?

You is your father's son through and through. The Ramdin blood strong. Not any and every body who reach up to the Big Apple does get through. It takes guts. I know plenty fellas who came up here and didn't last a good six months. The place too cold. They feel they're too big to pack grocery shelves or to take a little cleaning work. Missing the woman – all kind of excuse. Not you. You band your belly and now you have your reward.

And talk about coincidence. I got my birth certificate just days before my actual, real birthday. 'We', as in Uncle Hari, said this called for a celebration and started inviting one set of people. A crowded house with music blasting. I told myself it's only one night. Let the old timer have his party. I suspect Uncle Hari had other reasons for inviting his friends around. Sherry's been making a comeback.

Solo, try to stop Ian from calling Sherry all kind of name like Horse Face and Soucouyant.

You feel he will listen to me?

His blood never took to Sherry.

Don't bother with him. If she's the one you want he will have to fall in line.

He nudged me.

I'm so set in my ways I find it hard to adjust. And she done know me inside out. New broom might sweep clean but it's the old broom that know all the little corners.

More Saturdays than not she's by us. Sometimes I come home on a Friday and she's already here. I didn't need to learn my lesson twice. When she's around I make myself scarce. Ian doesn't bother with her. The real change is Katherine. The women them are tight. I overheard Katherine taking Sherry's side in some talk about Uncle Hari's laziness.

Girl, he's your father but if Hari want to see me during the week you don't find he could drive down the road? My days for running behind man done. Why I must always be the one going up and down?

I hear you. They've got to know times have changed. You go, girl.

For the first time in all these years I realised that Katherine probably missed having her mother. Without Sherry she was the only woman in the house. I never thought to ask her about that. All I know is that her mom ups and left Uncle Hari for a rich man and the man didn't want her children around. Even crazy Mammy wouldn't have let that happen. What was the name of that man she liked? Dev? Yeah, Dev. He couldn't come between us.

Party was for one o'clock. They forgot to remind everybody we're talking Eastern Standard Time, not Trini time. All three in the afternoon the first of Uncle Hari's liming partners were only now rocking up. The sound of voices filling the house sent me to my room. Since the Emergency night I get anxious when I'm around too many people. As the house filled up, the tension inside me moved from my feet to my legs and kept climbing. Hopefully downstairs, with plenty ol' talk and rum flowing, no one would even notice I'd checked out. Afterwards I cleaned up and blotted my scalp. They say you get your hair from your mother's side. Well, thank God for that because she has good hair. Thick and black. I wonder if she's gone grey?

Dennis arrived, took up a seat in the living room and didn't move except when he stretched to reach a rum or whiskey bottle. Pluto was supposed to be the guest of honour. Up until the morning he had said yes, he in that, but then work called and he bailed on us. That was fine. I haven't got used to all them gold rings and fat gold chains. But the biggest joke was when a man reached saying Pluto sent him. If it's not too much trouble Pluto would be well glad for a little home-cooked Trini food. And not to worry – he had walked with his own Styrofoam containers. Now that is boldfaceness. You're missing the party but you're sending for food.

People had been invited for lunch. Caribbean people didn't understand what that meant. It wasn't until all past eleven in the night that the last dregs were finally dragging themselves out the house saying this party was the bomb. Everybody put a hand and clean-up didn't take long. By midnight the whole place was back to normal. Uncle Hari slapped me on the back.

You had a good time?

Yeah, man.

I think the last time we had a big lime so was for my fiftieth.

He winked.

But that was just the other day.

Thanks for everything. I wouldn't be here if it wasn't for you.

Well, smile little bit then nah, man. Your face always looking so serious.

He pulled me in for a hug and whispered,

I have a special gift for you. Give everybody a chance to go in their bed. Then we go talk.

I would have preferred to go in my bed same time as everyone else. What kind of gift he had to give me in private? Tiredness was weighing me down. Sleep would be a gift. Not always checking up on me would be a gift. Health insurance would be a gift. The other day I had to go doctor when my cuts were hurting. Only a little infection that a week of antibiotics cured. If I spent fifteen minutes in the doctor's office I spent long. That cost me a day's pay. And the waiting room was packed so you know she's raking it in.

Sherry and Katherine went inside first. Ian was outside taking a smoke.

Hey, Solo. Look, Ian by the gate. He can't hear nothing. Come, let we talk. Man to man.

Man to man is always a bad start.

When you came up you were barely out of Pampers.

Uncle, I was almost nineteen.

Yes, but you was and you wasn't. Anybody could see you didn't have experience.

I blushed so bad my face felt it would burn off. What the hell. Where was this talk going?

Don't take stress.

He wiped his forehead.

Since you come up here, well, it's just that you never bring a girl home. Maybe you have a young lady that you don't want us to know about.

No.

So, normally, by your age.

He took a deep breath.

Look, by your age I was done married. You ain't even try out what it is to have a relationship. I fed up telling Katherine and Ian to carry you out so you could meet people. They tell me if a girl so much as give you a sweet eye you does run for cover one time. Well, mister, you can't hide forever.

It's not that. I'm happy by myself.

Uncle Hari rubbed his chin.

I fixed you up with somebody. She have experience. Maybe once you go with her you will find it easier to check out some of Katherine's friends.

You can't fix me up. How you know if she will like me? And what about me? I mightn't like she either.

Oh, she will like you.

You don't know that.

Trust me.

He moved in closer. I could smell the whiskey.

She's a professional. You understand? But don't hold that against her. She's my good friend. And this is a favour.

Don't say no and make me look bad, nah, man.

I was light-headed, headachy, nauseous and weak all rolled into this one body. Uncle Hari pulled a piece of paper out of his pocket and I glanced at it. In crapaud-foot writing was a name, address and Sunday 4 p.m. He shoved the paper into my jeans pocket.

It will take a good forty-five minutes by subway to reach from here. Relax.

Relax? I didn't know what was more shameful – that he knew I was a virgin or that he'd fixed me up with a hooker. A jamette. The last thing I wanted in this world was to hurt Uncle Hari's feelings but fucking hell. Nah, he gone too far. Only Uncle Hari. Mr Chetan would never in a million years do this. The man gone crazy. I shook my head.

No. This is not happening. Sorry. Night.

Lighten up nah, man. It's no big deal. Enjoy yourself for once.

Night.

All right, all right. You embarrassed. You don't have to be shame around me. We go talk tomorrow. And Solo, one day you will thank me.

My head was reeling as it hit the pillow. No way, no way, no way. I wasn't going by no whore. Nothing could be less sexy. Thankful? I should be thankful that people pitying me? Poor Solo. Can't even get laid. His uncle had to organise a fuck for him.

I dreamt I was in Midtown Manhattan looking for the address on the piece of paper. Freaking nightmare. I was naked – the only person in their birthday suit walking the streets while everybody else was in normal clothes. Her apartment was impossible to find. I would walk up to a building thinking I'd found the correct one only for the numbers to scramble up. The search went on and on. When I finally found the correct door, there wasn't a doorbell.

I woke. The bed was cold and damp. During my dream search for this blasted hooker I had sweated so much that it soaked my T-shirt. The sheet was damp. Even my pillow was damp. Without thinking I fumbled around for my wallet, parted my hair and slid the blade along the scalp. Pure relief flowed through my body and I sank back, exhausted. Paying for sex was for losers who no one would fuck. But why would anyone want to fuck me unless they were being paid? Yeah. I had loser stamped all over my fucking face.

BETTY

Now Solo's immigration was fixed I'm praying he will settle down and look after himself. The hardest thing is accepting that for his peace of mind – his, not mine – I must keep my distance. Mr Chetan bet me a hundred dollars that within a year me and Solo will be talking good again. I hope he wins that bet. It still made me cry to think it could be years before I saw my baby. Meanwhile, every so often, I call Hari to check what's going on. We've buried our quarrel for Solo's sake and, well, as you get older you realise it doesn't make sense holding on to any grudge tight so. And give Jack his jacket. Hari's been more father than uncle to Solo. Strange how life does work out, yes. I never thought I would be saying that about Sunil's wayward brother. I told Hari he's on my prayer list. He laughed. Solo is never out of my prayers. And Mr Chetan. Mr England's on there too but only just and I'm not sure for how much longer. I hurt his feelings when I said that I would rather go to the casino with the ladies than spend the night by him. He's not a big comfort and he's so damn clingy.

This week when I bounced up Tanty as usual at the prayer group she pulled me one side. She had a message for me. The pujari had done a reading.

What is a reading and who is a pujari?

Come to the temple and you go understand everything.

Anyhow, the pujari is like the pundit. When he give a reading is not he who doing the talking. It's really Mudder Kali talking through him. And Betty, Mudder asked for you.

How you mean she asked for me? She said, tell me what happening to Betty Ramdin?

This ain't no joke. The pujari said that I know a woman who is in great need of the cure and I must bring she to the temple. Well, I didn't know is who to bring. He said don't worry. The Mudder will make it known. As soon as he said that your face come in my mind as clear as if you was standing in front me.

Tanty, you're not making sense. I can't tell you the last time I was sick. I don't need a cure.

You might not realise it but you do. And don't think you can fight it. Mudder's calling you.

*

Tanty made it clear. One time visitors were always welcome but to get any real benefit you had to be devoted. Just like Christ doesn't take on people who only remember him when they need something, so Mudder, as they called her, wouldn't give assistance if I didn't come to temple regularly and do all the fast and offerings. Tanty kept pushing her story about me needing a cure. I tired tell she – nothing wrong with me. But she kept jook-jooking me. Mudder knew everything. If she thought I needed a cure then I had something wrong that even the doctors them could not see. They mightn't find out the problem until it was too late. Up to me if I wanted to take that chance.

I dropped Kali into a talk with Mr England the other day to see what he would say.

Oh no. Kali? Betty, don't touch that with a ten-foot bamboo pole. That is for backward people. They pretend to be worshipping but watch them. All they want is to drink rum and carry on bad.

He looked me in my eye.

Why? You worship Kali?

Nah. Tanty in the prayer group was telling me about a friend who went for a second opinion.

A second opinion about what?

Like if you're not sure whether to leave your job. Or you could ask what will happen to a court case coming up. Anything, anything. What will happen to your children.

And what problem you have that you need a second opinion?

None. Just curious.

Don't go. I know what I'm talking about.

He rocked back in the chair.

Let me tell you a secret, young Betty. When they catch Mudder's spirit they carry on wild wild. My grandmother took me to a Kali temple once. When my father found out my grandmother got in plenty hot water. Stay far.

Tanty said that part is what they call vibrating. And they don't take drugs. Tanty especially is not the kind to take anything. She's been dealing with her addict of a son for the longest while.

I don't want you going. In fact, you should stay far from this Tanty person.

Wait a minute, mister. I am the one who does put tea in my cup. You can't come and tell me who to see or where to go. If I want to go to a Kali temple I will drive my car and go there by myself.

I'm trying to protect you and you're carrying on?

He doesn't have to know although the way he's forever texting when we're not together he might very well find out. Me and Tanty can go by ourselves. He does have a point. I don't know what kind of madness happens in a Kali temple. But I'm ready to find out. I've missed my son grow from boy to man. I don't want to miss him getting married and having children. And I'm tired. I want my son back. If two prayers to this Mudder will help then I could do that easy easy.

MR CHETAN

Old fire stick easy fi catch
Falling in love again just like that

Aswad's song has been playing in my head nonstop. It started from the night of Mani's birthday party and it is still going strong. Texts have been flying left, right and centre. Within a week Mani was in my flat looking fit to be eaten raw with slight pepper on the side. I asked what excuse he had given the hubby. He shrugged. Anyway, that was their business. I had prepared a little food and we limed. But, man, between us the pressure was enough to buss a pipe. Once that tap was turned on we flowed in and out of each other for hours. We didn't stop until the well had run dry dry.

I can't lie. I've fallen hard. He's easy to talk to and I can tell him anything. In one man I've got hot and cute – hot with that hard body and cuteness for days with that dimple in his chin. Jackson was a muscle man and maybe he had a slightly better body. But Jackson was a man who always had to be right or have his own way. Mani's not like that. For all the Facebook wildness he's a gentle soul. And he's so cultured and sensitive he has my head giddy. I am bouncing around grinning like a fool. Even Solo said I sounded different on the phone. He made a joke about me finally linking up with a woman in my old age. Two things wrong there. Early forties are only ancient to somebody in their early twenties.

The other issue made me stop and think. It's time he knew.
I wanted to tell the whole world I'm in love. If I can't do that I
should at least tell my boy that I'd found the love of my life, or
rather my first love was back. Before my mind got tied up in
reasons why I shouldn't, I phoned.

> Solo, I have something to tell you. I've been meaning to say
> something for a while.

I took a deep breath.

> You know how you were joking that you thought I'd finally
> found a woman in my old age?

> I was right? Tell me I was right.

> I have somebody. But it's not a she. His name is Mani. Long
> time now I've wanted to tell you I'm gay.

> Okay. It's not a big deal.

I couldn't believe my ears.

> You're sure?

> Yeah. Like you forget I living in New York? That's nothing
> to worry yourself about. How'd you meet Mani?

When we finished talking I had to sit down and take it in. I felt
light, I felt happy and I had tears wetting up my face at the same
time. All these years hiding, afraid anybody suspected, and Solo
could not care less. I wish he was here so I could hug him up
tight tight. Without thinking I went in the kitchen and started
pulling out things to bake. Solo loved to huff down brownies.

While I measured out the flour, baking powder, cocoa and sugar I put on the TV for background noise. Headline news was that the leaders of the main churches – Catholics, Muslims, Hindus – were warning the government not to give the LGBTQ population protection under the Equal Opportunity Act. Imagine that. An hour hadn't passed since I had come out to Solo and I had to see all this hatefulness. How could a man of God demand not protecting people like me, saying we're 'infecting' society? Wasn't religion supposed to do the opposite? When Miss Betty asks me why I'm always hiding myself I will remind her that apparently, I am not a child of any god.

*

I've talked about Mani to Solo and Miss Betty. Jackson they never knew. At least with Mani they know he exists and I shared a selfie of us. I wanted him to meet Miss Betty but lover boy said he'd rather spend every single minute we had alone, just the two of us. At least three times a week he's down south. He is my world. I want to do things with him like go out for food or go for a drive to the beach but he has zero interest in leaving the apartment. And he gets away with it. Soong's Great Wall is my favourite Chinese restaurant and I am always begging for us to go. Guess what he brought with him the last time he came down? Chinese takeaway and yes, it was from Soong's.

Things have been going sweet for the past six months so I don't know why I went with my fast self and asked Mani how come he's with me. His husband was rich, better-looking – better everything than me. So why was his naked ass in my bed? I guess I was hoping he would say because he loved me

more than Patrick. Instead he made a foolish joke about the
first cock you get is always the sweetest.

> Eh, Mani, watch my face. I look dotish to you? I need to
> know where this is going.

> Why you're throwing talk like that?

> You know what I think? I think you're with me because
> your husband's stepping out on you. And you probably feel
> sorry for me.

He rolled off my chest.

> I don't know. Maybe it's both things. We had unfinished
> business.

He stared at the ceiling.

> And so you know, I don't have a problem with Patrick
> sleeping with other men.

I pulled his shoulder to make him turn around and face me.

> Forgive my simple mind but why all you bothered to get
> married if he horning you and you horning him?

> Marriage doesn't mean you only have sex with one person
> for the rest of your life. He sees other people. I see other
> people.

I had to laugh.

> So, wait nah. I am 'other people'? How much other people
> you have?

I'm here all the time. When would I be able to see anybody
else? There's just Patrick. I hope you don't think I'm going
to leave him.

Now I had to sit up.

Wow. All you does really do things different north of the
Caroni River, yes.

He grinned. The dog. I wasn't about to show him that he'd
landed a body blow.

Well, Mani, you're honest. I'll give you that. You don't give a
man any illusions.

He didn't look at me and the grinning stopped.

I've wanted to say something for a while but I never had
the chance. So, now you know. But I like seeing you. You're
cool with that, Chetan?

You ain't easy. Next thing you go tell me you want me and
you to sleep with all your other people.

He rolled his eyes. I wasn't finished.

I'm just asking. I don't know too much about all this kind of
sophisticated arrangements. Not my scene.

He reached for my hand.

Sweetie. Cool yourself.

A stronger man would have shooed him out and deleted his
number. Forget I loved him from the time we were small. He's
a married man in a complicated arrangement who had made

his loyalties as clear as the Nylon Pool water. But I wasn't strong and I did love him. I took his hand and sunk back in the bed. He dropped some hot and sweaty action on me and when he was ready to leave I kissed him like he was emigrating to Australia.

*

Until Mani reached on the scene I'd been going about my business thinking I was okay. Then braps, just so he landed up in my life. Even after he'd said his piece about loyalty to Patrick I didn't want to give him up. I am in love with him. Life's not easy. I find a wonderful man like Mani but something's in the way. I don't want to grow old sucking cock while parked up in the middle of a cane field. Too grim to even think about. And with crime out of control these days I know doing that is asking for a bandit to put a bullet through my head. That is no joke. I've read the blogs and Jackson had said the same thing. If the police think a murder victim is a gay man they don't bother to investigate too closely. I told Miss Betty all this only for her to twist up her mouth.

Let me remind you that your head ain't make to wear hat alone. What, the books and the TV are hugging you up in the night? Plus, you were stalking the man from long time before you and he got together. As soon as he said jump you were there asking how high.

So what you think? I should stop seeing him?

You have anybody else in the wings?

Not really.

Then wash your foot and jump in. You're playing with fire. But you done know that long time.

SOLO

It's not far but it's far enough. And most of all it's mine. When I close that door nobody can bother me and I don't have to hide nothing. Of course I talked to Mr Chetan and he said it was the right move for me although I don't know what he will think when he gets pictures of the apartment. He should be here. The way he has his apartment put away nice he could do the same for me. Uncle Hari wasn't so keen and he tried all kind of thing to get me to stay. He didn't like my block. It looked dangerous. I'm ten minutes from him but he said that ten minutes separated normal people from the hooligans and them. He said the building wasn't sanitary because he saw two cockroaches. Once you spray it's not a problem. But he made me feel bad like I was leaving him to live at the North Pole. Thing is, I knew I had to find my own place even if it wasn't the greatest. Shortly after I got my status fixed up, Sherry moved back in full time. Next thing you know Ian moved out to live with this girl because he's sure sure this is the one. And the way them always all over each other maybe she is it. And I see them every week. Come high, come low, we all go back home on Sundays to lime.

They're always chooking me to find out if I'm dating. I said I'm seeing someone but it's nothing serious. A half truth. Must be a year now since Uncle Hari fixed me up with Loretta and she and I now have an understanding. I see her regularly. It's helped me to stop cutting. When I feel like I'm tied up with

barb wire inside and I can't break out I get on the train from
Queens to Brooklyn.

*

Today the barb wire was choking me real hard, ramming into
my flesh. When I tumbled out on Flatbush Avenue my throat
was dry dry. Lucky thing my feet know Stop & Shop all by
they-self. Blindfold me and I can still find the cake section.
Aisle 3. Sometimes, if the shop's quiet, I close my eyes tight
tight and try to find a birthday cake. And candles. Can't forget
the candles.

Pushing the buzzer to Loretta's apartment above Eddy's
Laundry & Dry Cleaning sinks the wires deeper into my brain.
I'm grinding my teeth. Her voice through the intercom tight-
ens the wires banding my belly. My brain's clogged. By the time
Loretta opens her front door with the peeling dark green paint,
I'm no longer in pain. I am all pain.

Hi, how are you? Good to see you, Solo.

I am nodding, my eyes on her tired face, afraid to take in the
sight of her pale boobies or her shaved punanny through the
piece of red nightie she's wearing.

You've finished working on that new health centre in
Manhattan?

I wanted her to see me as a real man, with a little swagger, cool
as this fall evening. Instead I opened my mouth and all kind
of gibberish fell out. The mirror reflects a skinny Indian, eyes
big big like he's just seen a jumbie.

For me?

I give her the Stop & Shop bag and a small envelope. Although she knows exactly what's in the bag she plays along and acts surprised.

Oh my God. A birthday cake! One sec. I'll take it out the box.

I hang up my battered jacket and go through to the bedroom. The double bed is pushed up to the wall. She has crammed in a small, white table next to a plastic chair. I have that same chair in my apartment. My socks and sneakers I push under the bed. Loretta's already singing in her off-key voice,

Happy birthday to you.
Happy birthday to you.
Happy birthday, dear Solo.
Happy birthday to you.

Carefully, she rests the cake with five candles on the little table. Once I didn't walk with a cake and she had said, no problem, honey, and shoved an old birthday candle in a chocolate chip muffin. I'm shame to say but I remember letting out one loud steupse. The woman was only trying to please. But no. I needed a whole cake and five candles.

Make a wish. But don't tell me or it won't come true. Go on, sweetheart.

I bent down and sucked in the air around me. In one breath I out all the candles while same time spraying spit everywhere.

Loretta's clapping.

Wow, that's great. What a good boy. Good boy. Solo's a
good boy.

I can hear Mammy saying, make a wish. Apparently Daddy
used to tell me, Solo, boy, you go get married, drink rum, have
children and then dead.

I don't have to ask. Loretta's fingers are already undoing the
special belt I wear for us. She's ordering me, take down your
pants. Now. I tell her no.

Take off your pants. If I say get 'em off, then get 'em off now.
You're disobeying me?

I turn away. The belt lands on the back of my legs.
Bradaps.
Then a next one.
Bradaps.
Is licks in my tail. The belt swings in time with her words.

Take. Them. Off.

She lashes me even while I'm trying to be a good boy and pull
down my jeans.

Take that.

Bradaps.
When it's bad the pain inside coils the barb wire tight right
through my body. Loretta knows exactly how to cut me loose.
The belt swipes my bare bamsee and the noise in my head dies
down. I try to pick the jeans off the floor and connect with a
next lash.

Bradaps.

I need to hang up my clothes. That's what I'm wearing to go home. She can see what I'm doing but that's not stopping her. I fling the jeans and they land on the chair.
Bradaps.

Oh Lord. You hit my balls.

Can't take a little lash? Call yourself a real man?

Bradaps.
Bradaps.

Get that shirt off.

Between lashing me the linoleum on the floor was taking some good licks too. I wondered if the people in the laundry downstairs does hear what going on.

Solo! Come here. Take it like a real man.

For a slim thing she could well hit hard. I got one hard lash across my back and before I straightened up a next one flicked my leg. As I turned to one side she came again strong.
Bradaps.

Please don't hit me. I promise to behave.

Bradaps.

You're a pussy.

Bradaps.

Pussy boy.

Bradaps.

Stand up and take your licks like a real man. Pussy boy.

Now this was cut ass. My skin's on fire and I'm bawling. Just when I thought, nah, I can't take it, the blows soften and then stop. The brain fog is clearing. Each welt on my body has cut the barb wire. Quiet quiet in my ears I hear her,

You're ready? I want to fuck you.

I curl up on the bed. It's hard to see through the tears. Does she know how grateful I am? Beautiful Loretta. The flimsy nightie's gone and she's smiling like an angel. A dirty, kiss-my-ass angel all the way from St Lucia to the Statue of Liberty. I for one real happy she's here. Is not any and every woman will give you solid licks then fuck your ass because that is exactly what you're begging for. She looked me straight in the eye.

I'm going to fuck you so hard you'll be limping all the way back to Queens.

Give Loretta her due. That woman does keep she word.

BETTY

Mr England's always harassing my soul about where I'm going and who I'm with. Like I does ever be with anybody. I could be going to lime with his own cousin and his face would set up like he's being abandoned. And he hates Mr Chetan. I'm ashamed to admit it but the other day Mr England turned up unexpectedly and I hid inside. It was the first Saturday I had had to myself in a long time. Lucky thing I was staring out the kitchen window when he pulled up. My house is always locked up tight. The gate was locked and the house was locked. I sat down at the kitchen table and stayed quiet. He beeped his horn. He called out. I heard him shouting to the neighbour who was probably taking the breeze in his porch. As my car was there the neighbour said I should be home but then again I could have gone out with a friend. Mr England said he would wait. I was inside hearing all this while trying not to even breathe hard. Suddenly I remembered. My phone. I flicked it to silent and have mercy I didn't do it a second too soon. His missed call flashed up on my screen. A whole half hour, thirty full minutes, that man sat waiting before giving up on the chance to bother my soul.

This Sunday all I said was I have church things to do and I'm busy busy when in fact I've decided to buss it to the temple with Tanty. With this Kali business being a little shady, I thought they would worship in the bush somewhere. Instead we landed up in the heart of busy Tunapuna. I heard the temple before I went inside. Endless drumming – different from the deep, full sound of a tassa drum but, man, the rhythm was hard. Women were singing some high-pitched songs in Hindi. The only word I recognised was Kali. It sounded like they were throwing an Indian fete. And Tanty should've warned me about the no shoes policy. It was kind of late but I had a quick look. Thankfully even if the foot was looking dry my toenails were decent. My dry foot aside it was the black pants and green top I was wearing that made me easy to spot. Most, including Tanty, were in yellow. The place was a sea of yellow dhotis, yellow T-shirts, yellow saris, yellow pants, yellow skirt and yellow top. Even though I'm Indian I felt out of place.

All that rhythm was coming from three young fellas playing the flattish tappu drums. In front the drummers were two women sitting on a mat, singing into a mike. From nearby someone was blowing a conch shell but I couldn't see who it was. The singing and the drumming licking my chest had me dizzy. As we inched closer to the centre, I saw smoke coming from little flames set up all around the walls. Same time my nose started stinging from the smell of burning camphor. Then I spotted them. Women and men, eyes closed, shaking and throwing themselves about like they didn't care if they hit the concrete. A woman was flinging her long hair all about. Another one was holding her hands in prayer but shaking up like she gone mad. Suddenly a woman bawled out and that started more people screaming. They scream and then stop, scream and stop. It didn't sound like pain – more like pushing something out from inside your body. The drumming and the singing had them in a trance and, with their eyes shut tight, every man Jack looked like they were high. I leaned against Tanty.

That young girl going to get a buss head unless she stops flinging herself about.

They have people whose job is to make sure they don't hurt themselves. If they get hurt that mean they disobeyed Mudder. Maybe they drank rum before they came temple.

So this is the vibrating?

She nodded.

If you're true, pure, and you take the oath, you might feel Mudder in you and that is what does cause you to vibrate.

You ever vibrate?

How you mean, girl. I done do that plenty times.

Looking at them people lost in Mudder's spirit had me jealous. I don't know how to explain it. The place had a serious vibe but at the same time this vibrating was like a fete.

I picked through the yellow sea. Tanty had told me but I was still surprised to see two dougla women and a half-Chinee-looking man vibrating with all these Indian people. If they didn't drink rum or smoke weed, what did Mudder do to free them up so? That is what I wanted to know because even though I hadn't taken the oath I was feeling the vibes. Maybe it was the Shakti. Whatever it was I felt a connection, like a heat in my body. And it made me wonder what else was happening right here in Trinidad that I didn't know nothing about.

*

Hari knew that Solo was looking for his own little place but when time came for the boy to move out he took it bad. You would think Solo was his only child the way he was carrying on upset and depressed. Imagine I had to talk him through that. Me, who was missing Solo for years. Whenever he was down Hari would pick up the phone. I could never mind talking about Solo and it made me grateful to know how much Hari cared for the boy. Of course I didn't know the area where Solo was moving to but I was busy telling Hari not to worry. Solo will visit. Hari was always thinking people will take advantage of the boy.

From quite Trinidad I had to remind him you can't live your children's (or my child's) life for them. They must do their own thing. I felt like saying, now you know how my heart was breaking when he left my house still a teenager. I felt like saying it but I didn't. Two of we old now for that kind of botheration. Hari even invited me to come spend a two weeks by them. I said nah. I don't want to upset Solo. When he ready to see me he will come back. One day. I pray for that. Now Mr Chetan – he is the one that should go to see Solo. Tickets to New York real cheap these days. Everybody does be going to see family and shop until they drop. Mind you, I can't say if Mr Chetan will have the time to go New York. He might have other plans. I never know what's going on with him. All I can do is keep him in my prayers.

Tanty can't see me in prayer meeting without digging me to go temple again. I want to go and I don't want to go. No question they had a strong vibe there. Problem is if my church people or my neighbours found out I go to Kali temple that would be a next set of commess. And don't forget Mr England. He's not keen either. The church will say that worshipping Mudder is not the truth because the only truth is through Jesus Christ our Saviour. I'm sure the neighbours already have plenty to say behind my back as I live by myself. Worse yet, if they so much as hear a peep about Kali it would be, oh, that Betty Ramdin into black magic. Deedee, Gloria, even Mr Chetan – I can't see any of them too liking the idea neither. I could make the Presbyterian church my whole life and nobody would make an objection because that is correct devotion. This other thing's real different, too wild. Nobody must find out if I go Kali temple. Nobody. And that's only making me want to go even more.

I've heard of Mudder healing people when the doctors them clueless. Half the people in the temple came to ask Mudder to find them a good husband or help their children pass exams. What if I asked Mudder to bring Solo home? I'm so tired. Maybe it's my fate to be alone or stuck with people like Mr England sucking the life out of me. Some nights I cry until I'm exhausted from bawling into my pillow. I've lost my family. Mr Chetan's gone. Solo's gone. I don't have a soul left. Yes, I can manage. But what exactly is the point?

*

The temple was overcrowded. Tanty had tempted me back to hear what a real Indian pujari from India had to say. He wasn't speaking yet so Tanty and I made offerings to Mudder – a candle and cherries from my tree. It wasn't so long ago that

I was frightened to even look at this murti with her tongue hanging out, all them skulls and blood dripping down. Now I understand that, yes, she is terrifying but that is on purpose. Mudder is the destroyer of evil. She's also a mother and woman. Her foot is on Shiva for women like me to know that we don't have to take shit from no man. At least that is how I understand it. One man in particular is trying to put his foot on me. We go see about that.

I stood close to the drummers hoping the beat would drum out whatever was bothering my soul. Around me the incense and camphor were starting to burn my eyes. A woman vibrating near me jerked back and forth. Suddenly she dropped down, legs in the air, and started to bawl and push like baby coming, only her belly was flat as a sada roti. I was so fixed on the woman that I didn't notice the pujari until he put his hand on my shoulder. He was vibrating. Still in a trance, he led me to Mudder's feet, lit a camphor ball and put it on the brass plate.

> The Dark Mudder's calling you to do away with impure
> thoughts and deeds. Surrender to the loving kindness of the
> Mudder. If you are faithful and show your devotions she
> will help you see the truth inside yourself.

He chanted something in Hindi which I didn't understand and pushed the plate with the burning camphor up in my face. I was real scared because I had seen others put the burning camphor ball straight in their mouth. If it scalded me that was it. But man, I told myself, Betty, take a chance. I picked up the camphor ball.

I'm ready.

I closed my eyes and threw the flaming ball on my tongue and shut my mouth fast fast.

I didn't feel a thing.

I opened my eyes, took the camphor out my mouth and put it on the same brass tray. For the first time in I can't tell you how long I smiled from my heart. I wanted to vibrate, to dance away all the worries I was holding. In that crowded, loud, smoky temple I suddenly felt strong. I let the drum beat rock me until the energy, the Shakti, was flowing through my veins, warming me from inside, and when it reached my navel it exploded and I jumped up. I closed my eyes. Whatever was going to happen would happen.

I surrender.

My long hair is loose and the breeze is blowing through it. The white horse I am riding is going too fast but I hold on. When I swing my cutlass is not just one tree falling. The whole forest just drop down. At the top of the mountain I climb on a man and we fuck till I scream. Mudder lifts me as if I don't weigh an ounce and in the middle of the sky her bloody tongue licks me and I want to wrap myself around her leg. I pick up the baby and put him inside my dress. A hurricane is coming.

MR CHETAN

I passed by Miss Betty to return her dish. It's been in my cup-board since I don't know when. Soon as I stepped inside she dropped a quarrel on me. Oh, I don't make time for her any more. Everything is Mani this, and Mani that, like he is the only person on the planet. Thing is, I don't always know when he's coming over. How I'm suppose fix up a lime with Miss B when he might be free? Well, she didn't like that at all at all. Her mouth swell up like two bullfrogs.

Stop acting like a love-sick boy half your age.

That's not me.

Then stick must be break in your ears. I tired telling you don't build your whole life around somebody like him. But you're too damn stubborn.

It's a miracle we've found each other after all these years. I'm not giving him up. And if you ask me, that so-called marriage ain't all that solid. He tells me more about what going on in his life than he tells Patrick.

I ain't able with all this foolishness. I'm making coffee. You want one?

She walked to the kitchen with me seething behind her.

I will admit that when it started he wasn't serious. But oh gosh, man. That was nearly a year now.

He ever tell you he love you like he mean it?

I paused before showing my hand.

Every single day.

You're hearing things.

I rolled my eyes.

Miss B, believe what you want. I don't know why you're in such a bad mood.

Okay, but when he breaks your heart don't come running by me.

She handed me a cup of coffee. My hands were trembling with anger.

Since when I does come running by you with my problems?

Oh, sorry. I don't know the name but there was a man before Mani who left you high and dry. I didn't check on you then? Bring soup for you? It look like what I do don't count for nothing.

You see me, I just came to give you your dish and I think I should head out.

Yes. I think you should do that for truth.

For the first time ever I stormed out and didn't give her a kiss.

*

Mani and I had a good ol' talk remembering Point Fortin, the backwater we grew up in as children. Now it's a busy town with smooth barber-green roads all the way through. When we lived there it was a little village nobody bothered with. And it was a hassle to reach. People used to say that instead of potholes in the road we had a little bit of road around the potholes. Mani hasn't gone back since his family moved away. Mine might still be there. Or not. Over the years I've driven through but never stopped. Patrick's away for Thanksgiving so we have the whole weekend together. Left up to Mani, all he would do is go to the gym and relax at home. I think because he has so many events for work, when he's free he doesn't like going out. But I need to go out. I begged, darling doux-doux Mister Hotness, let we check out Point Fortin nah. I had to promise to give him a massage in the evening and for brunch he wanted sada roti, tomatoes choka, curry pumpkin and baigan choka. Mani was only bussing style because I would've done all that for him anyway and he knows it.

He finished at the gym earlier than I expected and the food wasn't ready.

You go chill out and I'll finish.

I can help. My hand ain't break.

Okay, you do the tomatoes choka. Let me concentrate on the roti. The baigan choka and the pumpkin done already and when I tell you the thing lash.

I got a high five and then kneaded the flour. While the flour was soaking Mani roasted the tomatoes directly on the gas flame. He let them cook without too much charring and I helped remove the skins. He mashed them to a pulp. I still feel washed with happiness when he's near me doing these ordinary things. Chopped onions, half a hot pepper and some minced garlic went on top the tomatoes.

You know how to chunkay the tomatoes?

Listen, I watched my mother cook so don't play like you're the only one who knows how to chunkay.

He poured smoking hot oil over the tomato mixture and I watched as he let the oil lightly fry the onions before mixing again with a touch of salt. He tasted it then offered me a little tups on a fork. Nice. Almost as good as my baigan.

While the tawah was heating up on the stove I divided my dough into three smaller balls. Mani asked how I managed to keep my tawah so shiny. I winked. He doesn't have to know all my secrets. (Sandpaper grade 180.) I rolled the first ball into a thin circle and laid it out flat on the hot tawah to cook.

Let me see if your roti going to swell.

Mani, stop putting your goat mouth on my roti. Please.

After about thirty seconds I flipped it over for the other side to cook. Then came the true test. I pulled the tawah to one side, exposing the naked gas flame.

Look and learn, Mani. Look and learn.

As I rotated the edges of the roti on the flame they puffed up perfectly. He kissed my nose.

You should open a food place or do catering.

I can't take that stress.

I was rolling out the second roti when my cell phone rang.

My hands in flour. Bring the phone and show me, please.

It was Miss Betty. Since our quarrel I hadn't called. This was the first time she was contacting me.

Talk to the woman. The two of you behaving so childish.

I didn't. Within seconds the phone pinged.

This woman like she won't leave me in peace. Let me see the message, please.

Otside ur house. U home? Hv sorrel 4 u.

He looked up.

Tell her to come in. I'd love to finally meet her.

I sighed.

Okay. Message her back and say I'm home.

Mani opened the door and introduced himself. I must say she was on manners.

You're cooking? I'm only passing through. This is my first set of sorrel drink before the Christmas rush starts and I know how you like it.

I looked at her holding two bottles of red sorrel and then looked at Mani. He nodded and smiled.

Stay, Miss B. I only have one more roti to cook and then we can eat.

We crowded around my tiny dining table and began dishing out. Miss Betty tore a piece of roti.

Your roti come out soft and nice. If you didn't have choka I could eat it dry so.

I done know my roti is the bomb but I didn't want to be obnoxious. Mani and I broke off a piece each and ate it by itself.

I tired tell him he should go into business. The man hand sweet. And no matter what state the economy's in, Trini people will spend money on food.

I rolled my eyes and poured the sorrel. Mani licked his lips.

Betty, this sorrel has a mean kick to it.

Fresh nutmeg.

Mani took another sip.

If it wasn't still morning I would sneak a little rum in my glass. But even without any liquor it's perfect.

Miss Betty was lapping up the praise. In no time the two of them were chatting away and I could barely add more than 'huh' to the conversation. Out of the corner of his eye Mani gave me a sly wink. Between bites the two of them argued about the latest layoff of government workers. Somehow from that they got to talking about parang music. As I scooped up the last of the tomatoes choka with a piece of roti it hit me that the only thing missing was Solo. If he was sitting here the moment would be perfect. I took a picture of the sorrel bottle with his mammy's hand-written label and sent it with my note:

U R missing out.
Come back 4 Xmas.

He texted back same time.

Will think about it. Possible.

BETTY

After weeks of avoiding him, Mr England catch me home. When I tell you the man looked bad. His clothes were all ramfled up and like he hadn't shaved in days. I offered him coffee but he didn't want anything except to have a heart-to-heart. I braced myself.

Don't give me that foolishness. I'm not asking you to marry me right now. I'm willing to wait. What more you want? Tell me. I'll do anything you want.

I told you already. It's nothing about you.

I'm not buying that. What it is you want that I'm not giving you? Tell me so I can do it.

He reached out and held my hands.

Betty, things were going so good. Now you don't want me. Tell me what to do. I'll do whatever you want.

I felt so bad I started to backtrack.

I'm sorry. I don't mean to hurt you.

You have nothing to say sorry for. Whatever was going on these past few weeks we can put it behind us and move forward. You're the one for me, Betty. The only one.

He stayed for dinner and I let him have dessert. I knew I was setting myself up for trouble. This was not what I wanted and I had to find the courage to end it tonight self. While he was snoring I tiptoed out the bedroom. From the cupboard I took the little Mudder murti Tanty had given me. I put it on the coffee table, lit a candle in front it, kneeled and began chanting the mantra:

> *Om Jayanti Mangala Kaali*
> *Bhadra Kali Kapalini Durga*
> *Kshama Shivaa Dhaatri*
> *Svaha Svadha namo-stu-te*

I can't say it's doing the things Tanty claims – like removing all darkness and impure thoughts from my life. For me it's a way to calm right down. I chanted must be two times and I stopped. The tappu drums were missing. A quick look on YouTube and I was swaying and rocking to the beat.

> *Om Jayanti Mangala Kaali*
> *Bhadra Kali Kapalini Durga*

I begged Mudder. If you're so powerful, why you don't bring back my son? Eh? Bring him back to me nah. Please.

> *Kshama Shivaa Dhaatri*
> *Svaha Svadha namo-stu-te*

I let the beat and the chanting take over and danced between the couch and the chairs and I didn't give a damn what I hit and what fall down. Mudder was vibrating in me, cleansing my mind and emptying out my body.

What the ass happening here? Betty! What you doing?
Betty! Is this some kind of obeah you working?

I knew he was talking to me but he could go to hell. I started
my mantra again.

Om Jayanti Mangala Kaali

Stop this blasted voodoo! What you think you doing?

I dropped to the floor and rolled around, still chanting.

Bhadra Kali Kapalini Durga

Betty, you're frightening me. Stop this nonsense now. Stop
it. This is black magic.

I felt him grab me but Mudder told me to stop being afraid.
With him or without him I'm just as alone and lonely. I don't
need this blasted man. I bit his arm.

What the fuck? You bit me. Why did you do that? I can't
believe this is happening.

Later, when the spirit had left, I looked around. Mr England
was gone. I don't think he'll be back.

SOLO

New York real big but where I'm living feels like a village. The people in the laundry and the bodega know my face and always say hello. When I walk around I feel comfortable that I know the place. Although my apartment is not the best I realise nothing's stopping me from giving it a lick of paint and fixing a few small things. The landlord's one cheapskate and I'm fed up asking him. The way I see it, I'll spend a little bit of money and feel a much bigger amount of happiness if I brighten up the place. Give it a month and I should have everything the way I want. Uncle Hari said he will come over and help. I know him. He will help with his mouth. I will be doing all the work and he will be sitting down ol' talking and laughing at his own jokes. I've been begging Mr Chetan to visit. He could stay with me. I don't mind sleeping on the couch and giving him my room. He sent two photos I'd asked for – a recent one of him and an old one of the two of us. I'm getting them printed on canvas and they'll be the first pictures I put up. Next Sunday everyone is going for lunch wearing white and we'll take family photos. Hopefully I'll get good shots so they can be printed and hung as well.

I hardly ever go by Uncle Hari them during the week but he wanted help fixing up Ian's old room. I went after work to see what we had to do. It must have been about six, six thirty maybe, when I rocked up. Sherry wanted to feed me straight away. I never say no to free food – especially from this house. That reminds me – I must look on Atlantic Avenue for frozen cascadoux. Don't ask me how to cook that fish but I volunteered to make it one Sunday. I'll have to call Mr Chetan for some cooking tips. Anyhow, I wasn't there a good five minutes when the phone rang for me. It's a good while I've been in my own place so I thought Sherry was making joke. And besides, who rings on a land line? I don't even have one. But she whispered – it's your mother calling. I rolled my eyes but Uncle Hari gave me a look. I took the phone.

Hello, Solo? That's you, Solo?

Mammy?

Solo, darling. He's gone.

She burst into tears.

What you talking about? Who gone where?

Mr Chetan.

I could barely understand what she was talking about because she was bawling hard hard.

A break-in. You know Trinidad. They couldn't just take what they wanted and leave people in peace.

She blew her nose.

What are you saying?

He's dead, Solo. They gone and stabbed him up right there.

She started bawling again.

No. You've made a mistake.

It's true.

No.

It's true, Solo.

No. They made a mistake. It's not him. I got a text from him yesterday.

No, son. I'm talking the truth. I know he was like a father to you. I'm so sorry.

No. I don't believe you. It's somebody else in his apartment.

Hari there? Put Hari on the phone.

Uncle Hari and Sherry were staring at me. I handed over the phone and sat down. It wasn't true. It couldn't be true. My phone showed he'd texted a joke at 2.30 p.m. yesterday. Trinidad was having some serious flooding but you know Trinis. Always making kicks no matter how bad things get.

Sign outside MANDY'S ROTI SHOPPE
after the flood:
CLOSED.
WATER MORE THAN FLOUR.

One minute he's sending jokes and now he's gone? He can't be.
I didn't cry. Over and over I asked Uncle Hari if he was sure that that is what Mammy said. Mr Chetan? My Mr Chetan? Dead? That can't be right. Uncle Hari was talking. Sherry was talking. I couldn't understand a word they were saying. My

Mr Chetan? Can't be. He's gone? I won't ever see him again? I kept telling myself that this was not happening. No. This was not happening. Mr Chetan cannot be dead. Mammy made a mistake. Not him. Not. Him. A scream was building up inside me and I started heaving. My entire body was on fire. I wanted to go home. I needed to go home. Right now.

PART THREE

SOLO

The moon can run but day will always catch it. I was back home for all the wrong reasons without time to think. We were up and down all over. As this was a murder, Mr Chetan's body went to the Forensic Science Centre in town, near Federation Park. Mammy parked the car and the smell hit me. The place was vamping.

Oh gosh, what's smelling so bad?

I'm afraid to know.

A man who was walking in the same time overheard us talking.

Wait till you go in the back. You will need a tub of Vicks up each nostril to remain in that room.

He wasn't wrong. But before that we sat down and waited. And waited. They had insisted we reach for 8 a.m. but 8 a.m. came and went. Nine came and went. Ten and still nothing happened. All this time we were in the reception area with that stench coming through. Plus, the formaldehyde was smelling strong. None of this felt real. I was here but not here. My head knew Mr Chetan was dead and his body was in the back somewhere. Only my head though. The rest of me was numb.

From what other people told us this place didn't work weekends and public holidays so some of the bodies like Mr

Chetan's had been stored elsewhere for the last three days. Mammy asked if I wanted to leave for lunch. I rolled my eyes. Who could think of eating? That smell was making a man feel nauseous.

My first full day in Trinidad and I'd landed up in this awful place. Me and Mammy are together after so long and I didn't know what to say to her. I'm trying not to think about why we're here so I played on my phone. She stared at nothing. No one in this room was happy to be here and on top of that to be waiting so long. The girls them behind the counter were the only people we were seeing and they started getting abuse. An old fella told them that they didn't care about poor people and how they were disrespecting all of us this Tuesday morning.

This centre only have fancy name to fool people. I lost my sister and all you have she in this nasty place stinking to high heaven. Man, all you can't treat people family so. I wouldn't wish this on my neighbour's maga dog who thief my chicken.

Well, the whole room cracked up and that broke the tension for a little bit.

After midday they made an announcement. Finally. And hear this: the reason we were all waiting was because no pathologist had turned up for work. The main man was off sick and the next one was off island. If we could hold some strain the Tobago pathologist was flying in now and everybody would get their case sorted today, please God. I thought Trinidad was better than this.

Two men steupsed and said they were waiting outside to see when this pathologist reaching. A lady said she was calling

CNC3, i95.5 radio and Ian Alleyne from Synergy TV because joke is joke. This government didn't have mercy for the horrors we were going through losing a loved one. On top of the distress all of we were facing they were making us hang around because nobody came to work today? What kind of madness was this? While she was shouting inside I heard cussing coming from outside. In the middle of all this confusion a young girl ran in shouting,

Fight break out. Help!

Straight away half the room emptied and the rest of us were looking through the windows to check who beating who. Cars were blocking my view. All I could hear was your mother fucking this and your mother fucking that. I stood up to get a better look but Mammy pulled my hand.

Stay out of whatever commess going on out there.

I gave her one stink cut eye and shook off her hand. Who she think she talking to? For spite I went by the door. She came close.

These days all kind of people does be carrying gun. Next thing a stray bullet hit you.

Don't tell me what to do. I've been looking after myself for years.

She sat back down quiet quiet. Police came and parted the fight. From what I could hear it was between a father and a wife over funeral arrangements for a body awaiting an autopsy. I took a seat, leaving an empty chair between me and Mammy, and went back to my phone. She didn't bother me again except once she offered me a Dinner Mint. I said no.

It wasn't until well after three that they called us to come identify the body so they could do what they had to do. I've watched endless TV shows with autopsies so I thought I knew what to expect. Well, TV is TV. Talk about sickening. The place was stink, stink, stink. Gurneys with dead bodies all over the place pushed up any old how. Every one of them, including our Mr Chetan, was covered with bloody sheets. And the rank smell, oh Lord. If somebody asked me what I thought hell looked and smelt like, I would show them this room. I glanced at Mammy. She was totally cool when she identified the body. Afterwards she ran to the washroom and was there long long. When she came out I could see her face was fresh red from crying. Me? I was okay for now but I wanted a razor blade bad. Thing is, I told Mr Chetan that I'd stopped cutting long time and that is the truth. This is the first time in ages I was tempted. For his sake I'm going to hold out or at least try.

We didn't get to sign off the body for burial until after five when it was starting to get dark. All the time we were in that horrible place we'd barely said two words. Plenty things were on my mind to ask Mammy yet she was the absolute last person I wanted giving me the details on how Mr Chetan ended up here. If she feel that I'm in Trinidad to talk to she nice nice she have another thing coming. Jesus, why they couldn't even cover the man with a clean sheet? Part of me was relieved we weren't talking. Prick me with a pin and I might have disgraced myself by crying like a little boy in front of all those people.

When we eventually hit the road back to San Fernando the traffic wasn't as bad as I remembered. A fair bit of the highway looked newly paved. Endless expensive cars were zipping about or maybe I just never noticed them when I was a kid. I tried to concentrate on the changes as we drove south. No new hospital, road or shopping mall could take away the pain of all the years I had spent away not seeing Mr Chetan, only to come back now he was gone. He's really dead? Yes. I saw the body. If someone offered me a pill to blank out the memory of him on that gurney, but it would cost five years off my life, I would have swallowed the damn thing now for now. I shut my eyes to see him alive, reading a book in the hammock on a Sunday with his glass of rum punch at the side. I would get restless in the afternoon and bother him to play chess. He always had time for me. More than that, he was always happy to be with me. Mammy interrupted my thoughts to ask if I had funeral clothes.

What happen? You don't think I have clothes? How much money you making?

She took a quick look at me sideways.

What kind of question is that, Solo?

You're the one asking me if I have clothes when I'm probably making more money than you.

I only wanted to know if in the rush you brought a dark pants and a good shirt.

All right, let us get something straight one time. If this didn't happen you would never find me here. I came for Mr Chetan and once we're done with the funeral I'm dusting it back to New York. I didn't come here for you.

She remained quiet. I looked out the window. Blood and silence were pounding like a steelpan in my ears.

Can I put on the radio?

She whispered,

Go ahead. Do what you want.

Only when the light came on as she opened her car door did I risk checking her face. She looked beaten. I felt sorry for raising my voice earlier but not sorry enough to apologise. All I wanted was a shower to get the smell of that place out of my clothes, my hair, my skin. Tomorrow we're tackling the funeral arrangements. I'm not looking forward to any of that. I don't remember anything about my daddy's funeral. I wish I did. This is real pressure.

BETTY

We ain't big people that the police need to worry will make papers. For that you have to know who to call up to get justice. And don't tell me this was a regular robbery and murder. Whoever did this didn't like him in particular. They've held somebody and apparently he confessed to killing Mr Chetan. So the police say. His cock-and-bull story was that he broke in to rob the place. Mr Chetan attacked him, he defended himself, and next thing the man was dead. He real dotish if he feel any court going to swallow that. The police them aren't giving us all the facts either. Piece piece the news has come through and we're getting it same time as everybody else.

Reporters who never knew Mr Chetan existed talking about him like they knew him in real life. Well, they didn't find out anything from me. I told them hooligans from the press straight: he was a decent, kind human being. If they wanted to print nastiness and tell a set of lies on the man to sell papers then let that be on their conscience. One paper reported the murder with the headline: 'Take Heed, All Ye Homos'. So, he deserved to die because he was gay?

I can't wait to see what that disgusting piece of shit who did this looks like. What devil stabs an innocent man forty-eight times? Yes, forty-eight times. I went in the kitchen, took a knife and I hit the chopping board forty-eight times. You know how long and how much energy that took? My hand

was tired after that. All for a wallet and a cell phone? Even if
the bandit was defending himself against scrawny Mr Chetan,
two stab and he would've gone through. And tell me why he
took the man blood and wrote 'buller' on the bedroom wall?
A few days after it happened I read in another newspaper that
the bandit had carved 'girl' on Mr Chetan's back. I went by the
police station and asked if that was true. I'm still waiting for
an answer.

What Mr Chetan must have gone through in his last hours
is too much for my brain to take in. One minute life was
good good and then bam. This kind of thing happened to
other people. We're simple people. We don't bother nobody
and look how overnight everything's mashed up. I will never
unsee that bloody sheet covering him. If God has any mercy
he would have taken Mr Chetan's spirit from this earth long
before I saw that black-and-blue body.

And where are all the people from work now, eh? And his
neighbours? I know the truth. People are whispering. Nobody
wants talk that they were pals with a buller man. Blasted
hypocrites. It's only when you're at the bottom of the well and
calling for help that you find out who will throw a rope. Somebody – I can't remember who – emailed me to say that I will
be fine because the Lord only gives us what we can bear. I
wanted to write back and say that is the most stupid thing
I have ever heard. We are forever getting more than we can
bear. Always. It's just that we don't have a choice in the matter.
Damn kiss-me-ass dotish people. What's happened here will
not get fixed just so just so.

Every morning when I open my eyes the first feeling I have
is that something bad is about to happen. I've stopped feeling

safe. Where he was living he had neighbours close close and he was still murdered, much more me alone in this house. Solo's here now but he won't be for long. And he's there one side trying not to see me or talk to me except when strictly necessary. I asked him if he wanted me to cook a nice curry beans and roti for breakfast and all he did was grunt, no. He made himself a sandwich and ate it in his room. Sitting down with me for a little five minutes seems too much for him.

In a way it's only right that Solo's still vex. I deserve it. If I hadn't gone and messed with that Kali business Mr Chetan might be alive all now. I went to Mudder specifically asking that she bring Solo home to me. Well, he's back. She answered my prayers. I should have known that Mudder wouldn't give without taking. All them hands she have is to give with one and snatch with another. So she had to make an exchange. Why did it have to be Mr Chetan who never hurt nobody? And why make the man suffer like that? Lord, what I gone and done?

I have a film playing over and over in my head. I got the call. I didn't bawl. It didn't seem real. Only when I reached by his apartment and I saw the police cars, lights flashing and a heap of people in the road – that was when my legs them left me. As they wheeled out the body I know I was screaming and scream-ing. I didn't care if I was in the way or who heard me. It was like somebody else was bawling and I was looking at them. The noise coming out of me wasn't human. The thing that scared me was I didn't feel I could stop. Strangers were lifting me off the ground and I was shoving them away.

One officer managed to pick me up and looked after me until I was quiet. Something about him felt genuine. He said he understood a little of what I was going through. In his line of work he dealt with this kind of thing too often. Officer Walker, Officer Jackson Walker. The day after the autopsy he passed by the house. Thank the Lord Solo was by the neighbour so I got to talk my mind. What they think happened is that the man forced his way in through the bathroom window and was probably looking to steal when Mr Chetan woke up.

You're sure you want to hear all this, Mrs Ramdin?

I'm very sure, Officer. Don't spare me.

He sighed.

The knife most likely came from the kitchen. He tied him up in the bedroom.

The officer stopped.

I think that's enough. You know the rest.

I wiped the water from my eyes.

Ain't I said I wanted to hear everything?

He shook his head.

There was an eight-by-ten photo of two men kissing. That seemed to set off the intruder. The injuries you know already.

Did he carve the word girl on his back?

Officer Walker looked at the ground. I barely heard him whisper, yes. One thing he said I should brace myself for up front is that nothing to do with the courts is quick. If this case came up before two years we would be lucky. And the fact of a homosexual angle meant nobody would make the case a priority – not the detectives, not the lawyers and definitely not the judges. Those were facts I had better swallow early. But he promised to keep the case alive as much as he could. Before leaving he asked me about the funeral so he could pay his respects.

*

Reverend came by the house. He wanted to know what to do for the funeral. I told him no service. His eyes opened big big.

Betty, people from work, his friends, our community, they need to pay their respects.

He was a quiet person. I don't think he would want all kind of people coming to maco.

I didn't say anything about people macoing. Mr Chetan was a good man. A Christian man.

I had to bite my tongue. If Mr Chetan was here he would be laughing because the last time he was inside a church was probably when he was a baby being baptised. What would you want, Mr Chetan? We didn't think we had to talk about things like what to do when you died because it wasn't time yet. You were supposed to live a good while longer. You were supposed to go completely grey. I would still be begging you to make sweet bread for me because you were the boss at that. We were supposed to sit down on a Sunday afternoon and complain to one another about back pain after picking pigeon peas from the garden. I would tell you to hush your mouth because I had stewed those peas as part of your lunch and as usual you had licked it down like you never ate my stew before.

If you want to keep the funeral part private, why you don't have a small wake the evening before? I could come and say a few words of comfort. We'll sing two hymns and say our farewells. You could talk. Or your son. I heard he came back from America.

I closed my eyes and held my head. Reverend had a point. Let everybody come one time, say what they had to say and done with that.

Burial is Monday. We could keep wake the Sunday evening.

Well, that is a little problem for me. I'm not here Sunday. As soon as church is over I have a function to go to. What about Saturday evening?

No. Anybody else free?

Leave it with me. I will find somebody. You mind if an elder comes for the wake and I will do the funeral proper?

No, Reverend. I'm not having any service at the burial.

Not even to say some last prayers?

No. He wasn't a religious man and I'm not going to turn him into one now.

All right. I never really hear people do it so but you're in charge. I will say prayers for him by myself. And as I'm here let us pray for mercy on Mr Chetan's soul.

We prayed and then he decided that I looked like I needed a sermon on forgiveness. Yes, forgiveness. Jesus forgave those who nailed him to a cross as an example of how to live. So, just like that, I must forgive the man who decided he had the divine right to take Mr Chetan's life? Man of the cloth or not, I threw Reverend's ass out of my house. Let them say what they want about me in church because I don't feel like I belong there anyway. Forgiveness? As he was leaving Reverend put his hand on top my head and said he forgave my rude behaviour because it was the grief talking. He would pray for my soul. All of this was part of God's plan and I must have stronger faith. Imagine somebody up on high wanted Mr Chetan to exit this world in such a terrifying way, begging for his life. What possible divine plan could involve this wickedness on the gentlest, kindest, sweetest man? Fuck forgiveness.

SOLO

If I'd stayed in New York, I don't think Mr Chetan's passing would've felt real the way it's troubling me now. Reverend somebody dropped by yesterday and he sat down in Mr Chetan's chair. I know the Reverend couldn't have known that chair was special but I was still angry like the man had deliberately gone and done me something. Whenever Mr Chetan was in the living room watching TV that was where he would rest himself. The whole time Reverend was visiting all I wanted was for him to get his backside off that chair. When I couldn't take more I stormed out the room without a word to the man. Mr Chetan might have moved out years back but as far as I'm concerned that other place never existed. For me he will always belong right here and that was his chair.

The cushion was still warm from Reverend's backside when Mani arrived. I knew exactly who he was from all the selfies that Mr Chetan had sent. Every ounce of me, body and soul, took to him. He opened his arms wide and hugged me tight like we'd been best buddies from long time. No wonder Mr Chetan loved this man. He sat next to Mammy on the couch and rubbed her back. She started crying one time. I was across from them in Mr Chetan's chair, watching as Mani's eyes filled with water too. I have never been the one to start a conversation. Never. Like some spirit came inside me and I found myself pushing up to say something.

What was Mr Chetan like when he was young?

Mani wiped his face with his sleeve and sat up.

I have a surprise for all you.

He took out his wallet and showed Mammy a black-and-white picture. I got up to see. He and Mr Chetan had gotten older but they both had the same face as these two boys, maybe thirteen, fourteen years old, sitting on a rocky beach, arms around each other's shoulders.

This was taken quite down by Icacos. He came with us on that trip and my father took pictures with his new Polaroid camera.

I stared at it for a long time. He put his hand out. I didn't want to give it back.

I'll get you a print.

Mammy piped up.

Solo will carry his back with him so get one for me too, please. You have any more pictures from long time?

No. That's the only one.

He looked at me and smiled.

You're too young to know but there was a time when taking a picture was a big deal.

He started scrolling through pictures on his phone.

I have hundreds. He used to get vex that I was always

taking selfies of us together but now I'm glad I didn't take him on. These last few days I can't stop looking at them and thinking that we never knew how little time we would have together.

He burst into tears. Proper bawling. Now Mammy had to hold him.

Mani, nobody can take away what you had with him. He's in your heart just like he's in mine.

Looking at them hugging up kinda made me jealous. I hadn't seen Mr Chetan for so long that I didn't miss him the way they did. I didn't lime with him, go cinema with him. He hadn't cooked for me since I was a boy. Yes, we texted each other all the time but it wasn't what these two had. I was missing a ghost. But ghost or not, it hurt bad to think of how he died. We're not Jamaica yet but the violence in this country is getting beyond a joke. Seeing his body was horrible. Whenever it flashes through my mind I want to run for a razor. I don't know how else to get rid of this pain. Problem is cutting will be dishonouring Mr Chetan and I can't do that. I mustn't do that.

Mani stayed for a good while talking, and in two twos he was in the middle of planning the wake. It took all my courage to speak up.

Mani, why you don't pass for me tomorrow and we could get through some of these things together? It'll be faster if the two of us do the running around.

I'll pick you up about nine.

BETTY

Just when I would rather stay in my bed and not see anybody I had to run up and down. Mani and Solo have their list but of course I need to check on them and there are other things I don't trust nobody to do. We have no idea how many people will show for the wake. It could be anywhere from ten to a hundred and I don't want to be in a situation where food done and not everybody got a share. I ordered dhalpourri roti from the hairdresser lady. I'm not sure which is the side line and which is her main business because more than once when she was covering my greys she was covered in flour. A man Deedee knew from her nephew's wedding is doing the meat. Twenty chickens and a goat going in the pot. Gloria said to leave the channa and aloo, pumpkin and the curry mango with her. A Muslim family on her street trying a thing and she wants to give them the business. I took out a set of cash to cover everything and when I tried to pay not one person would take a red cent. That touched me. What a world, yes. A man could get murdered for nothing and still we have good people like this who can't do enough.

Mani and Solo are now glued at the hip sorting out drinks, renting chairs, putting up a tarpaulin at the side of the house to make extra space. It would have been nice if my son spent time doing a few things with me. At least he seems happy when he's with Mani. I look at him and I can't quite believe he's here. And he's a big man, yes. He used to be a weak thing. Now he's fixing things and moving furniture like he was always in charge. I never taught him how to do anything practical and Mr Chetan spoilt him. But he was running cables for sound and climbing up to fix the tent. I watched with my mouth open wide wide. He's grown up nice.

After not hearing from the school piece piece they've been coming around. Maybe it was the shock or maybe they were looking at one another to check out what was going on. The music teacher's bringing her portable keyboard and her girl band to play guitar and sing.

With two days to go Mani pulled me aside. He wanted to talk in private – only the two of we. The house was full of people in and out so we went to the coffee shop next to the big Chinee grocery. This wasn't looking like good news.

Betty, Chetan ever talked to you about what he wanted?

How you mean?

I mean if he wanted a burial or cremation. That kind of thing.

No. And boy, if I tell you how much trouble I had finding a plot. Paradise Cemetery's full so I've given him the plot I had for myself. Hopefully I won't need it for a good long while.

So, hear what. Chetan left a set of papers for me to put in my safety deposit box. I clean forgot about them. This morning I checked and he had made a living will. You know what that is?

Tell me.

It's where you state what you want medically if you're not able to make decisions for yourself. It's useful if you're in an accident and you had a brain injury. Things like that.

Yes.

Well, he also put that he wanted to be cremated, not buried.

What you saying? Cremate? How we go do that now?

I know. But that is what he wanted. Cremation down by the creek.

He handed me a form Mr Chetan had completed. I knew that handwriting. Mani was talking the truth. I shook my head.

Jeez-an-ages, look at my crosses now.

I took a deep breath.

If that was what Mr Chetan wanted, then of course we don't have a choice.

The funeral home like they're accustomed to craziness because they didn't think it was a problem. Only trouble was Mrs Subjally didn't have staff to run around government offices in time for a Monday cremation. The best thing was for us to take the death certificate down Siparia and do everything today one time.

I was studying who I know in public health. My head real bad, yes, because it took me a good few minutes to remember that temple people must know somebody. Hindus only ever cremate and Kali people especially need fire when they're transforming out of this life. Tanty called she friend and the friend said she had one last cremation spot. It was for ten o'clock Monday but

I must come and pay for it now now. I said, give me an hour, even though I knew with traffic Mani would need a helicopter to reach there so fast. Well, we didn't need the helicopter because Mani's BMW had some good speed. I was only praying we reach body and car in one piece. By the time we saw the sign 'Welcome to Siparia' I was feeling sorry for the vehicle. Pothole or no pothole, Mani was getting Chetan's cremation spot.

Reaching Siparia turned out to be the easy part. We saw a sign for the public health authority. That was a clinic. Even the security guard didn't know which office we should go. He sent us traipsing in the hot sun to another building but nobody there knew about cremation spots either. All this time we were baking. Eventually we met someone who said we were close. Two minutes down the road and we would see a pink building on the right but we should hurry because the cashier took lunch from 1 p.m. to 2 p.m. and nothing involving payment does get done while she's eating. I couldn't believe a big government place would be operating so in the twenty-first century. I will have to hold my mouth because today wasn't the day to test the people. We buss through the door with a good ten minutes to spare. I told myself that was a sign. Mr Chetan wanted to be cremated and that is why we got here on time. Waiting until the cashier's lunch break was over would have meant we couldn't pay for the spot in time. This receipt had to take to the police station for us to get a fire certificate and they lock off issuing those at 3 p.m.

What we needed next was for Mr Chetan to look down and help us find the police station and we would be fixed. I saw a big blue building up a hill that could be a police station. I was half right. It was something to do with the police but not

where we had to go for this damn fire certificate. A man by
the gate told us to turn around and drive back down the road.

You will pass a shoe shop on the left. Then it have a small
road. Don't take that. Take the next one. Follow that until
you reach the first roundabout. Take the turning off your
right like you coming around yourself. You will pass a tall
breadfruit tree although the other day I saw they were
cutting down a set of trees in the back there. Anyhow, is
the third building on the right. And don't park where it say
'Reserved' because that is for the senior officers and them.
I think the fine is five hundred on the spot, yes. In fact, you
better park on the road in front and walk in.

As we waved him thanks and headed down the hill I asked
Mani if he remembered all of that. He laughed.

I think so but if you see a sign for the police station let's
follow that instead.

The police station was so old and broken-down-looking that
we passed it and had to turn around. I asked Mani to do the
talking, not because I can't, but I know they will listen to any
blasted man ten times faster than a woman.

Afternoon, Officer. We're looking to get a fire certificate.
You could help us out, please?

What you want a fire certificate for? Cremation?

We both nodded.

When is the cremation?

Monday.

Monday? And is now you reach here? All you lucky to even find me. On a Friday I does knock off early to avoid the traffic.

My friend was murdered, and we're trying our best to do what he would have wanted.

The officer looked at us.

Which one of all you is the next of kin?

I nodded. The officer stretched and got up.

You have the receipt from public health?

Yes, sir. Right here.

Chetan. That name's familiar. All you is the Chetan with a hardware in Penal?

Nah. We from up Sando side.

So, who all you related to? All you have any lawyer in the family?

Not really.

And all you expect to come Friday afternoon, not even Friday morning, and leave with a fire certificate?

He twisted up his mouth and went to a back office. It took a cool fifteen minutes before he came back.

I thought so. Boss say chief gone home already so it don't have nobody to sign the certificate. You have to come back eight o'clock Monday.

I could feel my skin getting hot from the inside like I was getting a fever.

Officer, we can't do that. The funeral home needs the fire certificate before they will carry the body to cremate. Ease me up nah. The man we cremating make the news. You remember the man they murdered and wrote things in his blood?

The officer's mouth dropped open.

Wait nah. This is for the homo who boyfriend stab him? So how come you is the next of kin? You is he sister?

Out of the corner of my eye I could see Mani was ready for him. I touched his hand.

Officer, he was murdered and it wasn't no boyfriend that they hold.

He twisted his mouth again like he'd sucked a lime.

All right. Wait. Let me see what the boss go say.

A good twenty minutes passed. The officer strolled out like he was going to lime in a rum shop.

The chief does be all about, so sometimes we get him to sign a few blank fire certificates and leave them here in case of an emergency. Boss letting me use one. This is a big favour all you getting.

That officer's ugly face with the gold front teeth in he mouth was suddenly the handsomest thing I had seen that day. Mani promised to write the station chief to say how helpful he had been in our time of need. I called Subjally's Funeral Home. All good. Mr Chetan's burning Monday morning ten o'clock sharp.

SOLO

Plenty people have asked me how we're related to Mr Chetan and quite a few thought Mammy was his ex before he turned to preferring men. I can just imagine the stupidness they're saying. I tried giving it straight. He lived with us for many years and was like family. If we were in the States, I'm sure out of politeness the talk would end there. Not Trini people. They act like they're entitled to know all your business. This woman came up to me, mouth full of cake,

You is the man son?

No. He didn't have any children.

Somebody tell me the dead was your father.

No.

I walked off to help take chairs from the van. She followed me.

So how you related?

I pretended not to hear.

I said, how you related to the dead?

I put the chair down.

How did you know Mr Chetan?

Me? I didn't know him. I just passed to drop the flowers Miss Gloria ordered and a woman, must be your mother, gave me a piece of cake. She was real nice.

Please excuse me.

I could not get inside the house fast enough. Once I locked my bedroom door I knew no one would bother me. Just ten minutes to myself. Things needed doing but I had to get away from all the madness. Later, when I saw Mani, I asked him what I should say to people like that woman.

Don't take worries. Tell them you're his nephew and your mother is his sister and end the story there. I knew this would happen. Ask Betty. From the start I told her to say she was his sister and shut down the macoing one time.

What will happen if Mr Chetan has a real nephew who turns up?

That blasted good-for-nothing family? Trust me. We ain't hearing from them.

If Mani was giving me a promotion to nephew I was cool with that. I prefer having an official title like I belonged to Mr Chetan. From now on it's simple. He was my uncle just like Uncle Hari.

Night time, after everybody had gone their way, I curled up in my old bed. I used to love this room. It's weird because Mammy kept all my old clothes and my school books. Everything is packed away neat neat in the cupboard. Why? I'm never going to need them again. Life was so different then. I've done my best to stay out of Mammy's way and she's kept far.

I can't sleep. All I want is a razor for a little relief. I don't feel like crying. I don't know what I feel except it's uncomfortable and painful and I want it to stop. I sent the New York folks a group message telling them about the wake tomorrow and then I started googling Mr Chetan. For every person who has sent condolences ten more are in the bush whispering and making up all kind of stories. Mani warned me about reading the blogs and online comments. I couldn't help it. I wanted every detail of what every person is saying about my Mr Chetan. These people didn't know the man from Adam. One blog said 'inside sources' confirmed 'two buller men had a lovers' quarrel' and that we should expect 'when two big man fight one must end up dead'. A next blog claimed they knew for sure he died during a rough sex game that got out of hand. The really evil ones posted shit like the only good gay man is a dead one or this was God's punishment of Mr Chetan. His sin was fucking a next man and they hoped the rest of bullers in Trinidad were taking note because the Lord was going to punish them the same way.

I phoned Mani. I was so angry I wanted to cuss every last one of those motherfucking idiots.

Calm down, Solo. Leave those cowards alone. We know the truth. That's all that matters.

How can people write these boldface lies and get away scot-free? We can't make them apologise and take it off the web?

Let me ask you something. What would Chetan tell you if he was here?

I sighed. My Mr Chetan was too good for this world.

He would say not to bother with them.

Exactly. I know it's hurtful. Believe me. It's paining me too. But writing back, tweeting, whatever, it will only make them feel important.

Mani?

Yes.

Can you come for me? I can't stay here tonight.

Something's happened?

No. It's hard being in this house. It's lonely. His room is so close. And me and Mammy, we can't be in the same place.

Look at me talking to Mani like this when it was only days ago I met the man. He will think something's wrong with me.

I noticed a little tension with you two.

I laughed.

Little? You're coming?

He said look out for him in half an hour. Mammy heard me moving about.

What are you doing this hour of the night? Where are you going with your suitcase?

I'm going to stay by Mani.

Why? What happened?

I don't want to stay here.

I could feel the tension rising.

You ungrateful, selfish wretch. What happen? Here not
good enough for you now you're living away?

I was surprised she raised her voice but I didn't take her on. I
opened the wardrobe to get my clothes.

I'm talking to you.

Leave me alone.

No. You're the one who is going by Mani rather than
staying with your mother at a time like this. We should be
a comfort for one another, Solo. A comfort. I raised you
practically by myself and this is the thanks I get?

Well, that was it. A bomb exploded inside me. I wanted to
slash every inch of my skin until my blood soaked a sheet like
the one that covered Mr Chetan and give it to her as a present.
Thanks for everything, Mammy.

You're a blasted hypocrite. You should see yourself. Acting
all holy. Making sure everything's fix up nice for Mr
Chetan. Did you look after my father like that? Eh? Answer
me. Did you give a shit about my daddy?

She burst into tears.

I'm sorry. I'm sorry, baby. I'm sorry.

I don't believe you cared one shit about him.

I swallowed the tears bubbling up in my throat and behind
my eyes.

You thought you could just push him down the steps? You're no better than the scum that killed Mr Chetan. You realise that? The only difference is you ain't get catch yet. Yet.

She wasn't crying so much as howling.

I've tried to tell you what I was going through but you don't have a heart. All you care about is your precious father. They say child will eat the mother but you know mother will never eat child.

You took my father from me and I want you to know I hate everything about you. If it wasn't for Uncle Hari, I wouldn't know a single good thing about him. I hate you. You hear that? I hate you.

She wiped her eyes with the back of her hand.

Well, Solo, do your thing. Do what you must do.

She blew her nose.

You want to call police for me? Call them. I never thought I would live to see the day my own flesh and blood would say he hated me.

She turned and went into her bedroom. I pelted toiletries into my suitcase. Mammy or no Mammy, I wanted to aim the cologne bottle straight for her fucking head. A framed picture of her holding me as a baby caught my eye and the bottle smashed that instead. Glass was all about on the floor, on my bed, and same time the place never smelt better. Mammy was back by the door. I could feel her standing there. I looked at the sparkling broken glass. After all that loud noise everything was so quiet. I bent down. With my right hand I chose a nice big piece of glass with a sharp point, held out my left hand and got ready to slice my wrist. This time I would do it properly and she could watch.

I don't know what happened. Mammy must have ninja genes because she got the glass out of my hand so fast and somehow threw me towards the doorway. I skid and fell half in, half out the room. She was screaming at me.

> If you want to kill anybody then kill me! Kill me and done the thing!

I got up slowly. My right hand had blood from a nick in my palm.

> Look me here. Come. You don't have to cut your wrists. Let we go to the police station right now. I will sign a confession and they can lock me up and throw away the key. Let we done this torment tonight self. Come, Solo. How much years now you wanted to see me punished? Well, you're getting your wish.

She picked up her handbag and opened the front door.

> Hurry up. I'm waiting. Leave your case. You'll have the house to yourself.

Through the open doorway I saw two headlights then heard an engine cut off. Thank God. I grabbed my case and ran outside. Mani looked at me and then up at Mammy.

> What's going on, Betty?

Mani, he's a big man. He can do whatever he wants. I ain't able no more. Solo flared up like a kerosene stove here tonight.

She turned and locked the front door. She actually locked me out.

BETTY

Solo stayed by Mani last night. He's bound to come back here today unless he's so bad minded that he misses the wake. Today is for Mr Chetan and I'm bone tired from saying what I needed to say. It's up to Solo. He can do what the ass he wants as long as he stays out of my way. Yes, he's my one child but I've taken my share of licks. If he wants to go back New York and stay there thinking I am the worst mother, and the worst human being in the world, that is his choice. Peace and love to him. The lesson of Mr Chetan's passing before his time is one I intend to put in practice. Make today count. If I drop down dead today I want to know I didn't hide from life. And who can't bring peace or add a little comfort to my life can move right along – from Mr England to Solo. Only people who treat me with kindness and respect the way Mr Chetan treated me have a place in my life.

Mani showed up alone two hours before things were due to start.

What happen? Like Solo's not coming?

He and Patrick are coming together. I wanted to be here early to help.

Things running so smooth I feel like I must be forgetting something.

I'm sorry about last night. I let him come by me because I thought it would do both of you good to get some space.

Thanks. I don't have time for Solo's foolishness today.

True. Let we get through this. But I wanted you to know I wasn't taking up for Solo.

Mani, don't worry your head. What I need is for you to find where we put the programmes them. Who will give them out?

Patrick could do that.

When Solo and Patrick arrived, I said hello. Mister Man mumbled something that could have been hello. What to do. You can't force understanding.

Reverend sent an elder everybody calls Uncle Baby. I've been calling him Uncle Baby for so long that I realised I didn't know his outside name or, if I did, I certainly haven't used it in a long long time. I asked Deedee but she and all didn't know him as anything besides Uncle Baby. I was too shame to go and ask myself so I grabbed Patrick.

Come, you don't look like you from around here. You see that man in the white shirt sweating? He's doing the service and I can't remember his good name. Find out for me nah.

Out of the edge of my eye I watched Patrick introduce himself. Uncle Baby caught him in an ol' talk about what I don't know. Anyhow, Patrick got away and whispered in my ear,

Mr Keith Bachan.

Keith Bachan? Thanks, Patrick. That's not ringing any bells
in my hard head. How he went from Keith Bachan to Uncle
Baby?

Ten minutes before we were due to start I looked around and
my heart nearly burst. The place was full, full, full. Standing
room only. I hope Mr Chetan was looking down and seeing
all this. He must be wondering who were all these people and
how they reach in his wake. On the dot Keith Bachan/Uncle
Baby called us to worship. The music teacher and her little
band led the first hymn, 'Be Thou My Vision', and then Solo
did the first scripture reading. He walked up to the little stage
like he knew what he was doing. I was proud. What happened
between us aside, Solo left here a shy boy and he reached back
a man. I closed my eyes and asked Mr Chetan to help bring
me and my son back together, please.

Solo read Ecclesiastes, chapter 3, verses 1 to 8. Even though
he was never a church man Mr Chetan liked that passage. He
was always quoting it. When Solo said 'a time to kill and a
time to heal' a shiver went down my spine. In the middle of all
this I suddenly remembered a day I was looking all about the
house for my shades. Mr Chetan could see it was on my head
but he didn't say anything. When he thought I had searched
long enough he looked at me serious serious and said,

> To everything there is a season, and a time for every
> purpose under heaven. A time to get and a time to lose. But
> Miss Betty, today is not the day to lose your shades.

And he took it off my head and handed me. I must have let
out one long steupse. Making me tumble up everything when

he knew I was carrying it around like a fool. To think he will never joke and laugh with me again. He should be alive. Why was he butchered by some disgusting scumbag? Why him?

Psalm 121 was read by the head teacher. He pushed up to be in the programme. 'I will lift up mine eyes unto the hills, from whence cometh my help. My help cometh from the Lord, who hath made heaven and earth.' In the end it's one God we're all praying to, although personally my God has deserted me.

Mani wanted me to do the tribute. Me? I can't talk good enough. People have to know what a wonderful man Mr Chetan was to me and everybody who knew him. And I didn't trust I could get up and talk in front all these people without breaking down. I begged Mani. He's educated and they go way back. And he did us all proud. He talked about Mr Chetan like he was a real person, not some saint we've lost. We sang 'When the Roll is Called Up Yonder', and shockingly in tune to boot.

It was then Uncle Baby's moment to give a short meditation. At least ten times I warned him – keep it short. Like his ears were clogged up when I was telling him. Give a church man a mike and a hundred quiet people and them does forget how to tell the time. He's clearly been watching the American preachers on TV. All fifteen minutes passed and he was now warming up.

My brothers and sisters, do you think Mr Chetan's going to heaven?

A few people said yeah and one woman in the back bawl out, amen.

I tell you, Mr Chetan will pass straight to the gates of
heaven because he has only to ask the Lord for forgiveness
and he gone through. That is our Lord. Always forgiving no
matter what sins we commit while on earth.

I was watching him good. Let him say one word about Mr
Chetan sinning for being gay and I will take that mike out he
hand so fast. I might look small and dotish but today wasn't
the day to cross me. Well, Uncle Baby surprised me.

Now, I want all you to think about something. How
much thousands of years people have been dying all over
the place. That is plenty dead. Think about it. How is
everybody finding place to live up in heaven? You think it
have room for Mr Chetan right now?

I can honestly say that after catching my ass on earth I thought
I was done. I didn't know that when I dead I go be hustling
for house and land again. Uncle Baby told us to calm down.
Revelation 21 gave the size of heaven and it was enormous –
1,400 miles square.

When they say square, they mean fourteen hundred miles
so.

He drew a line across in the air.

And fourteen hundred miles so.

His finger continued up to make a next line about the same
length.

All you know how big that is? Every man Jack go have place
to stay.

He wasn't done. He said Mr Chetan was a victim of violent crime that is out of control in Trinidad. In Revelation our Saviour thought this might worry us. Besides being a huge square, heaven has jasper stone walls reaching two hundred feet up in the sky. I was thinking that was better than any of them fancy gated communities they're building all over the place. Deedee squeezed my hand and whispered in my ear,

You think that go keep out all the Bad John them?

Why she wanted to make me giggle in the middle of all this? She whispered again,

Trini people smart, you hear. Them murderers and rapists and drug dealers go dig under that wall and come through. Oh, and don't forget all them thiefing politicians trying to get a piece of heaven.

I had to swallow the first proper laugh I've had in a while. I gave her hand a little squeeze. Uncle Baby lasted a good thirty minutes and afterwards people said I was lucky. When Reverend's not there to crack the whip he could go on hearing the sound of his voice for an hour easy easy.

People ate their belly full. Drinks didn't run out. Some men set up a card game in the corner. I looked around and I thought Mr Chetan would have been happy with how everything passed off and the crowd that came to pay their respects. Solo stayed close to Mani and far from me. I'm waiting. Even Solo can't keep this up forever – especially now. Mr Chetan would not want me and Solo to be strangers.

SOLO

Just now he will be ashes. I can't get my head around that. Uncle Hari called me. He said he's thinking of me and it gets easier. Mani said one day at a time. It's only since meeting Mani that I've realised how much Mr Chetan talked about me and how much he worried. That has been eating me up. I should have come back to see him long time and I didn't.

Solo, did Chetan tell you he made a will leaving whatever he had to you alone?

No. That's true? I mean, he always said I was like his son. And he would say whatever he had was mine. I didn't take him on.

Well, he meant it.

I said excuse and ran to the bathroom. This was too much. I crouched down on the cold tiled floor and bit hard on a hand towel. Mani can't hear me screaming.

I must have been in there a good while because Mani knocked on the door.

Solo? Solo, you don't have to hide in there and cry. It's okay.

I washed my face and opened the door. Mani was on the couch.

Come sit down by me. While you were crying in there I was crying out here.

I smiled as best I could. I slumped down by him and he immediately put his arm around my shoulder.

You're ready for the cremation?

Don't know.

It will be hard. And you have to be nice to your mom because it will be a tough day for her too.

I don't want to have nothing to do with her.

Mani sighed.

That's not going to work.

We sat in silence. Should I tell him about Mammy? Could I trust him? If there was ever anyone I could tell it must be this man.

Mr Chetan knew why Mammy and I fell out. Did he tell you anything?

No.

If I tell you it must stay right there. Even Patrick can't know.

Promise. I'm not going to spread your business all over the place.

You know, talking to you is like talking to Mr Chetan. The same calm, solid feeling I got from Mr Chetan I feel with you.

He smiled.

That is hands down the nicest thing anybody's said to me.

He ruffled my hair. Mr Chetan might be gone but thank God he left me Mani. I took a deep breath and told him the whole story of what Mammy did. Strange but he didn't look shocked.

You don't think she should have to pay for what she did?

What? You mean she should go to jail?

The way he said it made me feel bad.

Solo, you can tell me I'm fast and out of place but I find you're not studying what was going on with Betty and your daddy. We're not supposed to bad talk the dead but your daddy was like a lot of men I know. He might have been a decent person but once he drank he was something else.

But to me she had no right to touch the man, much more push him knowing he could fall and dead.

You don't feel sorry for your mom?

I paused.

He was always shouting. I remember being afraid of him.

Even as I said it I felt uncomfortable, disloyal.

I don't think he was too nice to me and Mammy.

Solo, not nice is when you taste a corn soup by the highway and you think it needs more salt. What your mother went through was hell. Chetan told me she still has pain from some of the injuries he did to her. Broken bones, gashes on her head and other things nobody should do to their dog, much more their wife. Part of the reason Mr Chetan loved Betty so much was because he admired the way she survived and quietly made a good life for you. She likes to act tough but a kinder soul you won't find. Trust me.

Her letters flashed in front me. Mani was talking but I was seeing Mr Chetan. I missed him. Mani rocked back in his chair. Something was bothering me, something I wanted to say, but I couldn't figure out what it was. With one hand Mani massaged the back of his neck. Suddenly it came back to me.

And Mani, this is the important thing I wanted to say. The night Daddy died. It was my birthday.

Mani let out a sigh like he was holding up the whole world by himself.

I don't want you to feel like I'm talking down to you.

His hand went back to his lap. I closed my fist. He must have seen my chewed-up nails by now. Still, no need to expose them.

Say I come and cuff you down. You might cuff me back then and there and nobody would bat an eyelid. They would say I cuffed you so you were in your rights to come back and box me. But when you're living with somebody who is always putting you down, beating you regularly, it can wear you down. The thing that finally tips you over the edge might be something little. After years of this abuse, who knows what made her lose it that particular night? Have you asked her? The way I see it she knew she was going to hurt him but she didn't set out to kill him. It wasn't like she pointed a gun at the man and blew his head off.

He got up.

I'm going to surprise the water by taking a shower. Chetan used to say that.

He ruffled my hair again. I gave in to what I was feeling and hugged his waist tight with my head buried in his stomach. I could feel his warm skin through the thin T-shirt. And he hugged me back. He kept hugging me and only let go after I had.

Solo, you're a good man. Chetan was proud of you. We'll get through this. I feel you're at a point where you must make up your mind about how you want to live your life. I'm not talking about Betty now. I'm talking about you. As you get older you will come to value the one or two people you have in your life that care. Really care. And your mother is one of the good people in this world. For all her faults, she will do anything for you.

As I watched him disappear down the corridor I realised something. If Daddy had not died, Mr Chetan would never have come to live with us. I wouldn't have had this second father. I can't imagine never knowing him. Life does work out in strange ways. And now Mr Chetan's gone and left me Mani – another guardian angel. I miss you, Mr Chetan. When you meet my daddy in heaven make sure you introduce yourself. Tell him I say that after he left, you took over. You were my next daddy.

BETTY

People at the wake wanted to know what time was the cremation and I told them, don't take it personally but the time does not matter. We're not having any more service than the one they just attended. It's not that I'm inviting work friends and leaving out church friends or vice versa. Nobody's invited. The only person I asked to come is Tanty. Through the temple she's done cremations by the creek and I figure she could give us a hand. But for the rest? The wake was their chance to pay Mr Chetan his respects. What more they want? Even the nice police officer came. He stayed a good little while talking to Solo and Mani.

Uncle Baby said it's a public place and if he wants to come he will come. I can't argue with that but if he's dotish enough to show his face it go be me and he. The headmaster and all held me down in a talk about the same thing. I told him it won't have no roti sharing by the creek. He laughed.

That is why you better give me a piece of foil, please. Throw in a roti and two-three piece of curry goat, let me carry home for the wife.

I shook my head. My people shameless, yes. I look like I'm running a takeaway restaurant?

But seriously, Betty. Why you don't want anybody there?

People not coming to maco. And you might need the little
support.

Thanks, but Solo and Mani will be there. I haven't made up
my mind if even Deedee and Gloria can come. They want to.

Let them nah. Sometimes it's like you've not said goodbye
properly until you see the body go.

I can't help that.

Well, you have enough to cope with. You do your thing
how you want.

*

Six o'clock bright and early Gloria called.

Me and Deedee decided that even if you don't want us there
we're coming. He was our friend too. We won't bother you
but we will be there. And really and truly you shouldn't be
driving. What time you want me to pick you up?

I didn't answer because I couldn't. Up to now I'd been man-
aging good good, staying focused. This morning I've been
crying nonstop.

I'm getting dressed. You go see me now now. Don't worry,
Betty. You know I love you like a sister. I'll be there.

On the drive to Subjally's Funeral Home I managed to keep from
crying. Mani, Patrick and Solo were already waiting outside,
looking grim. Tanty pulled up as we were about to walk into the

viewing room. They had him laid out real nice. I haven't been able to get into his apartment. Police are still doing their investigations so Mani bought a new set of clothes for him. Seeing him in a coffin made it too real. I bent down to kiss him and my legs decided they weren't holding me. I collapsed. Solo caught me and then Gloria and Deedee each took an arm and didn't let go. I could feel the grief heaving through my body. Deedee asked us to hold hands and she said a little prayer. I wanted to hug Solo. At least Mani and Patrick had him between them.

At the creek I realised why we had to book a spot. Each pyre was built on its own section of the hillside overlooking the sea. The funeral people gave us the option to wheel the coffin to the pyre or lift it in the traditional way. Solo, Mani and Patrick wanted to lift it. They started arranging with the undertaker how to hold the coffin when Officer Jackson Walker reach up. He asked to please allow him to pay his final respects. How I could say no? Seeing the body right after it happened must have affected him bad. The funeral director continued with the arranging.

It will be all you four men plus me and the hearse driver will make up the six to carry the casket.

Tanty squeezed my hand. She was reminding me of something I had told her in private. Her warm hand gave me courage.

I want to lift the coffin too.

The funeral director looked at me sideways.

Nah. You know how heavy this is? Leave it to the men. We will do we thing and you walk behind.

I shook my head.

No. I'm carrying Mr Chetan. It's the last thing I'm doing for him and nobody's stopping me.

My voice cracked at the end and the tears started again. Gloria growled at the man.

If you're putting people in height she needs to go in front as she is the shortest and I might as well go next to she to make up the six.

All you asking for trouble. That is not how we does do things.

Well, partner, is so we doing it today.

I'm only trying to protect all you. My insurance won't cover if all you drop the coffin or all you get injured.

Mani stepped in.

Sir, we understand. We accept full liability. Let them hold the coffin. Please.

And so we lifted Mr Chetan and walked from the hearse to the pyre with me in front, shoulder to shoulder with Gloria, Mani and Solo next, and Patrick and Officer Jackson Walker in the back. Tanty and Deedee walked behind with Tanty quietly reciting a prayer. Later they told me how proud they felt because in all the funerals they've been to, up and down Trinidad, this was the first time ever they'd seen two women carrying a coffin.

In the middle of the pyre was a hole. Before we pushed the coffin in, the funeral director took off the lid. We stepped to one side while he poured fuel on the wood. Mani was asking me something but it was like I'd gone deaf. The sun was hotting up. Gloria and Deedee held on to me by my elbows. The men had formed their own little group on the other side of the pyre. Mani walked over.

It's time to light the pyre.

You do it nah.

No, man. You do it. He made you his next of kin. His family.

Mani, you knew him the longest. You loved him the longest and he loved you. It's your right to light the fire.

Tanty made her offering to Mudder, asking that she sees Mr Chetan through his transformation from this life to the next. Using a banana leaf as a tray, she presented Kali with a red hibiscus, a little rice, lentils and a banana, that Mudder would take pity on his soul. She put the leaf tray on top the body and the whole world slowed down as Mani lit a torch and threw it on the fire. A scream came up from inside my heart and out my mouth. They probably heard me at the other end of the creek. Tanty was talking.

Betty, remember death is part of life. We mustn't be afraid
because is something all of we, rich, poor, man, woman,
every last body have to pass through. Bawl all you want.
Let it out. You don't have to believe but I know Mudder will
receive his spirit.

The little bit of breeze blowing had flames licking all around him now. You could see him in there burning. Through the flames I saw Solo on the other side. Patrick and Mani were holding on to him. Tanty seemed to be talking to the pyre.

Mr Chetan suffered so much he's not going to suffer in the next life. And I have no doubt Mudder will punish the demons who did this.

I could hardly hear all what she was saying. The grief was so strong I thought it would knock me out.

This fire's setting Mr Chetan's spirit free. Life and death come as one. They can't separate.

Loud popping noises were coming from the pyre. The funeral director told us they had set up a covered area and put out a few chairs for us to sit down.

Stay as long as you want. It will take a while for everything to burn. We will collect up all the ashes and you can pass for them tomorrow.

I didn't take my eyes off the pyre for the next hour and only maybe a quarter of it had burnt. I could still see his body. Patrick left and came back with a cooler of cold soft drinks. I took out a red sweet drink.

Hey, Solo, look your personal drink. An ice-cold red Solo.

He got up slowly and walked the few steps to me. I looked at my baby who didn't want me. I was done forcing love. I stretched out my hand so he didn't have to get too close to take the bottle. But he threw himself on me. I was shocked. Neither of us said anything. We hugged up tight tight and I knew we were both crying.

Death was all around as the sun moved higher in the sky and lit up the sea. For the next two hours me and my son sat close to one another watching the fire take Mr Chetan away from us forever. I'll never forget the sight and smell of his flesh burning. His flesh. The hot flames slowly ate his body and the pyre got smaller and smaller. Even from a good twenty feet away I was constantly wiping perspiration from my forehead. This was the first time I'd seen an open cremation. I think if I had buried him or used a crematorium it would not have printed on my mind the same way that he's gone. He's gone. Goodbye, Mr Chetan. Walk good in your next life. As for this one? You know what they say: wire bend, story end.

ACKNOWLEDGEMENTS

Coming to writing in the middle of my life means I arrived with accumulated debts I can never repay. The unwavering support of my partner, Avinash, makes everything possible and it is to him that I dedicate this book.

Luke Neima, my first reader, wraps brutal critiques in thick layers of kindness and diplomacy. The work feels as much his as it does mine but not enough to split the royalties. Louisa Joyner at Faber, an editor at the top of her game, what a privilege it has been working with you. Nicole Counts of One World – thank you for your sensitive and careful editing. Zoë Waldie, my agent – serendipity brought us together but it is your wisdom and integrity that continues to impress. Jeremy Taylor, thank you. Your faith and generosity propelled me into writing. Joy Mahabir, Tracy Fells, Allison Thompson, Constance Allman and the rest of my village – thank you for your time, loyalty and support. My parents, John and Lucy – a more enthusiastic cheerleading duo does not exist. Anish and Ishan, our beautiful sons, writing takes me away from you. This is what I give back with all my love.